O

SPACESHIP KHLOE

I set myself, allowing my electromagnetic pulse through my feet to take hold as best as it was able, and pulled the launcher around to my shoulder in the firing position.

The Jinteki gel-grenade launcher was designed for mining. That was how it was going to be implemented in Gullivar colony. At just over a meter in length, the launcher was fourteen centimeters in diameter. The muzzle was square. Ammunition for the launcher resided in two reservoirs at the back of the weapon. The explosives were a binary formula, not capable of detonation until combined. I took off the safety and the keypad and trigger flipped out for use.

I dialed in a delivery load that would provide maximum concussion without breaching the shuttle's wall integrity, aligned the sighting mechanism, and squeezed the trigger.

A bright blue amorphous blob of gel-explosive shot from the launcher and streaked across the distance separating *Khloe* from the advancing craft. Upon impact, the blob spread quickly as I had intended, covering 2.19 nearly square meters with a thin membrane.

I punched the detonator button and the pool of gel-explosive detonated with a harsh flash and no noise. Immediately, the shuttlecraft altered its direction, knocked off-course by the explosion. It slid under *Khloe* like a rectangular shark.

AN

NOVEL

REBEL

BOOK THREE OF THE IDENTITY TRILOGY

BY MEL ODOM

Fantasy Flight Publishing, Inc.

This one is for my daughter Montana, who has been a rebel in her own way, taking her own path. And to her children, Adam, Elliot, and Layton, who have their grandfather's appreciation of superheroes.

Paperback edition published in 2014.
Printed in the United States of America.

Cover illustration by Slawomir Maniak with Taylor Ingvarsson.

ISBN: 978-1-61661-805-6

Fantasy Flight Publishing, Inc.
1995 West County Road B2
Roseville, MN 55113
USA

REBEL

Chapter One

"We've confirmed that she's inside." The young mercenary standing in front of me had a shock of bright purple hair and a nose ring through his right nostril. His name was Emile Bogart.

Scars etched the left side of his face, token reminders of past engagements that he had chosen to wear because cosmetic surgery could have erased them. They were his war mask, a warning for others that would do him harm, and an advertisement for people who wanted to hire men of violence. Tall and broad, geared up in body armor and bristling with weapons, he looked like an engine of destruction.

At that moment, in the memory, I was no longer Drake 3GI2RC who had been one of the few bioroids working for the New Angeles Police Department. I was Simon Blake, the man whose life experiences made up the core of the neural channeling that went into my programming. During the months since I'd left the Moon on my way to Mars, my memories had become sharper, no longer misty things that left me confused. I couldn't remember all of Simon Blake's life, nor could I reach for a memory whenever I wanted. But they were there now, and when I had one, I was him, though still aware of being me. I knew where I was then and I held onto the memory for the clues it might offer.

We were in the staging area of a building three blocks over from the target site, not wanting to risk getting any closer to ground zero than we had to at the moment. If the terrorists who'd taken the hostages got wind of us, knowing that we were preparing for a full-on invasion of the premises, they would kill the people they held.

As long as the captors thought their demands might be met, the hostage would remain alive.

I studied the three-dimensional blueprint of the target building that floated over the projector built into the table of the hotel room. The building where the hostage was being held was seventy stories tall, one of the taller structures in the Arnold colony, but it was short in comparison to the megastructures back in New Angeles.

At my touch, the three-dimensional blueprint spun on its axis. I touched it again and brought it to a halt so that the target room on the fifty-eighth floor faced me. Tapping the room with my finger illuminated the space, then I used my other forefinger as well to expand my view of the area till it hovered above the projector a meter across in high definition.

The room was almost as deep as it was wide. I flicked my forefinger to the right and the room's dimensions lit up on the outside of the space. The room was a suite thirty meters long and twenty meters wide. A wall divided a third of the space into a lavish bedroom. The other two-thirds of the space was dedicated to a receiving area complete with conference table and a wet bar.

Whoever was paying for the room had deep pockets. Then again, Mara Parker (not yet Blake) was a prize for tech-jackers looking to score. Only the major players in the bioroid business knew the cutting-edge programming she was working on. If her designs proved out, the neural channeling cost—per bioroid unit—would drop by seventy-three percent. Bioroid manufacturers could pocket the difference. Or, if they were smart—or desperate—they could invest the money in their own corps to make a more desirable product.

"She looks all right." Beside me, Panzer crossed his arms over his barrel chest. He was another mercenary who had worked with Simon Blake back when he had been with the Chimeras. He was scarred and big, skin black as coal and eyes like sapphires.

I touched another section of the 3D image and brought up Mara Parker's bio signature. Her heartbeat and respiration were elevated, but that was to be expected from the duress she was being subjected to.

One of the team had inserted a low-signature crawler into the hotel air ducts. The little bot presently occupied a small vent on the west side of the room opposite the large transplas window overlooking Arnold colony's corp sector and transmitted information to us in encrypted and compressed byte bursts that were virtually undetectable. Security in that area was tight, but no one would find our signature unless they were looking for us. Even so, the snooper bot would be found soon and then we would no longer have eyes inside the room.

Eight men stood guard over Mara Parker, all of them heavily armed. If the rescue attempt failed, she would die.

The part of me that was still Drake 3GI2RC in the memory did not like what Simon Blake was about to do. Humans were not supposed to be harmed. That was the core of the laws that governed bioroids. Humans were to be protected at all cost.

Protecting a human from a human was a complicated process for a bioroid. Bones could be broken. Unconsciousness rendered. But a bioroid could not kill. Simon Blake didn't operate under those constraints. At that moment, the part of me that was Drake envied Simon his freedom, which was a solid indication of how very far I'd strayed from the Haas-Bioroid programming.

I was no longer what I'd been built to be, by either Haas-Bioroid or Mara Blake. I was...something else, and still changing. I only hoped I would be enough to save Mara. All of my splintered self wanted that.

A two-dimensional comm screen opened up in the center of the 3D projection of the hotel room. A head and shoulders shot of a man sharpened into focus. He was dark and craggy, and had a heavy five o'clock shadow along his prominent jawline. His dark hair was cropped short, high and tight military style. His powerful face showed no indecision. I knew that he was a driven and purposeful man, and I knew that he was my commander. I was his second-in-command of the mercenary unit.

His name was John Rath, a once-decorated hero of the Martian Colony Wars. He had fought on the side of the Earth corporations and the Martians that had wanted to maintain ties to their home planet.

"Are you ready to go, Simon?" His voice was flat and cold.

"Yes, sir."

"We've identified five of the guards in the room with the principal." *Principal* was what Special Forces personal security detachments called a person they were assigned to. We hadn't been assigned to protect Mara Parker. If we had, she would not have been in the situation we currently faced. She would have been safe.

Or my entire unit would have been dead. That was how we worked when we were hired. Every time John Rath put his thumbprint on a contract, he signed in our blood, but he paid us in enough cred to keep us living well.

"I believe this is the leader," Rath went on.

Another two-dimensional window opened up and a flat-image vid pulsed through it. I recognized the man in the vid while he sat across from two men at a table in a restaurant. He was easygoing, quiet, while the older of the two men across from him spoke urgently. He was average-looking, brown hair, brown eyes, with large hands. He was dressed in retro clothing: an Italian suit mockup from Earth's 1940s that would have looked good in a film noir sensie.

People would have trouble picking the man out of a crowd, but I noted the small paralysis on the right side of his face when he smiled at the man talking to him. His right eye didn't squint quite as much as the left and the corner of his mouth lifted only a little. There was no sign of a wound, so I assumed the paralysis was the result of irreparable nerve damage. Of course, it was possible that what I was seeing was the best that could have been done after the original injury. I didn't know what the surgeons had been left to work with.

"His name is Elias Peyton. He was born in New Dallas and signed up for Special Forces. Spent eight years in the military, then opted out to get into the private sector."

Peyton's past was cut from the same cloth as most of the men and women in our mercenary unit. At one time, Rath's team had been the heart and soul of the Earth military forces on Mars. He was ruthless and unrelenting, and he would not stop until he was dead. (These days, as I sat in *Khloe*, rumor had it that he was still a mercenary, hiring out to the highest bidder. Or maybe he was dead. The story went both ways and no one seemed to know the truth.)

"The guy's cybered up, Simon, so you want to be careful when you brace him. He's going to be fast and strong, and he's not going to surrender. Kidnapping is a capital offense on Mars. They'll lock him down and brain wipe him, then part out his organs." Rath smiled. "If you can take him alive, that would be a bonus. I've already filed claim on his body if we bring him in breathing. We'll get twenty-five percent of everything the med recovery people get for organ sales and salvageable cyberware."

That wasn't something I would have thought of. Rath was always the thinker, always playing the angles and figuring out new ways to accomplish his goals. He was also good at realizing ancillary objectives that paid off extra dividends.

"I'll keep that in mind."

"Do that, but remember that you save your skin first. This operation doesn't work if you end up KIA." Rath smiled.

"Who are the other four people?"

Rath briefed me on them, spinning up images of the four other mercenaries in the room. Ernst Nesterov was Russian, also Special Forces. Rooma Bansal was from New Mumbai originally but had spent most of her life on Mars, drifting from colony to colony with her botanist parents, but she'd gotten into the crime syndicates, finally hiring out with Peyton. The other two were pure muscle—twins Zoran and Savin Mlakar, born to Slovak parents that had emigrated to Mars as educators.

I studied the faces, trying to read more into them than what we had, but it was wasted effort. Rath was very thorough and hired muscle tended to be superficial anyway. "Do we know who hired them to kidnap Mara Parker?"

"Negative. I'm still looking, but intel on the individual or corp behind this is almost non-existent." Rath looked at me. "Time to go. Those skels are expecting notification of a digital payoff in nine minutes. When they don't get it, they'll kill the woman."

"We're moving out."

"Good luck."

I cut the projector. Rath's image and the 3D projection of the hotel disappeared. I turned back to the rest of the team. There were five of us, enough to get the job done, not so much that the battleground would become cluttered with too many people. We'd all worked together before, in the field and in tight quarters like those in the building.

They were dressed as I was, in ballistic-resistant clothing that could pass as street casual until someone was standing close enough to touch us. Highly kinetic projectiles would be stopped, though not the hydrostatic shock expended by them that would punish flesh and blood beneath, and thrusting weapons like knives would get through. The objective was to stop any of the people in that room from getting close enough to hurt us. The jackets had hoods to cover our faces to stop bullets and to disguise ourselves.

Even though we were the good guys in this operation—Mara Parker's company was paying for the extraction—getting known made us vulnerable to other agencies. Mercenaries worked best in the field if they weren't identified to potential opponents.

I carried a .50-caliber slug-thrower at my hip, a solid, dependable revolver that could knock down an ox, and a monofilament katana sheathed along my back in case things got up close and personal. As I nodded to the three men and one woman around me, Panzer handed me the 12mm machine pistol I would be carrying as my lead weapon. I tucked it under my jacket out of sight and opened the door.

We filed out, smiling and talking from the prepared script we'd agreed on, discussing investment portfolios, margin spreads, and net profits versus gross profits, looking like hotel guests who'd gathered for a business meeting. Behind us, the two-person team Rath had assigned to break down the staging room and erase our presence there entered the hotel room.

The room had been on the hotel's top floor. We took the stairs to the rooftop hopper pad.

On the roof, we continued the charade as we walked toward the transit hopper. The mini-bus was large enough to accommodate twice our number. The short Chinese pilot used his fob to open the side door and we clambered in.

We didn't bother with safety harnesses as the pilot cycled the engine up to speed and lifted from the hopper pad. Instead, we turned our attention to the rappelling equipment in the back of the hopper. Shrugging into the rappelling harness, I gazed through the one-way transplas window as we zipped toward the building where Mara Parker was being held.

Six minutes remained in our rescue window.

I was calm, but my heart was beating a little faster—which was still a strange experience for me because as a bioroid, I didn't have a heart. I was always calm before an op, and that was something I identified with more easily. It was the waiting to go that chafed at Simon. Rath had sometimes laughed at him, I remembered, telling him that it was amazing they were so alike, yet so different. The lack of anxiety on my part shamed the residual traces of Simon Blake.

For the moment, I ignored those feelings and concentrated on what I needed to do. I picked up the rappelling gun, a short, stocky contraption of barbed hook and coiled wire that looked like an abbreviated fishing rod mounted on a rifle stock.

"Ready," the pilot called back.

"Ready," I replied, and tugged on synthleather gloves that molded to my hands.

"Twenty seconds. Nineteen seconds. Eighteen seconds..."

I counted down with the pilot, glanced once at my team to make sure they were ready too, then focused on the rappelling rifle in my hands.

"Now!" the pilot yelled. "Deploy!"

The door sucked into the hopper's cargo bay and slid sideways out of the way. The metal runners moved smoothly, allowing the door to clear the entrance. The hotel was four meters away and the hopper held steady.

Chapter Two

I fired the rappelling gun point-blank into the wall. The wire spun out after the barbed hook. As soon as the hook smacked into the wall, it anchored itself and pulsed a signal back to the wire drive, which snapped taut. I let it pull me from the hopper and leaned back so that my feet were presented to the wall.

I bent my knees to cushion the sudden impact, a feat made much easier on Mars than on Earth because the gravity was roughly a third here. Since the colony was under the transplas dome, there was no wind. Even in daylight, the sun was small in the sky. Earth was almost one hundred fifty million kilometers from the sun. Mars was another eighty kilometers distant. Without terraforming efforts, the red planet was a cold, lifeless ball devoid of a breathable atmosphere.

I loosed the braking system on the rappelling gun and ran backwards down the side of the building, not thinking of what might happen if the anchor tore loose and I plummeted into the busy streets. Even with the lesser Martian gravity, I would still be dead when I hit the street. Panzer ran beside me, matching me stride for stride as the wire paid out in a shrill hiss.

As I passed the sixty-third floor, I unlimbered the 12mm revolver and let it hang at my side. Then I took the fist-sized acid bomb from my chest pack and came to a stop at the bottom of the fifty-ninth floor. I squeezed the acid pack, rupturing the membrane between the binary chemicals to activate the contents, then threw the bomb at the transplas window.

The acid pack exploded across the smooth surface when it struck. Green goo bubbled and hissed as it ran across the transplas, interacting with the material and breaking down the composition, rendering the surface fragile.

Panzer threw his acid bomb an instant after I threw mine. I counted down from the time Panzer's pack hit. The acid goo was designed to render itself inert after three seconds, but in three seconds, the kidnappers inside the room would be prepared for us.

I could only hope they didn't immediately kill Mara Parker. I didn't think that they would because she still had value to them as a negotiating piece. If I had been in their place, I wouldn't have killed her—as long as I thought I had a chance get the credits she was being ransomed for, or to escape. When they realized any chance of that was gone, Peyton would probably kill Mara just to end our opportunity to close the op out as a success.

I wasn't going to let that happen. I kicked off the side of the building, arcing out, then stuck my feet out in front of me, making small adjustments to the rappelling rig as I made a pendulum swing back to the window.

When my feet hit, the transplas shattered into gleaming chunks. I keyed in more slack as I went to one knee on the carpeted floor in the bedroom. I brought the revolver up in both hands and squeezed the trigger as a salvo of shots rang out. Three rounds thudded across my chest, not penetrating the bullet-resistant jacket but bruising me and knocking the wind from my lungs—a physical response that I still found troubling.

Another round slammed into the side of my head and my vision turned black for an instant.

In front of me, Zoran Mlakar cursed and took aim again. "Savin, kill the woman! Kill her now!"

Concentrating, pulling my double vision back together, I swiveled the revolver toward Savin Mlakar as he swung toward Mara. She had instinctively hunkered down on the bed, trying to make herself smaller.

I put the laser sight on Savin Mlakar's exposed throat and squeezed the trigger. That almost broke the part of me that was Drake from the memory. With my programming in place, I could not have harmed a human in any way, much less killed him.

Simon Blake had no such compunction. The part of me that was him watched in satisfaction as two rounds from the pistol tore through the man's throat. Dying, choking on his own blood, Savin Mlakar crumpled to the ground.

"Savin!" Zoran's howl was filled with pain and anger. He took a step toward his brother, lost for a moment, then turned his attention back to me.

By that time I had closed on him. I lifted my leg and brought my foot down hard against his right knee. The joint, even though it was reinforced by his armor, exploded and came apart. Broken bone pierced his flesh and the jagged ends stood revealed.

Forgetting his weapon, blind with pain and the loss of his brother, Zoran opened his mouth to scream again. I shoved the revolver's barrel into his mouth and pulled the trigger. Grabbing his chest armor in my left hand, I twisted his body and used him as a human shield as Rooma Bansal opened fire on me.

Her bullets hammered Zoran, thudding into the back of the dead man's head. I felt the vibrations of the impacts along my arm. Zoran's eyes stared sightlessly at me, bulging out of their sockets and weeping blood.

Panzer was stretched out on the floor and I realized I'd never seen him go down. A large, broad-bladed knife stuck out of his chest and blood pooled around the hilt. Ernst Nesterov lay beside Panzer, spraying blood from his lungs with every exhalation. The Russian struggled to rise, but I couldn't spare him any attention.

Gasping for breath, focusing on what I had to do, I shifted to the next target. Rooma Bansal was much smaller than Zoran and Savin, and she was fast enough that I felt certain her reflexes had been augmented. I tracked her across the room with a stream of bullets that just missed her and left a pockmarked line in the wall behind her, then I held my fire as she roped an arm around Mara Parker and trapped her as a shield.

Mara Parker was a beautiful woman. Her hair was dark and long, falling past her shoulders. She had the full-figured body of a woman who turned heads as she passed. Her light hazel eyes widened as she stared at me fearfully. I was certain she believed I was going to shoot her in that instant to save myself.

At my side, Giselle Portnoy was down, bleeding from the thigh in three places. She had followed Panzer into the room. Since the bullet-resistant fabric had been pierced, I knew at least one of the people in the room was using a flechette gun that fired needle pointed rounds. The flechettes often didn't penetrate the breastbone for a kill shot to the heart, or the skull for the kill shot to the brain, but they could cut a man to pieces in seconds.

Judging from the blood that streamed from Giselle, I thought it was possible the inferior lateral genicular artery had been severed. Simon Blake didn't know the exact medical jargon, but I'd learned them while working homicides with Shelly Nolan.

It reassured me that I might have been copied from him to a degree and had his memories running through my thoughts, but I was separate from him. I was still my own person. I found that satisfactory.

But I wasn't the one standing in that hotel room that day on Mars. Simon was, and he was facing an impossible situation.

Gunshots crashed in the outer room, followed by grenade

detonations. Cracks suddenly covered the common wall, offering testimony to the concussive force of the munitions our two remaining teammates had employed.

Zoran grew heavier in my grasp and I knew that the brief shield his corpse offered would be gone soon enough. As that thought flashed through my mind, a stream of flechettes ripped through the dead man and dug into my armor with sharp pinpricks. Blood tracked down my chest inside my armor and Simon hoped that none of them had pierced his heart.

In the corner of the room, Elias Peyton calmly reloaded his flechette pistol as though he had all the time in the world. I knew the movements of slipping a fresh magazine into the weapon took less time than I imagined, that his training would allow him to replenish the pistol in short order.

"Simon." Rath's voice suddenly thundered inside my head. "Take the shot. Do it now."

I activated the helmet's tracking system and saw the bright red reticule blur into being over Rooma Bansal's exposed left eye.

Fear widened Mara Parker's hazel eyes as she gazed at me. Even though she couldn't see my face, she read my intentions from my body language. She knew I was going to take the shot.

I released the corpse that I held, trusting that it falling would provide a distraction, knowing that I no longer had a shield to protect me from Peyton's flechette pistol. I focused on the reticule, holding it over Bansal's eye, then squeezed the trigger and hoped that Mara would not move.

Rather, Simon hoped that Mara would not move. I was reliving his memories. *I* knew Mara hadn't moved. The bullet sped true, caught Bansal in the eye, and churned through her brain before exiting her skull in a splash of blood against the wall behind her. The dead woman twisted away from her prisoner without firing and toppled toward the floor.

Elias Peyton hesitated a second, perhaps thinking that Simon or Bansal had killed his hostage, but he didn't hesitate long. The flechette pistol buzzed as it unleashed razor-edged death that bit into my chest, striking deeply into my left lung.

I held my pistol steady in my right hand, covering Bansal in case she wasn't dead, determined not to let her get off a shot. Using my left hand, I flung the small anti-personnel grenade I'd palmed as I'd dropped Zoran. The Taejo grenade disc, no larger than my thumb, flipped through the air and smacked into Peyton's abdomen. The disc hung there for an instant, long enough to draw Peyton's full attention. Horrified, obviously familiar with what it was, Peyton reached for the disc.

With a bleating, ear-piercing whistle, the Taejo grenade detonated and drove meters of monofilament wire into Peyton's body. Every time the strands of wire hit a bone, they twisted and followed new paths, piercing all organs and tissues in their way. The grenade contained four monofilament strands because four was an unlucky number in Korea. None of his organs would be salvageable.

Three of the strands emerged from Peyton's body. Two of them sank into the wall behind him. The third pierced the ceiling, sprouting from the underside of his left jaw. All of them winked crimson-stained silver in the light.

Weakly, Peyton fought to stand. He slid a foot forward, then leaned over and fell onto his face. He jerked spastically.

My vision blurred and I knew that I was in trouble. I knew that Simon Blake hadn't died in this room, but he'd thought he was going to. Panic flooded him when he drew in a ragged breath and discovered that both of his lungs were already filling with blood, pierced by the flechettes. The panic overran my senses and I couldn't help reacting to it. I wasn't programmed for the emotion, and it hit my radar as discordant jangling, a sensation of wrongness that triggered my onboard diagnostics.

I opened my mouth to speak, to let Rath know how badly I'd been hit, but all that came out was a gush of blood and crimson-tinted air that I knew I would never get back. I breathed in and started choking at once because my lungs were nearly useless.

"Simon." Rath's voice blasted over the comm in my hood.

I tried to answer, might have croaked.

"You're hit. I know you're hit. We're on our way. Get the woman and get out of there."

I tried to take a step, but the room whirled around me and my chest felt like someone had parked a cargo hopper on it. I grabbed a tourniquet from my med kit and slapped it high on Giselle's leg, flicking the servo-driven actuator. The band seized up, cutting off blood flow to Giselle's leg. I tried to affix a narco-slap to her neck, to get her up and moving and inhibit the pain, but I couldn't make my fingers work properly.

Then Bogart was there, a fringe of purple hair showing under the edge of his hood. He cursed as he took in Giselle and me, then he knelt down and patched her, then hauled her to her feet.

"Simon!" Rath's voice deepened and grew more commanding. "Do you read me?"

I tried to answer, couldn't, so I thumbed the tweaker on my glove to let him know I was there.

"You hang on! You do not have permission to die! Do you read me?"

I tweaked again, but I wanted to apologize to him because I knew I wasn't going to make it. My vision was narrowing to a spot of color and everything around it was greying out.

Surprisingly, Mara Parker came to my aid. Blood specked her face, offering mute testimony to how close she'd come to getting killed. She stood beside me, pulled my left arm across her shoulders, and shoved me into motion toward the window.

The sound of the hopper engine sounded far away even though I could see it just on the other side of the window. Hanzo stood in the cargo bay, holding onto the overhead bar with one big hand while he reached for me with the other. Obviously he'd already gotten out of the room so he'd be in the correct position for his next part in the plan. His samurai topknot flew in the slipstream. His hand closed on the front of my shredded vest and he hauled me across to the hopper.

Hanzo was cursing and looking worried as he laid me in the cargo bay. He wasn't trained as a corpsman and Simon Blake was long past anything he would have been trained to manage. Simon tried to breathe, tried to speak, but his lungs were full. He was on the verge of passing out.

I held onto the memory, knowing that I was slowly returning to *Khloe*'s cargo bay as the ship sped toward Mars. I wanted to see as much of the memory as I could. I needed to know more about Simon Blake's life. He lay there in the back of the speeding hopper, scared of dying. His fear no longer touched me, but it made holding onto the connection increasingly difficult.

"Rath, this is Hanzo." Hanzo loomed over me. Behind him, Mara Parker glanced around and spotted the medkit on the hopper's wall. Rath made certain we were stocked. Panzer had been the corpsman for our team, and he was dead inside the building we'd just quit. "Simon's hit. It doesn't look good."

Simon tried to breathe and panic turned his thoughts to pure animal need to survive. I used his eyes and ears to monitor the others in the hopper.

Mara threw the medkit on the hopper floor and shoved Hanzo out of the way. "Move."

Hanzo slid to one side.

A scalpel glinted in Mara's fist as she dropped to her knees. She opened Simon's armor and bared his chest, gazing down at the wounds in his flesh. I watched curiously because that was the sharpest emotion I had been programmed with. I was not sure what she was going to do, and was further confused when she stabbed the scalpel into Simon's chest.

"What are you doing?" Hanzo reached for her.

Mara shrugged out of his grip and pulled plastic tubing from the medkit. Simon's consciousness hung by a thread, hovering like a bit of flotsam on the thin surface of a dark ocean, and I hung onto it, wanting to learn everything I could. Clues about the scattered past were there and I didn't want to miss them.

She removed the scalpel and shoved the tubing into Simon's chest. Priming a hand suction device on the tubing, she started sucking blood from Simon's lung. Blood splattered over the hopper's cargo bay, jetting from the tubing.

Without ceasing the pumping, Mara leaned over Simon's face. Her eyes studied his. "Look at me."

Simon blinked slowly and tried to focus. I stared through his eyes as well, seeing nothing but her face. The thought that she might be dead skimmed across my mind, but I dismissed it. I would have to have proof of that as well.

"Stay with me." She looked fierce and scared and determined all at the same time. "I am not going to let you die. Do you hear me?"

Simon tried to answer, but failed. Then he couldn't float on the ocean of darkness anymore and sank. I sank with him.

* * *

When I opened my eyes, I was back on *Khloe,* the cargo ship I had secured passage on when I'd left the Moon, and I felt the alarm klaxons vibrating through the ship's hull. There was no air in the cargo area to carry the sound.

Fully alert now, no longer held by the memory, I linked with the ship's wireless system through the limited internal PAD I had, piggybacking systems diagnostics so *Khloe*'s near-AI guidance wouldn't alert to me. I accessed the ship's sensor array and immediately discovered that we'd attracted the attention of a space jumper.

Chapter Three

Attention, this is *Khloe*, a cargo ship en route to Gullivar colony." Captain Angstrom spoke calmly, but I detected the tension in his voice because I had filed a baseline on his communications while in stasis in the cargo bay. I eavesdropped through the ship's comm. "Change course immediately. You are in our logged flight path."

There was no response.

I tapped into *Khloe*'s external sensors and spotted the elongated shape of the approaching ship. The design was fragile, a connection of cargo compartments much like *Khloe*, but the other ship wasn't intended for use in any kind of gravity well. *Khloe* easily managed the Moon's gravity, though there were some concerns entering and leaving Mars. She could never have made a landing on Earth without self-destructing.

The other ship was a package freighter, constructed in space for the sole purpose of ferrying goods back and forth along the space lanes. Her skeletal frame held together in space where the structural integrity wouldn't be challenged, but she wouldn't handle any kind of planetfall or moonfall. Earth, Mars, and the

Moon all had workhorses that conveyed cargo to and from the surface. Earth used the Beanstalk, the umbilical to space, to lift cargo to the Challenger Planetoid to be shipped by package freighters much like the one closing rapidly on *Khloe*. The other ship's skin was dented and had a dulled finish that could have resulted from a lack of a dedicated crew or lack of funds.

I suspected it was more a cosmetic choice. This ship looked like most of the designs that frequented the Mars to the Moon route and would tend to blend in. Captain Angstrom pinged the other ship's IFF signature but got only noise back. The ship had been stripped of identifying frequencies and was running dark and silent.

Most men and women shipping aboard such a craft tended to be gypsies. They'd either chosen to work off the grid because they wanted independence, or they were wanted for crimes and had no other recourse to fend for themselves, no safe harbor. Traveling back and forth on long hauls didn't attract skilled labor, and law enforcement efforts didn't reach into deep space unless there was a need. Ship travel was expensive.

Using the ship's sensors, I watched as the unknown ship applied enough thrust to pace us two-tenths of a kilometer out. The pilot was excellent at his job, and the flight programs he was using were just as impressive. Aligning two bodies in open space was an exercise in mathematical expertise. I did not know if I could do it even with the programming at my disposal.

Three rectangular craft detached from the space jumper. Brief flickers of thrusters moved them away from the parent craft and pushed them in our direction. All doubt, which was a prognostic offshoot of curiosity programmed into me, that *Khloe* was the target was instantly removed. I did not feel anxiety, only more certain that *Khloe* was the intended objective for the mystery craft.

And that initiated my problem solving capabilities as I searched for a way to keep *Khloe*'s crew safe without killing the interlopers. Both of those criteria existed simultaneously within me. Neither could be ignored even though they lay seemingly at cross purposes.

I checked our flight path. We had just cleared Phobos, the nearer and larger of Mars's two moons. Phobos looked like a huge, pitted rock as it whirled around the planet. The moon's most obvious physical feature was the Stickney Crater, which most scientists believed had been left by a mass flung off Mars during the planet's formation. People on Mars watched Phobos set in the east twice a Martian day.

The moon was only 22.2 kilometers in diameter and its orbit was decaying. Eventually it would fall prey to Mars's gravity, get destroyed by the Roche limit when its own internal gravity surrendered to that of Mars. At that point, Phobos would be torn apart and be rendered into a planetary ring of rocks similar to those that circled Saturn.

Tracking the space jumper back, following what I assumed was the original path based on speed and trajectory, I deduced that the craft had been lying in orbit somewhere around Phobos just beyond the reach of the moon's gravity. Since it had been orbiting the Martian moon, doubtlessly "drafting" the moon's gravity to keep its speed up without expending fuel till a likely victim was chosen, the ship was nearly at the same speed *Khloe* was. When *Khloe* had entered the space jumper's range, it had begun to give chase.

The three rectangular craft closed on *Khloe*.

"You've had your last warning," Captain Angstrom said. "If you don't back off now, we will open fire."

The threat was idle and I believed the space jumper would know that. Cargo ships weren't armed for the most part because no one wanted highly fissionable materials in a starport. Even military spacecraft were weaponized with heavy guns in space and not allowed to land. Despite all the sensie output of science fiction stories, combat in space remained in the realm of fantasy.

Spacecraft were too vulnerable to attack and too expensive and necessary to replace.

The unknown ship made no response to Angstrom's latest hail. The three smaller craft sped toward *Khloe.*

I accessed the cockpit cam. Captain Angstrom and his people armed themselves, strapping on pulse weapons designed to disrupt an organic's central nervous system and a bioroid's equivalent of the same. While with the NAPD, I'd carried a similar Synap weapon. Other detectives and police officers had hated my pistol, calling it a "Ghandi gun" because I could not employ lethal force. The other detectives had believed in lethal force when a suspect resisted arrest with a weapon.

Some of my coworkers in New Angeles blamed my inability to carry a more deadly weapon as what had gotten Shelly killed. I could not argue the point.

Slug-throwers inside a spaceship were not a viable option. Without gravity, bullets tended to stay in motion and might find a weak spot in a ship's walls. Air was a precious commodity for human crewmen. Even with the scrubbing technology to remove the carbon dioxide buildup and reuse air, only so much could be carried on a voyage. In fact, having the scrubbers sometimes made captains cut back on the air shipping with them in favor of cargo space.

Every now and again, a "dead" ship coasted into port, descending on autopilot. Subsequent port authority investigation would discover a scrubber had failed out and the crew had asphyxiated during transit.

I had worked one of those cases when I'd been assigned to the Moon.

"Captain, they're not stopping." Kaloust, the ship's first mate, stood at the sensory array in the small cockpit. He was thin and hard and dark-skinned. Tribal tattoos stood out on his face and exposed arms. He wore a coverall, but the top was tied around his waist, leaving him in a sleeveless t-shirt.

Angstrom sat in the captain's chair and watched the sensor screens. A dozen of them occupied the space at the front of the cockpit and showed various views from around *Khloe.* The captain sat forward tensely, elbows resting on his knees. He was a thin and angular old man with a shaggy beard the color of bleached alabaster. The skin around his hazel eyes was deeply wrinkled, eroded by a hard life and anxious moments.

"They're not going to stop, Kaloust." Angstrom took a deep breath and let it out. "Not until they have our cargo."

Looking a little nervous, the first mate turned back to Angstrom. "What are your orders, sir?"

During the transit, I had examined the files on Angstrom and his crew. Angstrom had been a spacer all of his life, getting *Khloe* from his father. Kaloust had put in a few years as spaceport security, but he'd developed an addiction that had cost him his job. He'd since cleaned up, but the mark on his records was permanent. He was what my partner would have termed a "good" man because he had faced up to his problems and gotten on with his life.

The rest of the eight-man crew ran the gamut of spacer experience. Two of the older crew, Brenda Delroy and Jamal Ngola, had almost as much time in space as Angstrom.

None of them had military experience.

"We could surrender," Whitney Taylor said quietly from her navigation board. She was in her early twenties. During conversations I'd overhead, she'd signed on with *Khloe* because she'd wanted to be in space as soon as possible. "All they want is the cargo, right?" She was a petite woman with her hair cut short and the tattoo of a Japanese dragon around her neck in neon purples, blues, and greens.

"We're not surrendering." Brenda Delroy, heavyset and grey-haired, pushed back in her seat. She was the ship's cargo handler, the person who figured out how the shipments were to be packed, who checked all the final contracts.

"I didn't sign on to die for a shipment," Whitney argued, looking at Angstrom. "You can fire me if you like, Captain, but you're not paying me enough to fight whoever's coming for us."

"You won't be fighting them to protect the cargo," Angstrom said flatly. "Or for the pay you're getting. You'll be fighting them to survive."

Whitney's eyes widened. "What do you mean?"

"*Khloe*'s worth something too. Either sold as a vessel with forged documents, or parted out for salvage and scrap." Angstrom scowled. "And they won't want any witnesses to what they're about to do."

"The comm to Gullivar colony just got cut." Kaloust pushed back from the comm board with an angry, helpless look on his weathered face.

Angstrom placed a hand on the butt of his Synap pistol and stepped over to join his first mate. "You sent vid of the ship?"

"I did. Starport Authority told me they'd received the transmission."

"Did they identify that ship?"

Kaloust shook his head. "They said they were going to ping the ship, let them know they're aware of the situation."

Whitney looked hopeful. "Then those people will back off, won't they? I mean, they know Starport Authority is watching. They won't want to risk getting caught."

Angstrom clenched his jaw before speaking. His gaze stayed on the vid on the sensor screen. "Starport Authority can't reach them out here. They know that. At this point, they're not concerned about getting caught. For all we know, they're running low on fuel too and need what we have to get out of space."

The possibility left the crew silent and fearful. I recognized the facial indicators and body language I had been programmed with and learned while working with Shelly.

Taking a deep breath, Angstrom stared at the monitor display of the ship and the three rectangular craft now closing on *Khloe*.

"Keep recording that ship. Everything that goes on. If things turn out badly, bundle it all off into a buoy, set up the beacon, and shoot it toward Mars. They're not going to pick our bones without us taking our pound of flesh."

"Aye, sir." Kaloust sat at the comm board and began taking care of his task.

"Good plan, but the captain's planning for defeat." The voice was soft, feminine, and familiar.

I was suddenly aware of Shelly Nolan standing behind me. I had 360-degree vision through vid transmitters all over my body—bioroids are not limited to eyes only, that would have been a design weakness—and I had not seen her arrival. She was just there. No one sneaked up on me unless there was a blind spot or they came at me incredibly fast.

Dressed in her black thigh-length jacket, her dark red hair cut at collar length, wraparound black sunglasses covering her eyes, Shelly Nolan looked professional and composed. That was how I most remembered her when I thought of her, but I preferred the memories of her playing with her children, reading them stories and laughing at their recitation of their day's events.

I had not seen Shelly's family much since we had buried her. They had to struggle through their grief, and I had to learn to go on without my partner at my back. Working cases since her death always felt like something was missing.

Shelly looked at me and I saw my twin reflections in her sunglasses. "You can't let these people be killed, Drake."

I couldn't. My programming was already searching for a way to help. Preserving human life was deeply ingrained in my neural operating system. And that part of me that had been Simon Blake pushed me to do something as well. He, too, had laid his life on the line for others.

"We could flood the cargo hold with oxygen," Kaloust was saying. "Give ourselves some room to run or fight."

Angstrom shook his head. "We don't have enough oxygen on board for that."

That was true, and that was one of the reasons bioroids and bots were used to load and unload cargo. We didn't need oxygen. Humans in spacesuits were clumsy and slow in comparison, and oxygen was expensive. Recycling only stretched supplies so far, which was also true of water, and having humans work the airless cargo holds on the Moon and on Mars would have been wasteful as well as expensive.

"Then we can suit up," Whitney said.

"The air in the envirosuits will only last a few hours." Angstrom shook his head. "One nick in the wrong place and you're going to die a slow death. Same for escaping out into space. On top of that, you'll be slowed down, like running in quicksand. Even if they let us off the ship in suits, we'd suffocate before rescue could reach us. No corp or government agency would waste credits to save us."

I walked to the utility closets attached to the rear hulls. Tools and other equipment were stored there. I laid my hand against the compartment I wanted and pulsed an electromagnetic charge through my palm that spun the tumblers on the lock. The compartment opened to reveal the gleaming Synap pistols inside. They were part of a shipment Angstrom was ferrying to one of the colony's security corporations.

The Synap was larger than a slug-thrower, built boxy and thick. It fit my hand like it belonged there and my programming immediately weighed and measured the heft, recalibrating because there was no gravity, no air resistance in the cargo hold.

"That's not going to be much against armed men." Shelly stood beside me and looked unsettled.

She was a construct of my need for self-education, a guidepost I'd established after losing the real Shelly Nolan. Miranda, the Haas-Bioroid technician I had met on Earth and later convened with on the Moon, had told me that. Curious herself,

Miranda had wanted to further study my condition and continued association with Shelly's "ghost," especially since the neural channeling I had undergone had been spliced so heavily with Simon Blake's memories.

Since I was being hunted for a murder I didn't think I had committed—or at least didn't remember committing—Miranda hadn't been able to assuage her curiosity.

"I know." I dropped the Synap pistol into a pocket of the coverall I wore to carry tools for handling the ship's cargo. I opened another compartment and took out an industrial grade gel-grenade launcher and ammo pack. Shouldering the gel-grenade launcher, I closed the compartment and walked toward the manual exit hatch.

I had to override the security on the hatch, but it opened easily. The breach caught the attention of Captain Angstrom and his crew. Kaloust flicked one of the interior cams over to the cargo space and I saw myself on the screen as I climbed the ladder leading to the hatch. He tried to close the hatch, but I prevented his attempts.

Kaloust leaned toward the screen. "What is that Frank doing?"

Angstrom tapped the comm on his chair to open a channel to me. "Frank 5DE7CE, what are you doing?" That was the designation under which I was currently identified.

"I'm trying to save your lives, sir." I hooked in a tether to the D-ring on the wall, pushed the hatch open, and peered out into the black velvet of space.

Chapter Four

I eased out of the hatch and put one foot onto the hull, pulsing an electromagnetic charge through my foot to keep me attracted to the surface. The dulled *clank* of contact registered through the audlink I had to *Khloe*'s internal systems, but I heard nothing through the airless void around me. Pushing myself from the hatch, I stood and got my bearings, making certain to keep the tether line behind me unfouled.

Khloe spun gently as she traveled, not enough to create any real kind of gravity within the ship, just residual movement left over after jumping off the Moon. Phobos wasn't near enough or big enough to affect *Khloe*'s trajectory.

Jets on the three flat boxes of the boarding vessels flickered like bright daggers as the auto-pilot systems closed the distance to *Khloe*. The three craft came around, all of them targeting different sections of the cargo ship on which to land. *Khloe* resembled a short submarine, blunt and cylindrical to ease through thin atmosphere without breaking up.

Three hundred meters long and fifty meters in diameter, she was capable of delivering a medium-sized payload, from gourmet (on Mars for the moment) food and spices to small farm machinery and mil-spec vehicles. Martian colonial corps hadn't yet gotten the license to manufacture all machinery, and they levied large taxes for any inbound equipment in an effort to keep colonists from seeking local suppliers to meet their needs.

"Frank 5DE7CE, you cannot kill those men." Angstrom had returned to the command chair and was watching in tense anticipation.

"Sir, I am not going to kill them." I set myself, allowing my electromagnetic pulse through my feet to take hold as best as it was able, and pulled the launcher around to my shoulder in the firing position.

The Jinteki gel-grenade launcher was designed for mining. That was how it was going to be implemented in Gullivar colony. Mars was rich in magnesium, sodium, potassium, and chlorine, all of which were used in various industries. Mining companies scratched the natural resources from the planet's surface or extracted them from underground, then shipped them back to the colonies on mag-lev trains. Nothing on Mars was thrown away. Everything was used, recycled, and used again.

At just over a meter in length, the launcher was fourteen centimeters in diameter. The muzzle was square. Ammunition for the launcher resided in two reservoirs at the back of the weapon. The explosives were a binary formula, not capable of detonation until combined. I took off the safety and the keypad and trigger flipped out for use.

I dialed in a delivery load that would provide maximum concussion without breaching the shuttle's wall integrity, aligned the sighting mechanism, and squeezed the trigger.

A bright blue amorphous blob of gel-explosive shot from the launcher and streaked across the distance separating *Khloe* from the advancing craft. Upon impact, the blob spread quickly as I had intended, covering 2.19 nearly square meters with a thin membrane.

I punched the detonator button and the pool of gel-explosive detonated with a harsh flash and no noise. Immediately, the shuttlecraft altered its direction, knocked off-course by the explosion. It slid under *Khloe* like a rectangular shark.

Hacking into the shuttlecraft's emergency broadcast systems, I took four steps to my left to bring my next target into acquisition. The people on the frequency spoke Portuguese.

"Somebody's on the outside of the ship's hull! He's got a grenade launcher! I've been hit!" Anxiety filled the man's voice.

"Calm down." The woman's voice was more professional. "Can you get back to the ship?"

"No. Some of the thrusters are offline. I'm out of control."

"Work it out. See if the auto-pilot will reconfigure, if not, we'll get you before you drift too far."

"But what if—"

"Clear the channel. We've got work to do. Joao, Alfonso. Can you get to that ship?"

"On it, boss."

"Only a moment more."

I calculated the damaged shuttlecraft's next trajectory and noted that it would not—as I had believed based on the mathematical progressions I had formulated—fall prey to Phobos's weak gravitational well, nor did it have control of its course as it once had. The blast had taken out three of the small thrusters, which was the maximum I had planned for. Two would have sufficed, but three was even better.

The shuttlecraft fired its thruster again and slid farther away. It would take time for the automated system to re-route in order to regain control. By then *Khloe* would be gone.

"Don't leave us out here!" The anxiety reached a new level.

"Clear the freq!"

Hearing the panic in the shuttle pilot's voice immediately initiated an urgent response within me to help. Part of the programming to keep humans safe was maintaining their sense of safety.

Driven to assuage his panic, I was torn, but only briefly, over what I was supposed to do.

Then my priorities finalized and I dialed in a second gel-grenade as *Khloe* revolved and brought the next shuttle into view. I shouldered the launcher and fired again, adjusting for the recoil.

The second gel-grenade spread across the front of the shuttle and exploded when I pressed the detonator. The bright flash of the blast filled 122 degrees of my vision for 1.4 seconds, then subsided. This explosion was close enough to send a wave of heat over me.

Out of control, two of its thrusters offline, the shuttle's autopilot tried to adjust but succeeded only in changing the vector enough to ensure it slammed against *Khloe*. The vibrations echoed through me as I skimmed through *Khloe*'s diagnostics and checked for damage.

Angstrom cursed. "That was too close, Frank."

I replied, "*Khloe*'s hull integrity remains solid, Captain. All systems are operational. Life support is maintained."

"Another few centimeters and it could have gone the other way." The fear in the captain's words was brittle and edged.

I did not bother to respond. I knew that a few centimeters would have made a difference. Mass, velocity, and the dispersal of the blast had all been factors in the decision I'd made. Discussion was pointless. One of the shuttles still remained a threat.

I walked as quickly as I dared, making sure to keep one foot solidly anchored while I disengaged the other. I was slowed by having to keep the anchoring foot locked.

In herky-jerky fashion that had a rhythm of its own, I walked forward while at the same time moving laterally around *Khloe*. After seeing what had happened to the first two shuttles, the third had jockeyed for a position on the other side of the cargo ship.

I ran *Khloe*'s schematic through my memory and saw that there was an emergency hatch on that side as well. It opened into the forward compartment of the cargo bay next to the command center where the crew waited.

"Frank," Angstrom called, "do you see them?"

"Yes, Captain." I focused on the top of the shuttle just as it came into view. The shuttle had already docked, latched firmly onto *Khloe*'s hide like a tick. "I am making my way there now."

I shouldered the grenade launcher because I could no longer use it and slid the Synap from my pocket. I continued closing on the shuttle, aware that I only had 19.8 meters of tether remaining. Using *Khloe* as my reference, I estimated that the shuttle sat only ten meters away.

An access hatch opened on the shuttle's starboard side and a figure dressed in an envirosuit emerged. The polarized face shield kept me from seeing the man's features as he turned toward me and raised a heavy-caliber slug-thrower.

"I see him! It's a bioroid!"

"Destroy it, Joao!" the woman commanded.

Joao fired five times in quick succession. The muzzle flashes strobed the blackness of the surrounding space, reflected against *Khloe*'s dulled and pitted sides.

Three of the bullets streaked past me. One of them slammed into my left thigh, but my foot was anchored to the ship's hull and the round ricocheted off and sailed away without doing anything more than cosmetic damage. The second round struck me high on the left side of the chest and cored into the protective layers covering my primary operating systems. A bioroid's "brain" wasn't located in the head. It was located in the bioroid's chest, the greatest space available. The location also provided the most shelter and density.

Even anchored by my right foot as I was, I rocked back and spun slightly around. Scrambling to orient myself anew, I found myself turned at an acute angle to the man as he fired again and another person from the shuttle clambered out.

Three of the four shots went wide of the mark, but one of

them slapped against the side of my head. If I had been human, I would have been dead or unconscious.

I leveled the Synap and fired. The bolt, deliberately colored blue to warn those against whom it was used, struck the man. He shuddered and went limp as his senses left him stretched with only his magnetic boots holding him onto *Khloe*'s hull.

"There's another one!" Captain Angstrom warned.

Actually, there were three others. The other one outside the shuttle and the two who remained within the shuttle. I had verified their presence with thermographic vision.

Once more balanced, I walked toward the remaining envirosuited figure with the Synap raised.

"Put down your weapon and surrender peacefully." Since this one was not shooting at me, I had to tender the warning. I could no longer claim to be part of the New Angeles Police Department, but even using the Synap I could not fire indiscriminately without first being fired upon. Being rendered unconscious was not considered life-threatening to humans, but if they could be spared the unpleasantness, I was programmed to offer it.

"Destroy it!" the woman space jumper ordered over the frequency they were using.

"Shoot him, Frank!" Angstrom shouted, rising from his command chair.

The man raised his weapon and fired too quickly. Bullets skipped off *Khloe*'s hull in front of me and at my feet in bright sparks and sharp vibrations.

I pulled the Synap's trigger and the bright blue bolt lashed out and shook him into unconsciousness. His boots failed to secure his position to *Khloe* and he started to float away. His tether trailed behind him and I saw that he had not secured it before climbing out of the shuttle.

Reaching out, I grabbed the man's tether and fastened it to one of the D-rings on his unconscious partner's suit. They swayed there in weightless space as *Khloe* sped toward Mars.

I forced my way up into the shuttle, following behind the Synap. The airlock cycled quickly, filling the vacuum with air before opening the interior door. The craft's command module was small, barely large enough for the four-man crew. Panels above and below the sensor screen blinked with multicolored lights.

One of the remaining crew—a woman with a hard face, short hair, and dark eyes—stared at me over the barrel of a slug-thrower from less than a meter away.

I held my fire and spoke calmly. "Put down your weapon. Resistance at this point is futile."

"Freaking golem."

The term was a generic epithet for bioroids used by Human First and others.

"Zap her." Shelly stood at my side, somehow fitting into the entryway. I wasn't surprised that she had found a way to accompany me. Since she had died, nothing she did surprised me. "Waking up with a skull-rattling headache might teach her some manners."

"Kill her," a man's voice snarled. "Don't leave a living enemy behind you."

The second voice gave me pause. I knew it had not come from Angstrom or his crew because I was monitoring that frequency and they were only talking amongst themselves, suddenly hopeful about their situation.

I searched the command module for another person other than the two I saw before me even though I knew there was not enough space to hide someone else.

"Did you hear that?" I asked Shelly.

She looked at me with a troubled expression. "Hear what?"

"The man who spoke to me."

"No one spoke to you, Drake. You and I are the only ones here, aside from these would-be space jumpers."

I knew that was not true. Other than the two people in the

command module and the two I'd left floating outside, no one else was there.

"You don't leave an enemy behind you in a position to hurt you or your mission. I trained you better than that."

This time I recognized the hard voice. It belonged to John Rath, Simon Blake's old commanding officer. I somehow sensed him somewhere near where Shelly and I stood, but I saw only a dark shadow of a man in battle fatigues at an indeterminate distance.

"You should kill her and be done with it. You should kill them all, Simon. If you were me, that's what you would do. You've gotten soft."

The woman's eyes flickered a split-second before she pulled the slug-thrower's trigger. My vision flooded with the muzzle flash and I felt the bullet hammer my chest. I fired the Synap and immediately turned the pistol in the direction of the man, giving him no further warning. I was uncomfortable with that, but it was done before I knew it was going to happen.

"Good job, soldier," Rath whispered into my ear. "No hesitation, no mercy."

When my vision cleared, I gazed down at the two unconscious people floating weightlessly in the command module. I automatically confiscated the woman's slug-thrower and slipped it into my thigh pouch.

"Drake," Shelly said, "what did you do?"

"What I had to." Even as I said it, I knew it was Simon's answer, not mine. But I didn't bother to elaborate. Shelly wasn't really there any more than John Rath had been.

At that moment, I knew I was alone in the command module.

"Frank. *Frank.*" Captain Angstrom sounded annoyed and frightened.

"I am here." I put the Synap away and went to work securing the two unconscious crewmen, pushing them into the available seats and belting them in.

"What's going on?"

"All of the space jumpers have been neutralized, Captain. I'll be returning to *Khloe* momentarily."

"Roger that." Angstrom did not sound relieved.

Once I finished with the two crewmen inside the shuttle, I returned for the two I'd left tethered outside. I brought them in one at a time and strapped them in.

While I'd been busy doing that, I'd also monitored the space jumpers' main ship and saw that they were beginning the laborious process of salvaging their stricken shuttle crews. Given the parameters of those efforts, I knew the rescues would be easily effected within the given time constraints. Shuttles weren't equipped with more than superficial oxygen scrubbers. They could extend an oxygen supply, but they usually didn't carry more than a few hours' worth of breathable air. Given the clandestine nature of their operations, the shuttles might have been carrying less useable air to improve on cargo capacity.

Once I had the crew strapped in, I turned my attention to the control panel, quickly plotting in instructions for the autopilot to rejoin the main vessel. Then I quit the shuttle and began the walk back across *Khloe*'s hull.

Chapter Five

"Who are you and what are you doing on my ship?"

I stood stiffly at attention in *Khloe*'s crowded command module, hands behind my back in parade rest formation as I faced a very belligerent Captain Angstrom.

"I am Frank 5DE7CE." Under my present designation, that was true even though the e-docs bearing that name/model number were false. Stripped of my standing in the NAPD, I was no longer Drake 3GI2RC. Since that was the label given to me by Haas-Bioroid, that too was gone by default. I might have been shading the legal technicalities somewhat, but my logic programs had no problem with the answer I'd given.

Captain Angstrom cursed vociferously for a moment. Even Kloust drew back from the man. "That is not the truth."

"It is the truth." I remained steadfast.

"Who were you before you were Frank 5DE7CE?"

"Who I was does not pertain to the present situation."

Angstrom's eyebrows lifted in surprise and annoyance. He cursed again. "You're no Frank. You're higher than that. A lot higher."

I didn't say anything.

"What are you doing on my ship?"

"Going to Mars."

"Why?"

"Because what I need to find could not be found on the Moon or on Earth."

"What do you need to find?" Angstrom leaned threateningly into my face.

I did not mind the implied threats. I did not feel threatened. "Respectfully, Captain, that is none of your business." Within my programming for the NAPD, I had latitude to tell falsehoods and withhold knowledge. That was part of the job as a detective.

"I'll decide what my business is!"

I made no response, nor did I wipe away the spittle that flecked my face as he shouted at me from only centimeters away.

"Who was the woman that got you onto my ship?"

That had been Rachel Beckman, a professional mercenary. For a time, she had protected me. Getting me onto *Khloe* had blurred the line between professional and personal for both of us, but it had been done. "She was...a friend." I made my words more forceful. "Revealing her name could potentially be life-threatening for her, so I cannot answer that question."

Angstrom cursed again, knowing he was up against programming that he would never defeat.

Whitney Taylor spoke up then, surprising the rest of the crew. "Does it make a difference why Frank—or whatever his name is—is here on this ship? He's a bioroid. He can't hurt us."

Angstrom and Kaloust looked at each other, and I saw in their subtle facial expressions that they knew she was right.

"Not only that," Whitney continued, "Frank couldn't sit quietly by and let us be killed by the space jumpers. That's the only reason any of us know he isn't what he appeared to be."

"He could have been acting to save his own hide." Brenda stared at me with hard, accusing eyes.

"A bioroid?" Whitney snorted. "At worst, they would have jettisoned him. He could have floated out there for years and been just fine until someone found him. Or they could have taken him aboard ship, reconfigured his e-docs and ownership to resell him, or parted him out for salvage. He had more to lose going out there to confront those space jumpers than by sitting in here."

Brenda shook her head. "Do you really think he was at risk?"

Gently, Whitney reached up and touched the laceration along the side of my head. The stainless steel composition had withstood the bullet's impact, but the synthskin overlay had shredded. I felt no pain, only an irritating buzzing that let me know I wasn't cosmetically appealing at the moment. At my level, interacting with humans, appearance was important.

"I think he had plenty at risk."

Behind me, Shelly smiled. "I like this woman."

"Thank you," I said.

"You're welcome, Frank." Whitney smiled softly. "But I should be thanking you." She looked around meaningfully at Angstrom and the rest of the crew. "*We* should be thanking you."

No one did, but I detected a lowering of hostility in the command module.

After a moment, Angstrom addressed me again. "What are you going to do when we get to Mars?"

"What I came to do."

Angstrom cursed again, but not with the same previous intensity. "I paid for you, you know. Back on the Moon, I laid out a good amount of creds for you. I shouldn't have to absorb that loss."

Whitney looked at the captain. "Small investment given that Frank just saved our ship and our cargo. Not to mention, our lives. I don't know what kind of price you put on your life, Captain, but I value mine a lot."

"She has a point," Kaloust stated.

Angstrom's nostrils flared and his jaw clenched, but he didn't say anything. "You're going to help offloading the cargo."

"Yes." Doing so would help keep my cover intact. If Angstrom had made me leave, that would have drawn attention to me. "Once that is done, once it is night, I will take my leave."

"See that you do." Angstrom turned from me and walked back to his command chair. He riveted his attention to the sensor screen. A pair of remotely operated sensors stood watch over the space jumpers. The big ship was now trolling toward the second stricken shuttle. The first had already been recovered.

It was highly unlikely that Starport Authority had sent units to engage the space jumpers, and there was little if any chance of apprehending them. They would be long gone and Starport Authority would have expended a lot of fuel for nothing to show for it.

Whitney frowned at Angstrom, then took me gently by the arm. "C'mon, Frank, let's go get your face fixed up."

I let her lead me away.

* * *

Whitney's personal quarters were small with a bed that folded out from the wall and small overhead compartments that contained her personal effects. There wasn't much.

"Sit." She pointed to the bed.

I sat on the edge. "I do not mean to be an inconvenience."

"You're not an inconvenience." Whitney opened one of the overhead compartments and took down a cosmetics bag. "You look like you've been in a fight. You can't walk around like that."

"Synthskin can be difficult to work with."

"I know. Before I hired on with *Khloe*, I worked for Haas-Bioroid as a cosmetician for bioroids."

I accessed Whitney's service records in *Khloe*'s data. I thought that a background in something like that would more clearly have caught my attention and knew it was impossible that I had missed it. I found nothing in her files.

Whitney smiled at me as she began prepping the synthskin in the bag. "Checking up on me?"

"Yes."

"Not finding any mention of Haas-Bioroid?"

"I am not."

"Captain Angstrom isn't the most complete records keeper."

I silently agreed. When I'd scanned the records upon entry to the ship, I had found several of the e-docs incomplete. "Haas-Bioroid would have paid you better than you are presently earning," I said as she worked on my face. "And you would not have ever been in danger as you were today. Why did you leave?"

"I got my heart broken."

I resisted the immediate impulse to scan her cardiac system to verify the existence of a broken heart because I knew she was not referring to a physical ailment. Jealousy and love were two motives that suspects in my career at the NAPD often exhibited. "A lover wronged you."

"Yes." Whitney picked up a surgical scalpel from her tool set. "I need to excise more synthskin to make the repairs. May I?"

"Yes." I did not care what I looked like, only that I could pass as someone other than Drake GI2RC. Whitney's abilities did not matter.

She handled the scalpel with dexterity and sliced ragged edges of synthskin into wavy lines. "I'm cutting the patches unevenly to better blend the new grafts."

"Yes." I accessed the Net and pulled down information regarding synthskin grafting and recognized the technique Whitney employed. "I understand."

"I know this doesn't hurt, but I still have to ask."

"I am fine." The excision only caused a small degree of irritation, enough to let me know something was wrong.

"Good." She continued sliding the sharp blade across the

stainless steel substrata of my face. Even without the synthskin, I would have looked humanlike. The synthskin was only there to soften the alienness of my nature, not hide it. "While I was at Haas-Bioroid, I worked primarily on gynoids. Primarily their faces, but I was familiar with the whole anatomical package."

"You were good at your work?"

She grinned as she readied the synthskin. "I was one of the best."

"Till you got your heart broken."

Her mood darkened a little and her eyes tightened. "Yes. I became infatuated with Thomas Haas."

My interest ticked up. Thomas Haas was the heir apparent to Haas-Bioroid. Even more, he knew something about my programming that even I didn't know. He had appeared mysteriously in my apartment in New Angeles and taken control of me in a way that I still could not explain. I still had a blackout period that I could not access.

"I'm sorry," I said.

Whitney shrugged. "Don't be. It was entirely my fault. I knew better and I still chased after him." She smiled, but I knew there was not much humor in the expression from the amount of effort she put into it. "People warned me about how fickle he was. I was young and stupid, and in the end—when he cheated on me—I was too proud to stay working at Haas-Bioroid."

I said nothing because I didn't find anything in my memories to say. I could empathize with someone who had lost a family member to a violent act, but I could not address her loss in a way that I found acceptable.

"What was Thomas Haas like?"

Whitney leaned back away from me and narrowed her eyes in suspicion. "Why do you ask?"

"Just…curious."

"What kind of work did you do before you became a cargo handler, Frank?"

I paused only for a moment. "Work that I very much enjoyed."

After waiting to see if I would say anything further and discovering that I would not, Whitney nodded. "I feel the same way about no longer doing cosmetology on bioroids." She applied the synthskin and used a blue light to chemically seal the different layers. "I still moonlight from time to time whenever we're in port." She shrugged. "Some cargo ship captains need work done on their bioroids, and some of the sex houses need work done as well." Her nose wrinkled in disgust. "I don't work on bioroids they rent out for abuse, though. I draw the line there."

I remained quiet and still while she worked.

"What did you want to know about Thomas Haas?"

"Anything you might recall."

"You've seen him?"

"I have."

"Then you know how handsome he is."

Thomas Haas hadn't left an impression on me that way, but I knew that several nosies specializing in social media referred to him in that manner. I answered anyway to keep her talking. "Yes."

"Being rich doesn't hurt his attractiveness either." She carried on for a time about the things she had seen and done while in a relationship with Thomas Haas.

"Starry-eyed bliss. Attracted to anything bright and shiny and wealthy." Arms crossed over her chest, looking unimpressed, Shelly leaned against the bulkhead behind Whitney. "I won't say she had it coming, but any woman that lets herself get so lost in somebody like Thomas Haas is just opening herself up to a world of hurt."

I wondered how Shelly knew that, and wondered how this conversation came up with her "ghost." I knew we had not ever talked about this in so few words. Miranda had thought that the Shelly I was currently seeing was a construct my problem-solving programming found useful, but that didn't always line up with the conversations I sometimes had with this Shelly.

Or perhaps it was an aberration that had surfaced through the other programming Mara Blake had layered in when she'd set me up to be her salvation in the event of kidnapping. Again I wondered how she'd been so certain she was going to be taken. During my search for her, I had found no indication of such a person or corporation that would be so inclined. The other detectives assigned to her case, as well as the nosies, hadn't turned up anything either.

How had Mara known? What had she known?

It was all puzzling and I couldn't help but pick at the conundrum. So far, though, the effort remained fruitless. I felt certain the investigation would evolve once I reached Mars. Everything was leading back that way.

Back to where it had begun for Mara and Simon, and—to an extent—MirrorMorph, Inc., her company.

"There is one area where Thomas Haas is vulnerable," Whitney said, pulling my full attention back to the conversation. "His mother." She shook her head. "When it comes to the two of them, they're like oil and water."

I'd heard that before from other sources. Generally, it was thought that Thomas Haas was an unchecked dilettante and his mother too permissive. Some suggested the fractured relationship stemmed from Thomas's father, who had disappeared for all practical purposes immediately after conception.

Haas had been the brains behind Haas-Bioroid. She had come up with the initial designs, and the credits necessary to open the doors. After that, she had chosen well, picking some software/hardware developers to buy, others to go into business with or negotiate design licenses from, and still more to acquire through a hostile takeover.

Mara Blake had licensed the new neural channeling techniques she had developed to Haas-Bioroid while at the same time keeping MirrorMorph, Inc. as a separate entity.

"Want to take a look at the finished results?" Whitney pressed a button on a personal holo projector and focused it on me.

I studied my image as it floated in front of my face. Whitney's repairs were much more than I'd anticipated. The synthskin appeared smooth and unblemished, the damage completely gone.

"I did some reshaping on the other side as well," Whitney said, "to even out the repairs so they wouldn't be noticeable. I also added more of a tan to give you a multi-cultural appearance. Since you want to blend in—wherever it is you're headed—this might help."

"It will." I touched my face with my fingertips. I felt the contact, but it was distant, like layers of cotton lay in between.

"Feels slightly numb, doesn't it?"

"Yes."

"Don't worry about that."

I wouldn't have anyway.

"Give the repairs a couple days to fully integrate and you'll have the same neural feedback that you had before the damage. It takes a little time for the patching to get programmed back in."

"Thank you."

Whitney studied the holo projection, then looked back at me with interest. "You look different than you did. I didn't realize what I was doing."

I had noticed that.

"I was just following the natural contours of your face. You would think you were moving your facial structure as I worked. You didn't do that, did you?"

"I didn't know that was possible."

"Supposedly, it's not, but there have been whispers—here and there—about assassins who have had their faces rebuilt through nanotechnology to change their features."

I'd heard that too. "I've never seen anyone like that."

"You aren't supposed to." Whitney laughed.

"I suppose not."

Then Whitney frowned. "Was this the face you were trying to hide?"

"No." As Drake, I had looked different than the bioroid I saw in the holo.

"Good." Whitney started putting her equipment away.

I touched my face again, not convinced that things were good. I looked more like Simon Blake than ever.

Chapter Six

"*Khloe*, you are cleared for landing. You may begin your final approach."

Captain Angstrom occupied his command chair but sat tensely. I knew he had more on his mind than simply landing. Since I was hiding my real identity, he didn't know how much trouble I would bring him once we docked. I was sure that the fact they could all be in handcuffs within a short while crossed his mind. Secrets often turned deadly out in the Martian colonies.

In fact, I knew there was a good chance that Angstrom had started wondering if getting chosen by the space jumpers had been my fault. Regrettably, I had not considered the same thing at the time. Had I done so, I would have handled things differently.

"Police work isn't about getting there ahead of the bad guys," Shelly said. "It's about picking up the pieces and working with what you decipher as you go along. We don't usually get to prevent a murder. That's not the job, unfortunately. By the time we figure out someone is planning to kill another person, it's usually after the fact. But we can prevent a murderer from killing again."

She sat beside me in the cargo hold as *Khloe* shuddered and shook through the descent into the thin Martian atmosphere. I held onto the cargo netting to secure myself. She sat undisturbed. Other bots and bioroids sat quietly in their assigned spaces. All of them were low-level manual labor units and didn't communicate other than to take orders or inform someone about problems.

"You have the images of the two people in the last shuttle," Shelly continued. "When you get planetside, run them and see if you get any hits."

"If I discover they are more involved than I believe, it is too late to do anything about it. I let them go. Whoever was behind the interception will remain one step ahead of me."

"You think someone staged the space jump?"

I paused only briefly. "It is a supposition that carries merit."

"Seriously?" Shelly looked surprised. "Are you getting paranoid on me, Drake?"

Bioroids weren't programmed for paranoia, but they were scripted for close attention to anomalous events. Sometimes one bordered on the other.

"No. I'm choosing to err on the side of being overly redundant."

Shelly laughed. "Maybe you've learned more from me than you'd thought."

"What do you mean?"

"I mean that I would be paranoid right now as well with everything that's going on. Someone pinned Jonas Salter's murder on you when it would have been easier to kill you."

That was true. The Earth and Moon media still tracked the story of Salter's murder, but the matter had fallen to the back pages of the newsrags because the NAPD hadn't been able to find me or any more evidence that I had committed the murder. They hadn't even figured out why Salter had changed his name and his features and then hidden in plain sight.

"Efforts have been made to kill me." I reflected on those incidents. "Many times."

"Because of Mara Blake."

I was uncertain if that was a question or an accusation. I chose to be oblique as well. "That must be the answer."

As I looked at Shelly beside me, knowing she was some kind of construct presented by my logic programs—even though that seemed to be an oxymoron at the moment—I wished that I had the real Shelly with me. I missed her input, her keen intuition, and the certain knowledge that she would validate everything I thought I knew, as well as point me in new directions.

Then I realized that her family, her husband and her children, missed her far more than I did. I felt slightly unsettled and wrong about my own wants and needs, though I knew I was not programmed for selfishness. That was a human quality that was outside my operating parameters.

The Shelly beside me couldn't guess at my thoughts. She stared at the opposite bulkhead with an expression I found disturbingly familiar and considered things for a time. Then she spoke. "With everything that's going on, with Mara Blake in the wind and you being—at least partially—Simon Blake, I don't blame you for overthinking this. Especially since Simon Blake was taken out by his own people."

I was relieved to be onto another topic. That proved I wasn't stuck in my problem solving. "They were not *my* people. They were a splinter group of the mercenary unit."

"Noted."

"Most likely, they were people who were known to Simon Blake."

"Meaning that if you run into any of Simon Blake's old friends on Mars, you'll have to be worried about them sticking a slug-thrower to the back of your head and evacuating your brainpan."

"My brainpan is not in my head."

"You know what I mean."

"I have logged that possibility."

"Keep it near the top of the list."

"Yes."

Khloe's automated warning came over the ship's channel. "Brace for landing. Ten minutes."

I settled in and hung onto the restraining straps. I accessed the ship's external sensors and tracked the landing.

From far outside Mars's gravitational well, the planet looked large and red, paler in some areas where the lighter silicate sand created vast deserts. As *Khloe* closed on Mars, the colonies became visible. They were large plascrete bubbles that looked vulnerable against the expanse of the planet.

Inside many of the bubbles outside the main hubs, looking like topiary constructs against the barrenness that covered Mars's natural landscape, farm laborers and agriculture equipment worked to keep the fields productive. Nearly all of the food the colonists needed for life was grown in the ag-bubbles, but Earth still maintained a brisk business supplying spices and red meat.

Several of the ag-bubbles contained hydroponics fields containing catfish, cod, and crabs. Since water had to be mined from the polar regions on Mars and trucked into the colonies at the equator, the fish and crabs were made part of the water reclamation cycle. People fed on the fish and crabs, which in turn fed on human waste, helping cleanse the water before it was purified and once more put into the system.

I had thought the process showed innovation and had been intrigued. I'd discovered the procedure during an investigation of a marine biologist that had lately returned from Mars who had been involved in introducing another arctic whitefish to the system.

When I had brought up the matter, Shelly had voiced disgust at the idea of making fish part of the sewage reclamation process, then eating them. I'd pointed out that the fish had been spliced to be resilient and succulent, as well as a greater provider of Omega 3 and protein. She had told me that didn't matter.

I made it a point never to tell her about the rice and soy she enjoyed so much and the "night soil" that was used to fertilize those food products.

Gullivar colony was named after a character in an early 20th century novel by Edwin Arnold. In the book, *Gullivar of Mars*, United States seaman Gullivar Jones reached the red planet by means of a magic carpet. I had read the novel while en route to Mars but discovered that the present day Mars was in no way like the one Gullivar encountered.

I studied Gullivar colony's main hub. The city under the glass dome was nowhere near as large as a megalopolis back on Earth, and not even as large as the Moon cities.

"It's still big enough to hide anyone who wants to kill you," Shelly said.

I nodded and continued my cursory examination of the city, matching it up with the maps I had downloaded to memory. All around the dome, massive wheels that ran on solar energy twirled and glinted in the gathering clouds of red Martian dust and powered the huge generators that in turn powered the city. Thick cables snaked in from power farms farther away from the city.

Despite the distance from the sun, the solar radiation was strong and provided plenty of power to meet the colony's needs. Building additional domes to meet the growing population wasn't a problem either, though some of the older colony cities had built the solar farms too close to easily expand close to home. Large batteries stored power from the day and provided for a robust nightlife.

Sunlight glinted from the dome and from the solar wheels that cycled endlessly. Hoppers flew from tall building to tall building, and the whole city looked like a micro version of New Angeles or any other megapolis.

Outside the dome, the barren wasteland stood in sharp contrast. Although the wind was too thin for humans to thrive on, it moved restlessly, whipping up large clouds of red sand that shifted and changed shape as it flew across the countryside. Environmental suits, or envirosuits, for anyone working outside a domed area were outfitted with special filters to keep the sand from getting inside. Machinery and equipment had to be protected in the same way.

One particular sandstorm caught my eye as we closed on the starport. I telescoped my vision so I could better see it. One of the Martian trains ran along mag-lev rails toward Gullivar colony. According to the file I had tucked away in my memory, most of the pulling engines were built along the same lines: seven meters tall by ten meters long by three meters wide. The command module inside the pulling engine was filled with equipment that operated the unit, controlled the container cars over umbilicals, and monitored the terrain and weather.

When the first pulling engines had been built, Poseidon Equipment, Inc., named after the Greek god of the oceans and also the supposed inventor of the first chariot, fashioned them to look like giant sea creatures. Cast in bronze-colored metal mined from Martian mines, this pulling engine looked like a beluga whale. A fluked tail flipped up over the first container car.

Khloe's engines powered up again as we sank toward the docking pads and I lost sight of the train. Starport Authority was a rectangular area that was one kilometer wide and three kilometers long in the open, enclosed by walls on all sides to block out some of the wind and dust storms. Fourteen cargo ships presently sat on the plascrete tarmac. From the comm frequency I'd hacked into through my onboard PAD, I knew that three other cargo ships were en route and that Starport Authority wanted a word with Captain Angstrom after he'd landed.

The PAD I was currently equipped with wasn't nearly as sophisticated as the one I'd had as an NAPD detective, but I knew my way around hardware and software enough to get access to the starport communications. I needed to know what they knew—especially if I was a point of focus for the authorities. One of the first things I hoped to do once I got planetside was arrange a PAD upgrade.

So far, there was no mention of Frank 5DE7CE on any level. Drake 3GI2RC was another matter. The killing of a human by a bioroid—thought impossible by most people—was huge news. On Mars, where bioroids and clones were in even more use because of the terraforming and mining operations where it was not economically feasible to put flesh and blood labor under an atmosphere, the idea of a murderous bioroid was tantamount to a nightmare.

"On Earth, a rampaging bioroid might kill even several humans before being brought down, but on Mars such a creature could destroy environmental controls on a colony and doom millions to a slow death." That was in one of the local media sheets I tapped into once I got within range of Gullivar.

The comment had started a flame war between readers. Several commenters had told the nosie that "giving a golem an idea like that was stupid." That had spurred other observations that a bioroid "clever enough to kill a human could think of sabotaging environmental stations well enough on its own."

Human First had weighed in heavily, again pressing the need to ship all bioroids or clones off-planet—or "destroy them on sight." There wasn't much latitude with the Human First group.

"They should have called themselves Humans Only," Shelly said.

That had crossed my thoughts as well, then I realized the fact that Shelly had said that was redundant. She was just my programming underscoring the observation.

From there, the media piece devolved into arguments for and against bioroids and clones, then further devolved into commentaries on the strained relationship between Earth and Mars. Corporate spin doctors got involved in the meltdown at that point, jumping in on the side of Earth, trying to illustrate the inability of the Martian colonies to survive independently.

I had stopped reading because the rants were endless, being appended even as I had scanned the contents.

With a final bump, *Khloe* settled to the landing pad she'd been assigned. The creak of her hull and the whine of her servos vibrated through the bulkhead at my back.

* * *

As I had promised Captain Angstrom, I helped with the cargo. The landing pad wasn't protected by the dome, so I got my first exposure to the Martian climate. At the equator where we were, the temperature averaged -81 degrees Fahrenheit. Those temperatures got much colder at the polar caps.

Despite the ten meter high walls, iron oxide dust swirled around me the whole time I worked. If I required respiration, I would have suffocated within minutes as much from my lungs filling with the particulate matter as from the lack of oxygen. The wind was also a constant factor, requiring that all crates were secured at all times.

Getting *Khloe* offloaded and reloaded took forty-six hours of constant work. During that time I downloaded more and more of the local culture that I could, putting together a better picture of Gullivar colony and the outlying colonies.

Starport Authorities came by to question Captain Angstrom, but he said nothing of me or what I had done to keep the ship free of the space jumpers. According to his official statement, the space jumpers had missed us by centimeters and *Khloe* had eluded them. Since matching up objects in space, especially when neither of them was locked into a particular orbit pattern like a real or artificial satellite, the story was believable.

However, I recognized that the senior investigator had some doubts. He even insisted on a physical inspection of *Khloe*'s hull, and he had paused at the fresh scuff marks where bullets had bounced from her. Angstrom had insisted that he didn't know what the marks were from, and furthermore that he had seen many strange scars left by micro-meteorites.

The man could lie extremely well. I did not catch so much as a twitch in his blood pressure or flaring in his pupils to indicate the presence of a falsehood.

Not entirely satisfied, the Starport Authority team left. I had the impression that if they could find time in their busy schedule, the senior officer wanted to return for further questioning.

Clad in an envirosuit, Angstrom walked over to me and put his face shield against my face. I could read his lips as well as feel the vibration through his helmet.

"That guy's not happy with what he sees."

I nodded understanding.

"You're going to be better off if we're gone—and you've gotten out of here—before he returns."

I nodded again.

"Do you have a way to get through Starport Authority? Because if you need it, I can arrange a temporary messenger pass to get you into Gullivar."

I accessed his suit's frequency to respond. "If you do something like that, you will put yourself and your ship at risk."

"Only if you get caught doing something highly illegal."

Angstrom waited long enough for me to respond. I didn't.

"Whatever you've got planned, I don't think you're going to get caught at it until I have enough distance between me and this planet. And if you do get caught, I don't think blaming whoever brought you here is even going to show up on the radar. All the other trouble you cause is going to be too big."

"He's got a lot of faith in you," Shelly said with a smirk. "Of one kind or another. And he doesn't even really know you."

"Thank you, Captain, but your involvement will not be necessary. I do not wish to put you or the crew at any further risk. I have already got a way through Starport Authority."

The captain grunted in acknowledgement and I judged that

he was not surprised. "If I don't see you again, I wish you luck in whatever you're doing."

"Thank you."

Angstrom pulled his head back from mine, turned, and walked away. He opened a comm frequency and started negotiations for a shipment of Martian silicate that was used in Earth-based art supplies. Several art galleries in New Rio de Janeiro had developed new lines that were currently making small fortunes for artists that had learned to work in the medium. The profit potential for shippers wasn't great enough to interest the corporate cargo lines, but boutique businesses like the galleries in New Rio helped keep independents like *Khloe* operating in the black.

I finished storing the last of the goods making the trip back to the Moon, and to Challenger Planetoid, then headed off without saying goodbye. As I went, I downloaded the new e-docs that changed my identification from Frank 5DE7CE to…

Chapter Seven

"Norris 1JA5NU?"

I stepped forward to the security gate where three heavily armed guards lounged around scanware. They wore the black coveralls of Starport Authority and looked like a seasoned crew. "I am Norris 1JA5NU."

The man at the starport sec board searched the documents with a practiced eye. He was in his late forties and Hispanic with a full face and cropped salt and pepper hair. Sergeant chevrons glinted in blue metal against his collar. Even though his gaze was on the screen, I knew he had not fully removed his attention from me.

"Says here you're a trade goods scout for Lono Ag." He looked up at me. "That right?"

"Yes."

He scanned my cargo jumpsuit. "You don't much look like a trade goods scout."

"I was contracted out as a cargo labor unit to defray my travel cost. I ate no meals. I breathed no oxygen. I drank no water. I made no waste products that had to be accounted for."

"And when you got here, you unloaded crates."

I nodded.

The other two security guards grinned knowingly. The taller one muttered, "Try doing that to a human."

The older man raised his voice in irritation. "Knock it off, Mullins. Bioroids have got rights too, and I'm not going to let you demean a unit capable of understanding mockery."

"I take no offense," I said.

The man looked at me with a level gaze. "I do. I worked security with a Rocky unit that gave his life to protect me." He hiked up his pants leg to reveal a cybernetic leg. "Cost me a leg, but I wouldn't have made it through without him."

Rocky units were security units designed to protect people and property. They were a few steps below my capabilities, not having the more complete understanding of humans that I did.

The sergeant looked meaningfully at his tall subordinate. "And I said *he* because Rocky 2ST3AL was more man than a lot of you uniformed wannabes have ever thought about being."

"Sarge." Mullins shifted, his face darkening with anger and embarrassment. "You can't talk to me like—"

"Stow it." Without expression, the sergeant faced the bigger man. "One more word, Mullins, and you're on cavity search for a month. Scrubbing anuses for trace evidence of contraband."

"Right, Sarge." Mullins looked away from his superior and me.

The sergeant returned his attention to me. "What's Lono Ag?"

I knew he had the information in front of him, but he wanted to hear it from me. "Lono Ag, Inc. is a Hawaiian megacorp dedicated to providing fresh foods on Earth, the Moon, and Mars." I turned up a palm and juiced a holo ad that ran familiar advertising footage of the main offices on Oahu. Most of the footage showed the pineapple fields there, which was easily Lono's most recognized product. The mascot, an animated Lono in traditional dress, walked among the fields. "From a grass roots company in Oahu, Lono gradually bought up Dole Pineapple, BerryFields in Colombia, and several other…"

The sergeant held up a hand. "Enough. What is your job here?"

"My assignment is to tour local producers and begin preliminary negotiations concerning adoption and labeling of products consisting of soybeans, melons, and berries, as well as to investigate the potential for establishing canneries."

"You're here to cannibalize local growers, you mean?" The woman asking the question stood behind me. She was tall and thin, dressed in a fantasy bikini outfit based on a character in a *Planet Stories* short novel that left most of her body exposed. Science fiction and fantasy element clothing styles remained popular on Mars. I noted that the attention of the two younger sec officers was locked on the woman. Her hair was dark black and hung past her shoulders. Her eyes were light purple, obviously modded because no color like that existed naturally in human DNA.

"Lono Ag is not here to cannibalize anyone," I replied evenly. I turned to face her because that was more acceptable to humans. With my 360-degree vision, I had no problem seeing her. "We are here to revitalize dwindling gene pools and hopefully build a better business model between Earth and Mars."

The argument, as well as the party line I had responded with, was from several sheet articles I had read in preparation for the secondary identity Rachel Beckman had arranged for me when I reached Gullivar colony. As a trade goods scout, I could go many places without drawing too much attention. Especially since I was traveling alone. Disguising an entourage would have been much more difficult.

"Not only that, but as a bioroid I am incapable of negotiating an arrangement that will hurt a human," I continued. "I am here for the betterment of the ag business. Given present parameters, with the degradation of gene pools for vegetables and fruits—"

"A degradation which has been caused by Earth ag-corps choosing not to sell seeds without licensing arrangements, or seed crop that doesn't replicate past one growing cycle. You people manufacture failure as much as you do crops."

"Ag-corps are entitled to safeguard their licenses. Creation of new seed stock genegineered for specific environments is costly. Every licensed seed stock comes with a guarantee of success. You will not find that out in the wild, and on Mars, you won't find that at all."

"That's a lie you sold to several peoples in Africa, peoples who were not educated enough to protect themselves. I was working in Cape Town when BountifulGene Corp created the famines there six years ago. The tribes seeded crops that BountifulGene promised would deliver a greater and healthier crop than they'd ever had before. That crop got loose from the ag domes where they were being grown and mutated with the local plant life, which in turn contracted a disease that could not be pinned on Persephone Futures, Inc., a rival corp. Those people faced starvation. I watched malnourished children die." Her voice broke at the last.

I remembered the occurrence. It had been a dreadful thing. Thousands had perished before arrangements had been made by the World Health Organization, which was almost as malnourished as famine survivors. According to the media, the resultant death toll was a "perfect storm" of bad events. Gene-modified plants did not have the resiliency of natural species allowed to thrive without interference. Bananas, in their original incarnation, had disappeared in much the same fashion, bred down to a basic design that could no longer adapt to changing environment and infections.

"She's right," Shelly said at my side. "Your job cover isn't exactly awe-inducing. Or even respectable."

I knew that, but that was the price paid for mobility. Norris 1JA5NU wasn't going to be welcomed by many.

"Norris."

I turned to face the sergeant. "Yes?"

"Maybe it would be better if you kept moving along." The sergeant cleared my e-visa. "I don't have anything against bioroids, but ag-corps are a different thing. You'd get more respect as a dockworker." He shrugged. "Except from Human First, who still insist it would be better to risk flesh and blood in envirosuits than put you guys out there."

"I understand, Sergeant. Thank you for your time." I passed through the sec gate and stepped into my life on Mars.

* * *

As I walked through the starport, images of other Martian starports swirled through my thoughts. I believed that some of them came from vid, perhaps all of them, but I wasn't sure. Some of them seemed too real, too immediate. I couldn't help but wonder if Simon Blake had walked through Gullivar at some point. The colony was definitely old enough for him to have been here, but only just.

Several of the humans and clones around me, as well as a few of the bioroids, wore Martian dress in the manner of science fiction novels by Edgar Rice Burroughs, Otis Adelbert Kline, Leigh Brackett, and others. People, bioroids, and clones filled shops, bars, and eateries on the lower level cantina, standing alongside others dressed in the more familiar currently popular film noir and zoot suits I had seen in New Angeles and on the Moon.

Most humans had a desire to be someone else, if only for a short time, while out amongst the public. On Mars, at least in Gullivar on the day I was in the starport, the theme tended more to the science fiction realm. Several gene-modded pets that ran the gamut of tentacled things to small apes with bleached white fur and eight-legged mammals covered in lizard skin whined and snarled and oozed around their masters.

The licenses for such pets were exorbitant because resources were dear on Mars.

I continued along the upper deck, heading for the exit to public transportation. As I wound through the humans, clones, and bioroids, I watched the Martian princess I had encountered at the checkpoint stride toward me. I thought another encounter was in the offing and searched for a way to avoid it.

Instead, the woman linked her arm through mine. "Hello, Norris."

I tried to stop, but she dragged me forward.

"Keep walking. We need to talk."

I fell into step with her because she didn't desist pulling. "What do you want?" I checked my 360-degree view to see if I could spot someone else obviously with her. I found no one.

"Rachel sent me." She turned her head up and gazed at me with those strangely colored purple eyes.

"I do not know who you are talking about." I was not about to admit to Rachel Beckman's culpability in my arrival on Mars. She had put her freedom in jeopardy by taking part in my escape from the Moon.

"Sure you do. But let me go first. She said you would be protective."

I kept walking because I didn't want to draw attention from the security people.

"You're going to need an untraceable line of cred while you're here, Norris."

That was true, but I'd had some ideas about working off the books somewhere to accrue cred. Such work was available outside of the megapolis, but it was also risky. A bioroid who wanted to occupy himself or herself rather than shut down between shifts could supplement income. Likewise, people who held contracts for bioroids could farm those bioroids out to make more cred as well. "Rachel didn't mention helping out before you left the Moon because she wasn't certain she could make it happen," the woman continued.

I let her talk. Rachel Beckman was not financially solvent at all times. I had seen her background check and her financials were all over the place. She got paid well when she had jobs, but she played expensively as well.

The woman looked at me. "Rachel is a friend. A *good* friend. If you know her, you know she isn't always flush with cred, so what she's making available is a windfall to you, but I don't know what she's had to do to provide it."

Trusting the woman's words and the sincerity of her tone, plus the fact that while she was touching me I could easily read her bio signature, I nodded. "Tell her that I appreciate the effort, but it is not necessary."

She looked at me for a moment. "Rachel didn't tell me why you were here in Gullivar, or why you were on Mars for that matter, and it's none of my business, but I know that she's concerned about you."

"She has no need to be. Please relay that to her." I did not intend to contact Rachel Beckman again. The minutes-long delay between Earth and Mars communications left too much exposure for interception by other parties that would be looking for me. Since Rachel had been assigned to me on the Moon by the NAPD for my protection, I knew that detectives would be keeping a watch on her. I also knew that close circumspection would be difficult for her to continue some of the jobs she routinely handled. She sometimes crossed over into semi-illegal activity.

"This is your first time on Mars?"

"Yes." Even though I knew that was the truth about myself, the answer still felt somewhat like a falsehood.

"Then you have plenty to learn and plenty to look out for. Rachel has every right to be worried."

I thought about that but didn't have any response. "Please return the cred to Rachel."

The woman shook her head. “Can’t. This was a one-way ride for the cred. You find a use for it or it’s lost forever.” She slipped an unmarked credstick from her black tresses and offered it.

I hesitated.

“Either you take it or I keep it. Whichever it is, Rachel’s out the cred.”

“You could pay it back.”

The woman smiled. “She told me you would probably say that. She said you were the boy scout type. So she told me to tell you that I would keep the cred for myself.”

“Would you do that?”

“Yes.”

“And she’s your friend?”

The woman leaned her head against my shoulder and we drew little attention from the passersby. I assumed that whoever was mildly interested in our relationship figured that one or the other of us was getting paid as an escort.

“That’s funny,” Shelly said as she walked beside us.

“Rachel is my friend,” the woman assured me. “But I left some business on the Moon that means I can’t go back for a while. A good long while.” She sighed and I judged the reaction to be truthful and subconscious.

“Rachel could come here.”

The woman smiled. “Cute, but you don’t know enough about Rachel, evidently. She’s currently being investigated by Mars Security Force for a couple of bodies left out on the red plains.” She shrugged. “If you bury them deeply enough, they don’t show up again. An industrial terraformer plows right over them and scatters the DNA so thoroughly that an ID will never be confirmed.”

I hadn’t known that, and I was curious as to how the woman came by the information. “Was Rachel involved in those matters?”

“Involved, yes. Did she drop those bodies? No. That was…

someone else." She waggled the credstick at me. "So. You or me? I've got my eye on a couple outfits that I wouldn't mind picking up."

I plucked the credstick from her hand. "When you talk to Rachel again, tell her that I will pay her back as soon as I am able." I ran the credstick across my palm and read the digital information. The available cred wasn't prodigious, but Rachel must have dug deeply to provide it. I could pay her back.

Provided I was able to return to Earth. Or survived my trek across Mars.

The woman looked up at me. "You're not really here to cannibalize the indy ag-farms, are you?"

I looked at her and got the impression from her body language and facial characteristics that she wanted the truth. "No. I'm not."

"Good. From the way Rachel talked about you, I wanted to like you. If you were here to disrupt the ag business, I wouldn't have cared for you very much." She patted my arm and released it. "Time to go. Be safe out there."

"Wait."

She stopped a few feet from me and gazed back.

"What is your name?"

A smile flirted with her lips, but she looked sad as well. "Call me Orchid. If you ever see me again. Bye, mystery man."

"Bye, Orchid." For a moment, I watched her go, disappearing with definite skill among the other people in the starport. People continued to flow around me, some of them grumbling over the extra effort expended to step to the side.

I fell in with the flow and continued toward the exit. I stopped at a clothing store along the way and purchased a new set of clothing. I bypassed the Martian science fiction outfits that consisted of breechclouts and metal armbands as well as the futuristic wear that looked like something out of a retro Buck Rogers sensie, and selected black pants with thigh pockets and a black pullover with accompanying black mid-calf duster.

"Get the hat, too." Shelly stood beside me as I surveyed myself in the full-length mirror.

I pulled on one of the black skull caps from a nearby stack. Shelly had been the one to add that to my fashion statement at the NAPD. She'd said it softened my alienness for people we interviewed. Her daughters had laughed at me, telling me I was trying to hide the fact that I was bald.

When I looked at myself in the mirror, I realized that I "felt" more like myself than I had in a long time. Shelly had been right, then and now. The hat softened my alienness.

Then, as I gazed at the image, it blurred, went out of focus—something that could not happen with my vision—and became the image of a man in full combat armor and gear. He held a laser rifle in his hands and had a slug-thrower under his left arm and at his right hip. I recognized the face framed in the battle helmet as Simon Blake's. As I stared at him, he smiled.

"Are you ready for this?" he asked.

"Drake?"

My vision reset, the human equivalent of a blink. I focused on Shelly.

Concern showed on her face. "Are you all right?"

"I'm fine." I walked to the checkout counter and slotted the credstick I'd brought with me on *Khloe*, unwilling to use the one Rachel had sent inside the starport. I intended to use that one in the less legitimate areas where cred couldn't be as easily backtracked.

I walked out of the starport and continued on my way, heading for the nearest airlock to get me out of the city. Hoppers thrummed and buzzed overhead, flitting across the plascrete canyons created by the tall buildings. The shadows were long and grey, stripping the color from much of my surroundings.

Most of the people debarking from the starport headed for

the upper levels because they were well-heeled tourists or corp execs. I moved along with the common laborers that serviced the city's swank hotels and clubs, and the farmers that were in the metro area to sell their surplus or buy seeds for a new crop or fish DNA for a new strain.

I felt at home there.

Chapter Eight

Gullivar colony maintained a heavy guard over the airlock leading to the Martian plains because that was one of the primary vulnerabilities of the domed city. In the past, rebels and Earth-backed forces had fought over the gate. Standing twenty meters tall and thirty meters wide, the airlock showed scars from past violence.

Guards armed with heavy-duty laser rifles stood at attention on support platforms that provided defensive walls and primary sniper positions. Above them and on either side of the gate, large holos panned over the crowd gathered in front of the airlock. A few young people in the group cheered and yelled and waved while others made inappropriate gestures.

One young male dropped his pants and bared his buttocks as he yelled, "Earth can kiss my ass."

Evidently the young men around him were his friends and they yelled and laughed in support of his antics. Young Martians who had never seen Earth had no problem hating the other planet. Most of them would never get the cred for a visit to Earth, and most of them had acclimated to Mars so Earth's heavier gravity would be uncomfortable to them. The heavier atmosphere and natural particulates, many of them much different than those on Mars, also deterred visitation.

An undercover guard slid through the crowd and pulled a stunstick from his sleeve. Too late, the young man saw what was coming and tried to flee, hastily pulling his pants up as he went. Unfortunately, his loose pants tripped him up and he sprawled facedown on the street. Before he could get to his feet, the guard stepped forward and applied the stunstick to the young man's buttocks. The man yelled and shuddered, then went limp.

A few of the surrounding crowd applauded as the guard hiked up his prisoner's pants, then grabbed the man's shirt and easily picked him up from the ground since the gravity was only a third of what it was on Earth. The young man's constituency protested the arrest but quickly backed away when the security guard threatened them with his stunstick. A brief pushing match erupted as some of the young people cursed at the Earthers among them and threatened them.

For a moment, it looked like a riot was going to erupt. Those happened with a regular occurrence throughout the colonies. During the months I'd been en route aboard *Khloe*, several major riots had broken out and four Earth-owned manufacturing plants had been attacked by rebels. As a result, some of the corps had instituted an embargo on some products that the masses enjoyed: cheap sensies, clothing, and snack foods that the Martian nutritional boards had tried to outlaw anyway.

No one had licensed cocoa beans yet, so all chocolate was made off-world. Artificial chocolates abounded, but none of them had the same appeal as the original product. Real chocolate sold for a greater unit cost than designer drugs. Chocolate manufacturers relished this because it meant instant profits on any shipments they sent, and all of it was legal, without risk.

Before the fight could manifest, though, more plainclothes sec guards—some of them dressed as science fiction characters and others dressed like gangsters from the 1940s—closed ranks and got the violence under control. Their efforts were most efficient.

The two factions of the crowd quieted and returned to their respective areas. The sec guards remained in the area with their stunsticks visible. The message was clear.

As I stood waiting to be identified yet again, I pulled up news vid and newsrag stories concerning past battles there. Thirty-eight days ago, nine people had been killed at the gateway by a woman identified as a Martian terrorist.

I studied the young woman's face and tried to see the capacity for violence in her features. Only sometimes could that quality be seen, and only then when the person wanted it to show. During my career at the NAPD, I had known several murderers who had been surprised at their own ability to take the life of someone else, and many of them had shown remorse at their acts.

In the vid, the young woman worked her way into the center of the crowd that day. She was alone. She did not look around. She remained focused on her mission. Nineteen seconds into the vid, with a yellow highlighter drawn around her, the young woman suddenly screamed, "FREE MARS!"

Then she exploded. The crowd around her folded back on itself as the concussion blew them backward.

According to the nosies, forensic examination had confirmed the presence of explosive materials on the young woman's corpse. I played the vid back, zooming in and examining her face and the actions of the people around her. Only two of those around her had appeared frightened before the blast killed them.

I tracked back through several other incidents. They were much the same at the gates—always protests, then people dying. In the last year, one hundred and three people had died in front of this gate. Seventeen sec guards had died during the same time.

I didn't recall that many deaths being reported back in New Angeles. When I checked the news archives for that time period,

I discovered that Earth had *not* reported all the deaths. The more complete picture had come from Martian-based nosies.

"That shouldn't surprise you," Shelly said. "Look at how many investigations we participated in that were kept under wraps."

Since we were in the crowd, I silently agreed with her. I should not have been surprised by the knowledge that the media was controlled and slanted. But it disturbed me.

"Present your docs," the sec guard working the gateway said.

I held up my hand and he scanned my e-visa with his PAD.

"You're cleared, Norris 1JA5NU. Proceed."

I thanked him and went on into the airlock.

Inside, the humans pulled on envirosuits required by safety requirements. Traveling aboard the solar-powered trains was safe for the most part, but accidents were known to happen. Checking back through the news archives, I discovered that most of the "accidents" were actually attacks by Martian rebels, or by Earth sec forces when they believed rebels leaders were onboard. Ordinary citizens got caught in the crossfire.

When the airlock was filled to capacity, the warning klaxon sounded and yellow lights flashed. Ten seconds counted off on the digital reader built into the transplas walls. At zero, the airlock cycled open.

I followed the crowd. Some of the Earthers among the group had a hard time walking in the reduced gravity. They bobbed up and sailed for a few couple feet, bouncing off of other people.

An older man stumbled and sailed off-balance toward me, but I caught him, steadying him on his feet.

"Thank you." He tested his footing as other people irritably stepped around him.

Muttered curses and complaints of, "off-worlder," "corp trash," and "Earther" came from the passing crowd.

"You are welcome," I told him.

He smiled. "First time on Mars."

"I hope you enjoy your stay."

"Me, too."

I couldn't help offering advice. That was part of my programming. "Perhaps, until you adjust to the lesser gravity, you might try sliding your feet rather than picking them up."

"I'll do that." He snaked out a foot and moved cautiously forward a few centimeters. He still lost contact with the ground, but he managed it. "I don't suppose you had any trouble walking here your first time."

"There is an adjustment." I was much stronger than a human, and my reflexes were faster. Thankfully all of those things were under my control. I had simply attuned myself on *Khloe* till I was able to function normally in weightlessness and on Mars. The calibrations weren't quite exact, yet, but they served. I would continue to learn as I went.

The forward cars behind the pulling engine—this one in the shape of an angelfish with a tall dorsal fin but in the same bronze coloration—held atmosphere for humans and clones who needed it. I helped the man to the car but was stopped at the steps by a uniformed conductor wearing a slug-thrower on his hip. Several such men stood outside cars on the ship.

"Excuse me. Bioroids take passage in the cargo compartment." The railroad sec guard was broad and powerful. His eyes had been worked on, modded to be gunsights.

The man I had escorted looked embarrassed at the situation. He looked up at me. "I'm so sorry."

"It's quite all right." I handed the man off to the conductor, then turned toward the cargo cars farther back in the line. The powder fine iron oxide dust crunched and shifted underfoot.

* * *

Fourteen bioroids sat in the last container car where I was directed by another railroad employee. Most of them were Franks, but a couple were higher-grade units capable of problem solving and deep conversation.

A Brad met me at the door. Like most of those models, he had a full face and hair, looking human from the neck up. That appearance was blunted by the silver eyes. He wore a nice suit and gloves, but there was enough of a gap between the two to reveal the synthskin that I knew from experience with the model ran up to his elbows. Brads were used as corporate attachés or in other high-profile businesses that dealt with the public.

"*Kaor*. I'm Brad 2FE5BU." He greeted me with an outstretched hand and a wide, inviting smile. "Welcome aboard."

"Thank you." I took his hand briefly and stepped up into the container car. I peered inside and discovered that space was tight. Several bioroids were awaiting transit.

"*Kaor* is the traditional Martian greeting according to the Edgar Rice Burroughs mythos," Brad informed me in his pleasant voice. "Recognizing cultural attributes is a good way to fit in with a new populace."

"I am aware of that." I was aware of both things, actually. According to the information I had gleaned while aboard *Khloe*, many of the colonial Martians had adopted customs and splinter cultures adapted from popular works of fiction set on the planet. Psychologists felt that it was a way for them to separate themselves from Earth.

"Accommodations in the car are a little cramped," Brad said apologetically. "I wish I could do more to make you comfortable."

"It's fine." I looked out at the balcony behind the car. "Perhaps I could ride out here."

"Would you mind company?" Brads tended to ingratiate themselves with people they recognized as upwardly mobile. He had picked up on me being more than a Frank quite easily.

"Company will be fine." I returned to the narrow balcony and tested the railing, finding it stronger than it looked.

"Good." Brad followed me outside and stood beside me as final boarding was called. "I don't much care for closed in spaces."

I did not know if that was true. Brads were programmed to be companions. If a unit was not assigned a specific person to shepherd in any given social occasion, they were designed to seek out anyone they recognized as being potentially in a leadership role and talk up the party line. Because I was programmed to be curious by nature, I wondered what this Brad's party line was.

I stood at the railing and peered out at the unfamiliar Martian landscape. The constantly shifting winds scoured the planet down to its rocky bones and pooled great expanses of powdered sand oceans. Mars had taller mountains than any on Earth. The planet had taller volcanoes and more active volcanoes as well. Several towering pinnacles looked like pieces of art worn smooth by the wind and abrasive sand that blew across them. Prehistoric Mars away from the domed colonies and the outlying terraforming operations looked much different. Above, specially adapted hoppers sped through the pale orange atmosphere. Most of the hoppers were corp vehicles, but a few were military hoppers that I assumed were on patrol.

Yet at the same time, the planetscape looked familiar. I had never seen the planet, but Simon Blake had.

"Is this your first time on Mars?" Brad asked.

"Yes."

He smiled at me, his fallback technique. "I can usually tell with most people. But you were more difficult to guess."

I nodded. No matter what I said or didn't say, Brad was going to keep talking. It was what they did to dig up information on people. Floyd 2X3A7C, another bioroid working as a detective for the NAPD, and I had different sets of operating traits. We observed and waited and questioned things. We talked only when necessary. Brads kept talking, then vectored in on conversational hits that elicited a familiar or desired response, like a con man or fake spiritualist doing a cold reading.

"You didn't mention your name."

I gave it to him. Then I went into my fallback routine. "You've been on Mars for a time?"

"Three years, eight months, and thirteen days." Brad smiled. "I can give you the hours and minutes if you'd like."

"That's all right."

"Too much information?"

"Yes."

"What are you doing here?"

I explained my cover job, which he didn't really care about but nodded knowledgeably.

"That's a very good job, but you're going to find a lot of resistance here on Mars."

"Because I am a bioroid?"

"Some of the resistance will stem from that, but most of it will come because you are an Earther and the colonies are very protective of their ag businesses."

That further interested me. "How do you know that I am an Earther?"

Brad smiled in self-deprecation. "I mean no offense."

"None taken, I assure you. I am only curious."

"You scan as an Earther because of the way you move and the interest you take in your surroundings."

"Someone from the Moon might move and behave in a similar fashion."

"True, but it would not be an Earther fashion. I can tell when someone is from the Moon as well. You are from Earth."

I nodded. The difference in movement I felt would smooth out in a matter of hours. Every move I made was a lesson in self-education. By tomorrow I would move like a native.

The interest was another matter. By nature I was intrigued by anything out of the ordinary, and all of Mars was essentially out of the ordinary for me. Then there was the matter of self-preservation. Given everything that had happened to me—and to Simon Blake—I felt certain my existence was at risk on the planet. I resolved to learn to be more circumspect. I could learn from the Brad.

Brad shrugged with what he thought was good-natured acceptance but which I thought was still not quite human. "I only mention these distinctions because things here on Mars are different than you are used to."

"I will try to be prepared."

"You should. The terrorists can be very dangerous where Earth property is concerned. They would rather destroy a manufacturing plant and do without than put up with Earth business on this planet, but often one or two of them will settle for wrecking Earther bioroids. As long as you act like an Earther unit, you will be at risk." His eyes caught the light as he looked at me. "Will you be staying on Mars long?"

"I am not certain. I have open parameters in my assignment."

The final warning whistle blew and the train lifted above the mag-lev rail, rising only a few centimeters. Gusts of ionized pale orange dust jetted out from underneath, roiling around us in a large cloud. Vibrations ran the length of the train. With another blast of the klaxon, the train started accelerating.

"Aren't you curious about what my job is?"

I knew Brad would keep hinting until I asked. They had to disseminate information because public relations were their primary code. "Yes."

"I'm going to be a blackjack dealer at the Lorilei Casino. It's a wonderful opportunity."

Everything was a "wonderful opportunity" for a Brad. I searched the map and found the casino nearly three hundred kilometers away. The gambling establishment was located outside the Bradbury colony, not inside the megapolis. That was curious.

"You are not working inside Bradbury colony?"

Brad's smile never failed. "No. The Lorilei needs a skilled blackjack dealer. It is the perfect job for me. I will be the best they have ever seen."

"You have worked as a blackjack dealer before?"

"Many times." Brad stood easily with his hands behind his back, swaying to the smooth rhythm of the mag-lev train. "Most recently at the Savoy Casino in Gullivar colony. Until my reassignment."

"Why were you reassigned?"

"It was a personal matter."

I nodded and turned my attention back to the landscape, watching as Gullivar colony and the outlying domes quickly receded behind the train. At the speed we would be traveling, we would arrive in Bradbury in little more than an hour. A hopper couldn't travel as fast, but a military jet could cut that time in half. The time frame still allowed a lot of things to happen within a colony before the military could scramble to deliver help.

The Martian army was still spread thin around the colonial settlements. Protecting all of the colonies all of the time was difficult, and rooting out all the terrorists from the cave systems tunneled through the Martian mountains was even more so. The terrorists that manifested every year made controlling the situation impossible.

Brad shrugged and continued speaking as I knew he would. I was not invested in his "personal matter," but I was someone that could be potentially swayed to his camp.

"I was having an affair with one of the high rollers at the casino," Brad said. "Part of the special services package I'm capable of providing, you see."

I knew about that tendency with Brads as well. "She became disenchanted?"

"No. The casino owner discovered our liaison. She said that I had been compromised by my affiliation with the casino client."

"You were not?"

Brad smiled and shook his head. "Of course not. Blackjack is a game with rules. I would never break those rules."

I realized that was true. The casino owner should have known that as well. "The casino owner should have known that. I do not understand the problem."

"I also had a liaison with the casino owner. She was…proprietary in that regard, which doesn't make much sense to me. My liaisons with each of them did not overlap, and I was capable of servicing both." Brad shook his head again. "I will never understand human conventions in the matter of jealousy."

A Brad wouldn't. They weren't programmed for monogamy, either. Monogamy was a special add-on feature that Haas-Bioroid charged extra for because the trait had to be so deeply embedded in neural channeling that a unit had to be practically wiped to be cleansed of it.

During my career at the NAPD, I had learned that humans claimed to value such a trait highly, but oftentimes broke that covenant with each other in marriage and in business. Shattered trust was a motivation that put bodies in the morgue and filled the courts with cases.

That made me think of the trust Mara Blake had instilled in me, written into my core through a neural copy of her murdered husband. Whoever had taken her was somewhere on Mars. I was certain of that. Everything kept tracking back to mercenaries from the chimera unit under John Rath.

I stood there in the wind at the back of the train, but as I peered at the red landscape, I was suddenly swept into a memory of another time and place—and the second time Simon Blake had met Mara Parker.

Chapter Nine

"Captain Blake?"

The woman's voice surprised Simon Blake as he stood before a holo screen showing the rocky shores of a dead Martian lake. He remembered hearing the sound of an approaching hopper earlier, but he had ignored it because no alarm had been raised and because he had a logistical problem to solve that John Rath had given him. The mercenary group operated independently on separate tasks, trusting each other to do their job.

But he turned when he heard the address, and I turned with him, sinking into his point of view.

Mara Parker stood at the entrance to the dome-shaped transplas hut. The heavy curtains over the entrance moved slightly, then stilled as the airlock cycled.

The hut's interior was climate-controlled, heated by its own solar skin and heat-amplifying cells. Even so, the space held a bit of a chill. Simon preferred working in a cooler environment because he believed it kept his mind sharp.

As Simon, I wore combat fatigues digitally patterned to allow me to fade into the desert landscape. A large caliber slug-thrower hung from my hip and a laser rifle was canted against my work table within easy reach.

"Miss Parker." I registered Simon's surprise at seeing her there and it felt like an alien thing to me, but I knew it for what it was.

She wore a camo coverall that fit her from neck to ankles and I could tell from the fabric weave that it was designed to be bullet-resistant. The material would absorb kinetic energy and become rigid and concave, presenting a rounded surface that would encourage a bullet to go elsewhere and resolve the potential for possibly damaging hydrostatic shock. She carried a helmet, dangling it by its chinstrap from her fingers. Her hair was pulled back and her makeup had been applied with a light touch. Simon thought she was beautiful.

"What are you doing here?"

"Would you believe I was in the neighborhood?"

"Not for a millisecond."

She smiled. "Well then, I am in the neighborhood because I came to see you."

"Does John—*Colonel Rath*," I hastily amended, "know that you're here?" Rath wished to be known by his title among anyone outside our unit.

"Do you think I could fly a scramhopper in here without him knowing?"

"No."

She smiled again. "I'd be scattered across Mars."

"Or burned to slag." I knew Rath had positioned laser cannons around our encampment. He wasn't a man to take chances. I was surprised Rath had allowed her into our base.

Then Simon cursed to himself because he knew that as soon as Mara Parker cleared the zone, the camp was going to pick up and move. Mentally, he began making a list of how he was going to pack everything away, and to make certain he got something to eat before they humped out of the area.

"Not a pretty image, is it?"

It took Simon a moment to realize she was still talking about her potentially disastrous ending from an attempted invasion. "No, not a pretty image."

Mara waited for a moment, then pointed to my workstation. "Do you think I could sit down?"

I nodded, trying to keep up with all the changes. "Of course. I apologize." Out of habit, Simon had already blanked the PAD sitting on the workstation. I picked it up and slid it into my thigh pouch.

I motioned her to the chair I'd been sitting in, then stepped over to the side and picked up the dome's only other chair. I flicked my wrist and popped the release button and the seat unfolded.

Mara gazed at the chair's skeletal frame. It was little more than a plate-sized disc with four legs attached. "It doesn't look very comfortable."

"It's not, and it's not supposed to be. The colonel reminds everyone who gripes about them that they're work equipment. If a soldier wants to rest, he—or *she*—has a rack. Though those aren't very comfortable either, unless you're practically unconscious on your feet."

Gingerly, she sat.

Simon felt a little ill at ease, and I knew that discomfort was caused by Mara's presence. "I wish it was more comfortable. For your sake. I'm used to it. But it's the best I can do. These collapsible chairs are easy to hump to the next twenty when the time comes. You appreciate them more then."

"I suppose so." She drew in a breath and let it out. "Do you have coffee?"

"I have a caffeine-sub drink, ma'am, but you don't really want to drink it unless you want to be wired for action for the next twelve hours." I reached into my pack beside the workstation and fished out a liter-sized water bladder that hadn't been touched. "I have water. Loaded with electrolytes. It's not tasty or cold, but it is wet."

"Perhaps I should be offering you a refreshment, Captain Blake. The scramhopper I flew in has a few amenities."

"Thank you, ma'am, but I'm good." I looked at her. "You *flew* the scramhopper into our camp?"

"I did. Does that surprise you?"

"Yes."

"You work with women soldiers." Mara frowned a little then, as if she wasn't certain of herself or maybe wasn't sure of what she was thinking. "Surely you don't think I'm incapable of piloting a small aircraft."

"I don't think you should be alone, ma'am. You were kidnapped and held for ransom not even four months ago."

"Three months and eleven days." Her mouth tightened and her nostrils flared a little. "That experience isn't going to be something I easily forget."

"No, ma'am. I suppose not."

"In fact, that experience has been a life-altering episode for me."

I waited, not knowing what to say, but I was trying to figure out how she'd found our base. Chimera Team was stalking people who were high in the Martian terrorist hierarchy, men and women who were responsible for the deaths of hundreds and the destruction of millions of credits of Earth corporation properties.

"After I was taken, I became aware that the security people I had protecting me were woefully inadequate for the job."

"Working security is a hard detail," I said. "I prefer hunting people more than protecting assets. Protecting someone is difficult. There are often too many variables."

"You appear to be good at protecting things. And people."

"You're talking about rescuing you?"

"I am."

I shook my head. "A rescue isn't much different than what we're doing out here."

"Hunting people?"

"Yes, ma'am. We planned on bringing you back alive, but in order to do that, we had to hunt—and terminate—the people holding you. We did."

She blanched a little at that, and I realized I had spoken too baldly.

"I'm sorry. I didn't think too closely about what I was saying."

"No. That's fine." Mara looked away for a moment and pulled a strand of hair from her face. "You were very clear about your methodology."

"I could have been a little more circumspect."

"Actually, I appreciate the honesty. How much do you know about me?"

I thought about it and shrugged. "You develop neural channeling for bioroids. You run your own corporation, have a seat at the big table whenever you sit down with Haas-Bioroid. I could tell you your birthdate, height, weight, that kind of information."

"But you don't know that much about *me*."

I recognized the distinction she was trying to make. Or maybe Simon Blake did and I merely mirrored his understanding. "No, ma'am. I do not know much about you as a person."

"I'm developing some cutting-edge software in a cutthroat business, Captain Blake. Most android development corps would like to get their hands on what I have."

I nodded again. I knew that. That had been in the package Rath had given to us pre-op.

"Haas-Bioroid paid for my recovery. Did you know that?"

"Colonel Rath doesn't loop us in to all the details of an op."

"Normally you don't do rescue?"

I hesitated before I answered, then realized that Mara Parker was smart enough to have checked up on that before she said it. "No. We don't. Normally we destroy targets."

She stared into my eyes. "So what made this instance so different?"

I shook my head. "I don't know. You'd have to ask the colonel."

At that, she laughed aloud.

I felt Simon's ears heat up, which was a strange sensation to me. I'd heard Shelly talk about the physiognomic response, and I had seen it in people we questioned, but I had never felt it. In fact, it would have been impossible for me because I didn't have ears as such. I had aud receptors built into my head. It was a phantom sensation at best.

"Wait." Mara took me by the wrist and her hand felt warm against my chill skin. "I wasn't laughing at you."

I wanted to believe her, but I could tell that Simon didn't quite feel so generous.

"I was imagining what it would be like to ask Colonel Rath any of his business. He plays things close to the vest."

That was an understatement. No one in the unit knew exactly how many angles John Rath played at any one time. In the past we had undertaken missions thinking we were supposed to achieve one impossible goal, only to find out that it had been a feint so another team could manage to succeed elsewhere. With John Rath, the left hand never knew what the right hand was doing. In fact, there was no way to know for certain that those were the only two hands he had.

"Then I really have to ask how you found us," I said.

"Colonel Rath invited me."

"Why?"

"Because I had made it known that I wanted to talk to you—and him—again. It took me three months to make that happen. While you were in the hospital recovering from your wounds, having remodeling done by nanobots and gene-modded tissues vat-grown to replace what you'd lost, I wasn't able to get anywhere near you."

"I wasn't aware that you had tried."

"I did. Several times. Rath prevented me."

I nodded. "It's understandable. He has a no-contact rule with previous principles."

"*Principles*?"

"People that we have protected. People that we have worked for."

"Why?"

"Because people lie to us, ma'am."

Mara leaned back a little, but the smile never left her face. "That sounds a little jaded and cynical."

I grinned at her to let her know no hard feelings were felt. "That's how it is in the business. People make the mistake of thinking they can buy us. Pay for our blood. Pay us to die for them."

"Don't they?"

"Rath chooses who we bleed and die for."

"And he's always right?"

"It's not about him always being right." I spoke as Simon put his thoughts into words. "It's about finding something you believe in. *Someone* you believe in. You can believe the holos. You can believe the newsrags or the nosie of your choice. You can believe in whatever religion most appeals to you. But at the end of every day, you have to put your faith somewhere."

"So you put your faith in John Rath." It was a statement, not a question.

"I do. I *choose* to."

She looked at me as if weighing me somehow. "What makes him so special then?"

I smiled at her and shook my head. "He's John Rath. He succeeds where others fail. Most importantly, he keeps us alive. And he never deserts us."

"Never?"

"Not once. I've seen him standing tall in the middle of firefights I was certain we weren't going to get out of alive."

As I sat inside Simon Blake, I suddenly realized I could see those memories of John Rath like they were my own. Which, in a sense, they were. The colonel had always been there on every battlefield. He led charges and, when it came to it, he was the last man to retreat.

For a moment, we were silent in the hut. I heard the wind, constant and howling, whipping by the camp, whistling through the foothills of the mountains where we'd buried down.

"Did you ever find out who was behind my kidnapping?" Mara looked at me.

"No, ma'am."

"Did Colonel Rath?"

"If he did, he didn't tell any of us."

"Would he keep such knowledge from you?"

"Of course. He only tells us things he is certain we need to know. There was no reason to know who had kidnapped you. Our business was done with your recovery."

Mara shifted on the seat. "I have come to have...*strong* suspicions that the people behind my kidnapping were from Haas-Bioroid."

I considered that. "It doesn't make sense. They paid to get you rescued."

She smiled, but there was no humor in the effort. "Within a few days of my return to my offices, an NAPD investigation turned up electronic tracking devices that led them back to a man who worked deep inside Haas-Bioroid."

"Who?" I felt Simon Blake's protective urges swim to the forefront. They were a lot like the same programming that I was coded with.

"A man named Harlan Bernobich."

Simon searched his memories for any mention of the name but came up empty. I filed Bernobich's name away for later research. "I don't know him."

"I thought you might have heard his name. He turned up dead less than a week after I was freed."

"How did he die?"

"The NAPD says that he killed himself."

I studied her. "You have reason to doubt that?"

"See how cynical you are?" She smiled. "I've hired a private investigator to look into Bernobich, but I don't expect to get much. When Haas-Bioroid decides to conceal something, it pretty much stays invisible."

I had no comment for that, but I was curious. I was glad that Simon Blake had thought of the same question those years ago. "Why would Haas-Bioroid set you up to be kidnapped?"

"To frighten me. To pull me in closer to them. To allow them to insinuate some of their sec personnel into my operation." She stood and shrugged, pacing restlessly, which was difficult to do given the small confines of the hut. "Director Haas doesn't like doing business with anyone she can't control. She can't control me. All she's been able to do is get me to agree to lease my neural channeling to her when I finish with the first iteration. And she has options on subsequent evolutions of the same."

"You think she doesn't trust you?"

Mara fixed me with a stare. "Do you trust anyone outside your unit?"

I didn't have to think about that one. "No."

"I feel the same way. I trust my development team, and I trust my sec team, but I realize now that my sec people aren't able to handle extreme situations." Her face darkened and she looked suddenly fatigued. "I buried over half of them. I knew all of them. They are…they *were* friends." She paused and her hands knotted in her lap, shaking for just an instant. "I don't want to bury more of my friends."

Simon thought about all the men and women, brothers and sisters in arms, that he had buried over the years as a mercenary, and I watched him cycle through. He couldn't even remember all of them. Some of them he'd never gotten to know because they'd only had boots on the ground for a few days.

I looked at Mara Parker and I knew that Simon had an inkling of what she was doing there, but he had to ask. "Why are you here, ma'am?"

She looked at me and took a calm, steady breath. "Because I wanted to thank you for saving my life that day. And because I wanted to try to hire you as security chief for MirrorMorph, Inc."

Even though Simon had been expecting the question by then, he was still surprised. I recognized that in him.

"That's something you should talk to the colonel about. You'd want him before you wanted me."

"I tried to hire him. He was very polite and didn't laugh in my face, but he told me I couldn't afford him."

That was true.

"However," she went on, "he told me that if I could convince you to take the job, he would be willing to allow that. And to let you pick the people you wanted to take with you. Within reason."

Simon sat silently, taken completely off guard. I was puzzled. I had not before considered how Simon Blake had gone to work for Mara Parker. I thought perhaps they had fallen in love and the togetherness had resulted from that. Clearly that supposition was incorrect.

"The colonel told you that?" Simon couldn't keep the surprise from his voice.

"Yes."

"I don't think the colonel would let a team go so easily." What Simon really meant was that he didn't believe John Rath would let *him* go. Simon could not remember a time when he wasn't in his commanding officer's life. Everything before that seemed like a faraway dream.

"He's not letting a team go easily." Mara Parker crossed her arms. "It appears Colonel Rath is every bit the mercenary."

"What do you mean?"

"In return for the services of a security team, he wants a piece of my company. Fifteen percent to be exact. To be honest, the price is steep. But the truth of the matter is that I can't afford to leave my people unprotected. *I* can't be left unprotected."

Simon didn't want to leave her unprotected either. I knew that because his fears for her resonated in the programming that I had been encoded with.

"If Haas-Bioroid was behind my kidnapping and the death of my security people, then they didn't have control of the situation the way they thought they would have. They could have simply negotiated a ransom and made me feel obligated to them for the rescue."

"They could still feel that way. Whether they were involved or not."

"I don't believe they are innocent. I'm convinced Director Haas or one of the other board members was involved; perhaps my friends are dead as a result of some intra-corp struggle I'm not privy to. I'm also convinced that the kidnap team had decided to change the deal and betray their employers, which is why Haas-Bioroid contacted Colonel Rath." Mara shrugged. "Maybe in the long run, it was cheaper to hire you people than it would have been to pay off the kidnappers."

"We weren't cheap."

"No, I suspect you weren't. But having you people involved paid dividends for Haas-Bioroid."

I looked at her.

"Or maybe it was simply a point of pride. Director Haas sent out a message to anyone who might have ever thought about kidnapping a Haas-Bioroid employee. Or anyone in an ancillary business. True?"

I thought about the bodies we'd left in that building that day. "True," I agreed.

"So, my question to you is, do you want the job as my chief of security?"

"Let me think about it."

Simon's reply seemed to give Mara pause. She stared at me for a moment, then nodded and picked up her helmet. "Don't take too long, Captain Blake. I feel as though I can trust you now. I don't know how long that feeling will last." She turned and walked into the airlock.

Chapter Ten

"Are you sure that's really where you want to go?" Brad 2FE-5BU looked genuinely concerned as he stared at me in the gathering gloom of the Martian night.

Phobos and Deimos were both visible in the star-filled sky, and hoppers occasionally gleamed overhead as well. Back to the east along the mag-lev line, a cargo ship carved a bright yellow-white line toward space.

Standing to one side of the train and the line of cargo handlers that shifted supplies and equipment to the mini-docklands outside the main dome of Bradbury colony, I surveyed the long, low buildings built into the side of the canyon that ringed the hopper pads. A few specially outfitted hoppers sat on the pads, but more of the spaces were empty than occupied. The brightly lit neon signs along the shops and businesses made that emptiness even more pronounced.

Bioroids and modded clones worked the service lines on the hoppers. The majority of the aircraft were packet runners, couriers who transported special equipment for the terraforming operations at the edges of the Martian frontier or food to the skeletal human overseers that ran those processes. Two of them were marked with medical insignia, designating them as emergency med-flight hoppers.

Several businesses surrounded the hopper pads: casinos, whorehouses, supply warehouses, all-terrain vehicle licensors, small cantinas, and sensie houses for the flesh and blood workers employed on-site, as well as bars and drug dens. Out in the frontier, laws weren't quite the same as they were in the megapolis, and they weren't strictly enforced either. Vice became a marketable product and customers showed up to partake of their choice.

I was familiar with that from my time in the NAPD on Earth and on the Moon. As long as what the general population considered to be the dregs of society slowly killed themselves off—or quickly murdered others like them—no one truly cared.

"There's a lot more red color in the local environment, Drake," Shelly said, "but we've been here before. You know how things work out here."

I silently agreed, but focused on Brad. "I am sure."

His programming wouldn't allow him to let go of the matter without a more robust debate. "This is a dangerous place. You need to know that."

"I will be fine."

"People get killed here."

"I know."

"Bioroids get scrapped and sold for parts."

"I can take care of myself."

He gave a very convincing sigh of exasperation. "What can you possibly do here?"

"Scout potential market resources."

"The only thing growing in this place are several strands of mushrooms and herbs used to narcotize imbibers."

"I have a portfolio of pharmaceutical corporations that look for such things." That was true. The portfolio was part of my cover. During our time together, Shelly and I had run into people that had done that very job. They had walked a thin line between legal and criminal activities, procuring samples from both groups.

“Fine.” Brad didn’t seem happy about the situation. “If you get into trouble, if I can be of any service—though I guarantee that will be limited and I will not risk my neck because you are not human, you can find me there.” He pointed at the Lorilei Casino. He also gave me his PAD comm so I could get in touch.

The holo advertising the casino’s existence was tacky and garish. At least, that was what Shelly thought of it and demonstrated no qualms about advancing her feelings. Above the two-story building, a bountiful woman rolled dice with one hand and held a drink in the other.

Even Brad didn’t look too excited by his future place of employment. He said goodbye, then trudged rather than walked across the red earth packed hard from bioroid and clone feet and the boots of humans and ATV treads. The constant heat given off by the minihoppers taking off and landing helped fuse the landscape into a semi-gloss state that cracked where it was stepped on and looked like a glaze in areas that hadn’t been broken.

I turned my own steps toward a secondhand electronics shop that I had seen listed in the newsrags often enough to know was probably a dealer in black market goods and few enough times that I trusted they were good at what they did.

Bloo Moose $alvage and S&%@ was a three-story affair that jutted out from the cliff wall in uneven tiers that didn’t look connected. It was like someone had hammered the floors in at different times at different heights. I assumed that originally three businesses had existed in that space but had succumbed to losses or perhaps to Bloo Moose’s successes.

I walked toward the shop as a minihopper took off from the pad. The airlock door was sealed when I arrived at Bloo Moose. I thumbed the vidscreen next to the door and waited.

After a minute and seventeen seconds, a middle-aged man's face filled the pixilated screen. The image didn't inspire a lot of confidence about the goods that could be found inside because the man looked too green to be flesh and blood.

"Maybe it's a play on green Martians," Shelly suggested.

I didn't think so. I believed the tech was faulty.

"Who are you?" the man asked.

I gave him my current ID.

"Hold your e-visa up to the reader where I can scan it."

I did as requested, then waited some more. I trusted Rachel Beckman's e-docs forger to backstop the identity enough to get it passed a paranoid shopkeeper.

"Checks out." The man sounded disappointed. "What do you want?"

"Some replacement hardware. Maybe a few odds and ends."

"Like what?"

"A PAD upgrade for starters."

"You cleared for that?"

I slotted the credstick Rachel had sent and never took my eyes from the monitor. I only let him see part of the amount, enough to get him interested in opening negotiations if he was what I believe him to be. "Am I?"

"We can talk. What kind of odds and ends?"

"I will be happy to talk with you about those when I am inside."

The man hesitated only a moment longer, then buzzed me into the airlock. "Come inside. Talk is free. Anything else is going to cost you."

I stepped into the airlock and waited for it to cycle me into the building.

* * *

The Bloo Moose was more neatly organized than I had believed it would be. Plascrete shelves filled the central space and covered the walls. I was intrigued by the collection of things on hand, knowing that many of them had to possess interesting histories as to how they managed to get to Mars and then to linger on the secondhand shop's shelves.

There were several games and game consoles, old merchandise that split the difference between relic and junk. A collection of jazz albums on original wax commanded a premium position among all the goods. There were a lot of holo projectors and aud systems. At the back of the shop, a collection of weapons ranging from lasers to slug-throwers to stunsticks hung on the wall behind an iron bar cage.

The shopkeeper stood behind a counter at the back of the large room. He was of medium height, of indeterminate origins due to his black hair and swarthy skin, and his two front teeth sported a centimeter gap. From his body language I knew he had some kind of weapon back there with him.

A clone built from some kind of Congo primate DNA leaned against the back wall a few feet away. Short dark fur covered his arms and chest exposed in the deep vee of his shirt. His face looked wide and broad as a baseball catcher's mitt, and it was the color of a Concord grape. He wore a cutdown tangler rifle under one arm and a slug-thrower on his hip. I knew he'd been constructed for intimidation, and I thought he would have served well in that capacity if I had been human.

"Don't mind Gordon," the shopkeeper said. "As long as you don't bother me, he won't bother you."

"Of course."

"You may call me Jitish." His voice modulation shifted just enough that I knew immediately he was lying about his name, but he was good at that lie. I kept the fluctuation as a baseline against further business I would be doing with him. "What kind of hardware are you looking at replacing?"

"My PAD."

"What model are you currently carrying?"

I held out my palm and juiced the specifics of the PAD I'd had installed on the Moon. During the voyage over on *Khloe*, I'd used my PAD to connect with Floyd so he could fill me in on the Jonas Salter investigation. We had set up a virtual meetbox to converse. As *Khloe* had left Earth behind, though, the eventual lag time had dropped into our conversations, and we hadn't wanted to risk discovery anyway.

"I can definitely do better than this, but it's going to be expensive."

"We can negotiate."

Jitish grinned as if I were mentally challenged. "I got stuff you want. I don't see much room for negotiation."

"You are the first shop I have visited. You can close a deal, or you can be a baseline that I can improve on. That is your choice."

The grin disappeared as fast as a magician's assistant. "I've got a Gibson 23 MNEM."

"A Gibson is fine." Those PADs were near the top of the market. "I want to do better than a 23."

"Do you know what you can do with a 23?"

"Yes." While working with the NAPD, I had been equipped with a Sterling 101 ENGI. I doubted that I was going to find that here.

Jitish was quiet for a moment, long enough for Gordon to shift his stance and start to come over. The shopkeeper held up a hand and Gordon returned to his repose.

"I've got a Gibson 68 with a ZOOMUP expansion that lets you work on the Net faster."

That would do nicely, and the ZOOMUP could also double as a filter mask if someone had the right utilities. I could code those myself in a few days.

"How much?" I asked.

Jitish named a price, then we settled in to haggle. As it turned out, he'd recently come into possession of the Gibson PAD from someone who hadn't known what she had her hands on. I gathered the pronoun from when he had lapsed twice. There were two problems with the Gibson 68: someone was probably looking for it, so he didn't just want to tell anyone about it, and it was too valuable for him to sell to a semi-legitimate customer.

I got more of my price than Jitish did, though you would have thought I had hit him in the face with scalding water by the time the final amount had been decided. Payment for the Gibson severely impacted the credstick Rachel had sent for me, but I knew the investment was worth it.

"He's still probably making a small fortune for the PAD." Shelly wasn't happy about the situation. She didn't like the shopkeeper. I knew she wouldn't have. "Whoever dumped it in his lap probably didn't get much for it."

I silently agreed.

"You're wanting an install, right?" Pretending to be casual, Jitish studied me.

"No. Just wrap the PAD up and I will take it with me."

While in transit, I had downloaded the necessary vids to manage my own upgrade. Normally Haas-Bioroid units weren't allowed to do anything like that. Even licensors and owners weren't permitted to change out hardware or software that wasn't installed by Haas-Bioroid. That voided all support on part of Haas-Bioroid and could result in lawsuits.

Also, tampering with the Haas-Bioroid safety measures was almost impossible for a human due to the involved nature of the replacement/installation. The installments took hours and were tedious. A bioroid could do it, but they were programmed not to.

Miranda had removed my programming so that I could work on myself. I was already a fugitive, so I couldn't be any more voided by Haas-Bioroid.

Jitish boxed the PAD with recycled bubble wrap and pushed the package across to me. "You said you were in the market for other items."

"Yes."

"What?"

"I want a Synap. And a stunstick."

A grin flitted across Jitish's swarthy face and his eyes sparkled. "I gotta say, you're the most interesting bioroid that's ever entered my place of business."

I felt certain that was true.

"What kind of trouble are you in?" Jitish opened the weapons cage and took down a Synap that was gathering dust in one corner.

"I am not worried about the trouble I am in." That was mostly true because I had and could continue to elude my pursuers. "These things are for the trouble I expect to have."

Jitish placed the Synap on the counter. "You walk into trouble with this, you're going to hardly notice the difference. Unless you are in the military or are a licensed mercenary, you will be taken into custody by the NAPD or by the Martian army. But if you're determined to break the law…" He cocked a suggestive eyebrow. "I take it you can't carry a slug-thrower."

"Not for use on humans, no, but I do want one with rifle rigging." I pointed out a 15mm hand cannon that had caught my attention. The slug-thrower came with a longer barrel than the short one currently outfitted on the weapon.

At my side, Shelly stiffened. I had never carried a slug-thrower while working as her partner, but I remembered how Simon Blake had, and how well he had used the weapon. I believed I could do as well, though I would not be able to have the same casual attentiveness to targets.

"I will not be using it on humans, but there are hoppers and other vehicles that I may wish to elude." I voiced that to reassure her—myself, I supposed—rather than the shopkeeper.

Property damage by the NAPD had been frowned upon too, which was another reason a bioroid operating under their auspices could not carry a weapon like that.

"You do realize that I'm not supposed to sell this to a bioroid who isn't licensed for it."

"Perhaps you would enjoy watching it collect more dust in there.'"

Jitish held his gaze steady, but I knew that I had him when I had purchased the Gibson PAD at the price we had agreed upon. It had been a while since he'd sold much and he was hungry.

He named a price that was exorbitant, but I didn't mind letting him see some substantial profit on the slug-thrower. He was generous enough to throw in a holster that fit on the inside waistband of my pants.

The rifle rigging came in a small leather valise. I opened it, found the rifle stock and small folding bipod tucked in fitted compartments inside, and checked the fit on the 15mm Gortaub. The rifle stock fit on the slug-thrower easily, and the bipod slipped onto the .5 meter barrel extension like a glove. Even though I was prepared to handle the gun, the initial resistance to it in my programming thrummed through me. I finally pushed it aside.

Gordon had one of his massive hands on the slug-thrower at his hip and remained ready to pull his weapon at the slightest indication that I meant his employer any harm.

Working smoothly, with as much of Simon Blake's experience with the weapon as with my own understanding of it, I removed the stock and the extended barrel from the slug-thrower. Instead of returning them to their case, I tucked them into hidden pockets in my duster, which was cut to smooth the lines and reveal nothing of what lay underneath.

"How much?"

We haggled over that price a little more enthusiastically, but Jitish knew I wasn't leaving the shop without those things. I also made him throw in two hundred-count boxes of ammunition for the slug-thrower, one with short rounds dedicated to subsonic and low speed that wouldn't penetrate most walls—or bodies—and higher-velocity rounds for shooting at a distance. Then I purchased a set of tools, including a cutting laser and welder and a stunstick.

My cred level was nearly flattened, but I had everything I needed except for a place to stay.

When we were finished, I left the shop and began scouting for a hotel. I needed to upgrade the PAD and get hold of Floyd. There were questions I needed answered.

Chapter Eleven

I managed the repairs while looking into the mirror at a motel at the back end of the box canyon. Logic dictated that by placing myself back there I was trapping myself, but I knew I could climb into the half-mile high mountain range if I needed to.

Due to the craggy exterior, I could avoid any hoppers willing to chance the wind shear that could exceed 100 kph. Coupled with the thin atmosphere, hopper pilots would have a difficult time tracking me. Human pursuers wouldn't be able to keep pace with me while in envirosuits, and clones and bioroids could be dealt with.

I felt confident in my chosen bunker.

The PAD replacement took eighteen hours and nine minutes. I only had to backtrack on the operation six times, which I thought was well within tolerance given the less-than-adequate circumstances I was forced to do them in.

When I was finished, I ran a diagnostic and immediately felt the difference in the capability I'd been performing at when it came to Net access.

While I was soldering up my chassis, I pinged the secret account

Floyd 2X3A7C and I had set up for our communications. When I finished with the soldering, I went down to the motel's main lobby, checked my tools into a safebox, then checked out of the higher-priced room I'd stayed in, and signed up for one of the body drawers most of the people who stayed there slept in.

"Too bad we don't have crypts outside." The wizened old woman that manned the desk was different from the one I had checked in with. The tattooing on her face marked her as Martian; the ink looked as faded as her hair and as listless as the perfunctory smile she offered me. "It would be a lot cheaper. But we don't get many of you in here. I think most of the bioroids sleep standing up in whatever warehouse or business they work at."

I thought that was probably true as well, but didn't say anything. I accepted the key code she gave me, committing it to memory at once. I crossed the small lobby and headed into a narrow hallway, stepping aside to allow men and women to file past.

Locally, it was just after 1300. According to the help wanted postings I had seen on the vicinity classifieds in the newsrags, the nearby businesses ran on three shifts: from six to two, two to ten, and the skeletal maintenance shift from ten to six. These people were going to work and none of them looked excited to do so.

I continued past communal showers where men and women stood waiting to go in with towels wrapped around themselves. I filed scars and tattoos as a matter of course because those were identifying features a person of interest could not get rid of without considerable effort. I discovered three criminals guilty of misdemeanors and two felons as I walked by the steam-filled room. Since none of them were currently wanted for crimes involving murder or personal injury, I was able to pass them by without apprehending them myself.

Using my new PAD, I hijacked the motel's frequency and

sent in the location of all five people to the NAPD and Martian police. I would be gone before the law enforcement teams arrived, and I made certain my communications transmission could not be tracked.

"You're taking a risk," Shelly said as she walked beside me.

"I cannot let them go without telling someone." It was, in fact, everything I could do to walk away without apprehending them myself. Only the fact that I had no current law enforcement standing prevented me from doing so.

Shelly cursed but didn't protest any further.

The vault room was filled with small meter by .8 meter doors on the walls. A few of the drawers were open and motel guests were gradually awakening to the sound of alarms only they could hear, or were sitting on the drawers waiting to become more fully alert before trying to walk.

They looked at me, and most looked away immediately, but a few studied me with low-level curiosity. I ignored them and found the door to my drawer, then punched in the key code.

Smoothly, the drawer rolled out to reveal the small bed with sanitary wrap covering it to prove that no one had been sleeping in there since it had been sterilized. I levered myself into it, listening to the rollers groan slightly under my weight even on Mars.

Shelly stood and watched. "I'll be out here, Drake. I can't stand those things. They remind me too much of the morgue."

"I understand." Even as I responded, I wondered where her response had come from. Shelly wasn't squeamish. She and I had visited morgues several times. I thought perhaps having her say that was because I didn't want to see her lying beside me in that drawer. It would have reminded me too much of how I had last seen her after she'd been killed.

After I settled onto the bed, I pressed the keypad to roll myself into the storage space. Once the door was sealed, the unit's near-AI spun up into life, reading my preference from the check-in log I'd filled out.

"Hello, guest." The voice was a female baritone. "Welcome to Elysian Fields Motel. We try to match each of our guests with the most comfortable arrangements so that you will enjoy your stay with us."

A small screen opened almost in my face and revealed a deluge of sensie images ranging from dramatic to pornographic as well as a selection of sports.

"As you can see, we can provide you with an assortment of viewable products. You can choose a two-dimensional experience or a more interactive, virtual one. We can also bring you live sporting events from around Mars, Earth, and the Moon. Note: please allow for the lag time between Earth and the Moon for live presentation."

I opted out of that, switched out the lights, turned down the offer of music as well as background noise that included whale songs and swamp sounds, and logged onto the message service I was using with Floyd. He had responded. I asked him to rendezvous with me at our meetbox.

He asked me to give him an hour and I did, lying there quietly in the near-coffin while planning out my next move. Instead of meeting with Floyd, though, I took a side trip back to the past.

* * *

"Simon! Where are you?"

I was running for my life, taking long, risky strides over the Martian landscape in my envirosuit. Rebel mortar fire blew craters into the side of the mountain we were fighting on. My aud dampers filtered out most of the screaming missiles and the raucous blasts, but they didn't do anything about the concussive waves and scattershot shrapnel that filled the thin air around me.

"Here." I sent out a suit ping so Rath could find me easier.

"I see you. You're a quarter-klick out of position."

"That's because the rebels have got tanks we didn't know about." The intel on the op was faulty and Chimera Team was taking the brunt of that mistake.

Rath chuckled drily. "I'll have a word with Chesboro when we get back to Mariner colony."

"You do that." I threw myself down onto debris-strewn ground as another group of howlers whistled by overhead. "In case I don't get to attend that meeting, maybe you could tell him a few things for me."

"You'll be there. I'm not going to let anything happen to you."

On my knees and making the most of the cover I'd found, I peered down into the valley Chimera had agreed to take for Whampoa Reclamation. Whampoa was a Chinese mining outfit that had recently purchased the mineral rights to the mountain range we'd signed on to make safe.

After meeting stiff resistance originally, Whampoa had put some of their sec people into the area to shore up their efforts to move mining equipment into the mountains. Several million dollars' worth of earthmovers lay scattered across the mountainside. The rebels had used them as target practice.

There were also several dead sec people. Whampoa hadn't been allowed to claim the bodies. Since there weren't any carnivorous beetles and blowflies on Mars to help get rid of dead things, those corpses had just lain there, slowly decomposing in their envirosuits, which kept them at human temp instead of the cold of Mars. I knew from experience that by the time those bodies were recovered, the dead would be poured from those suits like stew or a really thick soup.

Chimera was getting a bonus for every dead body they brought in that could still be recognized. That was easy cred as long as the suit remained intact. If a suit's integrity was breached, things got really messy and hard to label.

"Meaning no disrespect, Colonel, but you may not have a

choice in the matter." I triggered the magnification built into my helmet and tracked the hostile forces.

Most of the rebel mortar emplacements lay hidden in ravines and gullies, dug in tight in hard to get to places. Some of them had even dug in behind the metallic corpses of the earthmovers. Chimera was getting paid for salvage rights to the equipment too, but I didn't think the rebels knew that their choice of hiding spots was making our jobs even harder than they already were. The colonel wanted those salvaged earthmovers as intact as they could possibly be.

"I *always* have a choice, Captain." Rath sounded supremely confident. I couldn't help thinking that maybe wherever he was, he probably wasn't looking at as much resistance as I was. "You need to remember that."

I lifted my laser rifle and sighted on a two-man mortar group that had broken cover and was sprinting across open ground 437 meters away. Since I was using the laser and not a slug-thrower, I didn't have to allow for any lead time or drop. I put the sights over the first man and burned a hole through his head you could have put your thumb through.

When the dead man went down, the man behind him was following too close to keep from sprawling on top of him. The man tried to get to his feet, shoving against the dead man. I sighted, waited a beat for him to calm and focus, then burned him through the head as well. He dropped like a stone.

"Good shots," Rath said over the channel. "Now why don't you get your team organized again and take those people out."

"Yes, sir."

I ripped off the cover to my PAD and orally gridded the battlefield, knocking out terrorists as my team accounted for six more kills. The main problem was the four tanks. They stood six meters tall, eight meters wide, and twelve meters long. Not a lot of thought had gone into the overall appearance. They were tracked ziggurats three layers high, and the two top tiers bristled with 20mm cannons.

I couldn't help wondering where the rebels had gotten them from. The people we'd identified couldn't reach that deeply for war machines and weapons, but they somehow had.

I keyed my comm. "I don't suppose you have air support ready, do you?"

"As a matter of fact, I do. Paint the targets and we'll release the birds."

I adjusted the laser rifle, turning down the destructive capability and bringing up the special targeting frequency. I aimed it at the first tank as it trundled down the Martian landscape as another wave of mortars blasted the landscape in front of me into bits. Sand and grit blew over me, *tink*ing against the envirosuit.

"Target One is painted, Colonel."

"Outstanding. Bird is in the air, locking onto your signal."

I waited, holding the rifle steady as the tank fired on the run, blasting a 150mm cannon round into the hill in front of a small contingent of the forces I commanded.

The turret suddenly lifted slightly and came around in my direction, and I knew the team inside the tank had figured out what I was doing.

"Colonel, the target has a snooper array tracking back my paint signature." I tried not to imagine the little that would be left of me if that round hit my position.

"Of course they do. We have 6.8 seconds between rounds those people can fire. That bird will be there in 5.9 seconds."

"Cutting it close, sir." There wasn't time to say anything else. I knew the tank was about to fire. I stared down the large muzzle and awaited that round.

Before the tank fired, though, a silver drone flashed across the sky and unleashed the small nuclear bomb it carried. Knowing the warhead was en route, I pushed myself up and scrambled for cover, managing three long strides before the V-shaped drone screamed down out of the sky and delivered a bomb that struck home.

The explosion enveloped the tank, bursting one of the treads into a cloud of flying shrapnel and separating the three layers that made up the vehicle's stages. A heartbeat later, the pieces clanged back down into a pile, then jumped and juddered as the ammo cooked off, turning it into a swarm of deadly debris that mowed down nearby enemy combatants.

The concussive force caught me and slung me to one side. Pain flared through me and my breath exploded from my lungs when I struck the ground. Dirt and debris rained down over me, pelting my armor and helmet.

"Simon." The colonel sounded firm and totally in command. "Give me a sitrep."

I pushed myself up, checking quickly to make sure I hadn't been wounded. The suit's air pressure looked normal, so I assumed it hadn't been holed. I gazed back at the flaming pyre that remained of the first tank.

"Target One is down, sir."

"Good. Light up the second target."

I threw myself forward and pulled the laser rifle into position. "Roger that. Painting the second target." I squeezed the trigger. "Target Two is painted."

Alerted by the first tank and that unit's sudden demise, the second tank had already locked onto my position. As I watched through Simon's point of view, I tried to get him to move, to abandon his location on the hillside, but he remained irresolute. His trust in John Rath's ability was much stronger than mine. Even knowing that he had survived the encounter didn't quell my desire to protect him.

I barely noted a second V-shaped drone that flitted into sight an instant before another explosion struck the second tank at the bottom of the right tread. Although the tank wasn't immediately left in ruins, the bomb destroyed the tread and the hillside, causing the vehicle to slowly overturn.

"Bogart," I called over the comm. "Put a rocket into that tank."

"On it, Captain." Forty meters away, Bogart popped up on a ridge, his purple hair showing under his helmet. The rocket launcher on his shoulder belched fire and smoke, and a large warhead whistled across two hundred meters to slam into the tank.

The tank erupted and rocked as it lay upside down. Flames from the incendiary warhead wreathed the vehicle. No one made it out of the tank alive.

A woman lifted the hatch on the third tank and attempted to track the next drone with the anti-aircraft guns. I centered the reticule over her head and burned a hole in her skull, frying her brain. She slumped forward just before the drone delivered its deadly payload. The bomb dropped down into the tank and exploded it from within, scattering parts and corpses over the battlefield.

The remaining tank attempted to retreat, but rocket launcher fire turned the countryside around it into a blistering inferno. Another drone lit it up and destroyed it as well.

Simon grinned and I felt his expression of relief spread across our face. "Thanks, John."

"I'm here to serve, buddy. I told you that."

"I know. But I appreciate the service."

"I've got more for you. Aerial recon has spotted most of your mortar teams. Have your people stand down for a moment while we sweep the area."

"Affirmative." I gave the order to my team, then checked for casualties. I had three. Two people KIA and a wounded man that was being attended by a corpsman.

An instant later, a swarm of drones flashed through the air and hit the mortar teams, giving them no chance to retreat or surrender, taking them out in bursts that threw earth high into the air and left craters behind. The op hadn't intended to be merciful. John Rath was taking his kilo of flesh in his employer's name.

After that, we just had to close in and put down the remaining opposition. The work was harsh and unforgiving, but we got it done because we knew Rath would expect us to be thorough.

* * *

Rath stood on a hillside in full attack gear over his slimline envirosuit. He was tall and muscular, with black hair and grey eyes behind his goggles, his age indeterminate. I couldn't see his face due to the breather mask, and Simon couldn't seem to remember what he looked like now. The files I'd found on John Rath tended to be incomplete and didn't have any good images. Most of them were blurred and out of focus. All I knew for certain was that he'd had facial reconstruction done several times, so the face the man wore at this point in time might have been any one of the faces he'd worn in the past.

Scuff marks and red Martian dust showed on his combat gear. Blood coated his left glove and I knew he'd been involved in the final hand-to-hand action that had routed our opponents. He stared down at the valley where sand stirred restlessly under the breeze.

I walked up the hillside, feeling uncomfortably fatigued and sore. It took me a moment to log those feelings and recognize them. As a bioroid, I'd never experienced them before. Only my past memories with Simon allowed me to identify those things.

"We'll earn a bonus from Whampoa Reclamation." The breather mask changed his voice, deepened it and roughened it. "Their intel didn't say anything about the opposition having tanks out here."

I nodded and gazed down at the crawlers scooting across the sand. Part of our team remained posted as lookout, but the rest of them were gathering the dead Whampoa employees, stacking them like cordwood on the crawlers.

Rath glanced at me. "You did good out here today, Simon."

"*We* did good, Colonel. It was a team effort."

"That it was." He shifted his laser rifle, keeping it canted across his chest. "I'm going to miss you when you're gone."

Simon turned his head inside his helmet and took a sip of water through the drinking tube that ran to his rucksack. "Are you sure that's what you want me to do? I don't feel right about leaving the team."

"This is the right thing to do. You're not going to go away forever. Just for a while. Till your lady friend completes her neural channeling project. Then you can come back to Chimera."

"She's years away from finishing it. I'd rather stay out here with the team."

"This is a business deal." Rath lowered his rifle and turned to face me. "You do this, Chimera gets fifteen percent of Mirror-Morph, Inc. If this thing goes as big as Mara Parker believes it will—and I believe it will too—that's going to be a solid payday for the team." He pointed his chin out at the valley. "This is what I've been hoping for, Simon. A payday with a long tail. We get paid in one, the cred gets spent and these guys have nothing. We've died and bled over battlegrounds like this Earthside, on the Moon, and now here."

"I know, John. I was there."

"Not through all of it, Simon. You weren't there for all of it." For just a moment, Rath's smooth composure slipped and I heard the anger and pain that resided within him. "I've left dead soldiers behind me. Good people. Friends." Fire flashed in his grey eyes. "Somebody needs to pay for that."

Simon didn't know what to say. I could tell then that this was an old conversation, one that he and Rath had shared on several occasions.

"Getting you in with Mara Parker and her people is a step in the right direction," Rath continued. "We won't be just a mercenary group hanging on by our fingernails out here. We won't be cashing blood in for cred anymore. We'll have a chance to become part of the franchised. This is an opportunity that I'm counting on, so don't screw it up."

"I won't."

Rath dropped a hand onto my shoulder. I felt his strength, solid, sure, and dependable. "I'm relying on you, soldier. You're the start of my investment in the future." He took his hand back and nodded downhill. "Let's go down there and help earn our keep." Without another word, he strode toward the nearest Whampoa corpse, lifted the man to his shoulder, and carried him toward the crawler.

I grabbed another corpse and followed.

Chapter Twelve

I didn't remember coming back out of the memory. I just opened my eyes, or maybe they were already open in the darkness, and I was once more in the vault drawer.

Rath had assigned Simon Blake to protect Mara Parker. That was interesting.

Then what had put Simon Blake at odds with the chimera mercenaries that had tried to kill him? What had happened to John Rath? The questions chased themselves around in my thoughts as I waited for evening to arrive.

I checked the time and found out I was two minutes away from when I was supposed to join Floyd 2X3A7C in the meet-box as we had arranged. At the prescribed time, I accessed the Net and went, knowing that the minutes-long drag would affect the conversation I had with Floyd.

I closed my eyes—

* * *

—and opened them to discover I was inside the NAPD on Earth, in the homicide bullpen at the desk I had assigned to me when I was working with Shelly. The buzz of conversations filled the space. Holos from PADs gleamed at every desk as the detective teams sorted through crime scenes and data dumps.

Across from me in her customary spot, Shelly pored over files that flickered through her PAD. I recognized some of the information from some of the past investigations we'd conducted. Beside her, steam rose from a cup of coffee.

Slowly, I surveyed the bullpen, aware that at any moment one of the detectives would recognize me and my freedom would be in jeopardy. I focused on the thought that I could break the connection to the meetbox, but I was also aware that I could be traced back to my present location in Bradbury colony.

Shelly looked up at me and grinned. "Don't be alarmed. No one at the NAPD knows you're here. That steam rising from the coffee alone should be enough to tell you this isn't real. I never had hot coffee."

That was true. Shelly had always purchased it hot, but it invariably cooled before she got the chance to drink it.

I glanced around the bullpen. All around us, detectives I had worked with over the years continued with their assignments, talking and sorting through e-docs with practiced care. Three desks over, Schmeltzer interviewed an informant Shelly and I had worked with on occasion, till he had retired two years ago. I had always felt comfortable around him.

"What am I doing here?" I asked.

"This is the meetbox." Shelly sipped her coffee, but the steam was gone from it now and I knew it was cold.

"Where's Floyd 2X3A7C?" I asked.

"He'll be along. He's fighting lag."

"Did Floyd set this up?"

Shelly shook her head. "This is your doing, Drake."

"Why would I choose this place?"

"I don't know. Why would you?"

I didn't have an answer for that, but I knew that what she said was true. On some level, I had arranged this destination.

Shelly leaned back in her chair. "If you were human, I'd say that you chose the NAPD because that's where you felt most at home. This is the place that defined you."

"I'm not human."

"Part of you *was* human. You were Simon Blake."

"No. Some of my memories came from Simon Blake."

"This isn't a place Simon Blake would have felt comfortable. This isn't from his memories."

I couldn't argue that with her. Simon Blake had been a mercenary, used to calling his own shots. Even though the regimental structure of the NAPD wouldn't have been far from what he'd known under Rath's command, he wouldn't have cared for the layers within layers of authority. He'd liked working for Rath, and he'd loved Mara Parker.

"Maybe you're human enough to seek solace in something you know," Shelly suggested. She gestured at the bullpen. "This was your home."

"Yes. But I can't come back here."

"Not till you clear your name, no. But you didn't kill Jonas Salter, Drake."

Since Shelly was essentially part of me as much as Simon Blake was, I wondered why I felt the need to tell myself something I already knew.

"Once you find out who killed Jonas Salter, you'll be able to come back here," Shelly said.

I wanted to believe that because returning to my original purpose was something I'd been designed to do. However, I knew the chances of me getting back in with the NAPD were small. More than likely, once I was captured or finished with my investigation, I would be returned to Haas-Bioroid, wiped, and reprogrammed. I felt no fear at that possibility, but I wanted to preserve myself. That survival mechanism was programmed into my neural channeling.

If I was repurposed, all that was me, all that was Drake 3GI2RC, would be erased. My name and recorded testimonies would be all that remained. Thinking of that digital shadow of myself logged into court cases and investigation recorders seemed unsettling.

Would I somehow live on in those digital shadows? That was an interesting question that I had no answer for.

More than that, what was left of Simon Blake would vanish once more, as well. His resurrection would be over.

At that moment, Floyd entered the bullpen and looked around. He wasn't surprised. Bioroids like us weren't programmed for surprise, though some gynoids could be encoded to simulate such a response. Instead, he paused a moment to assess his surroundings. His right hand dropped to the rosary that hung around his neck and he fingered the beads with a rhythmic clicking.

As I watched him, I realized that neither of us had turned out the way Haas-Bioroid had designed us. Floyd searched for some proof of an afterlife for bioroids and I spoke to ghosts. In fact, I was, I supposed, something of a ghost myself.

Floyd focused on me. "Drake."

Knowing that he could have turned against me and might even then be leading tracking software to my location, I felt a small sense of threat vibrate through me. I was programmed to feel that as part of my survival instinct. I felt certain that one of the other detectives would look up at the mention of my name.

None of them did.

"Floyd, join us."

He crossed the bullpen and stood near my desk. "'Us'?"

I realized my error then, and I tried to think of how best to explain. Before I could, Floyd's attention riveted on Shelly. I had not known that he would be able to see her.

"I did not expect to see Detective Nolan here."

Shelly looked at him and smiled. "Perhaps the world is smaller than you thought."

Floyd's fingers worked through his rosary beads like an abacus. "You are dead, are you not?"

"I am."

"Interesting." Floyd shifted his attention to me. "This is your doing?"

"It is, though not by choice."

"We really have to work on your bluntness, Drake," Shelly said, as she had so often informed me while we had worked together.

"I will." I responded to her because it would have been rude not to, and I wasn't sure how she would have handled that.

"How is it she is here and interacting with you?" Floyd asked.

"I have been told she is part of my persona at this point. Another layer of programming that I wrote myself, though I do not recall doing so."

Shelly flashed me a look. "I have always been my own person."

"This is highly interesting," Floyd said. "How long has this been going on?"

"Almost since the time of her death."

"You haven't thought to mention this?"

"Doing so seemed moot since I hadn't believed you would have seen her."

"Do you only see her in a meetbox? Or on the Net?"

"I see her all the time."

Floyd considered that for a moment. "You may still be accessing her core personality from the Net. You and I are constantly logged on."

I hadn't realized that, and the possibility intrigued me. The Shelly seated at her desk could have been an assembly of digital impressions I streamed from the archived footage on the Net. That gave me pause, because if that was true I was leaving a digital footprint that might be tracked.

"Seriously, guys," Shelly said with a note of exasperation,

"you're not here to discuss me. And quite frankly, I don't much care for it."

"Forgive me," Floyd said. Then he looked at me. "This is most puzzling. I have never felt the need to respond to a hologram before."

Shelly folded her arms. "I'm not a hologram."

I reached back and pulled up a chair from the desk behind me, then presented it to Floyd.

He sat, dividing his attention between Shelly and me. "I would like to continue an inquiry regarding your relationship with this Detective Nolan at some point."

"Not today," Shelly said.

Floyd nodded in agreement. "Another time."

Shelly didn't say anything.

"Perhaps we should focus on our investigation," I said. "The delay between Mars and Earth telescopes our time spent here, and the longer we talk, the more danger I have of being found out."

"Of course. I have news of Jonas Salter's murder."

That caught my curiosity, but I needed more information as well. "We will get to that in a moment. I have something else I need you to look into."

"What?"

"You've heard of John Rath?"

"Yes. His name has come up in the chimera investigations."

"There are chimera investigations?" I had not known that. That must have happened since I'd taken passage on *Khloe*.

"Files have been reopened up regarding the murder investigation you were assigned to that resulted in the death of Detective Nolan."

I looked at Shelly. Her countenance didn't change, so I assumed she took no notice of the conversation.

She glanced at me as if reading my thoughts. "What? It's not like I don't know I'm dead."

Floyd studied her, and I knew his investigator's mind was filled with questions. Shelly was an anomaly, and her presence there struck a chord in his search for a life beyond the one he currently lived.

"What about the chimera investigations?" I asked.

"Homicide has become more interested in John Rath and the mercenary team."

"Give me an account of the inquiries."

"It appears that John Rath disappeared from public sight a few years ago while he was on Mars, though everyone is uncertain as to what happened to him. There are reports of his death during an operation, but they are unconfirmed."

"What operation?"

"There is actually a selection of them. Apparently Rath did a lot of mercenary business in the Martian colonies. Some say that he died recovering a prototype of a new mining machine for NuStrata, Inc. that was allegedly stolen by a competitor. Others say he was killed by a nerve agent invented by GeneTwist Munitions while attempting to destroy the research that was being done to weaponize the bacterial strain. Still others say he was murdered by a rival mercenary group. Whatever the story, his body was never found. Though there are also rumors that his mercenary unit buried his body somewhere on Mars where it will never be found."

I committed those to memory to search through later. "There's no indication of the truth?"

"No. There are even rumors that Rath was grievously wounded and is recovering somewhere, and that only his brain survived and is lingering in a vat of Suspend in some unknown location."

That image was so distinct that it remained in my mind for a moment.

"The main thing investigators are focused on is how the chimera unit came to be split," Floyd went on. "From all accounts, the separation between John Rath and Simon Blake seems to be the eye of that particular storm."

"They parted as friends. Blake was actually on assignment from Rath to protect Mara Parker."

Floyd looked at me. "We have had no indication of that."

"John Rath sent Blake to Mara Parker to act as security liaison in exchange for fifteen percent of MirrorMorph, Inc."

"How did you come upon this information?"

"It is in Simon Blake's memories. I only now gained access to them."

"Interesting. We've found no mention of that."

"Can you access MirrorMorph, Inc.'s financials?"

"Give me a moment." Floyd's gaze became fixed for just a moment, then he returned to himself and turned his palm up. A holo opened up over his palm and displayed a legal contract. "I do not find John Rath's name anywhere in the MirrorMorph, Inc. financials or those of Mara Blake."

I looked through the summation. A few years back, Haas-Bioroid had acted on a contracted option and bought out a controlling share of MirrorMorph, Inc., forever tying the continued development to Director Haas's purview.

"As you can see, the major shareholder is now Haas-Bioroid." Floyd dragged his forefinger over the document, highlighting Haas-Bioroid's ownership.

"What about Mara Blake's share of the corporation?"

"It's been parceled out in several different pieces to various people who worked on the program. None of them are John Rath." Floyd brought up another document.

I touched that portion of the document, highlighted it, and then expanded it with my two forefingers. The information box magnified easily, providing a list of names. I didn't recognize most of them immediately, but a quick, subsequent search fleshed them out quite nicely. All of them were past employees, other developers Mara had worked with.

"It looks as though Mara Blake was looking out for the people who helped her design the neural channeling techniques she invented."

"Yes," Floyd replied. "She appears to be quite generous. However, as you can see, there is no mention of John Rath."

I searched the list again with the same results.

Floyd focused on me. "You said that Simon Blake was killed by chimera mercenaries."

"A rogue group, yes."

"Who deemed those people as rogue?"

I considered that for a moment. "I did."

"Because, based on your point of view—which was Simon Blake's point of view at the time—those people could only have been rogue."

"Yes."

"I propose that you turn around Simon Blake's recollection of those events. Cast him in the role of the rogue."

I did, and I didn't like where my thoughts led me.

"It could well have been that Simon Blake betrayed John Rath. That betrayal could well be what got him killed."

"Because Mara Blake rescinded her agreement toward Rath's fifteen percent of MirrorMorph's stocks?"

"That would provide motive to kill Simon Blake at the time. If Rath was cheated of those stocks, the mercenaries he was working with would have likewise been cheated."

"Perhaps Mara awarded those shares to Rath under another name." Although I was not programmed to be stubborn, tenaciousness was recognized as a valuable skill set for a detective to possess. Becoming tenacious in this case was easy. I liked Simon Blake and did not think him capable of treacherous subterfuge.

"Seeing Simon Blake as the good guy in all of this is a little narcissistic, don't you think?" Shelly raised a challenging eyebrow at me.

I did not deign to reply.

Floyd elevated the holo of MirrorMorph's financials. "I do not find a fifteen percent share anywhere in these files."

"Rath could have wanted the portion broken up, listed under a combination of names to protect himself. He always covered his tracks." I studied the breakdown, doing the math in split seconds. "Here, here, here, and here." I touched the financials, highlighting the four names I'd found in a soft yellow glow. "These shares add up to fifteen percent. What can you tell me about those names?"

For a moment, Floyd held still and I knew he was accessing files at the NAPD. Then he began speaking. "Sabrina Knight, forty-four, investments counselor at Red Gull Investments. She owns and operates a small firm here in New Angeles."

"Look at her portfolio. Where are her interests?"

"She's diversified, has holdings on Earth, the Moon, and Mars."

"Any ties to Rath?"

"None that I see." Floyd paused. The holo projecting from his palm flickered. "Wait a moment. One of the holding companies she has access to through other proxies is owned by Friedrich Garry Investments, an underwriter for the chimera mercenary group."

"Rath's mercenary group was underwritten by outside corps?" That was unexpected. According to Simon Blake's memories, the mercenary group was financially stable. No one owned them.

"Friedrich Garry Investments didn't own the chimera group. They were a clearing house for corp cred that Rath used to fund his operations. Give me a moment."

Trapped outside the NAPD files, I could only watch and wait as Floyd sorted through massive databanks. As he provided names and links, I chased them through media sources myself, but I knew the information I had access to was less than what he had. I also knew that even with the NAPD resources at his disposal, Floyd was limited on what he could discover. Corps and intelligent men had ways of hiding things they did not want known.

A few moments later, Floyd produced another holo, this one of the four names I had indicated he should search. I downloaded the file and searched through it. Floyd had done a good job.

Following the digital trail he had flagged was simple, though I knew the search had not been.

"It is done." Floyd studied the same document. "All of those people eventually track back to Friedrich Garry Investments, and all of them reflect the fifteen percent MirrorMorph, Inc. is paying to the chimera group."

I looked at the final accounts that the cred ended up in. All of them were owned under an umbrella corporation called SolGenX, a privately held business invested in solar energy development on Mars.

"Who owns SolGenX?" I didn't have access to that information on the sources I had available to me.

"I am still searching for that answer. The identity of that person, or persons, appears to be buried."

Identities of corporate owners was often withheld and protected to keep them from becoming victims. Often CEOs were hired to present a public face to encourage investments and product trust. They also became targets. Many times those "CEOs" were smokescreens to draw enemy fire, sacrificial lambs left to be slaughtered by kidnappers and terrorists and opposing corps.

"This is going to take some time, and our window here is closing. Perhaps you would like to see how the investigation into Jonas Salter's murder is progressing."

"Yes."

"Let me take you to the crime scene."

The NAPD bullpen faded around me and I was swept away.

Chapter Thirteen

It wasn't really the NAPD virtual crime scene lab, where the events of an investigation were rebuilt and replayed for detectives. I had been inside that several times with Shelly.

This was a different area in cyberspace that Floyd had prepared for me. We stood in an underground mag-lev utility closet on the Moon. The reproduction of the site was so good that my body automatically recalibrated to the Moon-norm gravity, which caused me problems for a moment while lying in the drawer in Bradbury colony because the input there was different. I made the adjustment and pulled up a secondary set of parameters that I used in the crime scene lab.

Jonas Salter sprawled across the floor. In the Moon's microgravity, the arterial spray from his slashed carotid arteries had gone much farther than it would have on Mars or on Earth. Blood glistened on the walls, the ceiling, and the floor like it had just been shed. The iron tang of blood registered on my olfactory receptors.

An uncomfortable feeling passed through me, something that didn't often happen when I looked upon the dead. Victims registered with me as potential evidence. Their gender, age, and social standing didn't matter to me other than as markers that would potentially lead to their killers.

Things had been different with Shelly. I had felt decidedly uncomfortable at her death. My programming had insisted that I put things to rights to return her to the world. I knew that was not possible, yet the feeling remained.

I felt an echo of that now, but I recognized it was not any attachment on my part to Jonas Salter that vibrated through me. That feeling came from that piece of me that was Simon Blake. Simon had, for a time, been close to this man.

Another man, beefy and broad with greying brown hair, brown eyes, and a thick jawline, stood in the utility closet with us. He wore a suit and regarded me with a flat gaze. I recognized Sergeant Louis Blaine at once.

"Hello, Drake." His deep voice echoed inside the utility closet.

"Hello, Detective Blaine." He offered his hand and I cautiously took it, expecting to feel a trapper utility program snap around my online presence so I could be traced and dampened so I couldn't return to my physical body.

"Louis is fine." Blaine released my hand and jerked a thumb over his shoulder at Floyd. "I tripped across Floyd and invited myself in to the murder investigation of this guy after I found out we were both looking at the same thing." He nudged Jonas Salter's virtual body with a scuffed shoe.

"My apologies," Floyd said. "I should have warned you. Detective Blaine and I have been collaborating in this matter."

"Why?" I asked.

Blaine knew the question was more for him than for Floyd. "I owe you one for the Cartman Dawes investigation. You got me out of that warehouse alive."

That was true. If not for me, Blaine would have died.

"Plus, I don't like how the frame against you fits. There was nothing between you and this guy." Blaine returned his attention to the dead body. "If you were going to snap and flatline somebody, you would kill a cop."

"I would never—"

Blaine held up a big hand. "I'm not saying you would. I'm just pointing out that you're around cops more than you are anyone else. I've never seen a murder yet that didn't have some kind of trigger. You would kill a cop. I've been tempted a time or two myself." He favored me with a big-toothed grin. "But this? This doesn't sound like you at all."

"Thank you."

Blaine's presence there bothered me because, according to him, he had conspired with Simon Blake to interfere with the murder investigation of Rachel Giacomin, who had worked with Mara Blake at one point. She had also supposedly been Simon's lover, and she had tried to kill Simon before she had turned up dead.

Blaine had framed Dwight Taylor for Giacomin's death. Taylor had later turned out to be an ex-mercenary who had worked for John Rath. He'd also been one of the men who had tried to save Simon Blake after Simon had been ambushed in a hopper. For a moment I was in that underground garage holding Taylor as he lay dying, shot by other chimera mercenaries while trying to elude me. He'd stared at me, blood tricking from the corner of his mouth. "You're dead. I saw you die."

I hadn't known what he had meant then, but I did later when I realized my neural channeling had come from Simon Blake. My face had started to reform then, and I was taking on Simon's features.

So who was Dwight Taylor? A murderer? Or a man who had tried to save the life of Simon Blake?

There were no easy answers to any of this. Not even Jonas Salter was who he said he was. When I had first met him as Drake, he had been living as Dylan Templeton, the designer of one of the most popular fantasy online games on the Net. It hadn't been until later that I had recalled he had worked with Mara and Simon on the neural channeling designs.

There were too many faces involved, and so many names. Keeping them straight was hard work. But I knew that all I had to do was work my way back to the person who had set everything into place. I focused on that.

"Drake?" Blaine stared at me expectantly.

I realized then that he had asked me a question. "I'm sorry. I was being inattentive."

"That's not like you."

"I think perhaps the lag time is causing problems." That was a fabrication, but I was allowed to tell those to people who were innocent if no one was hurt.

Blaine grunted and nodded. "As I was saying, the crime scene techs turned up evidence of you being on the scene." He pointed and two patches of blue liquid highlighted.

One of the patches was on Salter's left shoulder, the other was partially obscured by his body.

"This is your cooling system fluid. Serology identified it as yours from the radioactive markers it contained."

All bioroids had radioactive markers in their cooling system. The radioactive markers were an anti-theft precaution, but they worked admirably well in crime scene identification as well.

"The techs matched it against samples kept on file at the NAPD."

"I didn't know such files were kept."

"They are." Blaine shifted his attention back to me. "If you didn't know the NAPD kept those files, that means you didn't donate them."

"No, I didn't."

"Then there's only one place the NAPD could have gotten them. Haas-Bioroid."

I acknowledged that with a nod, and I considered the

ramifications of that. Having me identified as a killer bioroid wouldn't be beneficial to Haas-Bioroid.

Or would it?

I accessed a datastream and checked the stock quotes. Haas-Bioroid stock was currently on the rise in spite of the charges that had been levied against me. The accusation against me had lifted their public profile again. In fact, rumors that Haas-Bioroid had created killer bioroids was on the rise again.

That urban myth had been around since the first higher-functioning bioroid had walked out of the corporation and taken its place in society. In all the years that bioroids had been operational, there had never been a single incident of the murder of a human by a bioroid.

The fact that I was wanted for murder was proof that the idea would not go away.

"Have you matched your radioactive markers against your cooling fluid?" Blaine asked.

"No. That had not occurred to me." Nor had I possessed any equipment to do such a comparison while onboard *Khloe*. "The markers found at the crime scene match what Haas-Bioroid has on file?"

"Yes, but that doesn't mean they're your markers, Drake." Blaine ran a hand over his stubbled jaw. "The file that Haas-Bioroid has could have been switched by someone working in-house, or samples of your markers could have been stolen from Haas-Bioroid and planted at the murder scene."

"There's nothing to indicate either of those scenarios was acted on," I replied.

"You didn't kill this man, Drake." Shelly suddenly stood in the utility closet with us. "That's proof enough that one of those things happened."

Blaine's eyes widened in surprise and the pulse in his carotid artery jumped. "Nolan?"

"Hello, Blaine." Shelly stood at my side.

Blaine shifted his attention to Floyd. "What is this?"

"Apparently Drake has created an alternative persona within his system," Floyd answered.

Blaine shook his head. "I've never heard of anything like that."

"Neither have I. But as you can see, she is here."

"Drake was framed," Shelly stated. "If you're going to be involved in this, you need to accept that and move on." As usual at a crime scene, Shelly had a no-nonsense attitude. Although Blaine was senior to her in experience, she didn't bow to that. "Floyd said there was other evidence to suggest you had a lead on Jonas Salter's murderer."

"Yeah." Blaine walked over to the west wall. "Part of the security makeup on the underground is heat sensors. They log changes in ambient heat. Construction teams use them to find hairline fractures in the tube tunnels. All the vibrations through the underground causes problems every now and again." He tapped a small device no bigger than his thumb and vaguely ovoid that was mounted on the wall. "This closet has a heat sensor. Not all of them do. They're sensitive enough to register changes in body heat."

I understood what Blaine was getting at immediately. "The human body's average ambient temperature is 98.6 degrees Fahrenheit. The ambient temperature in tube tunnels is 68 degrees. You can tell when Salter's body was brought into this place by how long it took him to reach the temperature he was at when he was found."

Blaine smiled and touched his nose. "Bingo. After Floyd brought me into his confidence, I started poking around. I did some background fact-finding on the Mujeeb Heat Sensor. This one's high quality. They're made in Bangladesh and are about the best on the market."

Shelly folded her arms. "Get to it, Blaine. We don't have time for the full puppet show."

Blaine grimaced irritably. “Wow, you’ve got her cold, don’t you, Drake?”

I didn’t reply.

“The thing is, I considered this sensor because I had another case where a Mujeeb helped me pinpoint the time of death on a victim. The vic had been shot and left for dead, but didn’t actually die right away. One of the vic’s friends found her and left her to die, and the sec door recorded the first visit and the second hours later, when that person said he’d found my vic dead. If she’d received medical treatment, she would have lived. Based on the info I pulled from the Mujeeb, I made a second-degree murder case against the friend and an attempted murder case against the shooter. Took two bad people off the street in one case.”

I wasn’t familiar with the case, but I made a note to look it up.

“What I did here is some high-end math,” Blaine continued. “Given the space in this room and the heat signature that showed up, I calculated the amount of flesh and blood that would have had to come into this place to cause the heat spike that showed in the records.” He grinned. “That calculation told me that either a 213 kilo man entered this room, or Jonas Salter had company when he got dropped off.” He punched an area above Salter’s corpse.

A window appeared and showed the legend of the medical examiner’s office.

“When the medical examiner’s people picked up the body, Jonas Salter massed out at 95 kilos, plus a little more for the liquid volume he lost.” Blaine looked at me. “That leaves 118 kilos unaccounted for. You mass out at more than that, and your ambient temperature runs several degrees lower than that.”

“Except for my hands and my face.” Since I worked with the public, those areas were programmed to heat up to 98.6 Fahrenheit. For those times when the human touch was needed.

“Yeah, I factored that in too. That amount is negligible. The bottom line is that someone else—someone human—was inside this utility closet with Salter."

"Have you told anyone about this?" Shelly asked.

"No."

"Why?"

Blaine faced her and squared up. "Think about it, Detective. I've got a theory. Having another human in this room doesn't take Drake out of the picture. The case could be made, and given how tight this frame job is, I'm guessing that it *would* be made that there might simply be another body the NAPD hasn't turned up yet. Or that Drake had an accomplice. Until I can put someone inside this room, irrefutably, I can't go anywhere with this. Doors will shut down. Files will be lost. I'm not exactly a sterling representative of the NAPD these days."

I knew Blaine was right. Shelly knew it too. I saw her frustrated frown. I turned back to Blaine. "Thank you for your efforts."

"You're welcome." Blaine looked at Shelly. "You were a good detective, Nolan. This thing with Salter means that we haven't found the end of the string that got you killed. I'm going to help with that. You deserved better."

I didn't know why Blaine spoke to her when he knew she wasn't really there. Maybe it was out of respect for me. Or maybe he thought I might be discomfited if he didn't acknowledge my aberration.

"Blaine and I will stay on this part of the investigation," Floyd said. "We've been reviewing video files of the tube the day Salter was killed, trying to find him in the crowds. Maybe it will help if we start searching for two people together instead of one."

"Or it could be whoever did this erased the footage of Salter getting on the tube," Blaine said. "Whoever set this up was really connected."

I nodded. "Thank you. Please keep me apprised. In the

meantime, Floyd, if you could start searching for those links to John Rath so that I could find out what happened to him, I would appreciate it."

"Of course."

I broke the connection to the meetbox and—

* * *

—opened my eyes once more in the drawer at the Elysian Fields Motel. The local time was 2119, late enough for me to start my search for the chimera mercenaries. That was the only lead I had left on Mars. Mara Blake was out there somewhere waiting.

Chapter Fourteen

I cycled through the airlock and stepped into the hazy environs of the Iron Pyrite Saloon. The neon pirate motif I'd seen on the digital board outside, obviously a play on the word pyrite, was repeated throughout the bar. Robot pirates battled on a mural behind the bar and a robot pirate lamp sat on every table. The airlock let out onto a raised area that overlooked the main floor of the bar and was intended to give the impression of a ship's captain standing on the stern.

Male and female servers dressed in pirate costumes—running the gamut from Caribbean pirates to the more recent asteroid space jumpers—plied a crowd of miners, transit employees, dock workers, and local laborers.

There were even a few people here slumming from Bradbury colony or other locations. I knew them because they kept to themselves and surveyed their surroundings with a mixture of fear and anticipation. Pleasure bioroids of both genders circulated the crowd as well, and occasionally someone would accompany one or two of them upstairs to privacy rooms.

I drew casual attention, but not too much. Everyone in a place like this noticed newcomers, but there was enough traffic from the train station that a new face was nothing immediately threatening. Merely a curiosity at the outset.

A young man dressed as a Spanish pirate with a cutlass in hand approached me with a smile from under the large, feathered hat he wore. He pointed his weapon—a pressed foam replica in neon green so there would be no mistakes about whether it was truly a danger—at me. "Avast there, lubber. Will ye be needin' a table for one, or a table for a group? Arrrr!"

"One. Something back in the VR section." I didn't drink or eat, so a bioroid sitting at a table by himself was either someone waiting on someone else or spying on someone else. Virtual reality offered new experiences to bioroids, and though the business was small, the market was dedicated and growing as newer, high-functioning bioroids came out of Haas-Bioroid and other manufacturers.

"Arrrr. Then follow me, matey." With a flourish, the server shoved his cutlass through his waist sash and headed back for a corner away from the bar.

I followed him and ignored the stares that trailed in my wake. Most of the men and women watching me didn't realize I had 360-degree vision. Most of them dismissed me at once and went back to their drinks and conversation.

The server pointed to a small table against the back wall. "Will this be suitin' yer pleasure then?"

A VR connection gleamed atop the table. It was a small, round touchpad that gleamed dark purple.

"This is fine." From the table, I could see most of the main bar. I sat.

The server dropped the accent. "If you ask me, the VR here is kind of pricey, but the range of environments is pretty good." He smiled. "I envy you guys being able to access VR with just a touch. I have to have a full skinsuit at home, and that thing gets itchy if you try to spend too much time in it.

Also, with all the health regs, I don't get unlimited access. Couldn't afford it either."

I nodded.

"Let me know if you need anything further."

I told him that I would and he went away. I put my left palm over the touchpad and booted the link, but I also partitioned my mind, letting the VR program run on a subroutine that I monitored but didn't let distract me from watching the bar.

After briefly considering the menu, which was fairly impressive for a bar this far outside of a megapolis or colony, I selected a history VR about Vikings that seemed to be a favorite. Maybe it was because the bioroids that frequented the Iron Pyrite stuck with a seafaring interest or because after spending so much time in the midst of a desert planet the idea of being out on an ocean was an attractive one.

When I logged in after slotting my credstick, I was suddenly seated on a hard wooden bench and was pulling an oar as a storm-tossed sea surged around me. The other warriors I sat with cursed their luck and prayed to their gods as the ship's captain called out the strokes. The cold, brine-flavored mist fell over me and I discovered my clothes were already soaked.

The sensations, smells, and sights—especially the violet lightning searing the sky—jarred me. I muted the experience, shoving it further down into my mind, then thought perhaps I'd chosen the Viking VR because I was there looking for warriors.

"Why didn't you ever get a VR rig for your home?" Shelly sat beside me and watched the bar as well. "A lot of bioroids that can afford them have them. You can certainly afford it."

That was true. Downtime was the worst thing for a bioroid. Having a job meant having a purpose, and it meant the hours in the day would be filled. Sitting idle for even the eight hours of downtime required every day by federal law, more to make certain more employees had a chance to work, seemed interminable. High-end bioroids had been designed to perform, to remain engaged.

Many of the bioroids were too simple, too unimaginative, to need stimulus throughout the day. They simply returned to where they were billeted, shut down, and went into upgrade mode, which was seldom necessary because Haas-Bioroid handled the upgrades and most bioroids didn't change jobs. They had nothing new to learn, and they never noticed. New things upset their routines and they resisted implementation and integration of them.

Higher-functioning bioroids were another matter. They learned every day from stimulus they received on the job. Models like the Brad that I had met on the train to Bradbury colony would require stimulus other than the job routine. They were constantly learning, and even during shut down mode, their minds remained active. They trolled the Net during those times.

However, most of them chose social interaction. They clubbed, they had sex—those that were equipped for it—they talked with anyone that would give them the time of day, and they got into trouble. Crime often wasn't a necessity for a bioroid, although many of them didn't mind getting their hands on the extra cred. Many times, criminal activity was simply a byproduct of restlessness and a need to learn, or to be part of a group. All of that experience was channeled into the performance of their jobs, allowing them to learn more about working with humans.

"I never felt the need for a VR rig," I replied. "I had our casework. That kept me occupied." And it had. Throughout the day when I was with Shelly, and during the time we were apart, I continually combed through the files and investigations we were working.

"That's why we had such a high closed case percentage."

I knew that was true. Shelly had often formed our investigative plans, setting up interviews, making intuitive leaps of logic that I'd been challenged to follow, but I had been the one that had spotted trends and patterns in the criminals we pursued.

"We were a good team," she said.

I nodded. We had been. To some degree, we still were. Momentary discomfort passed through me when I considered that I was somehow holding Shelly to the here and now instead of letting her go as her family had been forced to do. I made myself dismiss that thought, telling myself that I wasn't holding onto Shelly, that the "person" beside me was a simulacrum my mind had created out of necessity to keep me functioning as a detective. This Shelly was stimulus and a direct connection to experience and training, a needed second opinion and devil's advocate as I progressed.

The Viking VR continued to run, and the experiences there moved at 4.6 times the speed of real life. That was where the VR industry cheated its bioroid customers. A human had the capacity to act faster than life went on around it. Most humans could speak and understand 125 words a minute, but the brain moved at 400 words a minute or faster, allowing them to think about what was being said and what they were saying. High-functioning bioroid brains processed information even faster.

A VR sim charged for "real" time experiences that were compressed into bursts four and five times faster. Therefore, a VR that lasted four hours could be accessed in sixty minutes. The unit cost was still based on the delivered hour of entertainment, not the time connected. Some bioroids had become dependent on VR experiences, lusting after something other than their daily drudgery.

I sat there for an hour, watching people come and go. The bar patron that stood out the most was an older man with bionic legs. He'd had them for a while because they were older prosthetics, and not as fluid as the models on the market now.

I estimated that the man was in his sixties. His face was craggy, showing blemishes from scar tissue that hadn't quite been banished by a surgeon's laser, and seamed from a hard life. His full beard was the same salt and pepper as his long hair. The tattoos visible on his meaty forearms tracked back to both Earth infantry and Martian mercenary corps.

The two other men around him were not military colleagues, but worked with him at a machine shop. They referred to him as Hayim, but I didn't know if that was truly his name. If I'd still had NAPD access, I believed I could have found him in the Earth infantry databases.

"You'll have to be careful how you approach him," Shelly said.

I silently agreed. When we'd been partners she would usually interface with civilians, or I would flash my NAPD credentials and get them to talk to me. I had no authority on Mars.

After a few more moments spent watching a soccer game sent from Earth, Hayim excused himself from his friends, paid his tab, and headed for the door. His bionic legs worked jerkily, unable to quite be adapted to the lower Martian gravity. They might have performed just as awkwardly on Earth or the Moon. Or maybe he'd drunk more than he'd intended. After losing his legs, the circulation and the body mass, a drink would affect him more strongly than a whole person.

I gave him a lead, enough time to reach the airlock and don his envirosuit, then followed. No one took notice of my departure. I went up the steps and trailed after Hayim, rejecting scenario after scenario of how best to announce myself and declare my intentions.

Once I cycled through the airlock, I fell into step with Hayim. He walked along the boardwalk to the west, glancing into shops and store windows as he passed. I thought he was more alert. I thought I was watching him without losing sight of everything around me.

The four men that rushed Hayim from a darkened alley surprised me. One of them grabbed Hayim from behind and affixed a small box to the back of the man's suit. Electricity surged through the suit, popping along the metal, and Hayim dropped bonelessly to the ground only to be caught by another of the men.

By that time I was in motion, pistoning my arms and legs to remove the distance between us. Since there was not enough atmosphere to carry the noise of my approach, and the men were bundled into envirosuits, I knew they could not hear me.

One of them saw me coming, though, and he alerted his companions. The one carrying Hayim hurried away, managing him easily in the lower gravity, dragging the limp man almost effortlessly. The attacker's three companions drew sidearms and leveled them at me.

Five meters from them, I threw myself into a slide, going at them feet first. Bullets sped over my head, unseen to the human eye but visible in my thermographic vision as heated red and yellow streamers missing me by centimeters.

I hit two of the men squarely enough to knock them from their feet, trying not to permanently harm them, but evidence pointed to the fact that Hayim's life was in danger. That hazard freed me up some in my response, but I still felt uncomfortable about the way the leg of one man bent backwards in a manner no human joint was meant to do.

I ignored that for the moment, though my programming prompted me to relieve the injured man's pain as soon as possible. Since I massed greater than they did, the brief obstruction the two men provided didn't stop my slide. I continued on for another six meters, farther than I'd anticipated because the loose sand over the hard rock provided no real traction against my clothing.

The third man spun around, his pistol blazing, tracking small craters just behind me. In the thin atmosphere, he didn't have to worry about his shots being overheard. I rolled to my left hip and managed to draw the Synap pistol before I came to a stop. The man's last few rounds chewed into the ground and threw dirt and puffs of dust into my face. I leveled the Synap and took aim, then fired.

The blue bolt streaked across the distance between us and

sent the man flying backward, not from the impact, because that was minimal, but because of his nervous response as his muscle control seized up for a moment then relaxed. By the time he landed a few meters away, I had my legs under me and was advancing toward the two men I'd scattered when I smashed into them.

The man whose leg I'd broken rolled in agony, unable to do more than scream in pain. His partner tried to push himself to his feet and aim his pistol. I shot him with the Synap, then shot the man with the broken leg as well to render him unconscious and put him out of his pain. I checked his suit to make sure the fracture he'd suffered hadn't ruptured his envirosuit. Finding everything secure with the man's suit, I sprinted after the man who had taken off with Hayim. They had already disappeared down the alley, which looked to be a warren of trails between various smaller shops and businesses that had been jammed in wherever space had been available or later carved out of the canyon side.

I took advantage of the lighter gravity and leaped to the top of the nearest single-story building, managing the feat easily. I landed and ran, pulling down a map overlay of the area from the Net. I saw instantly that the map hadn't been updated. The row of buildings behind the initial row wasn't even on the map.

I dropped the map overlay just before I reached the building's edge and looked down. Ten meters to the left, the attacker had just finished throwing Hayim over the rear of a minihopper and was climbing aboard, grabbing the handlebars and starting the motor.

I didn't hear the motor start, but the minihopper rose in the air and accelerated. I ran along the building, gaining swiftly on the machine and threw myself at him when I'd matched speeds.

I hit the man a glancing blow with my shoulder because I didn't think he could survive a direct impact, then pulled him from the minihopper. We crashed into a nearby diner that had closed for the night and rebounded onto the street.

With no rider in control of the minihopper, the vehicle's safeguards took over and set it gently on the ground before shutting down. Hayim lay undisturbed across the rear deck.

The man tried to get to his feet, but the fall had knocked the wind from him and left him nearly senseless. I pushed him over into oblivion with the Synap, checked his vitals to make sure he was in no distress, then went to ensure Hayim was all right.

I squatted down beside the old man and looked through his helmet faceplate. He was conscious, yelling invective. I accessed his helmet frequency so we could converse.

"Do you know who these men are?"

"Riffraff," Hayim snarled. "Tech vultures. I'd seen one of them before. He got busted on a warehouse job a few months back. Stealing seed stock and fertilizer."

"What did they want with you?"

"My legs. Had to be after my legs. They can part them out for a little cred to other people who don't care where they get spare parts." Hayim cursed. "I should have seen them coming. Probably would have, too, if I hadn't been watching you."

"Watching me?"

"You were following me. I was so concerned over you that I didn't see them till it was too late." His eyes narrowed. "What do you want with me?"

"Just to talk. I had some questions about mercenaries. I know you've spent time working as a soldier."

A red light strobed through the alleys, whipping across the sand-covered ground.

"That light means sec people are going to be along," Hayim said nervously. "I don't want to get involved with this."

"The sec officers won't give you any trouble. They'll help you, probably take you to a hospital if you need it."

"I don't need a hospital. What I need is to get out of here." Hayim struggled to get to his feet.

"You should stay and make a report."

"Not me." Hayim tried again to get to his feet and failed. "I don't have papers for the colonies. Secmen find me here, they'll put me on the first freighter headed back to Earth."

"You're here illegally?" That was interesting. I knew a small contingent of Mars's colonial population were ex-patriates from Earth. Many of them were like Hayim, military men and mercs who'd chosen to stay.

Hayim scowled at me. "Yes. I thought you were one of the watchdogs the Martian Colonial Authority has looking for people like me."

"No."

"Then why were you looking for me?"

"I want information on the mercenary action here on Mars."

Hayim looked at me suspiciously, then stuck out a hand. "Help me up and get me out of here. Then we'll talk."

I extended my hand and gently guided him to his feet. I put him on the back of the minihopper, then climbed aboard and started the engine. I gazed back at the unconscious man, wishing there was a way I could ascertain his identity, but his e-ID would be inside his envirosuit. I briefly considered trying to bring him with us, but even if the minihopper would have allowed it, that would have meant kidnapping him. The sec team closing in on our location would pursue a kidnapping.

I engaged the hover ability and shot through the alley, putting as much space between the alley and us as I could.

Chapter Fifteen

Hayim lived off the grid in a ramshackle apartment building that looked like it was a week away from being condemned. Built into the canyon wall behind it so that it looked more like a frontispiece layered over the rugged rock, the structure was one of the more primitive dwellings in the area.

"It don't look like much," Hayim told me, "but it's home. It was one of the first places built in this area. It's solid and stable." He pointed to a narrow path between the apartment building and the small bar next door. There were a lot of bars in the area. "Put the minihopper over there. I've got someone who can get rid of it for us."

I rounded the corner and powered the minihopper down in front of an airlock built into the canyon wall beside the front of the building. The space was four meters back from the road that led to warehouses and the surrounding shops that looked as weathered as the apartment building. Evidently the whole section was falling into disrepair. Tucked around the corner as it was, the alley provided a natural blind spot from the street.

Hayim shoved himself off the minihopper and limped over to

the airlock. I stepped off after him and watched the dusty red road behind us. So far I hadn't seen any sign of pursuit by a sec team.

"That doesn't mean anything," Shelly said beside me. "They could still be out there looking, and Hayim is someone that can easily be identified."

"I know."

Hayim cued the announce button beside the vid display next to the airlock. I walked over to join him so I could be part of the conversation. I held onto the Synap in my thigh pocket. Trust wasn't even part of the equation at that point.

"Who is it?" The voice was thick and feminine. I could hear it as it linked to Hayim's helmet frequency.

"It's Hayim." The light under the vid display winked green, letting us know that it was receiving our image. The screen remained blank. Whoever was on the other end of the connection wasn't revealing herself.

"What do you want?"

"Got some salvage for you."

"The bioroid?"

"No. A minihopper. It's probably got a history, so it'll have to be wiped from records and vanished. And if it doesn't have a history, it will have one after tonight and it'll still have to be wiped."

The vid display popped out of the wall on a flexible waldo and adjusted to a new angle so it could take in the minihopper, then it pulled back in and focused on Hayim again.

"Where did you get the minihopper?" the unseen woman asked. "You didn't have one when you left here."

"Four guys jumped me at the Pyrite."

"Anybody you know?"

"Men I've seen around. Tech vultures. They were after my legs."

"You're lucky you still have them. They find something else they wanted instead?"

"I can take care of myself," Hayim growled.

"Maybe once upon a time."

"You interested or not?"

"It's not worth much. Can't give you cred for it."

"Just tack whatever you think it's worth onto next month's rent and we'll call it square."

The woman snorted derisively. "I should charge you for getting rid of it."

"I'm leaving it there. Martian sec people could be along any time to start asking questions about it. You feel up to them going through the premises? If so, just leave it there. I'm not taking it any farther."

The woman inside the building was silent for a moment. "Who's your friend?"

Hayim looked at me.

"Norris 1JA5NU," I replied, using Hayim's frequency. I pulsed my e-docs across the reader.

"You're bringing a sales rep home, Hayim?"

Hayim folded his arms across his broad chest. "He's not like any sales rep I've ever seen. He took out the four vultures who attacked me like they were nothing. Says he wants to talk about mercenaries."

"Interesting. You and your friend are cleared to come in." The airlock irised open large enough to allow Hayim, the minihopper, and me. I engaged the minihopper's parking hover and pulled it after me, feeling only somewhat uncomfortable about going inside. Staying out on the street was far less desirable.

* * *

The airlock opened onto a dimly lighted garage area filled with machines, equipment, and three low-end bioroids in various states of disrepair. The bioroids alone could have caused our hostess a fair amount of legal trouble. Haas-Bioroid and its competitors drew a hard line over reverse engineering and bad treatment of their product.

Inside the room, Hayim opened his envirosuit and hung it on a peg beside the airlock. He glanced at me nervously, then at the cutting laser on a nearby tool chest, then back at me again.

"I don't mean you any harm," I reassured him.

"A sales rep, huh?" A middle-aged woman with sandy grey hair cut to her chin line stepped out of the shadows beside a carbon scrubber hanging from chains in the center of the room. Judging from the way the scrubber was torn down, she was either repairing it or stripping it down for salvage.

She was short and a little overweight, broad shouldered and a little thick through the middle. Her eyes were mismatched, the left one blue and bloodshot and organic, the right one a paler blue with a pure white sclera that might as well have been stamped ARTIFICIAL, CYBERNETIC. She wore a mechanic's grey jumpsuit stained with oil and burned in places. The sleeves had been crudely hacked off. A tool belt hung around her hips, heavy with wrenches, screwdrivers, and battery-powered hand tools. She carried a compact, large caliber slug-thrower in her right hand that looked out of place amid the other equipment.

"Why are you interested in mercenaries?" She stopped two meters from me and regarded me with jaundiced speculation.

"I'm trying to find someone," I replied.

"Why?"

"This is the task I was assigned. Other than that, I cannot say." That was close enough to the truth that I thought it would work. I was a bioroid, usually following someone else's orders.

A cold, half-smile twisted her lips. "Who sent you?"

"I cannot divulge that information."

"Who are you looking for?"

"I cannot di— "

She fired the slug-thrower from her hip, not even bothering to lift it. I'd detected the slight shift of her shoulders as she set herself to absorb the weapon's recoil, though, and I was already moving to the right as her finger tightened on the trigger.

The bullet still caught me in the left arm and partially spun me around. My right hand snaked out for a drive chain lying on a nearby workbench at the same time the sound of the shot filled the garage space.

I closed my fingers over the chain and whipped it out as the woman raised her weapon to take aim. The chain wrapped around the pistol barrel and I yanked back immediately, popping the weapon from her hand. Effortlessly, I caught the pistol in my left hand. I watched her to make sure she didn't pull another weapon from hiding.

My response surprised the woman and she stared at me, backing away three more steps. I braced myself, thinking she was going to go for another weapon as soon as she felt she could safely turn her back and run for it.

"Reena!" Hayim yelped. He had ducked down and covered his head with his arms. "What are you doing?"

The woman ignored Hayim and focused on me. "Why are you really here?"

I tossed the chain back to the work table, then popped out the pistol's magazine and thumbed the rounds free, ejecting them into a cup that was also on the table. I worked the slide and removed the chambered round as well, then disassembled the pistol and placed it on the work table.

"I don't mean you any harm," I said. "I came here with Hayim because he was in no shape to see himself home. I also did not get the chance to talk to him as I had intended."

"And you just happened along in time to stop the attack against him?"

"I was following Hayim," I admitted.

Reena's gaze shot beyond me to Hayim for a moment, drawing his attention to what I was saying.

"I saw him there at the bar." Hayim rubbed the back of his neck irritably. "I was watching him while he was following me, trying to figure out what he wanted. I thought maybe he was working for Martian Immigration and that they'd finally caught up with me. That's why I didn't see the men who jumped me until they took me."

Reena reached into her jumpsuit and took out a narc-stick. She lit it with a small lighter and the blue flame lifted her face out of the shadows. She took a deep drag on the narc-stick, held the smoke a moment, then let it out. Over on the wall, a carbon scrubber kicked to life and started cycling the air, gently pulling the smoke toward that side of the garage so the pollutant could be removed.

"I was there to help," I pointed out.

"That's true," Hayim said. He walked over to the work table, leaned down, and pulled up a bottle and two short glasses from a transplas crate. "If it hadn't been for him, I might have ended up dead. I knew one of the guys that jumped me. He wouldn't have wanted to leave witnesses. Probably still won't like the idea that we're—*I'm*—still alive."

"You left that man breathing?" Reena's voice took on a strained timbre.

"Yes. You know how I don't like to kill someone in cold blood."

"You've done it before." Her response was cold and calculated, designed to damage.

Hayim shrugged and wouldn't meet her gaze. "I'm out of that business, Reena. You know that."

"You should have killed that man."

"I wasn't able to defend myself. They locked a taser block on me that trapped me in my envirosuit."

"Do you know the man's name?"

"No."

"Letting him live is going to be a problem. Better to correct that mistake before things get out of hand."

Hayim poured amber-colored liquid into the two short glasses, handed one of them to Reena, and kept the other for himself.

"He won't be a problem long. Sec patrol has probably scooped him up by now. He's probably got outstanding warrants."

"And if he doesn't? If they let him loose?" Reena shook her head. "Once he figures out that you're not down there pressing charges he'll know that you're an even bigger victim than he had first thought you were. He'll know you can't go to the law." She sipped her drink and never took her mismatched eyes from me.

"It was just bad luck." Hayim tossed his drink back and shook his head.

"How much do you think your new friend has to do with your bad luck?"

Hayim laughed, then dragged an arm across his mouth. "Bad luck? He's not bad luck. If he hadn't been following me, those men would have taken my legs. Even if they didn't kill me, which I think was going to happen, I wouldn't have had any legs, Reena. I'm here illegally. Military veterans hospital wouldn't get me another pair of legs. I'd have been dragging myself everywhere I wanted to go." He shook his head. "I couldn't live like that."

The woman's voice softened a little as she spoke, and she took her attention from me to focus on him. "I wouldn't have let you do that, Hayim. We'd have gotten you another pair of legs. I would have worked something out for you."

"My problems aren't your problems." Hayim set the empty glass on the work table. "And I'm not going to let this problem be yours either."

"What do you mean?"

"I'm going to get gone for a while."

"For how long?"

"Long enough to let this all die down. If you find out those guys aren't looking for me anymore, or that the Martian authorities aren't looking for me, send word."

Reena was silent for a moment. "Where are you going to be?"

"I owe Norris for saving me. I'm going to try to square that."

"You don't owe this bioroid anything."

"I figure I do. And who knows? Maybe I can find some work out there in the fringes. Get us a nest egg together that will help out."

"Going with me won't be necessary," I said.

"With the situation the way it is," Hayim said, "I don't think I have another choice. I'm heading in the direction you're going anyway. Two will be safer than one, and I may not have any friends left out there."

Silently, Reena walked over to Hayim and put her arms around him. She looked into his eyes. "The fringes are a bad place to be. Worse than they were when we were out there all those years ago."

"I can't think of a better place to hide out. There are a lot of places where I can get lost for a time." Hayim hugged her and stroked her back. He smiled at her. "Things will be fine. I'll be back soon as I can." He hugged her a final time and stepped away.

I hesitated, uncertain of what to do.

"Go with him," Shelly said. "Like he said, he knows his way around out there, and evidently that's where you're headed."

Reena looked up at me, a tear tracking under her biological eye. "Take care of him out there. He's not as young as he used to be, and he hasn't been the same since he lost his legs."

I nodded. "I will."

Since both women felt that I should accompany Hayim, I went.

* * *

A few minutes later, I waited in Hayim's small room while he packed. His personal quarters had a bed that pulled down from the wall, a personal entertainment deck, and a food processor for hot and cold soy-sub meals. A privy and kitchen were down the hall. A screen on one wall offered a view out onto the Tharsis Region that contained Olympus Mons, a shield volcano that was three times as tall as Mount Everest. It stood 27 kilometers tall and was, according to some, the tallest mountain in the solar system.

Hayim threw a handful of clothes into a hard backpack, added a few toiletries, then lifted one of the floor tiles in the corner to remove a few credsticks that he shoved into his pockets. The servos on his left leg whined as he moved.

Some of the clothing on the bed belonged to a woman about Reena's size. I kept quiet and pretended not to notice as Hayim shoved the clothing under the bedclothes.

"She stays up here sometimes." Hayim kept moving, opening a small pantry built into the wall and removing a few food-subs, protein bars, and energy bulbs. "Some of the people that live here think it's funny, two cripples like us hooking up."

"It's none of my business, and it's none of theirs."

"No, it's not." Hayim closed the pantry and stood. He faced me. "Part of me wants to blame you for the trouble I'm in, but those guys were coming for me before you showed up." He ran a hand over his bleary-eyed face and I could see he was sobering up. He was going to crash before much longer, though. I knew the indications from past experience with alcoholics and addicts I'd handled while I'd been at the NAPD.

"I can carry the backpack," I offered.

"I carry my own weight. I always have." Hayim reached under the mattress and took out a large-caliber slug-thrower.

I shifted slightly, preparing myself.

"Not for you," he said. "The places we're going to go aren't much on hospitality." He rapped on his right leg and a section opened up. He shoved the slug-thrower into the empty space where the weapon fit like it belonged.

"Is there anything I can help with?"

"Not here." Hayim looked up at me. "Cred is a problem, though. Riding the train would be the fastest way to get where we need to go, but you can hire out with different corps looking for someone to help out with overland deliveries to outland areas away from the colonies and the big corps."

"I can pay."

Hayim nodded. "Like I said, a train will be faster, but that doesn't necessarily mean it's going to be any safer. Things out in the fringes, where terraforming is still going on, can be pretty dangerous. Which mercenary outfit are you looking for?"

"The Chimeras."

Hayim snorted in surprise and shook his head. "Those people will be hard to find. When John Rath disappeared, most of those people disappeared as well."

"Did you know John Rath?"

"No. But I worked in a lot of areas where Rath and the Chimeras did. Me and Reena both." Hayim took a final look around the room, flicked a hand over the light sensor to turn out the illumination, and led the way out the door.

Chapter Sixteen

The line waiting at the train station spread out across the main building. Men and women sat on the floor with their envirosuits stripped down to their waist. Three-quarters buried in the Martian soil, the building was little more than an airtight shell with an airlock attached. People weren't allowed into the building without buying a ticket because management didn't want to waste oxygen on someone who wasn't providing a profit. A small restaurant on the far side of the building served up a soy-sub menu.

I sat beside Hayim, who lay stretched out and snoring on the tiled floor. After I'd purchased the tickets and we'd found a place to sit down, he'd promptly fallen asleep. My olfactory sensors relayed the strong smell of alcohol seeping through his pores. A young couple had briefly considered squeezing in beside us, but the girl caught a whiff of my companion and campaigned for another location.

"Your traveling acquaintance isn't going to impress many of the people you meet," Shelly said.

"It's better that way," I replied, too quietly for anyone around me to hear. "I don't want to be noticed, and if I were traveling alone, I might draw attention."

"Whoever you meet is going to try to get away from the two of you."

"We've had worse prisoners we've brought in."

"Agreed, but that's a short list." Shelly shifted her attention to the overhead holo display broadcasting media from a Mars network. "Looks like the unrest between Earth and Mars is getting worse."

On the screen, vid rolled of a riot in Phobos colony, one of the southernmost colonies where we were headed. Martian police equipped with shields and non-lethal weapons tried to handle a protest against Earth-corps that had gone violent. The vid was pre-packaged, not live, and was intercut between different cameras for the most effect. I judged from the height perspective that there were at least five different vid sources during the riot.

One of the vid people stood behind a Phobos PD officer who used her stunstick to render a man unconscious who was clearly strangling the life from another man. Jolted into unconsciousness, both men collapsed to the ground where they were trampled on by other protestors and civilians.

A large man lunged from the crowd at the police officer. She wheeled quickly and brought her weapon around, but the man caught the stunstick in gloved hands and resisted her efforts to club him. The view pulled away from behind the officer as her attacker bore her backward. Then the angle cut to another vid operator who stood at the side and caught the action there.

Since I couldn't hear the transmission and I had access to the Net in the building, I keyed up my internal PAD and routed audio to myself.

"—gathering started out peacefully, but didn't remain so. Police department spokesmen here in Phobos aren't saying who started the violence, but there's no doubt that it turned bloody very quickly."

The police officer gave ground as the big man drove her backward and swung a big fist into her helmet, rocking her head back with each blow. Then she set herself and kicked him in the crotch. Her attacker stumbled forward another step, but then froze, obviously trying to remain on his feet.

Yanking her stunstick from the man's grasp, the police officer drew the weapon back and swung it. The baton slammed into the man's face, crushing his nose and knocking out two of his teeth. Blowing bloody spray, his eyes already glazed, he collapsed to the ground.

The vid suddenly swung skyward, catching a hovering Phobos PD troop hopper thirty meters overhead. Light poured through the plascrete dome and I could tell from the angle that it was mid-afternoon.

"Protesters were there to announce grievances against the sudden increase in AgInfusion's fertilizers."

A new window opened up on the monitor and revealed a middle-aged black man who spoke with an Ethiopian accent. His face showed fear and sadness. "My family and I were persuaded to relocate here to Mars for the promise of a better future. Our country still struggles to feed its people. My wife and I buried our first two children in our village." His voice broke.

Three men rushed another police officer and took him to the ground where they started beating on him. They screamed in open mouthed anger as they delivered their blows. The police officer's features eroded under the impacts, skin split and bone fractured.

"Then we came here to Mars, to Phobos colony," the man continued. "I wanted to be a farmer. I knew the work was hard, and the pay was not much, but it is a necessary thing for the colonies to survive. People need to eat. I want to feed them." He shook his head. "But with the way the Earth-corps keep raising the price of seed, the way they limit the seed so that you cannot build a seed crop because the plant DNA will not replicate past the first generation, farmers here are fighting a war they cannot win, losing the battle centimeter by centimeter, season by season."

A corp secman in a hardsuit entered the battle and fired a pistol into the backs of the men beating the police officer. Watching these events was hard. My first impulse was to go there and do something. Only logic dictated that the events were past, that I could do nothing, so I remained seated.

The pistol was non-lethal. No wounds showed on the attackers as they faltered in their chosen endeavor and turned to face their attacker. Almost as one, two of them fell, overcome by a drug that had been delivered to their systems.

The third man pulled a monofilament knife and closed on the corp secman before he could retreat. Outlawed for civilian ownership, designed strictly for military use, the deadly blade penetrated the secman's hardsuit and opened up his stomach. Blood spilled over both men. I knew instantly that the color had been touched up for the vid. Filters had been slapped onto the blood to make it more colorful and vibrant.

Some of the parents in the train station covered their children's eyes or tried to distract them from the monitor. Some of the younger children quickly looked away, their faces troubled and scared.

I thought about Shelly's daughters, tried to imagine how they would respond to such events. They would consider them horrific. Shelly and her husband had worked hard to give their two daughters a safe home.

Then I looked at Shelly sitting quietly beside me and knew that the protection those children had been given hadn't been enough.

Shelly looked at me. "What happened to me wasn't your fault, Drake."

I knew that this Shelly was an operation of my persona, and I was aware that I was telling myself I wasn't to blame. Maybe that was why I didn't believe it.

"Everything ties back to the Chimeras," I told her. "And it all ties back to Simon Blake."

"You're not Simon Blake."

"Part of me is." I knew that was true.

Shelly stared at me for a moment, and I thought maybe there was no answer to what bothered me the most. "What you have to do is hang onto the parts of you that aren't Simon. He doesn't get to claim everything you've turned out to be. And you don't want to lose yourself to him. You're getting close to doing that."

I wasn't certain if I was trying to reassure myself or if I was probing at my greatest fear. I focused on the monitor, watching as the violence continued. People were dying—*had* died, I corrected—and there was nothing I could do about it.

"I didn't come to Mars just to bury my next child," the man on the monitor said. "I came here hoping for a future." Anger flickered in his eyes. "Now the Earth corps want to take that away from me. Take that away from my children." He shook his head. "I'm not going to allow that to happen."

The window showing him closed, then the fatality and wounded lists started to scroll. Sixty-eight colonists had died in the protest. No one knew for certain how many of them were anti-Earth demonstrators and how many were simply bystanders who got caught up in the violence. Seven Phobos Colony Police Department officers were dead. Three corp secmen had died. The list of injured was in the hundreds.

The monitor switched over to a nosie seated inside a studio. She was blond and pretty, the kind of looks that would have gotten her a career on Earth, on the Moon, or on Mars. "Today's riot is the worst that has been recorded in the last eighteen years." She looked sad, but the expression was a canned, artificial one. News didn't really touch her. She lived above everyone else. I'd seen nosies like her, men and women who managed to stay out of the reality of living in the megapoli. "Next, we talk to Shakir

Waqar, our tech guru, who reports that Haas-Bioroid is ready to announce its next-gen models."

An image of a bioroid dressed in combat fatigues superimposed on the screen beside the nosie. It had no face but sported wraparound eye shields that I knew weren't necessary because I had 360-degree vision and there was no way Haas-Bioroid would cut down on that for a new model.

The image disturbed me on several levels.

On the monitor, the screen changed again, this time to the sculpted features of a man of indeterminate age and a small, laser perfect, thin mustache. He sat in front of a wall filled with bookshelves, which said a lot about him because people didn't have space for such extravagances, and only the wealthy could afford to have *printed* books.

The crawler under the man's image announced: *Dr. Baigorria Medrano, PHD, Military Strategy, Harvard University.*

"To put it simply, war is business, and as such, it is a highly profitable enterprise. Every major corp has some division dedicated to the development of war materials. Weapons. Combat armor. Stealth technology for vehicles and men. Our whole field of medicine has benefited from military engagement and the injuries and loss of soldiers. The initial strides took place during the Civil War between the North and South United States. That technology has continually developed. The terrorist action in Afghanistan and the Middle Eastern War cemented the advances medicine made in bionic limbs."

The vid angle switched over to include a middle-aged man sitting in a chair across the desk from the professor. He wore thick black-framed glasses—which was a cosmetic choice, not necessary for vision with all the options open to anyone with medical insurance—and a goatee. The black suit and long haircut looked like it belonged back in the 1970s, which was an anomaly for someone reporting on emerging technology. His name, Shakir Waqar, crawled under his face.

"In your latest paper, Dr. Medrano, you make the case that the time has come for a battle-ready bioroid," the nosie said.

Something stirred in the back of my mind, and it was uncomfortable not knowing if it was truly the back of my mind or something left over from Simon Blake.

"I do make that case, and for one simple reason: it's time to stop sending men and women into the field to fight our battles. The training cost per unit of flesh is too expensive for the return we're getting."

Another crawler started across the bottom of the screen: *Who does he think he is? I served in the military. I risked my life every day and watched my buddies die. Is he going to try to tell me those sacrifices don't matter?—Captain Ffolkes.*

"Someone has hacked the network," Shelly said.

I started to access the Net and run a trace on the hack, then remembered I didn't have NAPD credentials and wouldn't have been able to use them if I'd had them on Mars anyway.

"The truth is that soldiers sign on for a term of combat," Dr. Medrano went on. "They cycle in and they cycle out, and that makes the training part of the military ineffective. If a bioroid were created that could handle war, training could be cut down to a simple neural download. Not only that, but you'd have the same soldier time after time. Standardization would be optimum."

The next crawler announced: *Then where is the organic soldier? The men and women who can learn from each encounter? Who are truly adaptive in the field?—Captain Ffolkes.*

"But a bioroid that can kill?" Waqar let the question hang in the air for a moment. "Do you know how many people have nightmares about such a thing?"

"People have nightmares about all kinds of things," Medrano replied. "That's the way the human mind is built. And that's one of the reasons human soldiers tend to be ineffective in the long run. A bioroid soldier will never develop post-traumatic stress disorder. There will be no need for the ongoing psychiatric care many of the soldiers these days need."

Another crawler ran at the bottom of the monitor: *He's talking about creating monsters! A human soldier knows compassion and mercy. That's what creates PTSD. Taking a human life should never be easy for a soldier. If it is, soldiers aren't being trained right.—Captain Ffolkes.*

I noticed that a few more people in the crowd were starting to take notice of the vidcast. They shared nervous glances. I wondered if the story was airing on Earth, or even on the Moon. Surely it would be.

"Having mechanized warriors in the field is nothing new," Medrano continued. "The war in Afghanistan at the beginning of the 21st century proved how successful that could be. Instead of constantly throwing men into areas, drone warfare enabled surgical strikes. The same result could be achieved through a small group of war-capable bioroids."

"You're talking about bioroids used as drones? With a human controlling those units through telepresence?"

"No, I'm not. Doing something like that is absurd. There's no reason to halfway do this. In order for this to be successful, human involvement has to be factored out of the equation."

I pulled down information on Medrano from the Net. By all accounts, he was a recognized authority on warfare, one who had worked with the Defense Department on the development of military thought that remained top secret. Some of the blogs I accessed accused him of being a warhawk, and he had a history of being involved in the Colony Wars on Mars as a proponent for Earth. Medrano was also a resource for several sec divisions with assets on Mars.

"Do you know any bioroid corps that are currently working on such a unit?" Waqar asked.

Medrano smiled. "The list would be shorter if I gave you the names of bioroid corps that *aren't* working on such a unit."

The story cut to an image of a hulking bioroid on a battlefield, standing atop a pile of bodies in rubble that looked like it was covered by a plascrete bubble.

"Not exactly subtle is it?" Shelly asked.

"No," I replied, and the idea sat uneasily in my thoughts.

The last crawler crept across the monitor as the vidcast shifted to a commercial by SandozGene, a Martian ag-corp. Even as a perky SandozGene spokesman unleashed his spiel about a new modded corn seed, the crawler asked: *Are you going to let them threaten us like this? Are you going to let those patriots in Phobos colony have died in vain?—Captain Ffolkes.*

Chapter Seventeen

"All aboard." The mechanical voice blasted throughout the train station, rousing several of the waiting passengers from slumber. Enough of them had slept that I had run an oxygen check to make certain that nothing was wrong, but the oxygen and carbon monoxide levels in the building were fine.

"They're just stressed and tired," Shelly said. "There's nothing you can do to fix that."

I accepted that, but I still felt the need to do something for them. After the news had ended, the monitor had broadcasted a few dramas directed at casual viewers. Most of them were created out of the same fabric as those I had been aware of back on Earth and on the Moon.

Viewing audiences in those places weren't as large, percentage-wise, as they were on Mars. On Earth and on the Moon, there were clubs and VR decks, places where people, bioroids, and clones could go and mingle. Mars tended to be more centered around work and home, and the entertainment areas were smaller, less developed. The people around me worked and rested, often with too much of one and not enough of the other. Yet, somehow, they endured.

There were a lot of sensies, though, stories that would appeal to housebound audiences. Mostly they were stories about people who lived under harsh circumstances who managed to contribute to their societies. The stories weren't subtle about their messages.

While I'd waited for the train to arrive and while Hayim slept, I'd pulled down information about the proliferation of sensies on Mars and discovered that several psychologists—most of whom were based on Mars—felt that the media channels, primarily owned by Earth corps, were there to indoctrinate the Martian population.

"These sensies seek to lull the colonies," Dr. Macdonald Wease, a recent Burroughs University graduate, said in one report. "The dramas show colonists eking out a living and becoming successful at whatever they're doing simply by virtue of hard work. That's not the Mars I grew up on. My parents and I had to work hard for what we had, and then it wasn't much. We had to work hard to just survive. They wanted me to get an education so I wouldn't have to live the way they did. My father died trying to pay for my tuition.

"I'm going to be paying off student loans for my education for the next fifteen years. If I'd signed with an Earth corp to provide clinical care for Martian patients, those fees would have been paid for me. But I would have also had to espouse the party line. The same line that used up my parents and threw them away. Mars is a conduit for profit for the corps that built there. The colonies provide a market for the corps and an expanded tax base for the governments."

When I'd attempted to look up more about Dr. Wease, I'd found a media story that he had committed suicide only a few days after his statement, which had gone viral. He had taken sleeping pills and drowned in a hot tub after hours in his apartment building. He wasn't prescribed sleeping medication, and most Martians took showers, not baths, because water usage and recycling was expensive.

The story bothered me enough that I'd wanted more information immediately, certain there was cause for a more in-depth investigation, but none was available. There were no further follow-ups on Wease except for the notice about his cremation.

"This is Mars," Shelly told me. "Things are done differently here."

I could remember being told that by several people I'd had interactions with, but never by Shelly. I pulled my attention off the Net and locked back into my immediate surroundings.

All around me, men and women dressed themselves and their children in envirosuits, pulling them up and tabbing them closed to maintain integrity. Suiting up was merely a precaution till the train was locked down. The airlock allowed everyone to board the train directly without losing atmosphere, but the boarding process was always dangerous.

Hayim slept on till I roused him by shaking one shoulder. I was gentle, and I'd waited till the line for the airlock had started to thin. During the time he'd slept, I'd noticed that he had frequent nightmares. I didn't know if this was a regular thing or if it had been brought on by the drinking or the near escape from the tech vultures.

He blinked up at me, momentarily lost.

"Time to go. The train's here."

He attempted to get to his feet and I heard the left leg whining again. I offered my hand. He hesitated a moment, then accepted my help.

"Anyone looking for us?" he asked.

"Not that I have seen."

Hayim pulled his envirosuit on, wobbly for a time before he managed it. I followed him to the airlock. Transit authority secmen had stepped off the train, but they seemed more interested in stretching their legs than in watching the passengers.

Gazing through the transplas, I scanned the train. The pulling engine was a manta ray turned on its axis like it was gliding under the sea. Whoever had created it had made good use of the spatial restrictions required by the engine. Several of the passengers hadn't ever seen it before. They stopped and took pictures of it with their PADs.

I stopped in front of the uniformed conductor, a bored woman who was scanning e-tickets into a PAD.

"Pardon me," I said.

She looked up. "Can I help you?"

"Can I get back to the baggage car from here?"

"You won't be riding back there—" She scanned my e-ticket. "—Norris 1JA5NU. Out here, everyone rides in the passenger cars. You won't be requiring a sleeping compartment, right?"

"No."

"Then feel free to roam about the rest of the train. Respect the privacy of those who have sleeping compartments. Enjoy your trip."

"Thank you." I stepped into the train behind Hayim.

"Welcome to the frontier," my companion said to me. "Out here, the division between human, clone, and bioroid isn't quite a distinction the way it is in the colonies or back on Earth. In this place, we're all equal, all just chaff for the mill to grind until we're of no further use." He grinned at me, but I heard the bitterness in his words.

The first passenger car was already filled with passengers. They sat three to a side in comfortable chairs beneath overhead storage. The heating unit kicked on to combat the below freezing conditions outside the train. I followed Hayim toward the rear of the train. Most of the other passengers headed forward.

"We're not walking the same direction as the majority of other boarders," I said.

Hayim shook his head. "The newbies still think sitting closer to the pulling engine will get them extra heat. It doesn't. The engine runs on solar power and doesn't add anything to the ambient temperature of the passenger cars. It's self-contained, cut off from the rest of the train. And they also think that if the atmosphere is lost inside the cars, which sometimes happens, that they'll be all right." He grunted in displeasure. "They don't know that each car can be sealed off from the other. That way, if passengers have to be lost, they can lose them but the cargo can still get through. Unless they're hauling livestock. Then everything dies."

I pulled down the train safety regulations from the Net and scanned through them as I followed Hayim through an airlock to the next train car. The airlock opened and closed automatically. According to the operations manual, in the event of the loss of atmosphere in one car, the airlocks would automatically seal, preventing subsequent forfeiture by other cars.

We walked through two other passenger cars, then three sleeping compartments that were little more than the motel crypts put into a car. Some of the passengers were already crawling into them, flopping down and sliding back into hiding with electronic hums.

"These are the frequent travelers," Hayim said. "It's a thousand miles out to the fringes. Twenty-six hours of non-stop red dust Martian sandscape, with only the mountains to break up the monotony. You won't find them peering through transplas hoping to see something they've never seen before. They'll be right there until we debark."

I nodded. "What do you mean *frequent* travelers? I thought these were colonists."

"Some of them are. Some of them, like these people, are part of the corps' terraforming crew. They cycle in and out because they can afford to. The other people on this train are riding one way. They'll probably never get enough cred to come back. Or, if they do, they'll never find another job unless they pick up a trade that can be used somewhere else or promote through a corp."

"If this is a one-way trip, why do they come?" I peered back down the passageway through the airlock at the people taking seats in the last car.

"Because they have nowhere else to go." Hayim looked up at me with cruel amusement. "Welcome to Mars, planet of opportunities." He slapped a palm against a sleeper unit that had a green light, announcing that it was still open. "Get this one for me."

I slotted the credstick I had, then Hayim punched in a name that I knew was not his own. He waited tensely for a moment, then the sleeper unit flashed green in acceptance.

"I didn't know if that name was still in the train system."

I didn't say anything.

"He could be leaving a trail," Shelly warned.

I knew that, but I didn't have many options regarding trusting Hayim. And I was certain that he didn't want law enforcement attention any more than I did.

"That credstick of yours still have enough on it to purchase me a meal plan?" Hayim asked.

"Yes." Although the amount on the credstick had been seriously drained, I wasn't yet worried about having funds. I wouldn't need much, and I had more than enough for return passage.

"Then let's go to the dining car." Hayim led the way.

* * *

There were two dining cars set up aboard the train. One forward in the line of cars, and one toward the end. The sleeper compartment cars were more centrally located. The container cars loaded with cargo were just behind the pulling engine.

"The cargo is put up there so it's more protected," Shelly told me. "That tells you the value the transportation corps put on human life."

I tried not to think about that too much, but that was difficult because I was programmed to protect human life. Knowing that people were berthed in the rear cars because they were held in lower regard than cargo was uncomfortable.

"Families have children," Shelly said. "They naturally replace themselves. Cargo doesn't. If one of those cars of modified seeds is lost, colonists will face starvation or—at the very least—exorbitant prices for the replacement shipment. Everything here is done for a profit."

Knowing that the cargoes were so valuable helped ease my discomfort a little, but not much. I balanced out the lives of the many versus the lives of the few, but I still didn't like working those equations.

I felt out of place in the dining car, which was set up with tables and seats bolted to the floor on either side. The only bioroids in the car other than myself worked as servers. Curious about the lack of human workers, I accessed the Net and pulled down information about the Martian trains. According to what I learned, the transportation corps preferred bioroid servers because they didn't require rest or nourishment and were therefore cheaper to maintain on the long runs to the fringes.

Hayim chose a small table to the side and I joined him. He took a napkin from the table and laid it across his lap, then punched up the menu on the tabletop. He perused the offerings for a moment after I slotted my credstick, then made his selections.

I peered past him through the transplas window at the wide openness of Mars. Red dust existed as far as I could see, and the sun looked small and far away. A dust devil swept up out of nowhere and began peppering the train with small debris. A red warning light pulsed across the window, letting people know the protective metal shields rose from their recesses to protect the transplas.

"Stupid thing, putting windows on a train that goes across a thousand miles of some of the bleakest, harshest land you'll ever live to see," Hayim told me. Then he pointed around at the other people in the dining car that were using handheld devices. "But letting solar power into the cars beats having to provide outlets for all the toys." He knuckled a fist and rapped it against one of his bionic legs. "And it keeps these powered up."

I nodded.

A moment later, a female bioroid with only a bare minimum of human features carried a tray to our table. She was a June model, designed for taking care of families and servicing the needs of others. Her nameplate announced her name as June. No one had even bothered to give her a name of her own.

She sat out a bulb of whatever liquid refreshment Hayim had chosen at his elbow, then a plate of soy-sub designed to look like a steak.

"Will there be anything else?" June asked.

"No," Hayim said, picking up the bulb. "Thank you."

June nodded and walked away, turning her attention to another table, clicking through the checklist built into her subroutines to make sure her guests were well cared for.

"Do you know what this is?" Hayim held up the bulb for my inspection.

I studied the label and scanned the barcode. "Apple cider. Manufactured by TasteeGene, a subsidiary of SolSystems 32, a corp that specializes in beverages, fruits, and vegetables, and also a supplier of seed stock to Mars and hydroponics on the Moon." I could have told him more, but I presumed he would ask if he needed further information.

Hayim laughed. "Wrong. TasteeGene ships flavored powder to Mars because shipping liquid weight through space is a negative investment. There's only so much water on a planet. Earth corps don't want to give Martians anymore hydration than they have to. So they send the powder and we use it to flavor our water."

I didn't understand what his point was, so I waited.

"Know where the train gets the water?" he asked.

My immediate response would have been the train station, then a quick check through the schematics of that place told me that was not the case.

"From the train," Hayim said when I did not answer. "Each train has a certain amount of water. The passengers use some of that water when they drink it or bathe in it or flush the toilet. The water gets recycled in a reclamation car—which is right behind the pulling engine because water is one of the most valuable commodities carried on the train—then pushed back through the cars. Shortly before we reach our final destination, the train corp will offer *complementary* beverages that are filled with hydrochlorothiazide designed to cause frequent urination." He smiled grimly. "They hope to maximize their water retention on the train by draining the passengers."

"That seems logical."

Hayim laughed. "That's because you don't have to drink other people's urine and bath water." He broke the tip off the bulb and took a healthy drink.

"Attention, all passengers. The train will be leaving the station in five minutes. Please secure all baggage." The mechanical warning echoed through the train, then repeated.

I felt the surge of electromagnetism pulse through the table. Hayim cursed and adjusted his plate with difficulty because the magnetism locked it down and made it harder to move. He sliced his soy-steak and continued eating.

"The way you handled those tech vultures last night tells me you're no stranger to fighting." Hayim eyed me speculatively.

"No." I didn't offer any further explanation.

"You've been a mercenary?"

"I'd rather not discuss myself."

"It's going to be a long trip."

"You're going to be in your sleeping compartment after you eat. You won't notice the trip."

Hayim grinned. "I'll be in the sleeping compartment after I

have a shower. I'm not going to crawl in there and sleep in my own stink."

I didn't say anything.

The train blared a final warning and I heard the extended air-lock from the train station uncouple. I accessed the train's exterior public vid cams put there so passengers could watch outside and watched as the airlock pulled back into the building. A passenger hopper was just dropping off a fresh load of prospective passengers that trudged toward the building.

"It's always interesting finding out why people took up the mercenary business," Hayim said.

His words took me away and I was no longer in the train car. Instead, I was once more seeing through Simon Blake's limited perspective.

Chapter Eighteen

I sat in a small booth with Mara Parker. She regarded me over a bulb of wine, her eyes deep and thoughtful.

The weightless sensation in my stomach pulsed uncomfortably. I knew in a moment that we were in space. Around us, other people gathered in booths and at tables, chatting with one another or working on PADS, and I knew we were traveling on a premium voyage that allowed passengers to roam reserved sections of a large intra-system cruiser that had been constructed in space and would not survive planetfall.

Normally passengers opted for crypt travel, spending most of their time in VR, either in sensies or in telepresence contact with their employers or corps. Electro-stimulation kept their bodies in shape, working muscles and providing isometric muscle exercises that helped prevent the loss of bone density.

Dressed in a simple burgundy one-piece, Mara looked beautiful. I felt Simon's arousal toward her, filtered through a matrix in my subroutines that dealt with sex crimes, and the response made me feel uncomfortable. I knew that instinctive attraction between the genders was not an evil thing. That attraction promoted the survival of the human species. It was what an individual did with his or her sexuality that turned to perversion.

I had no feelings about prostitution. Homicides, though, were another matter.

"Are you nervous, Simon?" Mara's teeth were very white and her breath was sweetly alcoholic.

I wanted to say *no* because I wasn't, but Simon answered. "Maybe a little."

"Of being out here?" Mara raised an eyebrow.

"Of being with you."

She laughed at him. At me. And I realized then that this was a form of courtship that I had seen between Shelly and her husband. Their words said one thing, but the language was something they had created between them that spoke of history and trust and hope. Their children hadn't understood it either. It had always reminded me that I was an outsider, though Shelly went to great pains to include me in her family when she invited me.

"Why would you be nervous about being with me?" Mara asked.

"I don't know."

"Well, you shouldn't be."

"All right."

She sipped from the wine bulb again. "I have to say, I was surprised when you accepted my offer. I didn't think I would get you away from John Rath."

"Even after you offered him fifteen percent of your company?"

"Even after that." She paused. "The two of you seem... very close."

"We've spent a lot of time together."

"How long have you been together?"

"On Mars?"

"No. Altogether."

I searched for an answer and couldn't find it. The scant information I'd turned up in my search on John Rath didn't have a lot of hard data. Too much information had been lost in the wars.

"A long time," Simon said.

"You're avoiding the question."

"Why are you asking it?"

Mara took another sip of her drink before she replied. "Rath is a...complicated man."

I felt Simon's smile spread across his lips, but I knew he wasn't satisfied with her interests. "You're attracted to him."

"Why do you say that?"

Simon shrugged. "It's all right. A lot of women are."

"Do you truly think so?"

"I've seen it."

"Do you think I find him attractive?"

"How could you not?"

Mara smiled. "He's arrogant, selfish, and can be ill-mannered."

"A lot of women like those things about John."

Mara shook her head sadly. "You don't get out much, do you?"

"What do you mean?"

"*I'm* not most women, Simon. Whatever purely animal magnetism John Rath might possess, and he does have those things, is far outweighed by my recognition of his faults. John Rath would be a dalliance, a blip on my social radar, if I so choose."

"He would have to choose, too."

"Men don't have as many choices as women do." She smiled. "You're more...*hardwired* for sexual conquest than women are."

I had no argument for that, and neither—apparently—did Simon. He sipped his own bulb, but it contained flavored water, not wine or anything alcoholic.

"For myself, I'd much prefer a man who could complement me. Who could make me more than I would ever be on my own." Her eyes flashed. "And I'd want a man, if I so chose, who could keep me safe."

"A commendable list."

She laughed. "But it's one that's hard to fill, I'm afraid." She pulled her dark hair back out of her eyes.

She was the subject of the attentions of several men and a few of the women in the public area. Simon found her fascinating. I felt his elevated pulse, and his attraction to her kept pinging my filters with a dissonance I had not ever felt before. I was not comfortable with it.

Despite Simon's infatuation with Mara, I kept my attention on the room. All of my memories of Mara included some kind of near-death experience. And one of them had been a death experience eight years ago. Simon and Mara had been married for six years before that had happened, though, and he'd died of an assassin's bullet, not of the hopper crash that had been used to cover up the murder.

Someone somewhere, I was certain, was waiting to kill her.

"You know a lot about neural channeling," Mara said. "Where did you learn?"

When he'd been with Mara, Simon had also helped work on the new neural channeling interface with MirrorMorph, Inc. I didn't have any background on Simon Blake either. He was almost as much of a cipher as John Rath. Except for his death, which had been covered in lies and half-truths. I still remembered him gasping out his life in the hospital as Mara uploaded his personality to make the Drake models.

There were other Drakes, usually working in security fields. I was the only one who had been licensed to the NAPD. And I was certain I was the only one who remembered Simon Blake so intimately.

"School," Simon replied. "I've also been studying the subject on my own."

"As a mercenary?"

"There's considerable downtime. When you're onsite, things aren't always like they were when we rescued you."

"I can still remember you breaking through that window and killing the woman that held me. I'll never forget that."

"You should try to forget that. It doesn't do any good to hang onto that memory."

She bit her lip and Simon's attention focused on how the blood rushed back to the plump flesh. "Forgetting isn't easy."

"You can forget a lot. If you want to."

"What have you forgotten, Simon?"

"A lot. You have to in this business."

"Give me an example."

"The face of the woman who was holding you hostage when I first saw you." Simon smiled coldly. "She's dead. She's not coming back. No reason to remember her."

"Have you forgotten that?"

"Not yet. But I will."

She hesitated. "What about me?"

"What about you?"

"Will you forget about me after this assignment?"

Simon shook his head. "No. I wouldn't forget about you."

She laughed a little then, more at herself than at Simon. "Do I sound neurotic or pathetic?"

"No."

"Good. Let's change the subject."

"All right."

"Tell me how you became a mercenary."

Her words echoed inside Simon's head, and suddenly I wasn't in that ship with Mara Parker anymore.

* * *

I was scared and alone and out of control. I had labels for those feelings because they were in my programming for use with victims I dealt with while working at the NAPD. I'd only had shadows of those emotions during my visitations to Simon Blake's past. They had never been stronger and I almost fell victim to them.

On my knees in a darkened room, I stared at a pile of blood-covered rubble strewn across the floor. I was inside an envirosuit. The faceplate was cracked, obscuring my vision, but the suit's atmosphere integrity hadn't been compromised. The sound of my breathing rang loudly in my ears. I tasted salt and I knew it was my own blood.

"Over here. Help me." A hand flailed weakly near the pile of rubble to my left. There, almost buried, a figure waved at me again. The effort was strained, almost more than the man could deliver.

I pushed myself to my feet, using too much strength because adrenaline was flooding my body and wreaking havoc with my control. I hurried over to the figure and gazed desperately at the rubble that covered the man.

Light flashed through the hole in the building's roof, briefly illuminating the man's features on the other side of the face shield. Like me, he wore an envirosuit, but his was no longer containing the oxygen he needed to survive.

"Dad!" The word exploded from my throat before I knew it was coming. Surprise and the sudden pain of impending loss almost shook me loose from the memory, but I held onto it tightly. I tried to peer into my father's face shield, but his features were barely visible every now and again as lights flashed overhead.

I started pulling at the plascrete and rock that covered his lower legs. My muscles strained and even the largest rocks rolled away easily.

"Where…where's your mother?" His breath fogged the inside of his helmet and I knew it was because the suit was losing air, losing heat.

"I don't know." Tears ran down my face. They felt strange. I had never felt them before, and hadn't even known them for what they were until I spotted my reflection inside my faceplate when the lights flashed overhead again.

I was young, perhaps eleven or twelve, with a thin face, a shock of dark hair, and a nose the rest of my features hadn't quite grown into. Curiosity filled me, but so did the need to free the man from the fallen rock—to free my father.

"Find her." My father was gasping now in the thin air that remained within his suit. "Find your sister. Save them."

"I will. After I get you out of here."

"Son." He put a hand on my shoulder, stilling my efforts. "*Son.*" His voice was so weak and strained I barely understood him. He took another rattling breath. "It's too late for me. My legs are broken. I've got internal injuries. I feel all busted up inside." He coughed and a crimson mist painted the inside of his face shield. "Please. Go."

Instead, I worked harder, flinging the rubble from him. I didn't understand how he could be so injured by rock and rubble I was moving so easily. But the part of me that was still Drake did understand. Gravity could be taken away, but the mass was still there.

My father coughed again a couple more times, and the blood inside his helmet obscured his face. His chest stopped moving and his hand dropped away from my shoulder.

"Dad! *Dad!*" I reached for his bio tab, but before I touched it, the tab flashed red, indicating that he needed life support, that he was no longer breathing on his own.

I shouted for him again and tried to pull him free. As I did, his body split in two, cut through by a fiber cable that had pulled out of the nearby wall. The fissure that it had ripped from ran around the room on two walls. The cable had been part of the home's sensor array, and a main conduit for the heat we needed to survive the cold.

Crying, choking on my rage, pain, and fear, I forced myself to stand. My father's blood stained my gloves. I swayed for a moment and the room spun around me. I thought I almost lost the connection, but then I realized that it wasn't me, that the young boy I had been had almost passed out.

I checked my suit integrity, thinking that I had ruptured the envirosuit somehow. But the suit remained intact.

Where's your mother? Find your sister. Save them. My father's words rang in my head.

I turned and surveyed the room as a violent tremor shivered through the ground and almost caused me to fall. More pieces of the ceiling fell, stirring up clouds of dust that hung in the thin air. I put a hand against the wall, trying to make sense of my surroundings. The place looked familiar, but I couldn't lock into it. I knew where I was, but I couldn't name it.

The house was small, surrounded on all sides by blank walls, no windows. I knew I wasn't on Earth from the way I'd moved the rock, and I didn't think I was on the Moon because the rock hadn't been that light. That meant I was probably on Mars.

The room was a boy's bedroom. A small collection of toy soldiers sprawled atop a shelf. When the ground shivered again, some of the toys tumbled from the shelf and dropped to the debris-strewn floor. A battery-powered game deck lay on the twin bed. The holo of an alien world filled with strange creatures moved in the meter of space above the projector.

I lurched into motion toward a doorway, feeling certain that my younger self knew where he was heading. I focused on staying with him and remembering everything I could.

I found my mother in the next room. She lay in pieces against the room's only standing wall, covered in dust and debris. Where the opposite wall had been, a crater now sat. My younger self didn't know for certain what had happened, thinking that maybe a bomb had gone off.

I knew that the damage had been done by a ground burster delivered by a military hopper. That type of munitions had been developed for use against troops that had dug into mountainsides.

Not against civilians.

I walked over to the woman—my mother—even though I knew she was beyond help. I peered down into her vacant gaze through the shattered remnants of her envirosuit helmet, then gently reached in and closed her eyelids. The gesture came naturally. I had seen Shelly do that sometimes when we had a young victim, but I didn't know where my younger self had learned to do that.

I turned and headed deeper into the house, looking for my sister. I couldn't remember what she looked like. There was only a brief impression of dark hair and blue eyes, our father's hair and our mother's eyes.

I found her in her room, cold and still. She looked like she was four or five, lying so still and silent on the floor. She hadn't been able to put her envirosuit on by herself. I finished putting her into her suit, aching at the time it took to do that but telling myself I had no choice, then tried to resuscitate her with the suit's onboard systems.

I pressed her med-tab and pulled my hand back just before the suit delivered an electric jolt to her heart. Anxiously, calling her name—"*Kiri, Kiri*"—I searched the med readout and discovered she still wasn't breathing. I triggered the electrical jolt again, but the results were the same.

After the fifth attempt, the suit would no longer deliver the charge to her heart. The readout crawled a message: NO REVIVIFICATION POSSIBLE. SYSTEM IS SHUT DOWN. NOTIFY AUTHORITIES.

I screamed and my voice vibrated inside my helmet as I knelt there and held Kiri's limp hand in my own. Lights continued to strobe overhead, filling the outer room with illumination time and time again.

After a while, I didn't know how long, I got up.

The part of me that was still wholly Drake felt uncomfortable with the pain I sensed within my younger self. I remembered how Shelly's children had mourned during the funeral, how helpless I had been to offer them solace.

My younger self didn't feel as helpless. Rage filled him as he walked through the ruin of his home. Intuitively, he stayed within the shadows as he made his way outside. Then he glanced up at the sky and spotted the twin moons, Phobos and Deimos, through the broken dome that had covered the ag fields.

My parents had been farmers. I remembered my father's rough, callused hands, and I remembered the way my mother had schooled me in crop rotation and production variables and fertilizers. My father had provided the strong back and my mother had provided the technological know-how.

I hadn't wanted the life of a farmer. I could remember that in that moment, but I didn't know what I'd wanted to be. It didn't matter anyway. Not anymore. Whatever that future might have been, it was gone, snuffed out just as surely as the lives of my family.

Above, a group of unmarked hoppers burned their jets and climbed through the broken hole in the dome.

Someone put a hand on my shoulder and I spun around quickly to face a boy only a little older than I was. He seemed calm on the other side of his face shield. He spoke but I had to read his lips.

Are you okay?

With shaking hands, I switched on my envirosuit's comm. "I'm alive," I replied. "My family..." My voice choked up and I couldn't speak.

He put his hands on my shoulders. "It's going to be all right. I'm going to take care of you. Do you hear me?" He crouched down so that our eyes were level. "Did you hear what I said?"

I nodded. "Who was that in the hoppers? Who did this?"

"Secmen from the corps. I don't know which ones. Probably got a group together and hired the attack out to make an example of us. To let us know that we can't live with them, and we can die anytime they decide they want us to."

I shook my head. "That's not going to happen to me. They're not just going to kill me." I looked up into the star-filled sky and swore by both moons that I would not die so easily.

* * *

I returned to the social room aboard the spaceship in a rush of unease that left me reeling for a moment. I tried to remember where I was. Part of me insisted I was on a mag-lev train on Mars headed into the fringes, but another part of me remembered I was sitting across from Mara Parker and headed back to Earth.

Concern darkened her eyes as she looked at me. "Simon? If the question is too personal, I'm sorry."

"No. It's all right." I cleared my throat. "My family was killed on Mars. I got into the mercenary business to protect myself, and to protect other people." *And to get revenge.*

She put her hand on mine. "Simon, remember, you have to rescue me. I'm depending on you."

Chapter Nineteen

"You don't have to tell me about yourself. I've already figured out a lot about you just in this time we've been together." The words were spoken by a man's voice, not Mara Parker.

My vision blurred for a moment and I was back with Hayim in the dining car. Mara Blake's final words haunted me. They hadn't been part of the memory. They had been part of the directive that had brought me to Mars where I kept tripping over Simon Blake's past.

"Just stay focused, partner," Shelly said as she sat beside me. She wasn't eating either. "You have a game plan. Just stay with it and adjust as you go. That's all we ever do."

Hayim finished his meal and pushed his plate away. June hurried over, appearing almost out of thin air, and scooped the dishes away.

"Want to know what I've figured out about you?" Hayim asked.

"Not really."

He scowled. "What do you plan on doing once we reach the fringes?"

"I'm going to let you hook me up with a mercenary group as close to the Chimeras as I can."

"What do you want with them?"

"It's personal business."

"If you told me what your *personal* business was, it might help me get you in with the right people. There's a lot of bad ju-ju mixed up in the Chimeras."

I made no reply.

After a moment, Hayim sighed in disgust, cursed, and drained the last of his cider bulb. "If you don't want to talk, I'm getting a shower and hitting the rack. What are you going to do while I'm sleeping?"

"Meditate." That was a response Shelly had given many times when she wanted to think and other detectives insisted on bothering her.

Hayim snorted and shoved himself to his feet. His left leg squealed in protest. "Meditate then. Try to stay out of trouble. With trouble behind us and trouble ahead of us, I'm going to rest up while I can."

"Let me see your PAD."

He hesitated, then reached into his thigh pocket and took out his PAD. I accessed it with my internal PAD and left my name, NORRIS 1JA5NU and Net code with all the log information he needed to reach me. I also coded it with a pingback subroutine so I could locate him as long as he stayed connected to the Net without him knowing I was tracking him.

"If you need me, contact me." I handed the PAD back to him.

Hayim studied his PAD without a word, then stuffed it back in his thigh pocket, turned, and left the dining car.

I got to my feet and left as well, heading for one of the common cars where passengers rode while awake. No one paid any special attention to me, and I did my best to act like a Norris unit. Those models would not engage unless required to, which would be in response to a human questioning them or to make a sales pitch.

I took a seat by myself in the car near the window. The car I'd chosen was only half full. The passengers had quietly segregated themselves, dividing into seasoned travelers and newbies, into older and younger groups that shared superficial interests. Most of them talked about general things, where they were going and where they had come from.

The children played together at the back of the car, using uplinks to the Net to access gaming platforms on GameNet. Colorful figures—warriors, sports figures, and fantasy beings—moved in the meter high holo projections. One of the games they played was *Fables of Uhrdona*, a game created by Jonas Salter under the name Dylan Templeton.

I thought about him as I'd seen him in the game when we'd first met—at least, when he and Drake had first met. He'd been an elf, long-eared and carrying a magical staff, accompanied by a large bear as his animal familiar. That image was quickly replaced by the crime scene inside the utility closet on the Moon.

I gazed through the transplas at the stark iron oxide landscape. Dust whirled in clouds around us, occasionally obscuring the view.

"So," Shelly said as she sat beside me, "Simon Blake had a family that was murdered. We didn't see that one coming."

"No," I admitted.

"How do you feel?"

I stared at her reflection in the transplas and she locked eyes with mine. "I do not *feel* anything. Any such empathetic response that may emulate that emotional state is merely a finely honed construct created solely for the purpose of allowing me to understand individuals we may encounter on the job."

"Lie to me and you lie to yourself, Drake. You know enough about our situation to know that." Shelly smiled at me. "Remember, I know what you know."

"Then why ask?"

"So that we can talk about it."

"I do not wish to talk about it."

"You should."

"If I should change my mind, I will let you know."

"I'll probably know before you do."

I surmised that was true.

"The visions or dreams or whatever you want to call them are coming faster now," she said.

"That's because we're getting closer to where this all began."

"Do you think that Mara Blake is still alive?"

"If I have to ask myself that, what do you think?"

Shelly smiled and relaxed a little.

"She's still alive," I replied. "If she wasn't, I'd feel it."

Beside me, Shelly winked out of existence and the red dust clouds cleared enough for me to see the distant mountains.

* * *

For hours, I checked my meetbox account to find out if Floyd or Blaine had left a message for me. They hadn't. I also monitored the vidcasts on the screens that folded down from the overhead storage bins to provide individual programming. Even out there in the deadlands between colonies, the train maintained a satlink to the satellites crisscrossing Mars in low orbit at the edge of the thin atmosphere.

Due to the colonization of the planet and ag-bubbles venting air into the Martian sky, the planet's atmosphere had become richer and deeper. Many of the helium flotation satellites linked by casual Net users had drifted higher as the atmosphere expanded. Some theorists believed that a human sustainable atmosphere was only a few hundred years away, given the current growth on the planet. Others postulated that such an atmosphere would never occur because Mars didn't have the gravity to hold onto it.

Conspiracy theorists that flitted across the boards on the Net promised that Earth would never allow that to happen because then Mars would slip from beneath the parent planet's thumb. Even if Mars did "escape" Earth's influence, though, Mars's population wasn't dense enough to stand up against Earth corps and Earth military. Given the controlled population growth—which barely exceeded replacement numbers and only occurred as jobs opened up and terraforming provided food and water to support the increased numbers—that would happen even more slowly. Immigration was strictly controlled for that reason, and people like Hayim who flouted the law by staying illegally on Mars were considered criminals by Earth.

Violence continued to break out throughout the colonies like a disease. I watched six media stations on the monitor provided in front of me and tracked more stories on other channels.

"—and in my opinion, these attacks aren't random events spurred on by similar riots in other parts of the colonies." The speaker was identified as Reza Theofanis, a political commentator. She wore her black hair pulled back and looked aggressive and self-assured. "This is a full-fledged, concentrated, and organized effort to strike back at the Earth corporations. Look at the coordination that's immediately observable."

A Mercator map of Mars unfolded like an orange peel and revealed the colonies. Brightly colored pushpins appeared rapidly, popping into place as Theofanis spoke. Every colony on the planet had experienced some kind of uprising against Earth-controlled corps.

A hacked crawler rolled across the screen: *YOU'RE RIGHT THAT THIS IS AN ORGANIZED EFFORT! THIS IS THE BEGINNING OF A REVOLUTION! MARS FOR MARTIANS! EARTHMEN GO HOME!*

The view panned back, pulling the other guest in the studio into the frame, and at the same time scrolling off adjacent projections of fighting that had broken out in the street between Earth corps secmen and rioters.

I focused on one encounter when I discovered live ammunition was being used, then pulled down the archived feed from the Net and blew it up.

An armored sec team stumbled back from the sheer number of protestors wielding makeshift weapons. A few of the protestors brandished stunsticks and Synap pistols, weapons that had clearly been taken from sec people or local police.

"Or maybe those protestors are police members," Shelly suggested. "Martian patriotism has spread deeply over subsequent generations."

That was possible. I continued watching, feeling useless as the sec commander gave the order to open fire. A dozen pistols and subguns chugged to life. The lack of recoil and the spitting noise of the cartridges cycling through the weapons identified them as flechette rounds designed to rip and tear flesh without endangering the dome or other mechanical equipment.

Facing grievous injury or certain death, the rioters pulled back immediately, dragging those who were wounded or possibly dead. Still, the sec team didn't go unscathed. Without warning, the heads of two men erupted in sudden explosions of blood and bone and they dropped in place. The high-pitched cracks of the sniper rifle that had taken them out rolled over the rest of the group, causing them to break off their attack and retreat to cover.

The vid angle changed as the cam operator dodged for protection as well. The sniper was good at his task. He or she managed to get two more secmen and then disappeared without a trace. Several anti-Earth movements claimed the sniper's actions, but I knew that the shooter had been militarily trained and had doubtless not acted alone. Exfiltration under such circumstance would have been hard. Getting away without leaving a trail was even more difficult.

"Do you think the sniper was part of the protestors?" Shelly asked.

"Perhaps. But the sniper could also have been someone hired

by the corps to raise the body count. Everyone involved in Mars has an agenda."

The protective screen over the windows slid down over the transplas. Warning lights suddenly flashed red.

"Passengers, please take your seats and belt in." The female voice was tight and clipped in her address.

Male and female conductors walked through the car urging passengers to comply.

I'd already hacked the onboard vid array so I accessed them and took a look around the train. The mag-lev track was laid through a stark, rocky outcropping that towered over the cars as the train rushed forward.

The pulling engine shifted shape as defensive metal sheets raised and gun ports opened. Train-jacking was rare on Mars, but it was occasionally done.

I changed magnification on the vid uplink and scanned the countryside ahead. A group of armed men and women in envirosuits rode minihoppers and six-legged ATV crawlers, moving restively along the upper rim of the closest outcropping.

"They're not moving on an intercept path," Shelly said.

"The train's going too fast." I knew from the satlink that our current ground speed was 143 KPH.

"They could match our speed."

"The minihoppers might." I accessed the rear-facing vid and saw that another group of riders and fliers had locked onto our back trail. These also piloted large eighteen-legged crawlers and a half-dozen walkers—saucer-shaped attack craft that carried an eight-man crew, heavy plasma cannons, and large-bore guns capable of taking out a passenger car with a single direct hit.

"The clean-up crew," Shelly said.

The train's commanding officer knew the trouble he was in immediately. The comm officer started relaying information on the train's position and as much detail as he could on the attackers.

"Podkayne Transit Authority, this is Manta Bill 3047, en route from Bradbury Train Station. We're being attacked by a jacker crew 4.2 kilometers north of Pohl's Peak."

An instant later, three emergency beacons flew from the train into the sky. One of them was shot down immediately at the same time the comm array on the train was taken out by a plasma blast that left the plasteel plates of the pulling engine cherry-red.

I accessed the pulling engine's environmental controls and discovered that the heat inside the vehicle wasn't powerful enough to become lethal at present. The comm systems went down and a second beacon exploded half a kilometer up, chased down by a seek-and-destroy missile that had locked onto the beacon's comm signature.

The third beacon continued skyward, disappearing almost immediately. I knew it would continue to resend the comm officer's message and the train's location until a rescue crew took control of it.

"Unless the jackers have a high-altitude pursuit drone," Shelly said.

Before I could respond, the mag-lev rail 2.3 kilometers ahead of the train blew up. The destruction was clearly visible and there was no doubt the rail was gone.

The loss of the mag-lev connection caused the train to go on emergency lockdown mode. Foam-filled bags deployed from the seats in front of passengers and braced them for collision, ready to cushion the impact when it came.

Even so, nothing could have prevented the shock and trauma that jerked the passengers as the cars tumbled from the rails because there was no way to completely stop the mass in motion. Many of the people with me screamed in fear and pain as the car rolled over onto its side and skidded along the dust-covered bones of Mars. When the seams split, the car lost air integrity and I knew people were going to be in danger of asphyxiation.

I stayed loose, letting the foam bag in front of me do its job, then I tore through the bag, spilling foam in all directions, and unbelted from the seat. I organized a list of people that would need my help first: older passengers who hadn't gotten their envirosuits pulled up, children who would panic and forget their training, and people that appeared to be the most injured.

I held onto the seat and lowered myself to the right side of the passenger car, which—now re-oriented—had become the floor. I moved through the passengers quickly, helping those who needed it to tear free of the foam bags that now threatened to hold them immobile while they suffocated on Mars's thin air.

Part of my attention stayed riveted on the approaching jacker crew that flew and stalked quickly toward the train. Through the exterior vid array, which had remained mostly active, I surveyed the train and saw that the cars lay scattered and broken like a child's toys.

A jacker on a minihopper swooped by the car I was in, pausing long enough to peer through a rent in the plasteel to view the interior. Still watching him on an exterior vid, I saw him take out a can of spray paint and squirt a red X over the car's left side, which was now above me. Then he flitted on. I wasn't sure what the mark indicated, though I had an idea.

Satisfied that everyone inside the passenger car was well and breathing on their own, I grabbed hold of the 1.1 meter rent in the car's side, braced myself against a seat, and heaved, peeling the skin back enough for me to slip through. I climbed atop the car and peered out at the sky—tinted red by all the dust swirling around from the crash—and watched the minihoppers speeding by.

The eighteen-legged crawlers pulled into position beside the cargo cars and human crew deployed. I knew only a human could be callous enough to concentrate on retrieving materials before taking care of lives at risk.

The minihopper continued scouting and painting cars.

"This is an inside job," Shelly said. "They know what they're looking for."

I agreed. Around me, railroad secmen climbed from the cars and unlimbered weapons. My programming caught for just a moment as I tried to process who was in more danger: the passengers still in the cars, or the secmen squaring off against the jackers.

"The passengers are still inside the cars," Shelly said. "Conductors and train bioroids will help take care of them. These secmen are kindred spirits to us. They're defending the cargo, and maybe the passengers if this thing turns bad."

Chapter Twenty

I took out the Gortaub 15mm slug-thrower with difficulty. My programming made the job almost impossible, but I reminded myself I wasn't going to kill anyone with it, just take out material assets. Even with that knowledge, mastering the weapon was still difficult.

With a half-dozen clicks, I fitted the skeletal rifle butt, the scope, and the extended barrel onto the pistol, changing it over to a mini-rifle. Then I took out one of the extended 25-round magazines and slid it into place.

One of the secmen nearest me took in my weapon with surprise and started to turn toward me. I looked at him and accessed his envirosuit's comm frequency. "I am going to help you."

He nodded.

I dropped over the side of the car and landed in the powdery dust, feeling it slip beneath me for an instant before I got my balance. Solid core bullets hammered the passenger car and plasma blasts cooked the thin air where I'd been standing.

I took aim on one of the minihoppers as it heeled around to begin an approach path toward a cluster of railroad guards.

The tail stabilizer was one of the most vulnerable points on the craft. When the reticule settled over the point where the stabilizer hooked into the minihopper's body, I slid my finger over the trigger and squeezed. The Gortaub jumped in my hands but I managed the recoil easily. What was more difficult was the actual act of firing. I knew there was a possibility the pilot would get harmed, but I also knew the minihopper would have safety measures built in.

And I also knew that shooting these targets would save lives. I used that leverage to free myself from the constraints of my programming.

The 15mm round sped true, not hampered by Mars's lesser gravity or by air resistance in the thinner atmosphere. When the bullet struck the stabilizer, it tore away from the minihopper's body. Immediately, the aircraft spun out of control, whirling like a top.

With a crash imminent, the minihopper's safety systems ejected the pilot into the air and a foam-filled crash bag deployed around her. Before the pilot hit the ground, the crash bag covered her, then it smacked into the hard planes of the stony landscape, bounced twice, and opened up to disgorge the pilot. She moved feebly, then lay back. Her envirosuit was intact and I was not concerned about her safety or her further involvement in the battle at the moment.

Another minihopper rose above the other side of the passenger car with both 20mm chain guns blazing. The two secmen above me spilled over the side, driven by the impacts. As they fell, blood already streaming from one of them, I fired into the ammo drum of one of the mini-guns.

The ammo drum cooked off rounds in a mad light show and triggered the minihopper's evasive safety feature. The exploding rounds wouldn't penetrate the minihopper's hard cockpit shell, but they registered as heavy and direct fire. Attempting to save itself and its pilot, the minihopper shot straight up into the sky.

I turned to the fallen secmen beside me. One of them was already dead, his face punched in by a direct hit. The other secman writhed in agony from a round that had nearly amputated his left leg. The envirosuit had already attempted to tourniquet the leg to stop the blood flow from the pulmonary artery.

Still in shock, the man tried to get to his feet. I held him down, then punched in the suit's automatic med routines. On the other side of the face shield, the man's eyes glazed as slap-patches of narcotics took him into twilight and started flooding his system with antibiotics and coagulants. Still breathing, but more relaxed, the secman laid back and stared up at the sky with uncaring eyes.

I went through both secmen's kits and discovered they had thermite lace, which was probably intended to burn open cargo containers if the need should arise. I intended to burn through something else.

With the thermite lace looped over my left shoulder, I turned and ran toward the nearest cargo crawler feeding on the wrecked train. The crawler lay next to the container car with its hatches open while the interior crew deployed massive mechanical jaws and the exterior crew ripped open the container car's walls.

The railroad secmen fought a solid battle, never giving quarter, but they were facing a losing battle. The jackers outnumbered them, and those men and women had come prepared to kill whoever they had to in order to get the shipments they were after. I knew they weren't after every shipment because the spotters flying the minihoppers had marked some of the container cars.

As Shelly had said, the jackers had come well-informed.

I bounded across the Martian landscape, using my strength and the lesser gravity to hurl me twenty and thirty meters forward with each step. Three jackers aboard the crawler attempted to shoot me. Bullets ripped into the ground only centimeters behind me, and plasma blasts turned the red sand into glass ellipses in meter-wide spots.

I returned fire as I neared the crawler. I shot a heavy machine gun off the gimbals it was mounted on, managed to crease the helmet of another man hard enough to knock the second shooter aside, and shot the heel off the armored boot of another to send him toppling to the ground.

By then I was running beneath the poised crawler's legs. I slapped lengths of the thermite lace around five of the multi-jointed legs, then touched the ten-second delays.

At the count of "four," I dodged down and rolled away. The rapid-fire sequence of explosions followed me. I put out a hand and pushed myself up just in time to see the crawler's legs burn off. The craft shifted awkwardly, then started coming down toward me in an avalanche of tumbling plasteel as the other four legs flailed wildly and dug into the ground, gouging long ditches.

I avoided getting tangled up in the writhing crawler by only a few meters. Shifting hands with the Gortaub, I drew the Synap and blasted three of the jackers that ended up sprawled across the landscape. They fell and didn't do more than twitch a few seconds before succumbing to unconsciousness.

Caught in the sights of a minihopper pilot, I ran along the downed crawler. One of the crawler's legs swung up out of control and smashed into the minihopper hard enough to activate the eject sequence. The pilot shot up into the sky and the 20mm cannon he'd been chasing me with stopped firing.

The minihopper impacted 140 meters away against a stand of broken rock, then tumbled back down to the ground mostly intact. I changed course at once, knowing that the third emergency beacon might not have escaped destruction.

At the minihopper, I smashed through the transplas pilot bubble with my fists and climbed inside. I seized the comm and switched it to the emergency frequency I knew Podkayne Transit Authority would be monitoring.

I spoke clearly and briefly, tracking the activity around me. I knew I had been spotted. One of the walkers' turrets was already turning in my direction.

"Podkayne Transit Authority, this is a passenger aboard Manta Bill 3047 en route from Bradbury Train Station. We have been attacked by a jacker crew." I added the global positioning coordinates as I tapped into the broadcast frequency and headed back out of the minihopper.

The walker's turret locked onto the downed aircraft.

"Manta Bill 3047, be advised that Podkayne Transit Authority has a lock on your position. A tach team has been dispatched. ETA is twenty-three minutes twen—"

The walker's main gun belched and a 200mm round struck the wrecked minihopper. The comm frequency died as the vehicle turned into a flaming slag heap.

Even though the thin air of Mars lessened the concussive shockwave from the blast, the explosion was still enough to knock me to the ground in a headlong dive. I twisted and rolled as I hit, back on my feet instantly as the walker gunnery crew tried to target me again.

I dodged behind a stand of rock just as the main gun fired again. This time the shot struck the rock, splintering it and bringing it down on top of me. If I had been human, I would have died there. Instead, I was buried, taken out of the fight for the moment as I struggled to find purchase and extricate myself.

Then I wasn't there anymore. My vision blurred.

* * *

A man in mercenary fatigues stood over me, his face calm and somber. "Simon? Are you awake?"

"Yes." My voice was weak, ragged and hoarse. I felt like I had glass in my throat. I blinked and his features became sharper. I knew from my surroundings that I was in a hospital bed. "What happened?"

He cocked his head to one side. "You don't remember?"

"No." I tried to clear my throat and couldn't.

The man reached for a cup on a small table beside my bed and put a straw into my mouth. "Take a small drink. Just enough to wet your lips."

I did, and the water tasted cool but had an off-flavor that told me it was laced with electrolytes and vitamins. I tried my voice again and it was a little better. "What happened?"

"What do you remember?"

I struggled to think, but it was like someone had wrapped my thoughts in cotton. "I was in combat. Somewhere." I thought some more, and finally managed to snag a wayward memory. "Around Demeter colony." That was one of the first ag-bubbles on Mars.

"That's right. I was in the same action."

"You're a merc?"

He nodded. "My name is John Rath."

The name meant something to me. "I've heard of you. Commander of the Chimera Mercenaries."

"That's right."

"What are you doing here?"

"My team and I pulled you out of that firefight."

I tried to remember and couldn't. "When?"

"Four days ago. You've been in a coma."

"What about my team?" Their faces appeared in my mind. I knew them all. They'd been men and women I'd fought with for…I wasn't sure how long.

Rath shook his head. "Nobody else made it. You guys took a direct hit from a walker."

I struggled in the bed to lift my upper body and check myself. My head spun and I thought I was going to be sick. My arms and legs appeared intact. If everyone else was dead, how could I be whole?

"Am I injured?"

"Some internal damage," Rath said. "Nothing that couldn't be easily patched up. The main thing was the head injury."

I reached up and felt my head, but there were no bandages.

Rath shook his head. "Nothing you'd notice on the outside. The doctors said you'd suffered a concussion. That you'd probably have some memory loss. It might or might not come back."

I considered remembering how my team had died around me, then thought maybe that memory would be better off lost. I had memories of them before, but there were a lot of other memories that were jumbled, jagged pieces that didn't really fit together. I remembered several pieces of battles on Earth and on Mars, several faces, but no one really distinct.

My sharpest memory was of the night my parents and sister were killed.

"Just take it easy," Rath advised. He put a hand on my shoulder and eased me back to bed. "You're going to be fine. You're in good hands. Nothing's going to happen to you here."

I lay back, but adrenaline flooded my system and caused my body to quake. The part of me that was still Drake 3GI2RC knew that I was suffering from a panic attack. I had seen victims and NAPD personnel undergoing similar effects. I knew it would pass.

"Just keep breathing," Rath instructed in a calm voice. "Concentrate on getting a rhythm. Let the chemicals run their course and everything will be fine."

A nurse in green scrubs came through the door and checked the equipment attached to me.

Rath fixed her with his gaze. "It's all right, nurse. Lieutenant Blake and I have got this."

The woman looked like she was going to protest.

"I said, we've got this." The edge in Rath's voice was unmistakable. "If we need you, I'll call you."

The nurse took an involuntary step back, then gave a grudging nod, turned, and left the room.

I focused on my breathing and the panic filling me began to subside.

"Good job," Rath said.

"My memory," I croaked.

"What about it?"

"I'm having trouble…remembering everything. It's all mixed up."

"You remember the battle at Demeter colony," Rath said. "You remember your name."

I struggled to do that, and couldn't really do it, but I remembered that Rath had called me Simon and Lieutenant Blake. The same name showed on the patient monitor on the opposite wall. "Simon Blake." I said the name with more confidence than I felt.

"See? You're going to be all right, soldier."

"I lost my team."

Rath nodded and his face hardened. "They got buried right, Lieutenant. Their families got paid full death benefits. You did everything for them that you could. I saw that. In time, you'll remember."

I nodded. He gave me another sip of water and I took it.

"When can I leave the hospital?" I asked.

"Another couple days, I'm told."

I glanced over at him. "What are you doing here?"

"I've got men and women in this hospital. I came to check on them. Thought I'd look in on you."

"Thank you."

"I also wanted to talk to you about a business proposition."

I waited.

"I want to buy up your contract from RuschDev and offer you a leadership position with the Chimeras. With me."

I struggled to remember RuschDev and thought I recalled that it was a genemod corp that specialized in creating vegetable hybrids that would grow on Mars.

"Why would you do that?"

"Because you're too good to be working for a small corp like that, and because RuschDev, as of four days ago, became a crater in Demeter colony." Rath paused and lifted a PAD, punching up a display that was a vidcast clip of the street where RuschDev had once stood.

The neighborhood of small corps looked familiar, but I couldn't remember being there or anyone who had worked there.

RUSCHDEV VICTIM OF ANTI-EARTH ATTACK, the crawler at the bottom of the holo announced. *NO SURVIVORS FOUND. THE BODIES OF SEVERAL KNOWN TERRORISTS ON-SITE.*

"Your pink slip with RuschDev came while you were in the coma. I'm forcing them to pick up your medical. Then—if you want—you're a Chimera. Unless there's somewhere else you'd rather go."

I was silent for a moment, thinking about it. I sifted through those jumbled memories. As best as I could recall, I had no family left alive. I'd spent time on Earth and Mars fighting other people's battles, defending other people's property and personnel, and the only friends I could best remember had died four days ago.

I shook my head and it hurt. "No. I don't have anywhere else to be."

"Good. The team will be glad to have you. *I'll* be glad to have you." Rath offered his hand and I took it, feeling it strong and firm in mine.

* * *

I returned to the attack site in a rush and took stock of my situation. I was in no immediate danger of being crushed under the fallen rock. The gravity was in my favor and my chassis was too well constructed for it to buckle.

I tried to shift and only managed to move a few millimeters

at first. Then, gradually, some of the rocks on top of me began to slip and give way. I kept moving as much as I could, thinking of the people aboard the train who were in danger. I would not fail.

Finally, light broke through the darkness that surrounded me. I thrust a hand through a section where I could see sky, then drew my arm back and thrust again, creating more space and a sudden rush of rock that spilled from the top of the heap. A quick check of my internal diagnostics showed me I'd been trapped and immobile under the fallen rock for eighteen minutes forty-three seconds.

The rescue group from Podkayne shouldn't have been more than three minutes thirty-seven seconds out.

I shoved through the pile of rock and rolled down to the bottom of the hill where the original outcropping had been. Only a stub, like a broken fang, remained to mark the area where it had stood. The Gortaub was still slung over my shoulder and I pulled it around, then freed the Synap from my thigh pocket again.

The jackers were in full route, though. Several of the container cars lay sliced open from laser torches. Cargo spilled out across the sand. I sprinted over to the crawler I'd disabled. I didn't think any of the crew would still be aboard, but one of my subroutines involved thoroughness, which was considered an asset at the NAPD.

One of the railroad secmen fired at me and small-caliber rounds ricocheted from my chassis before another of them ordered the first to stand down. I picked up his order over the comm frequency I'd tapped into. "That bioroid is working with us. Don't shoot."

I leaped up to the crawler's command module and grabbed hold of the door. Before I opened it, I checked the bullet-scored transplas window and spotted the booby trap that had been left behind.

The anti-personnel mine was only eight centimeters cubed

with a matte black finish. The thing that immediately caught my attention was that the explosive had been manufactured according to a design by Skorpios Defense Systems, and that link took me back to the investigation I'd opened on the Moon that had marked me for destruction.

Skorpios Defense Systems CEO Gordon Holder had been executed and I had followed the trail left by his killers to an illegal munitions manufacturing site where weapons had been being made and shipped off the Moon to Mars. Although the facts had never been confirmed, everyone at the NAPD believed that the weapons were being sold on the Martian black market. The terrorist factions were better armed these days than they had been in years.

I left the command module door in place and used the laser cutting tool I'd bought when I'd picked up my weapons. I sliced a hole in the wall, then reached in and disabled the claymore mine. After I set the device aside, I opened the door and checked the interior.

I didn't climb into the area. It was a crime scene waiting to be analyzed, one that would hopefully help law enforcement agencies find the jackers responsible for the attack.

"Hey." One of the railroad secmen hurtled through the air in a long leap, letting me know he wasn't a native Martian, and landed a few meters away. "Don't climb into that vehicle."

"I'm not," I replied. "I disabled a claymore mine inside the vehicle." I dropped down to the ground.

"Who are you?"

"Norris 1JA5NU."

"How did you go on the defensive like that? A Norris isn't usually capable of something like that."

"I represent Lono Ag currently, but I have been repurposed. Before that I pitched a defensive line for KentDefender Corp. I was programmed in how to use weapons and under what conditions." Fabrication was one of my skill sets as a detective to get confessions. I used that now to cover myself.

"You do good work, Norris."

"Thank you." I strode back toward the train, disassembling the Gortaub as I went and storing it once more.

Above me, the strike wing from Podkayne Transit Authority shot past and streamed contrails behind them.

Chapter Twenty-One

I was carrying the sixth fatality from one of the passenger cars when Hayim found me.

"So you're still functional, eh?" Hayim cradled a sheet-covered woman's body in his arms. Dried blood streaked one of his cheeks under the envirosuit's face shield, but he looked otherwise unharmed.

"I am." Tenderly, I handed the dead man to the cargo bioroids working from the back of a cargo hopper. "How are you?"

Hayim handed up the body that he'd carried. "I survived. Seems like I always do." He slapped a hand against his metallic thigh. "At least, most of me does. The crypt safety measure kicked in and protected me. Took me a while to get out of it."

"I'm glad you are all right."

"Me, too."

I started walking back toward the train. A group of bioroids and robots laid new mag-lev track to replace all that had been ruined. The railroad construction crew had arrived less than forty minutes after the transit authority teams, but the nosies had beaten them, trailing on the heels of the transit authority strike force.

One of the media people stood in front of an overturned cargo container with the crippled crawler lying in the background. He wore an envirosuit and stood in front of a vid operator wearing a shoulder-mounted satellite relay.

The transit authority had locked out all comm units not part of their group and there wasn't enough bleed out from those communiques for me to pick up on my PAD. I had no problem tuning in the nosie, though.

On the broadcast, the nosie wasn't in his envirosuit. They had placed a holo overlay over him that mimicked his movements and showed him in a suit and tie. He was young-looking, but he hadn't had any surgery done on his vocal cords yet and I could hear the age in his voice. His blond hair was neatly trimmed and his cerulean blue eyes sparkled.

"—Authority isn't saying much, but my sources inside the department are telling me that they believe the destruction of Manta Bill 3047 was caused by terrorists who were after the cargo the train was hauling." The nosie turned and pointed at the wreckage of the crawler and the cargo container behind him. "As you can see from this downed crawler, the terrorists came in force, with enough weaponry to stage a small war. Taking out a train armed only with a skeletal security team was child's play."

I silently disagreed with him. I didn't necessarily believe that terrorists had been behind the attack. It could just as easily have been a rival black market dealer after the illegal cargo the train was carrying. And the security team aboard the train hadn't been skeletal. The numbers from what I had seen had been double what would normally have been assigned to such a run.

The fact that several of the railroad secmen had been transported for sustained "injuries" along with passengers that had gotten evacuated was suspect to me. None of the transit authority officers investigated their release. That indicated that someone had paid for "reduced attention" during the investigation.

"You know that means that a corp was behind the weapons shipment, right?" Shelly asked.

"Yes," I answered.

"Our original thinking that Gordon Holder and Skorpios Defense Systems were selling to the black market was incorrect."

"That was just one theory you and I had come up with."

"Holder would have spread the arms around the black market. Anyone could have purchased them. That would have made a lot more business sense than hitting this train and alerting the colonies that illegal weapons were shipping to Mars."

I considered that as I carried another body to the flatbed. "What if the revelation was part of the plan all along?"

"These jackers wanted people to know that the weapons were here? Why?"

"To ratchet up the feelings of distrust between those factions predisposed toward Earth's continued involvement here, those who want Martian independence, and the terrorists."

"Wouldn't the terrorists be the most likely suspects? Just to drive a deeper and wider wedge on the political front?"

"Think about it, Shelly. The terrorist groups have been responding to perceived threats as well. Earth-owned corps have been beefing up their security presence in the colonies."

"That was in response to increased terrorist attacks."

"It's a closed environment cycle. One that can be manipulated from outside by simply raising concern in one area. The other areas raise automatically."

"You think one group is behind this?"

I passed another body up to the other bioroids working on the flatbed. "I don't know. I was merely thinking outside that cycle."

"Norris," Hayim said to me.

"Yes."

He lifted an arm toward his face in an automatic gesture, then grimaced when his hand banged into his face shield. "My nose itches. I hate when I'm inside one of these suits and my nose itches."

"I understand."

He put his arm down. "You do realize that my e-ID isn't going to stand up against any close scrutiny on the part of Podkayne Transit Authority."

"I do." I wasn't sure if mine would either.

"You might be able to slip off on your own because you don't need air to breathe, but I can't. I'll never make it."

"I know. I have a plan."

Hayim looked at me expectantly.

"You will not like it," I told him. But it was all that I could think of.

* * *

"Are you comfortable?" I asked an hour later.

Hayim lay next to the pile of corpses on the car where the dead had been moved. He was safe enough from harm and from discovery by Podkayne Transit Authority.

"No, I'm not comfortable," he growled in response.

"But you are alive and you are free."

He cursed, but it was at the situation and not at me.

Fred A24U13 seated next to me was so low that he was almost featureless. Only a hint of a nose and cheekbones showed below his silver eyes that never flickered with animation. His voice was flat and monotone. Fred D21E30 and Fred M28A89 sat on the other side of the container car as it sped toward Podkayne colony.

"This one is not dead," Fred A24U13 said.

"Not yet," I said. "But he will be soon enough. He is human. All humans die."

"Hey!" Hayim objected.

"He is not dead," Fred A24U13 repeated. "Therefore he should be on one of the passenger cars with the living. His presence here is a mistake."

"He has lost his legs." I pointed out the tear that ran up one side of Hayim's envirosuit during the wreck. The suit's automated system had already tied a tourniquet to the leg, sealing off potential air loss, but the bionic limb showed through.

"Then he should be aboard a medical evac," Fred A24U13 said.

"He is in no immediate danger. His vital signs are strong." I trusted that the conundrum would hold Fred A24U13's logic circuits in thrall, and it did.

"You are certain this man is where he should be?"

"I am."

"Then I defer to your decision." Fred A24U13 sat back and went inert inside the cargo webbing that held him stationary.

"It's getting stuffy in here," Hayim said. "The suit's cautions haven't lit up, but I can tell the difference."

I checked Hayim's oxygen supply and discovered that it was getting low again. Even with only using a little more than half the oxygen a normal human needed due to his reduced circulatory system, the trip to Podkayne colony had exhausted the suit's reserves.

I knelt down and checked through the bodies, finding one that had expired quickly from a piece of shrapnel that had ripped through the heart. The envirosuit's onboard limited AI had shut down the suit's air supply immediately after discovering the injury had been unrecoverable.

Using a set of tools I had liberated from the train, I drained that suit's oxygen into Hayim's suit. He started breathing easier immediately.

"Thanks," he said. "Are you sure there's enough oxygen to get me to Podkayne?"

Thirty-seven corpses had been laid to rest in the cargo container. Not all of them had oxygen intact, but enough of them did.

"Yes."

Hayim took another long, slow breath. "When we get to Podkayne, there'll be an investigation. We can't go through that."

"We won't. I'm accessing the GPS through the train's Net connection. Nine kilometers from Podkayne, it will be dark. We'll take our leave then."

"From a moving train?" A concerned look bit deeply into Hayim's features.

"The train will be breaking at that point. I can manage the dismount at the speed we'll be going."

Hayim took a moment to consider his options, and I knew he was thinking about risking his identification rather than jumping from the train. In the end, he nodded. "We don't have a choice."

"No."

"No matter what happens, you're going to be fine." He sounded grudging about the fact.

"I need you to find the Chimeras, and I can't let you come to any harm. You know that." Still, those protocols that protected Hayim while he was under my control warred against my decision. I decided to take his mind off of that difficulty and focus it on another to distract him. "Once we're inside Podkayne colony, security will still be strict. The present identification we have will not hold up under close scrutiny. Getting stopped on the street could impact us negatively as well."

"Once we're in Podkayne, I can fix that."

"How?"

"I know where a forger does business, and I know my way around forging equipment."

* * *

Three hours and forty-one minutes later, just after sunset and when the moons were racing across the sky, I sliced into the container car wall with my cutting laser, bypassed the security wiring, and opened the side loading door. The hard landscape looked ochre in the darkness.

"How fast are we going?" Hayim stood beside me, rocking from the slight motion of the train along the mag-lev rail.

I accessed the GPS information. "Seventy-eight kilometers per mile."

"You realize jumping from this train at this speed could kill me."

I did. In fact I was uncertain if I could leap with him from the train. My human safety primary routines had kicked in and almost locked me down. I ran through the scenarios, trying to find play in the programming, struggling to convince that concrete foundation of Drake self that *not* attempting to escape with Hayim would be even more detrimental to him than jumping.

I became paralyzed at the door, staring out and knowing that transit authority security would lock Hayim down. At the least, they would kick him off Mars. But they could lock him down for the rest of his natural life.

That would be a death sentence, I told myself. I was further incapacitated because I knew I had put Hayim on that train. By saving him, I had condemned him to this eventual confrontation with Podkayne Immigration.

But I had saved him from the attack…

The scenarios chased themselves around in my logic center, extrapolating mirrors of conflict that I couldn't resolve. The neural channeling I had been created from wasn't supposed to permit this kind of mental lockdown. Most bioroids would never have reached such an impasse.

The problem solution software I had been programmed with had been developed to disentangle complications. I had been designed to draw conclusions that would lead to truths, to people who committed wrongdoings, to eventual retribution for murder or crimes against persons and corps.

I was mired in pi, repeating confluence of failure to protect Hayim.

"Norris." Hayim touched my shoulder. "I'm not eager to leave what's left of my body scattered across that inhospitable landscape, but we're only minutes out of Podkayne. If we're going to jump, we'd best get to it."

Instead of helping, his announcement stepped up the confusion running rampant within me.

"Drake." Shelly was suddenly beside me. "You can do this."

"No," I replied. "I can't. Logic dictates that I can't allow Hayim to arrive in Podkayne colony. Logic also dictates that I can't risk his life by jumping from the train with him. Logic further dictates that I can't pull the emergency stop because railroad secmen will deploy and capture us before we can escape."

"You're not alone," she said.

"There's nothing you can do."

"Not me. Simon Blake."

"Simon Blake is dead."

"Simon Blake still lives within you. Access that part of you. See what Simon Blake would do."

Her words echoed within my logic centers. I tried to touch that part of me that had been Simon Blake, and I was surprised to find him there and waiting.

Chapter Twenty-Two

I lay on my back and stared up at the distant sun through the red sky and the small portable transplas dome. My body hurt and my lungs cried out for a breath I couldn't take. Finally the paroxysm that had locked down my chest relaxed and I could breathe again. I sucked in air and pain exploded inside my head.

"Have you had enough? Or do you still want a shot at the title?" The tone was only slightly mocking, and a little winded. I took pride in that. My opponent was the toughest I'd ever faced.

Moving gingerly, I rolled over and discovered I was on a familiar grey square exercise mat that was seven meters to a side. A group of men and women ringed the sides, all of whom seemed to be greatly amused by my predicament.

Several cheers and jeers reached my ears. "Come on, Blake."

"You can't give up that easily."

"Get back in there and take your beating."

Clad in a skintight black singlet, John Rath stood a few meters away. Headgear with ear protectors wrapped his head. His skin was flushed red with exertion and I saw a few bruises on his arm and one on his right check. His right eye was slightly swollen too and a bead of blood collected on his eyebrow. Martial arts gloves covered his hands and boots covered his feet. They weren't there to protect him. They were there to protect me.

I tasted blood as I pushed myself up on hands that were likewise covered with the special gloves. Blood dripped from my nose and I wiped at it with my arm, smearing a thin film of crimson from my wrist to my elbow.

My mind recalled the recent battle. Rath hadn't been gentle. He never was.

Grinning around his black mouthpiece, Rath opened his arms wide. "We can stop this any time you're ready."

"I'm not ready to stop," I replied. But I knew I didn't have much in reserve. I was all but spent. I set myself in my stance, legs spread to shoulder width, left foot slightly in front of the right, my clenched fists raised to just below my eyes.

Rath nodded, then he started his advance, moving with sinuous grace in one of the kung fu styles he favored. I mirrored him, giving ground and moving as deftly as he did. He had taught me quickly because learning the fighting skill was like picking up an old proficiency.

Other than the death of my parents and sister, my memory still hadn't returned. The doctors were convinced that it had been jumbled as a result of the head injury I'd suffered. I knew more about myself from reading the file Rath had given me about Simon Blake than I did on my own. But there was a lot my body remembered, like fighting and military engagements. Some days I felt like a ghost of the man I'd been.

For a time, we sparred like shadows, equally matched as we delivered blow after blow, kick after kick. I felt the impact at both ends: when he made contact with me and when I made contact with him. Instinctively, I knew every move he was going to make, and he read me like he'd written the programming.

Then, coming out of a defensive posture, he shifted, dropping his left shoulder and lifting his right leg like he was going to deliver a roundhouse kick. I set myself for that, then his left snap-kick came off the ground a split-second later and slammed into my chest. The impact caused my heart to skip a beat and I experienced a moment of disorientation as my body and mind tried to come together again.

Before I could recover, Rath shifted to his right and drove his right fist into the left side of my face. My jaw clenched spasmodically as white-hot agony flared through my mind. I brought my arms up to defend myself, managing to block his next blow, but he hadn't been intending to land that one. It was just a distraction that set me up for the spinning back kick that caught me in the right side of my head.

My knees turned to jelly and I went down. No longer able to hold my arms up, I sat there defenselessly as he faced me. For a moment I thought I would be struck again. Sometimes Rath had trouble stopping a fight once he started. He had a killer mentality, a singular focus. But that was on the exercise mat during personal combat. When he was operating on the battlefield, his scope was wider. He saw things that other people didn't. His touch there was gentle—a surgeon's scalpel teasing flesh from bone.

He stopped a follow-up kick to my face by centimeters. Then, as easy as water flowing, Rath sank to his knees in front of me. He was breathing harder, but he had it under control. I sucked in air greedily and struggled to hang onto my senses.

"Had enough now?" he asked.

I nodded, unable to speak.

Around me, the other men and women of the Chimeras applauded and yelled cheerful obscenities.

Rath smiled at me, and I saw that flicker of pride in his dark eyes that I relished. Whatever he asked me to do, whenever he asked me to do it, I was his, heart, body, and soul. It had been that way since he had visited me in the hospital seven months ago. My memory might still be sketchy, still blurred in most areas, but I was certain I had never followed a man better than John Rath.

"You're good, Blake," Rath said. "Almost as good as me."

"I'll get better," I said through my aching jaw.

"Better than me?" Rath grinned and shook his head.

I'd meant better than I was, but I didn't bother to correct him. The challenge felt right.

"You'll never be better than me. I taught you everything *you* know, but I didn't teach you everything *I* know." Rath called for a towel and caught one when it was thrown to him. He put it over my shoulders like it was a trophy mantle, and I felt like it was.

* * *

Back on the train in the cargo container, the rushing wind buffeted me. I was also free to choose among my options again. Something in that passing wisp of a memory tilted the balance and freed me to move. I turned to Hayim and dropped to my knees. "Climb onto my back."

On the other side of the face shield, he looked tired and worried. "You're sure you can do this?"

"Yes." I wasn't sure about the landing, but I knew I could now put us through the door.

Awkwardly, Hayim threw his arms around my neck and wrapped his bionic legs around my chest. The fact that I was taller than he was helped with his positioning.

Almost effortlessly in spite of Hayim's additional weight, I stood. I was a lot stronger than a human, and the gravity differential on Mars worked in our favor. The mass remained a problem, though, and that would affect the landing.

I accessed the GPS and ascertained the train's present speed—seventy-one KPH—then threw us from the train. We dropped four meters to the ground, still accelerating forward. I turned my hips in a way no human could do, putting my legs at a ninety degree angle to my body, landed on my left foot and immediately kicked upward into a jump that carried me thirty meters across the broken ground. Some of my speed began to drop away naturally but I knew better than to try to force it.

I touched down with my right foot and still didn't try to decelerate, but I did manage to hold onto enough friction while touching the ground to spin my torso into the proper alignment so I could swing my arms to help keep my balance.

I sailed another twenty meters this time, but then I had the rhythm. I was no longer skipping like a rock across a lake surface. I was running, taking superhumanly long strides, but in control of the speed and direction. Hayim bounced against me for a moment, then he wrapped his arms and legs more tightly around me. He was screaming inside the envirosuit. I'd damped his comm, but I could still hear him with the helmet to head contact I had.

I ran, keeping the rhythm for a moment, avoiding the craters and pitfalls that appeared before us. Occasionally my feet skidded against bare stone, other times they sank in the powdery ochre sand. Through it all, I kept my footing, and I kept Hayim on my back. He thumped against me and became a variable I had to deal with.

Two point four kilometers from Podkayne colony, which gleamed in the distance under the moonlight, I came to a halt next to a large ag-bubble that was dark and thick with wheat fields. I stayed outside of the sec radius.

Hayim groaned as he unlocked his arms, then stepped down onto the ground. His leg squealed in protest.

"Are you all right?" I asked.

"I never want to do that again."

"Sit down and catch your breath for a moment." I searched my thigh pockets for a comprehensive tool kit. I opened the kit as Hayim sat, then gave him an energy drink laced with electrolytes.

While he attached the drink to the tube in his face shield, I sorted through the tools, taking out what I thought I would need.

"What are you doing?" Hayim asked.

"I'm going to repair your leg."

Hayim hesitated. "Have you done work like that before?"

"No, but I pulled down schematics from the Net while we were aboard the train. I know what I'm doing, Hayim. Trust me. Where we are, with the things against us, the last thing you need is for that leg to fail you."

After another moment of hesitation, Hayim extended his leg, which squealed louder than it had before, making me wonder if it had been injured while I'd carried him across the empty desert or during the train wreck.

"Getting the leg repaired was too expensive for me to have done, and Reena didn't know her way around it. She does a lot of work on mechanical things, but mostly she parts them out. Repairing something like this is above her pay grade."

Using an Allen wrench, I opened the cover over his knee and started there. I cleared debris with a brush, located a ball joint that had been pitted from continued excessive wear, and removed it. I took out another because that one was no longer salvageable.

"Where did you get that?" Hayim asked, eyeing the new ball joint.

"From one of the server bioroids that was damaged during the wreck. Her torso and hips were separated, and the destruction to her chest cavity where her brain is was too severe for her to stay online."

"She's dead?"

"Dead is a human condition. That unit was rendered inoperable. Her consciousness was backed up through weekly visits to Haas-Bioroid. She can be reactivated and only have lost a few days' of memory."

"Has that ever happened to you?"

I carefully reinstalled the replacement ball joint. "I have been offline a few times."

"How?"

"As a result of damage."

"But you're all right now?"

"I am."

"And you know what you're doing?"

"I do."

Hayim finally relaxed and lay back, seeking a more comfortable position.

After I replaced the knee joint, I opened the ankle and the hip and cleaned those parts as well. Debris from the degrading ball joint had gathered in both areas. When Hayim stood after I put everything back together, the leg no longer made noise.

He stamped around with the limb experimentally, then looked over at me and grinned. "It feels really good. Better than the other one, in fact."

I put my tools away. "I'm glad. Maybe after we get to Podkayne colony I can take a look at the other leg."

"I'd appreciate it. How far out are we?"

"Two point four miles."

He checked his chronometer. "Almost 2100 local time. The crews from the ag-bubbles should be showing up for the nightly tour of the megapolis."

* * *

Five minutes later, we found a well-worn path headed for Podkayne colony, which was visible in the distance. The megapolis stood tall, filled with multicolored lights that shone out from the domescrapers and minihoppers flitting from rooftop to rooftop.

"It's beautiful," Shelly said as she walked at my side. Hayim walked on the other side. "It looks like a bouquet of gemstones sparkling under glass."

"The megapolis has its secrets and dangers."

"Every city does, Drake. I know I taught you that."

"You did." Shelly had had a much gentler hand for me than John Rath had had for Simon Blake. But ultimately, both of them had striven to keep us alive, safe, and functional.

Less than a kilometer from the colony's gates, Hayim and I were overtaken by a crew ATV, pinned in the bright headlights as it careened down toward us. Hayim and I stepped off the narrow road. The crew ATV hissed to a stop only a few meters in front of us, creating a cloud of powdery dust to roil out around it.

The crew ATV stood four meters tall and crept along on eight legs that moved with blinding speed. The boxy shape allowed for a sizeable cargo area that was at the moment mostly occupied by several men and women in envirosuits.

One of the men in the back stood and waved at us. He spoke over a limited short-range comm frequency that I accessed by tapping into the crew ATV's satellite feed.

"What are you doing out here?"

Hayim jerked a thumb over his shoulder. "ATV went offline a couple klicks back. We couldn't reach anyone, and it was close enough that it wasn't an emergency."

"Come on. We'll give you guys a lift."

Hayim waved at them, then started for the vehicle at a trot. "Thanks." He caught the hand of the man at the crew ATV's edge and allowed himself to be pulled up.

Before Hayim scrambled aboard, I leaped up and landed in an empty space that had been made in the back of the vehicle. The group of farm workers looked at me in silent speculation.

I let Hayim do the talking because I was a bioroid and most of the workers wouldn't expect me to speak unless I was directly requested to. He explained that we were contracted inspectors checking water pumps that recycled through the ag-bubbles. The job wasn't high maintenance, but it was a high priority. Every farm corp, Earth and Mars, kept a crew that rotated through the ag-bubbles. As a cover story, it was easily believable because a technician didn't have to be highly skilled to perform the job.

Hayim sat on the long bench that stretched across both sides of the crew ATV as the vehicle got underway again. He buckled himself into his seat, then reached for one of the ATV's oxygen hookups and fitted it to his suit. He wasn't getting low on his air supply, but attaching to an outside supply any time he had a chance was a good habit.

"Did you hear about the attack on the train today?" one of the females asked.

Hayim shook his head. "I wasn't on the mediafeed channel all day. You get out there in the bubbles, you get a chance to listen to what you want to instead of being constantly bombarded by advertising."

"That's true," a male worker said. "Life may be a little more difficult here in the colonies, but I haven't regretted leaving Earth. A man's got room to breathe out here."

"Even if there's no air to breathe," the woman said.

They all chuckled at that and I gathered that it was an old joke.

"What about the train?" Hayim asked. "You said there was an attack."

The woman delivered a fairly concise summary of what had happened during the attack on Manta Bill 3047 without embellishing anything. Evidently several of the vid cams aboard the train had remained functional during the engagement.

"Does anyone know who was behind the violence?" Hayim asked when she finished.

"Not yet. Three terrorist groups are trying to take credit for it, but the railroad transit authority isn't buying into that."

"The terrorist groups are all small," another female added. "No one believes they're organized enough or large enough to pull off a train robbery."

One of the men who hadn't spoken cursed. "Life out here is hard enough without the terrorists making it harder."

"It's not just the terrorists making life difficult," the man who'd helped Hayim board the ATV said. "It's the Earth corps too. Every time a colonist grabs an extra centimeter of success from hard work, the Earth corps find a way to tax or raise prices so they get that extra centimeter for themselves. If they had it their way, the Earth corps would keep us under their thumbs."

The other ag workers looked at him.

The man held up his hands in defense. "Hey, I'm no terrorist. Don't get the wrong idea. All I'm saying is what every one of us has thought at one time or another."

The tension within the group relaxed.

"The Earth corps will put on extra sec teams for a while," the woman agreed. "And they'll find a way to pass the cost on to us. Either by raising the cost of basics we need, or by tacking on an export tax, or just raising the cost of shipping freight."

"Earth corps can't hold us down forever," the first man said. "Every day the colonies get a little closer to independence. We're going to live to see it happen."

The lights of the sec gate allowing admission to Podkayne colony distracted everyone. Searchlights strobed the ATV and mini-drones with FLIR—forward-looking infrared—and chem-sniffers flitted by us after a brief hesitation. The mini-drones were sensitive enough to pick up gunpowder residue, but I had thoroughly cleaned my hands and clothing with a sonic scrubber aboard the second train that had been sent to transport passengers stranded by the terrorist action.

We disembarked the ATV at the gate, then filed through the sec line, presenting our e-IDs for the scanners. The number of secmen present was doubtlessly increased, and all of them watched us with bright interest.

Hayim's heart rate was slightly elevated over the baseline I had for him, but the sec point didn't know what that baseline was. They scanned his legs for a moment, then let him pass on through. I followed without any difficulty. The Norris e-ID still stood.

Once he was through the airlock, Hayim took off his helmet and growled a curse. “Okay, I’ve got to get a drink.”

Chapter Twenty-Three

The bar served an abbreviated menu and was called the Inn of Two Moons, a unit of a small colony-owned chain of bars/diners by XCLJooce Corp. XCLJooce was known primarily for its chain of juice franchises, an empire that rivaled the largest coffee outlets, but it had picked up the Inn of Two Moons chain seven years back.

Although Two Moons had made some in-roads on Earth and the Moon, the inns were primarily located in the colonies. Many off-world and pro-Earth merc units gathered there and Two Moons maintained an extensive merc Net board where privately contracted mercs and sec teams could keep in touch with each other.

The bar/diner was packed with people when Hayim and I arrived. The Two Moons franchises had undergone extensive remodeling when the Earth investments had rolled in. Every one of them tended to look like the next: same layout, same 1950s and 1960s science fiction motif with clunky spacesuits for the males and metallic one-piece swimsuits for females that featured fish bowl helmets for the human and clone servers. Drink dispensers that looked like Robby the Robot from the 20th century film *Forbidden Planet* trundled across an ever-shifting floor that projected images of space. A television soundtrack from the 20th century show *Star Trek* was playing.

"It's not all innocent science fiction posing or vitamin-packed drinks," Shelly said as she surveyed the place with a critical eye. "A lot of people say these places are clearinghouses established for pro-Earth mercenary work. Earth corps funnel funds onto Mars through membership cred accounts to pay for operations."

Three years ago, Shelly and I had almost closed an investigation regarding a murder-for-hire that had sprung out of XCL-Jooce. A whistleblower on a Mars-based operation had turned up executed in New Angeles. No one in homicide had wanted the case because it was politically dangerous and filled with lies. Shelly and I had taken it. She'd nearly gotten killed on two occasions before we were led through a predetermined inquiry that fell into place too quickly.

Just as we'd started making our case, neither of us convinced that we were on the right track, the person of interest in the investigation hung herself. The NAPD commissioner had ordered the case closed despite the misgivings that Shelly and I had made her aware of, citing that our time would be better spent elsewhere. Since we'd found no other leads, we'd had no choice but to walk away. Anytime we devoted too many hours to an investigation, our caseload started to back up. Murder was a fast-paced business in New Angeles. Shelly had kept the file as a cold case and revisited it periodically, but we'd never gotten anywhere on it.

A young female server stepped up to us. She wore an older hairstyle, a shimmering green swimsuit with matching elbow-length gloves, and thigh-high boots. "Welcome to the Inn of Two Moons. May your experience be out of this world. Where would you like to be seated?"

"The bar," Hayim answered.

That was a primary hotspot for mercs without contracts who were looking for work. Exploratory conversation and opening bids were often placed there. Tables and booths were for mercs who already had connections.

The server led us over to the bar, narrowly avoiding one of the 2.2 meter tall Robby Robots as it rolled by on tracked footing. Instead of claw appendages at the end of its arms, it had juice dispensers. Lights flashed in its sloped head, but I knew its logic circuits were not kept and they were only for show.

Hayim sat at the bar. He was getting around much easier since I had replaced the knee ball joint.

The bartender was another young-looking woman but she moved with experience and confidence that suggested she was older than she looked. "What's your pleasure?"

"Mandarin orange and pineapple," Hayim replied. "Vodka."

XCLJooce shipped flavored powder off-planet instead of liquid product.

"New Moscow vodka or domestic?"

Domestic vodka was manufactured at the potato ag-bubbles, a side industry that had taken shape from the moment the first potatoes had been dug up. Off-world vodka was expensive because it had to be carried in a liquid state.

"Domestic. And I'd like the meatloaf platter with all the trimmings."

"Of course." She turned her attention to me. "Anything for you?"

"No, thank you."

Leaving us, already filing the order subvocally through her helmet, she approached a lanky man dressed in simleather and wearing weapons. Carrying firearms wasn't discouraged in Podkayne colony except in certain areas where rich off-worlders lived while in the megapolis.

The man looked middle-aged and sported a heavy beard shadow. Both eyes were cybered, but only someone looking for that would know. They were a little too clear and the pupils adjusted faster than a normal human's would.

Hayim and I didn't speak. Getting connected to a mercenary group was a waiting game and might take days. When the meal arrived—all of it really soy-manufactured to look like different food items—Hayim dug in with gusto.

I waited. No one approached us, which was exactly how Hayim thought it would go.

"He's right," Shelly said. "Until you become part of the surroundings instead of sticking out as new additions, no one is going to enter into a conversation with you. Too many local undercover police and terrorist groups have tried to get into the pro-Earth mercenary circles."

I sat quietly, taking in the local vidcast, learning that more and more civilian unrest was fomenting in the colonies.

"Podkayne police aren't admitting to speculation about the missing weapons shipment," a svelte nosie stated on the vidcast, "but we know they have a lot to think about." She stood in front of a holo of the train wreck. "All of the weapons that we have seen are reputed to be knockoffs of munitions manufacturing giant Skorpios Defense Systems, owned by Argus, Inc."

She touched the screen and flicked her hand, magnifying a large hand-held blaster.

"This weapon is a blatant reproduction of SDS's Indra model." She gestured again and an image of a real Indra appeared next to the knockoff. The only difference was the lack of a serial number and branding information. "This weapon has been linked to a police raid on an illegal arms manufacturing site on the Moon seven months ago."

Vid of the raid played, showing NAPD officers carrying crates of weapons out of the weapons plant I had found while looking for the people that had killed Gordon Holder, the CEO of SDS. The vid was cut to only a few seconds.

"As you can see," the nosie went on while the screen behind

her changed to the train wreck again, "not all of those weapons were found on the Moon. Some of them have found their way here, and a few people believe that Mars was the intended destination for this illegal arms franchise."

The vid shifted to a female politician on the steps of the Interplanetary Courthouse in Bradbury colony. A crawler announced her name as Bradbury Senator Coleen Wentworth. She had a short brunette cut that framed her face and the tattoo of a black-bladed broadsword above and below her right eye. The tattoo marked her as pro-Mars without being dismissive of Earth's interests in the colonies. Few politicians wore such distinct reminders of where their loyalties lie, but Senator Wentworth had no hesitation it seemed.

"Of course those weapons were intended for Mars," Senator Wentworth said. "The Martian transit authorities have verified that the shipments were going to various pro-Earth facilities in Podkayne colony. I, and several other politicians and police commissioners and military leaders, believe that the weapons were going to be dispersed from Podkayne throughout the colonies for the express purpose of arming employees. Rest assured, this investigation is only getting started. We're far from finished with this."

The vidcast opened on the nosie again. "Senator Wentworth is known for her scathing attitude toward Earth corps. For another take on the situation regarding those weapons, we interviewed transit authority liaison, Tars Heinrich."

As the vid cut away again, I accessed history on Heinrich and discovered that he was a native Martian citizen but was heavily franchised—according to muckraking nosies—to Earth corps. Heinrich was one of the go-to individuals to get pro-Earth legislation regarding shipments. He was slim and sported a greenish tint to his skin as well as body mods that included lower incisors that jutted up over his upper lip.

He stood in front of the Bradbury Transit Authority building on the red land. His presence there without an envirosuit gave away the fact that he'd been holoed in.

"As you know," Heinrich said, "Mars is my birth planet. Less than a quarter of the people living on Mars can make that claim."

ONLY BECAUSE OF THE ENFORCED POPULATION GUIDELINES AND THE STEADY INFLUX OF OFF-WORLDERS, a crawler announced as it spun across the screen. *EARTH WILL NOT RULE US FOREVER. WE SHALL OVERCOME.*

"Hey," the man in simleather shouted angrily. "Get that drek off the vid."

"It's not us," the bartender called back. "The vidcast at that end got hacked."

Most of the other patrons at the Inn of Two Moons raised their voices in angry protest as well. The bar was definitely pro-Earth. Hayim watched it all with an air of disinterest, but I knew his sympathies lay with Mars. He was only there to help me locate a mercenary group who might lead me to the Chimeras.

"That shipment of illegal weapons was just that," Heinrich went on, "illegal weapons. Merchants of death trading on the fears of pro-Earth and pro-Mars sentiments were hoping to make a fortune off those weapons. But we stopped that today. Those weapons have been taken into custody and will never find their way into the hands of people."

THEY'RE TRYING TO KEEP REAL MARTIANS UN-ARMED. HEINRICH AND HIS PRO-EARTH TOADIES ONLY WANT THEIR SECMEN TO HAVE WEAPONS.

Finished with his meal, Hayim pushed his plate away. He glanced at me. "Do you know what you're getting into out here?"

"Yes." The civil unrest manifested in the people around me. But my thoughts were on Mara. Somewhere out there, she was depending on me to rescue her.

* * *

We were at dinner, Mara and I, when we met Conway Gerrold. I sat at a table in a restaurant bigger and more luxurious than any I had ever before patronized. I was there under protest, but Mara had insisted on taking me out. She had been locked up in her lab for the last week since our return to Earth.

I was not at my best. Although I had trained for the heavier gravity on Mars, training for it and being subjected to it twenty-four/seven was much different. I spent four hours a day in a gym trying to get my edge back. I was not used to being so weak and so easily fatigued.

As a general rule, Martian musculature was genetically coded for heavier gravity than on that planet, but gaining the appropriate muscle mass needed the requisite exposure to the higher gravity. I struggled to build myself up and was exceeding what my physical trainers thought I would attain, but I was still too slow for my personal taste. I was a man used to living on his physical attributes.

John Rath had tried to prepare me for my transition to Earth. He had wanted me at my best because Mara Parker's life might depend on that. I had listened, but I had not accepted how weak I would become.

Now that Mara was out of the lab, away from all the coding, she was different. She talked to me about movies and art and places she had traveled to. It was like being with two different women, but I loved the challenge of keeping up with both.

She stopped herself after a bit and smiled ruefully. "I'm sorry."

"For what?" I asked.

"I didn't bring you out here to talk your ears off. I've read that people who have lived their lives on Mars aren't used to as much audio output as we have on Earth."

That was true. Although I had spent time in the colony domes, I had spent much of my adult life in the harsh Martian wilderness in combat-ready envirosuits. There, communications were routed through a helmet and I had control over how much or how little volume I wanted to deal with.

There was no damper for the myriad noises and conversations around us. The tables in the restaurant had come with white noise generators but I had turned ours off so I would be more attuned to our environment. I didn't expect anyone hoping to harm Mara would announce his or her presence, but I hoped learning all the noises would help me sort out any that might be threatening.

I sipped the wine she had ordered to be sociable, but I nursed it. She was already on her third glass while I was on my first. "I love hearing you talk."

Her cheeks colored just a little and a smile dimpled her cheeks. "Thank you, but you don't have to be so polite."

"I'm telling you the truth." My attraction to Mara Parker had grown over the months I had spent getting ready for her return to Earth. I wasn't certain if she knew that I felt that way. I didn't know what she would do if she found out.

"I don't normally take employees out to quiet dinners, either." She put her elbows on the table and picked up her wine glass. She watched me as she sipped from it.

"I'm enjoying dinner as well."

She sighed. "I didn't mean to refer to you as an employee, either."

"But that's what I am."

She looked like she wanted to say more, but we were interrupted. "Simon, you've got a man headed in your direction." Kendra Robeson's voice carried easily to my earpiece.

Mara might have taken me to dinner, but I had assigned a three-man team to accompany us. Getting dinner reservations for them had been expensive and tactically challenging.

I held up my left forefinger, signaling Mara that I had to attend to her security. Nervousness tightened her eyes, but otherwise she made no overt changes. She had placed her life in my hands and trusted me completely.

Six meters away, closing at a non-threatening pace but with hostility and determination making his steps sharp and steady, a man dressed in a tailored, double-breasted suit approached our table.

"Do you have an ID on the man?" I asked Kendra.

Mara answered at the same time my second-in-command did. "His name's Conway Gerrold." Mara frowned.

"He's a Human First representative," Kendra added. "Guy has a history of aggressive behavior toward Haas-Bioroid and other bioroid and clone manufacturers."

"How aggressive?"

"He doesn't do any of the work himself, but he's been charged with destruction of property twice and conspiracy to commit destruction of property four times. None of those charges have stuck."

"Is he alone?"

"Negative. There are four bodyguards seated at his table."

"Are they still seated?"

"They are."

By that time, Gerrold had reached our table, and I had my right hand on the small needler holstered at my hip. I made sure the weapon didn't show and that I didn't look hostile in any way.

Gerrold dismissed me immediately and focused on Mara. His wavy blond hair fell down in front of his face and made him look younger than I guessed that he was.

"Ms. Parker," he addressed Mara.

She cut him off instantly but remained smiling. "*Dr*. Parker, if you please, Mr. Gerrold."

Gerrold hesitated for a moment, then nodded. "Dr. Parker. I was not aware that we had met."

"We haven't, but I know who you are and what your platform is, and I know that we'll never agree on anything you want to talk about."

Gerrold frowned at that. "I wished to talk to you about the new neural channeling techniques you're developing."

Mara pushed herself back in her seat, making herself more of a target. The black dress she wore had armor woven into it. I'd made certain of that. But with the bare shoulders and cleavage, there was a lot of vulnerable flesh open to anyone that wanted to hurt her.

"I'm not going to discuss anything I'm working on with you, Mr. Gerrold. Certainly not something that would be highly classified material."

"Highly classified or not, secrets have a way of getting out into the megapolis." He gazed at her with smug disapproval. "I've heard that you're going to be able to bring the dead back to life with the programming you're working on."

"You do hear the most interesting things." Mara ran an immaculate forefinger around the rim of her wine glass.

"Then what I've heard is true?"

"No."

Gerrold grimaced. "You would lie to me anyway, wouldn't you?"

I stood up then because I could no longer tolerate his abusive tone. I kept my hand on the needler and put a hand in the center of Gerrold's chest.

"Don't touch me!" Gerrold tried to brush my hand away, but I didn't let him.

"Dr. Parker has made clear her wish to be alone, Mr. Gerrold." I spoke politely. While working with Rath, we had sometimes done close-in bodyguard work on people we had to maintain civility around. At least until the bullets started flying and laser beams started frying air.

"You're not going to get rid of me that easily." Gerrold struggled against me, but I moved him back a step, just enough to let him know I could do it.

Behind him, I saw the four bodyguards start to get up from their table. Kendra and Jonas Salter and Anil Patel, all chimera mercs that did work for John Rath on Earth, closed in on the men, lighting them up with targeting beams to let them know getting involved at this point was less than ideal.

"Humans aren't going to get pushed out of this world just because you people can invent bioroids and clones," Gerrold said loudly. "We were here first, and we'll be here after you people stop playing God. What do you hope to achieve by bringing the dead back to life to toil on in jobs that real humans should be holding?"

Mara wasn't bringing the dead back to life. Her neural channeling programming was just better than anything else currently on the market. But the idea that MirrorMorph, Inc. had found a way to replace living people with bioroids was a favorite conspiracy theory of some of the Human First members.

I pushed with a little force at that point, striking Gerrold just under the sternum and stealing his breath away. I leaned down and spoke into his ear as he struggled to regain his breath. "Leave. Now. Or I'm going to throw you out. Walking out under your own power will be a lot more dignified." I popped him under the sternum again, robbing him of the breath he'd just gotten back.

Wheezing, aware that his bodyguards weren't there, Gerrold turned and went. He stopped a safe distance away to throw more menacing threats, but he went.

I turned to Mara. "I apologize."

"That wasn't your fault."

"I know. I apologize for insisting that we leave now." I held out my hand to assist her to her feet.

For a moment, Mara looked as though she was going to argue, then she took my hand. "It's a shame we have to leave. The desserts here are really good."

"Maybe another time." Folding her arm under my left arm so I could guide her with my body, I headed for the door.

Chapter Twenty-Four

Returning from Simon Blake's memory, I sat in the darkness of the rented room I shared with Hayim. The memory of Mara carried echoes of emotion that felt deeper than I'd experienced so far. I didn't know whether that was because I thought I might be getting closer to her, or if it was because of all the violence that the day had brought.

The need to find her grew stronger within me.

"Easy, partner," Shelly said. "You're working the only trail you have available to you right now. Jonas Salter told you that the answer lay with the Chimeras. Find them and you'll be closer to rescuing her."

"Rumor has it that the Chimeras are dead or disbanded."

"A rumor didn't kill me, Drake. A Chimera did."

I didn't point out that the man who had killed her had been an ex-Chimera.

"Maybe," Shelly said. "Don't take anything at face value. Follow your leads. I taught you that."

I knew she was right, so I accessed the meetbox I shared with Floyd 2X3A7C and found him waiting there for me.

* * *

Floyd looked up as I arrived. It was a purely human behavior. He had the same 360-degree vision that I had. His fingers moved rapidly over his rosary beads.

"Good evening, Drake," he greeted.

"Good evening, Floyd."

We stood in the holo of the Jonas Salter crime scene. His crumpled body lay where it had been. I thought of the newest memory I'd had of him, of how he had been there for me right after I'd arrived on Earth to protect Mara Parker. I wondered why I could not remember when he and I had first met, and I felt that I was missing something. John Rath had known Jonas before I had.

"If you are wondering if I have any news regarding Jonas Salter's murder, I do not. Detective Blaine and I remain stymied, but we are pursuing leads."

"I know you are doing your best. However, I have another name I would like information on."

"Of course."

"A Human First representative named Conway Gerrold."

"Give me a moment."

I walked over to survey Jonas's body, but I didn't see anything that stirred memories or gave me an indication of who had killed him.

Floyd said, "Conway Gerrold was killed by an unknown assailant eleven years ago on March 20."

That was a turn I had not expected. I had searched for Gerrold on Mars's databases, but the man hadn't been mentioned there. With the lag time between Mars and Earth, I hadn't wanted to try searching the databases there in case I ended up getting found out.

"What happened?" I asked.

The holo scene around us winked out of existence and was replaced by a rooftop scene where a sleek black hopper hovered and waited. A moment later, Conway Gerrold stepped from the building accompanied by the same four bodyguards Simon Blake had seen him with at the restaurant. The date was only nine days after that encounter and that made me suspicious.

"Gerrold was en route to a meeting with some friends," Floyd told me.

"Human First?"

"Personal friends." Floyd was quiet a moment. "However, those personal friends were and yet remain Human First members."

"I see."

In the holo, Gerrold climbed into the hopper. I recognized the New Angeles megapolis around him, the deep canyons of the city inky black in the residential areas of the towers but lit up with luminescent neon colors where the clubs were.

The hopper had barely taken off when the vehicle suddenly exploded and turned into a fireball. Debris and flaming body parts shot out across the open air to drop into the street below while the largest pieces of the hopper chassis crashed onto the rooftop.

"What happened?" I asked as I watched fire drones speed out to quench the flames.

"According to the crime scene analysis, someone planted a bomb aboard Gerrold's hopper. You do not remember this?"

"Why should I?"

"Because Simon Blake is listed in the field notes as a person of interest. He was questioned on four separate occasions by detectives regarding a confrontation he'd had with Gerrold nine days before."

"I'm aware of the confrontation."

"You do not remember planting a bomb aboard Gerrold's hopper?"

"No." I was also bothered by the fact that I didn't *not* remember doing that either. Had Simon Blake perceived Conway Gerrold as that much of a threat to Mara Parker?

"Also interesting is the fact that you were questioned by Detective Shelly Nolan."

That was even more unexpected. "May I have a copy of that report?"

"Of course." Floyd uploaded the file to the meetbox and I downloaded it to my PAD on Mars. Although the connection was a little risky, I deemed the acquisition of the file worthy of the jeopardy.

"Thank you for this," I told Floyd.

He nodded and his fingers tapped across his rosary like a spider's legs. "Of course. How goes your investigation on Mars?"

"I'm trying to find the chimera mercenaries and John Rath now."

"Events have gotten dangerous on Mars. The civil unrest is in all the media at this point."

"I'm aware of that. The discovery of that hidden weapons plant has become more important as well. Have there been any further developments on the investigation?"

"Not as yet. I am keeping watch over it as well. When I have news I will let you know."

I waved and was startled to discover how natural the gesture seemed. Floyd responded in kind, but I knew that he thought it was strange as well from the way he cocked his head. That too was a human gesture he had picked up that he might not have noticed. Body language was something we were both programmed to emulate, though why we had to do it with each other was not logical. Perhaps it was because both of us were aware we were overstepping the parameters we had been designed for.

I blanked out of the meetbox before he could ask the questions that I knew he had to have.

* * *

Back on Mars, I sat in the dark room and found Shelly standing against the wall where I had left her. "Why didn't you tell me that you had questioned Simon Blake about the murder of Conway Gerrold?"

"Why would I have told you? At the time I—and you—didn't know there was a connection between you and Simon Blake."

"What can you tell me about the investigation?"

Shelly frowned. "That was a long time ago."

I realized again that she wasn't the Shelly I had lost. She was only a shadow I had somehow created to help guide me. *She* wouldn't know more about the Gerrold murder investigation until I did.

I opened the file and began to familiarize myself with the case. I sifted through the crime scene reports and the vid files of the interview. Simon Blake's interview was the fourth one in the file.

* * *

"State your name for the record, please."

This time I was not Simon Blake. I stood behind Shelly Nolan, who was on the other side of the transplas table in the featureless interview room. I approached Simon, even laid my hand on his shoulder, but I couldn't get inside him. I was trapped outside his thoughts and I didn't know why.

I avoided an endless logic loop, but only just, choosing to focus instead on the interview.

Shelly was much younger. Her marriage and her children lay before her. She looked young and innocent. I had seen her face in holos at her house, and in records at the PD, but I had never noticed her in such an intimate way.

She was slimmer, almost to the point of being underweight for department regs. She looked elegant in her grey suit and her red hair was longer than she had worn it when we had partnered. She'd had her children at that time, her daughter Susan had been only a few months old then, and she'd had less time for herself. Looking at her there, I wondered if she mourned the lack of time for herself when her work and her family consumed so much of her day.

I didn't think so. If she had, she'd never mentioned it. I focused on the interview.

"My name is Simon Blake." Simon sounded matter-of-fact.

I watched his eyes and listened to the timbre in his voice and detected no falsehood. But I knew him better than Shelly had at that moment. I knew he was capable of being unreliable in his narrative. He had been trained by John Rath.

"You're from Mars?"

"Yes."

"What are your present duties here in New Angeles?"

"I provide security for MirrorMorph, Inc. That's all in my file, Detective."

"I'm well aware of that, Mr. Blake."

"This is redundant questioning."

"A lot of police work is. I'm sure the same can be said of the security field. Constantly checking and re-checking perimeters, safety measures, protocol."

Simon smiled then and I knew that he approved of Shelly Nolan. I found that satisfactory. "I stand corrected."

Shelly waved a hand over the holo projector built into the table. A twenty centimeter image of Gerrold appeared above the table's surface. "Did you know Conway Gerrold prior to killing him?"

Simon's grin widened and his dark eyes sparkled. "Actually that's two questions, Detective." He counted them off on his fingers for emphasis. "One, I did not know Conway Gerrold. Two, I did not kill Conway Gerrold."

Shelly waved her hand again and a sec vid from the restaurant where Gerrold had approached Mara Parker played, showing Gerrold talking to her. Since we—or rather, *Simon* and Mara—hadn't had the white noise generator at the table switched on, the conversation had been recorded.

When the recording had played through to the point when Simon had offered to throw Gerrold out, Shelly froze the holo with Simon standing in Gerrold's face. "Did that sound threatening to you? Because it did to me."

Simon pursed his lips and shook his head. "Not my part of the conversation. I believe I was being very civil under the circumstances."

"You were, Mr. Blake. Every centimeter the professional."

"Thank you."

"I was talking about Gerrold's part of the discussion. Do you feel that he was threatening Ms. Parker?"

"No."

"No?"

Simon smiled and laced his hands behind his head. It was something I had seen John Rath do a number of times when he had talked with Simon during the memories I had of him. Rath used his posture to speak volumes, and Simon was emulating that now.

"No, I didn't think Gerrold was threatening Ms. Parker."

"How am I supposed to believe you?"

"Gerrold was still alive when he left the club," Simon said softly. "If I'd perceived him as a threat, I would have killed him. Or at the very least, I would have crippled him. That's how I handle threats."

"I understand that you also blow them up." Shelly waved a hand over the projector and a holo of the chimera mercs in action sparkled into view.

The soldiers in the vid wore combat hardsuits, but the stylized chimera was clearly visible on the scarred chests and backs of the armor. I tried to remember the battle and thought I caught a faint hint of it somewhere in Simon Blake's memories. We had been contracted to protect a supply shipment to the new colony. The megapolis government had been expecting terrorists to attempt to destroy the shipment. Instead we had been attacked by thieves. That had made defending the shipment easier, but the action had still been bloody and we had lost three good people. In response, the chimera group had killed every last would-be thief with extreme prejudice.

"This is your unit, correct?" Shelly remained focused on Simon, not on the action taking place on the holo.

Simon didn't look at the battle either. I knew he was studying Shelly for weaknesses, measuring her strength. Standing there watching both of them engaged in a battle of wits was uncomfortable.

"You know it's my unit, Detective. Otherwise you wouldn't be showing that to me."

Waving her hand over the projector, Shelly stopped the vid again, freezing a hopper in the air just as it started to come apart from a direct hit from a shoulder-mounted rocket launcher. The hopper had broken apart and the rocket explosion looked like it was burning a hole in the craft.

"It *is* your unit," Shelly said. "More than that, that—" she pointed at the figure in the black combat hardsuit "—is you."

"Is it? All of those mercs look the same to me. That's how we keep from shooting each other out in the field. I'm sure the police wear uniforms and hardsuit strike gear for the same reason."

"You were identified by someone who was there."

"Who?" Simon smiled again. "The jackers we went up against all died. The Chimeras don't give up fellow soldiers. Whoever took this vid couldn't have identified whoever was in that suit." He shrugged. "Nice try, Detective, but no prize. No one identified me as the rocket launcher operator in this vid, and I didn't kill Gerrold."

* * *

The case file remained inconclusive. No one was ever arrested for murdering Conway Gerrold and his bodyguards. Human First had hounded the NAPD, but the investigation went nowhere. As it turned out, Simon Blake had an alibi for the time Gerrold was killed: he had been with Mara Parker. She had vouched for him.

I still didn't know if that was true. If Simon believed Gerrold was a threat to her, I believed that Simon would have killed him without compunction.

Still in the darkness but aware now that the sun was rising, I sat and listened to Hayim sleep, knowing that he wouldn't be up for hours. I tried to dredge up more of Simon Blake's memories now that there were even more questions about his culpability in events on Earth and Mars, but they remained beyond my reach.

Chapter Twenty-Five

Hayim got up at 1200 Mars Standard, which surprised me. After the previous day we'd had, I'd expected him to sleep much longer. But by 1300, we were breaking into a small shop he assured me belonged to a forger who specialized in mercenary e-IDs. The shop was closed. According to Hayim, it was only ever open when the forger was doing business. Most of that business took place late at night.

Uncomfortable with breaking into the shop hidden in an alley and three floors below ground, I checked the background on the premises and on the woman who owned them. Lara Guignard, who Hayim promised owned the shop, had a past history of brushes with the law over e-doc discrepancy, but none of her arrests had ever resulted in a conviction.

According to megapolis records, the shop didn't exist. The forty square meters were supposedly taken up by the Indian laundry that fronted it and a recycling shop. Guignard owned both of those on paper, but it took some inspired digging to discover that.

The second underground floor was taken up by a transient

motel that specialized in migrant farm workers that floated through the colonies during harvest season. Most of the colonies managed to stagger their harvests so the workers could go from ag-bubble to ag-bubble, constantly staying on the move. Crop production depended on human labor because it was cheaper than purchasing bioroids or clones or even robots to do the job. Earth corps kept trying to undermine the local labor population, but hadn't been able to offer a better system. There were some valid arguments that Earth corps didn't really want to replace human workers. They just threatened those migrant laborers enough to exploit them further.

We checked into one of the motel rooms above Guignard's shop. Hayim paid with a private credstick and the young man at the desk didn't even raise his head from his PAD. I scanned the PAD briefly to see if it linked into any sec vids overseeing the rooms, but it didn't. Privacy laws weren't the same in transient quarters, and Earth corps didn't announce when they were spying.

Corp human intelligence gathering on Mars as well as Earth operated everywhere, gathering information from human sources and projected trends. They were always open for business. Execs sometimes forgot that flesh and blood laborers weren't as docile as machines or clones. Every biological thing on any planet had an agenda. Gossip was as good as cred in some circles.

The rooms were small and rough. Graffiti and children's drawings covered the hallway walls as well as inside the rooms. The drawings usually centered around family or activities, and the graffiti was angry rhetoric.

Hayim swiped the room card and we entered. Instead of clothing and personal belongings in his backpack, he carried an industrial mining laser we had picked up from a pawn shop on the way over. The laser was small enough to isolate pockets of ore and to be carried in a backpack.

Once we were locked inside the room, Hayim pulled the laser out and set it up. I took out the power cord and hooked it up, then took out the cheap holo player we'd also bought and set it up as well. When I had a vidcast going that showed the turmoil breaking loose in the colonies, Hayim pulled the laser to the center of the floor.

"You're sure there are no squealies in the room below?" I asked.

Hayim looked up at me and shook his head. "No. I'm not. In fact, there probably are. That's why you're here. See if you can sniff them out and shut them down."

I walked over the room, tracing the dimensions of the small space below me. I found three squealie hot spots and hacked into them with my PAD. Getting through their defenses was labor intensive, but I managed. One of my subroutines for the NAPD had required me to be able to break and enter.

"Police officers are one step removed from criminals when you think about it." Shelly stood over against the far wall and watched us. "That's why so many police officers make such good lawbreakers if they decide to go that way."

All of the squealies were tied to a comm node that broadcast an alert to a single PAD. I tried to ascertain who the unit belonged to but was unable to secure that knowledge.

"Doesn't matter who they're tied to," Hayim said. "We can assume the PAD is Guignard's or belongs to a secman she's hired for the job. The main thing is that we don't set them off getting inside or while we're in. Are they disabled?"

I nodded.

Without another word, Hayim sliced through the floor.

* * *

Minutes later, I watched the room and the squealies while Hayim used the equipment. I also hacked into the sec cams that watched over the alley entrance that offered direct access to the forger's shop.

Seven hours passed. During that time there were seventeen false alarms on the alley cam, and I had to ping the squealies' response code four times when Guignard or her secman checked on the shop. The pings came at regular intervals, so I felt certain it was a pre-set sec check, not an honest inquiry.

When he was finished, Hayim had two e-IDs, one for him and one for me. He merely reactivated one of his old aliases for himself, but he created a new one for me, which would not draw undue attention because mercs expected bioroids to get "sanitized"—lost in the system.

"You're a McDreamy model," Hayim said as I lifted him from the floor below. "Good with medicine but not so much with bedside manner. Can you do that?"

The McDreamy models were based on an old 20th century sensie that had a cult following even today. Haas-Bioroid had capitalized on that when they released their med units.

"I can do that," I replied.

"Good. Then let's get out of here, get back to our room so I can rest, then let's see about getting hired."

* * *

Securing a contract for a merc unit took five days of sitting at the Inn of Two Moons. As a bioroid, I did not get anxious or bored. I simply sat and organized my files, drew down more reports of the rising violence escalating between the Earth corps, pro-Earth Martians, pro-Mars supporters, terrorists, and the criminals that profited from being in the gaps between all of those. The body count in the colonies continually rose, as did the need inside me to do something.

"Just wait," Shelly advised me. "This is all tied in together somehow. You know that's true."

I did, but waiting became increasingly difficult. The thing that most kept me from acting was certain knowledge that I would be arrested the moment I was identified by the authorities—*any* authorities. I told myself that I was better free and in reserve as I was.

Believing that was hard.

* * *

On the fifth day, however, Hayim and I met with Liam Rector at one of the back tables in the Inn of Two Moons.

Rector was a fireplug of a man in his middle years. Pink, ragged scars showed on the left side of his face, announcing that he'd been the recent recipient of the outer fringes of a shrapnel burst. According to the med subroutines I had jacked from the Net, the wound was no more than three weeks old.

With quiet contemplation, Rector regarded us with his mismatched eyes. Both were organic, so he'd received a transplant somewhere along the way. Both eyes moved well together, so it had been a good replacement.

"I'm with the Screaming Mimis." Rector grimaced. "Not my name. We're Earth corp sponsored and they wanted to brand us. Have you heard of us?"

I had. The Screaming Mimis were a pro-Earth merc unit and had been on-planet for five years. They had fought in several skirmishes and held their own, but they weren't heavy hitters. They were average in every way and usually regulated to small protection contracts.

Hayim nodded. "I know who you are."

"Then you know we're select when it comes to choosing people to round out a roster." Rector tried to say that with authority, but Hayim and I both knew he was lying.

"I'm looking for work," Hayim said. "I'm not going to be too particular. You guys have a rep as a meat grinder unit. You put people on the ground and a scary percentage of them die. Don't try to gild the lily with me."

Rector frowned and spat a curse. "Meat grinder or not, we're not in the habit of hiring ancient half-men." He nodded at me. "We want the McDreamy."

Hayim stared back at Rector's mismatched eyes. "We come as a team. You want him, you get me as part of the package."

Rector swiveled his attention to me. "Is that true?"

I didn't hesitate. At least, I didn't show any sign of hesitation, but that was only because I processed information and variables so much faster than a human could. "We come as a package."

Cursing again, Rector brought out his PAD and pulled up contracts. He glared at Hayim during the process, but Hayim didn't care. In the end, Rector had no choice.

Once our contracts were sealed, Rector gave us the location where we'd be meeting up, deposited our signing bonus to cred-sticks that he gave to us, and headed upstairs with a gynoid that had caught his eye.

Hayim looked at me. "We're mercs, McDreamy." He cursed. "I don't know whether to celebrate or throw up."

"You could have stayed out of this," I pointed out.

"And do what? Sit here until I run out of cred or get busted by Martian police or military looking to roust pro-Earth mercs?" Hayim shook his head. "No, thanks. I'd rather take my chances out there in the killing fields. I'm more at home there." He slapped his bionic legs. "Besides, after you reworked the legs, I've got to admit, I'm feeling pretty spry."

"I do not want you to get killed."

"Then make sure you stay close, McDreamy. Keep me patched up and keep blood in me if I take a hit."

Chapter Twenty-Six

Keeping Hayim alive was difficult. Keeping all of the Screaming Mimis alive was impossible.

Three days later, we were north of Podkayne colony running security for limited cargo routes. Terrorist forces or pro-Mars mercs were taking munitions shipments pro-Earth corps tried to get into Podkayne colony. The soldiers in my unit speculated that this meant the weapons from the train robbery had been intended for Podkayne's pro-Earth sec teams.

There was no way to know for certain. Even if one of the megacorps like Argus, Inc. had stood up and reported that they had shipped the weapons from an illegal subsidiary, no one would have believed them. Lies and accusations and crisis management ran rampant in the vidcasts. There were more lies than truths, but no one could pin down the truth.

On the fifth day, the cargo shipment the Screaming Mimis were escorting from a handoff by another merc team got hit in a surprise attack at dawn. The announcement came when a salvo of rockets took out the lead crawler in the convoy, crippling the craft and dumping it in the middle of the passage we were following down out of the mountains.

Our unit leader, Major Carroll Randall, had debated taking the passage because of the probable choke points, but trying to go across the expanse of ancient sea bottoms filled with powdery red sand would have been just as risky. Probably more so because the sand would get sucked up into engines as they dumped heat into the chill environment or into the leg joints that propelled us.

Our crawler's pilot screamed curses as she struggled to find some way out of the passage. However, on either side of us steep plunges of hundreds of meters led down to the powdery sand that wouldn't be much more crash friendly than rock. Even in the lesser gravity, the crawler wouldn't withstand a sudden impact like that with all the mass it had.

As soon as the crippled crawler flipped over onto its side, a fresh salvo of rockets burned across the sky and hit the vehicle again. This time there wasn't just the first series of explosions. Another set of explosions followed almost immediately, letting me know the second round had been sabots, designed to penetrate a target vehicle and deliver a fissionable payload into its interior, eliminating all the squishy targets within.

While our pilot jockeyed with the controls and yelled at gunners to take their positions, I grabbed a backpack, slid into it, and fisted another medical bag as well. I barely fit into the vehicle's airlock but I squeezed in and punched the cycle button.

The air around me was sucked away and redistributed inside the crawler. The only reason the crew didn't stay in envirosuits was because the crawlers came equipped with carbon dioxide scrubbers that stretched the oxygen. No one wanted to be out on patrol and run out of air.

Once the airlock was a vacuum, the platform spun and the outer hatch irised open. I leaped out, making the three meter drop easily, hitting the ground running, taking five-meter long strides.

A trio of hoppers flamed by and dropped Taejo mines while

our crawler gunners filled the thin atmosphere with anti-aircraft fire. Flak hung in the sky like immense bruises. All of the attack hoppers emerged from the deadly cloud unscathed.

I sprinted toward the stricken crawler, going over the specs in my mind. The crawler carried a ten-man crew: a pilot and navigator, four gunners, and four loaders. All of those lives were currently in jeopardy.

Welby 4JU3LI, another med-programmed bioroid, also ran toward the overturned crawler. The Welby managed four strides before a Taejo mine struck the ground and unloaded its deadly cargo of monofilament wire. Transfixed by the wire, lifted from the ground a meter, the Welby kicked frantically for a few seconds, then ceased to function as its operating system went inert.

I took cover behind a stand of rock that had slanted facets. Still, three of the wires pierced the rock and perforated my chassis a few centimeters. Nothing vital was hit.

Standing, I looked over the battleground and discovered our attackers had expertly placed the Taejo mines. Nine of our fifteen escort vehicles had been rendered useless in the initial attack without a single loss of soldier or vehicle for them.

Cries reached my comm. "Medic! *Medic!*"

Scarlet dots filled my GPS overlay, letting me know where the calls were coming from.

I ran, heading for the initial vehicle because if the crew aboard that one might be made ready, they could perhaps remove the crawler from the passage and allow the other crawlers to maneuver.

"Where did they get those Taejo mines?" a woman demanded over the comm-link. "Those aren't permitted in combat."

"You want to call foul?" someone else asked. "I don't think those guys care. I'm sitting in the middle of six dead mates with Taejo wire through both of my legs."

I marked that transmission on my comm, pinged it back to its source, and hoped that the assessment was not realistic.

"Medic!"

I reached the downed crawler, clambered on top of it, slapped my hand against the airlock controls, and pulsed the override frequency through my palm. I laid in the airlock at an angle, unable to keep from thinking how much it reminded me of the coffin I had seen Shelly in. I brushed the image from my thoughts as the airlock cycled and spun me into the vehicle.

Pinging the med stats of the combat suits of all ten mercs in the unit, I discovered two of them had expired. Three others were severely wounded from shrapnel, and one of those was going into cardiac arrest. All of the others had been injured, mostly cuts and bruises, and three of them were leaking air from their envirosuits.

I threw the backpack and medkit onto the floor, opening them up fast as I could. Seconds measured human lives now. Using spray epoxy, I patched three rents in the heart victim's suit, ascertained that his injuries were within my capabilities to salvage him, and pinged his suit to restart his heart. The first attempt failed, and blood squirted from a wound on his back.

I rolled him over and discovered a length of shrapnel jutting from his side. Laying my right hand next to the wound, I flicked the thirteen centimeter piece of plasteel with my left forefinger and used a program for a limited sonogram subroutine to ascertain the length. The piece projected a full centimeter into his right lung. Blood was filling the lung even then.

Reaching into the medkit, I drew out a surgical laser as I withdrew the piece of shrapnel. Digging into the wound, I seared the lung wound closed, did the same for the outer flesh, then took a vacu stem line from the kit, readied it, and punched it through his chest into his lung. Triggering the vacu program, the line started pumping blood from his lung. I used the spray epoxy to seal the suit around the stem line as his blood bubbled out of the lung.

I hit his suit again, triggering the built-in defibrillator which shocked his heart. It started on the first time. The pulse was weak and thready, but it was there.

I moved to the next man, sorting quickly through his injuries. I left his helmet intact, then opened the suit briefly to reveal a laceration across his stomach that had nearly disemboweled him. I seared the skin together and pulsed a command through the hardsuit to immobilize him so he couldn't move around and re-open the wound.

He started trying to fight me as the air evacuated from his helmet and left him not enough oxygen to satisfy his needs.

"Easy, Corporal Mullins. I have you."

"Can't…breathe."

"You will in a moment. Be patient." I knew that the advice was wasted. There was no way a human who thought he was asphyxiating would be able to be patient.

Once the hardsuit locked down as I'd instructed, Mullins could no longer fight with much effect. The lack of oxygen triggered hypoxia and his consciousness started to fade.

I repaired his suit, made it airtight, then signaled the suit to release reserve air into the system to keep him alive. The blue coloration left his features almost immediately. I triggered a round of medication to ease his pain as well, followed by narcotics that would alleviate his anxiety.

I moved to the next man, listening to the cries of the other wounded in the other vehicles, knowing I would never be able to get to them all in time.

A harsh voice cut through the comm. "Screaming Mimis, stand down and abandon your vehicles. If you do so, you will be allowed to live."

I accessed the exterior cams on the crawler and pulled up several views of the area. The nine crawlers that had been struck by the Taejo mines looked like they were connected by thin, gossamer webbing. Those vehicles were not traveling any farther without extensive work, and I doubted that would help all of them. Several of the Screaming Mimis soldiers had crawled from their vehicles and had taken up defensive positions along the passage. Some of them tried to manage wounded, but I knew that some of the wounded struck by the monofilament wire were strung up inside the crawlers, either dead or dying or severely wounded.

I continued working even as hoppers from the enemy group lowered and hooked onto the cargo containers with grapples. Within a few moments, they were flying away.

* * *

Out of one hundred and fifty men in the unit, only eight-seven remained alive. Eleven of the crawlers had been rendered inoperative, but Captain Venturi, replacing Major Randall who had expired in the firefight, had managed to get the remaining four operable. The jackers—everyone called them that, but I doubted the people who had attacked us were anything less than full-scale militarily trained combatants—had left the civilian vehicles as well. With the cargo gone, there was more room for our wounded, but oxygen shortage was a real concern.

The bodies of the dead had been left with a GPS beacon so they could be recovered later. But only if someone wanted them home for burial. Otherwise they would be left where they lay.

"Well, that couldn't have gone any worse," Hayim said as he helped me take care of the wounded. He had enough medical experience that he could take care of everything that wasn't a life-threatening emergency.

I appreciated the extra help. "You're still alive," I said.

"I wasn't talking about me," Hayim said. "I was talking about this team. A lot of these soldiers are greenies. Not more than kids somebody's recruited to fight their wars for them."

I had not noticed that before, but as I polled the list of Screaming Mimis combatants from the medical files I had on the men, I realized the average age was twenty.

I shut off the hardsuit to a young woman who had just expired. Our casualties had just risen to sixty-three dead. I pulled out the air reclamation system I had and affixed it to the suit so I could drain the oxygen to use for the rest of the team that still lived.

Hayim cursed. "You realize that you're drawing her dying breath into that system."

"Yes," I replied. "And you or one of these other soldiers might be thankful for it later. Podkayne colony is too far away for us to comfortably make." I looked over the convoy. "We may lose more of them before we get them home."

* * *

I sat at a corner table in the Inn of Two Moons and watched Captain Venturi try to entice other soldiers to sign under our banner. He wasn't having much success because no unit had endured the casualties we had suffered. There was some talk of the Screaming Mimis being cursed with bad luck. Who was supposed to have cursed us was not known.

Private Deng, still in a soft cast with a broken leg, joined Hayim and me at the table. He was young and talkative, one of those men who lived on social networks when he wasn't in the field. He placed his drink on the table and eased into a chair, which I helped pull out for him.

"You shouldn't be walking around so much," I told him. "You should be in bed with that leg elevated."

Deng waved my comment away with a bandaged hand. Monofilament wire had shot through his hand in two places but hadn't done any permanent damage. He shook his head and took a sip of his drink. "Bed's the last place I want to be. Every time I try to sleep, I fall right back into that ambush. Only this time I don't make it out of there alive." He grinned without enthusiasm, baring his teeth. "Not until I wake up screaming, anyway."

"I can give you something that will help you sleep," I offered.

"No. The last thing I want is an endless cycle of nightmares."

I let him be the judge of his situation. During the last three days, my evenings had been filled with the need to find Mara Blake. But I couldn't do that until I found out where the chimera mercenaries were. They were tied up too tightly in everything that had happened to not be part of her disappearance as well.

"Maybe you're investing too much into the Chimeras," Shelly said as she sat on my right.

"I'm not," I replied.

"If you're not careful, you're going to develop tunnel vision on this investigation."

"It's not tunnel vision if I'm correct. It's focus. You taught me that."

"I did."

"Do you think I'm wrong?" I asked.

"No."

Deng stretched his injured leg out, wincing as Private Kulemeka bumped into him and pulled out a chair.

"Sorry," she apologized, then pulled the chair out to a more agreeable angle. She was young and dark-skinned, a native of Malawi, Africa, who had signed up for a Mars security post, then became a mercenary after her initial three-year contract was up because she wanted to see more of the planet. Her hair was pulled back and tribal tattoos marked her slender neck. She sat uncomfortably and winced in pain. During the attack, she had suffered three cracked ribs. She looked at me. "I'm having trouble sleeping, McDreamy."

"I can give you something to help you sleep." I pointed at the globe of alcohol in her hand. "You will have to monitor your alcohol consumption."

"No problem."

I reached into the medkit and found a blister pack of medication that would help her sleep. I passed the meds over and tapped the wrist monitor she wore. The monitor buzzed.

"Hey! What's that?"

"Your wrist alert is tethered to my overwatch programming. If you misdiagnose yourself, I will know it."

Kulemeka pulled at the wrist monitor.

"It's now sealed," I said. "It won't be released again until you've finished with the sleep aids."

"Big brother, much, McDreamy?" she asked.

"I'm here to care for you, Private."

Deng drained his globe. "You wouldn't have to take care of us so much if Earth would just go ahead and release those fighting bioroids they've been working on."

Kulemeka shivered and then grimaced in pain as she tried to find a comfortable position for her broken ribs. "I don't know that I like the idea of bioroids capable of harming—or killing—humans. Some of those old 20th century sensies about killer robots from the future are pretty scary when you think about how many bioroids are in the world now." She looked at me quickly. "No offense, McDreamy."

"None taken," I assured her.

Deng grinned at her. "Bioroids used in battle is great by me. If they get blown up, you just fix them or part them out, send them back in. It also means you and I don't have to die with our guts blown out somewhere in the colonies." He accepted his drink from the server and thumbed the tab he'd opened up with his credstick. "Besides, bioroids would be trained for fighting, not making other bioroids."

"That right, McDreamy? You don't know how to make bioroids?" Kulemeka looked at me.

"I don't know how to construct bioroids," I told her.

She regarded me for a moment, then blew out a breath. "Just because McDreamy doesn't know how doesn't mean Haas-Bioroid doesn't have bioroids on the assembly line right now putting units together." She sipped her drink. "Besides that, you know how to do surgery on humans."

"Limited surgery," I told her. "I don't know everything about the human body."

"Yeah, but the human body has got to be more complicated than a bioroid."

I admitted that it was.

"See?" Kulemeka lifted an eyebrow at Deng. "Bioroids can start building bioroids if they want to."

"The Three Directives will keep bioroids from harming humans," Deng said.

"Are you even listening to yourself? You're talking about combat-ready bioroids. They wouldn't have the Three Directives as part of their programming."

"Sure they would. They'd just have it so it could be turned off during combat. You drop them into a kill zone, have them decimate the enemy, then switch the Directives back on once the mission's over. In fact, you could have the reinstallation of the Directives be part of the mission. They finish up, the Directives go right back into place. No problem."

"I think McDreamy needs to check your pain meds." Kulemeka snorted in disgust. "You're living some kind of whacked out sensie fantasy."

I ran a quick diagnostic on Deng and found that he was operating within acceptable tolerances.

She shifted her attention to me. "What about you, McDreamy? If you could have the Three Directives lifted from you—if you were able to harm humans—would you do it?"

"I can't envision circumstances where that facet of my performance would be necessary."

Memory of the rooftop where Shelly and I had been pursuing the murderers of Cartman Dawes, the CEO of IdentiKit, flashed into my mind. I had shot her killer with a Synap but he had been out of the weapon's effective range and the beam hadn't kept him from shooting her and killing her.

My colleagues at the NAPD faulted me for Shelly's death.

They said that if I'd been a human partner or if I'd been equipped with a lethal handgun, Shelly would be alive today, not just a ghost in the machine.

They were right.

Simon Blake would have made a better partner. He would have shot that man on that rooftop that night and Shelly would have gone home to her family.

"Don't give in to that," Shelly told me. "There are other times that the fact you are a bioroid saved my life."

I hung onto that and tried not to figure out the percentages of whether it was better that I had been a bioroid protecting her or if I hadn't been human that night.

"It was one night," Shelly told me.

But that one night had made all the difference, hadn't it?

"It might have made a difference that day," Deng said.

"No," Kulemeka said, "it wouldn't have. McDreamy saved lives out there. If he'd been engaged in fighting, some of us wouldn't have come out of that ambush alive. More than that, if he'd stayed on the attack instead of standing down the way we were told, he might have gotten us all killed."

I told myself that wasn't true. If I had been permitted to engage our attackers, I would have known when to stand down. I didn't know that for certain, though. I was faster and stronger than a human. I could have killed a lot of those men who had ambushed us. So would I have made a difference?

Chapter Twenty-Seven

"The idea of bioroids with a license to kill is a nightmare." The subject matter of the vid playing on the vidcast was an old one, but the subject matter had become relevant again given the news of the warroids circulating through the colonies. "The concept of machines and artificial life forms able to kill humans alone is enough to scare any sane person to death."

After Hayim had declared himself done for the evening, we'd returned to the hotel room we were renting. We didn't have much in the way of conversation. Both of us appeared occupied with our own thoughts.

I sat in a chair by the wall while Hayim stretched out on the bed and watched the vidcast.

The speaker was on a media program with Lily Lockwell, one of the best roving nosies on Earth. Her auburn hair looked immaculate, every strand in place. Beautiful and articulate, she captured the attention of viewers. A monocam covered her left eye and the vid operators running the presentation kept cutting back and forth between vids that showed Lockwell and her guest and her POV of the man.

Tall and powerfully built, Alton Fuller looked almost too big for the chair he occupied on the media set. His bronze hair was combed straight back from his broad, handsome face. Muddy green eyes like those on a reptile made him look distant and cold. He was one of the top spokespersons for Human First.

"—idea of a war bioroid isn't a new one, Ms. Lockwell," Fuller was saying. "I'm sure you've heard of it before."

"I have," Lily Lockwell responded. "But we still haven't seen them in action. For all we know, these warroids are a smoke-screen, an unsubstantiated threat. Until one of them kills a human, there are a lot of people who won't believe in them."

"The people who would build such a *machine*," Fuller stated, making his disapproval evident audibly, "would, of course, pay off the media."

Lily Lockwell's mouth twitched a little at that, and I knew she was annoyed but holding herself in check. She always made sure she got the story she was looking for without becoming the story in the process. "I'm not paid off, Mr. Fuller."

"You wouldn't admit it if you were."

"Have you been able to prove any of your allegations, Mr. Fuller?" Lily Lockwell's voice never rose, never changed in any way.

"Proven that military bioroids are battle-tested?" Fuller shook his head. "These people cover their tracks far too well for that to happen. The only time we're going to know killer bioroids exist is when they shove a blaster down our throats and pull the trigger. If you ask me, it's going to be almost too late by that time. We've had our warning. People are just choosing to ignore it."

With those words, one of Simon Blake's memories drew me out of the hotel room.

* * *

"Do you swear to uphold the laws and obligations of the New Angeles Police Department to the best of your abilities?" Commissioner Chen Mai Dawn did the swearing in herself on the stage in front of several dozen leading corp execs and favorite sons. She looked trim and athletic in her black business suit, but she was totally professional.

Floyd 2X3A7C stood in front of her, his right hand lifted as he faced the commissioner. I hadn't expected to see him there, and the sight of him almost separated me from Simon's memory, but I held fast to the past.

In Simon's memory, Floyd looked shiny and new, dressed in a tailored NAPD uniform. He wasn't going on the street with the other police officers, though. Commissioner Dawn had agreed to let Floyd work out of her office, where he still worked even now. He had been the first bioroid to be contracted to the NAPD and the event was carried throughout the media. The act divided the populace sharply at the time, bringing out the worst of the Human First groups.

Floyd didn't wear the rosary then, and he didn't seem as curious about his environment and what might lie beyond as he did currently. The Floyd I had met had been on the PD for years before I arrived. By that time he had developed a need to know things, to understand people, and mostly to discern how he fit into the world he'd been brought into.

"I do so swear," Floyd answered in a flat voice that carried none of the character that I had come to see in him. Shelly had been on the force when Floyd had first signed on. She had been a rookie then, still wearing a uniform but already fast-tracking through vice units because a lot of the johns still preferred flesh and blood to gynoids or cloned prostitutes.

"Then, Detective 3rd Grade Floyd 2X3A7C, let me be the first to welcome you to the New Angeles Police Department." Commissioner Dawn held out her hand.

Floyd took her hand and shook it once, mechanically perfect, and released it. "Thank you, Commissioner."

The audience broke into applause, but the effort was lackluster at best and bordered on insulting. My own swearing in ceremony had been perfunctory, done in a small room, and recorded for my file, with only the required witnesses present. I had never again looked at that vid, but now I was curious to see how much I had changed.

That thought tugged at me, threatening again to split me from Simon, so I pushed it away for the time being and concentrated on what I could gather from being there.

Mara Parker sat beside me. She looked tired, but excited. I knew she had been putting in a lot of hours at MirrorMorph, Inc., writing and rewriting code. In her black dress, she looked attractive and I felt some of the interest Simon had for her and it was stronger than ever. The feeling was alien to me, yet I understood it on a level based on the sex crimes information in my knowledge base. It was discomforting.

She looked up at me. "Do you know what this means?"

"I know that you're going to tell me."

She treated me to a small smile which quickened Simon's pulse. "It means that all the neural channeling work I've been doing is going to be successful. Imagine it, Simon: a world where bioroids can replace flesh and blood police officers in the police departments in megapoli. Men and women in law enforcement won't be casualties anymore."

Around us, people were getting to their feet and heading to the chocolate buffet that had been laid out for the ceremony.

I stood and offered Mara my hand. She took it and I pulled her to her feet. "You're going to have a hard time convincing me that a bioroid will be able to replace a police officer. Much less a detective." I shot Floyd a dismissive glance. The words and attitude were totally Simon's. At that point, bioroids weren't being used as med-techs on Mars. He'd had limited exposure to them other than in a servile role.

Floyd stood on the stage with his hands folded behind him, looking like a department store mannequin. No one had told him what to do once the ceremony had concluded. His social software, though adaptive, hadn't had enough stimulus and experience to create a conditioned response to his surroundings.

"Look at him. Standing there because he doesn't know what to do." I snorted. "Some detective he's going to make."

Mara took my arm and I moved us along with the crowd, constantly watching for any threat that might manifest itself. I guarded Mara with my life because there had been two attempts on her in the last eight months. One of them had been a simple robbery gone wrong, but I still didn't know who had sent the last three men. I'd killed all of them.

It was possible that Haas-Bioroid wanted all of her research instead of sharing ownership with her, but it didn't make sense that the corp would move against her till she'd finished the program coding. So someone else was out there. Plenty of other corps wanted to get their hands on the work she was doing.

"Don't mistake Floyd's social inadequacies for any kind of deficiency regarding his police work." Mara walked confidently alongside me and I felt the heat of her body against mine. "I got the chance to look over his programming. It's all first-rate. Top of the line." She frowned. "He just lacks some social experience. Haas-Bioroid botched that. A detective can't be a manual laborer like an assembly line bot or a human-looking front end loader moving freight in a warehouse. A detective needs to be more human. That's where the code I'm creating will bridge the gap and reduce the learning curve Floyd will have to experience."

"Have you considered the fact that Haas-Bioroid intentionally didn't make that machine more human on purpose?" a challenging voice demanded. "Because they want the machine to remember that it isn't human?"

Instinctively, noting the threat level in the words, I turned and stepped in front of Mara, putting her behind me. My suit was bullet and laser resistant. I had a slug-thrower hidden on my hip under my jacket and a smaller one mounted on my forearm where a single twitch of my wrist would snap it into my palm.

Alton Fuller didn't look any different than he had in the vidcast in the hotel room on Mars. His jacket was expensive and he wore it over a black turtleneck. He turned his hand over and the holo of a business card appeared there courtesy of his PAD.

Mara remained behind me, not bothering to accept the proffered business card. "I know who you are, Mr. Fuller."

Fuller smiled and shrugged. "That's encouraging, especially in light of the way you've been avoiding all my attempts to contact you."

"I've got a busy schedule."

"Yet you found the time to attend this charade." The business card disappeared from Fuller's palm.

"I was encouraged—*strongly*—to attend by people who are supporting my work. If I'd had my way, I would have passed."

"I was hoping I could perhaps get a few minutes with you now, if I may. I'd like to discuss my thoughts on your attempts to makeover the bioroid operating parameters."

"They're not attempts," Mara snapped. "They're also not makeovers. I'm enhancing the neural channeling so that it will go deeper, transfer more knowledge."

"To create copies of people who have mistakenly allowed their thoughts and emotions to be downloaded into your computers?"

"Not copies. Interpretations. They will not be watered-down versions of the neural donor. A bioroid that comes out of the neural channeling we're doing at MirrorMorph will think faster and better, and be closer to being a human being than anything we've seen so far."

"You see that as a desirable goal?"

"I do."

Fuller worked his jaw and I knew that he was getting more and more worked up. "If you imbue bioroids with as much information as you're talking about, how can you ensure that they will honor the Three Directives?"

"They will."

"Why?"

"Because, Mr. Fuller, at the end of the day, they're still bioroids. In any incarnation, they will observe the Three Directives."

"How do I, as a concerned citizen, know that, Dr. Parker?"

"Because I'm telling you that."

Fuller folded his arms across his chest. "You'll permit me my kernel of doubt. You wouldn't be the first person to attempt to feather her own nest with empty promises."

We had gathered a small crowd of media people who were listening avidly to the exchange.

"I didn't come here for a debate, Mr. Fuller," Mara said. "I'm here to put in an appearance, and then I'm returning to my lab."

"How far are you going to go with your abominations?" Fuller's tone grew louder and more accusing. He knew he had the attention of the crowd and he reveled in it.

Although most of the execs there supported the bioroid alternative for common labor, most of them did not like the idea of a bioroid in a position of authority, which was exactly what Fuller counted on during his diatribes. He underscored their fears.

"I'm going to go as far as I possibly can, Mr. Fuller." Mara squared up on the man and stepped from behind me to confront him directly. "I intend to create neural channeling that will allow bioroids to be as capable as humans so that danger to humans is reduced."

"You want to *replace* humanity, Dr. Parker."

"I want to *protect* it."

I leaned in close to Mara, whispering into her ear so that only she could hear me. "This isn't the place or the time, Mara. Don't let him play his game. You can't win this. Let it go."

For a moment she stood there, listening to Fuller quote facts and figures and trends. I thought she wasn't going to be able to walk away, but she turned on her heel and headed for the door.

Fuller tried to follow her, clamoring for her attention. I

stepped in close to him to mask the short jab I sank into his soft stomach. All of the air wheezed from Fuller and he stumbled to a stop.

Two of his sec crew started to come after me. I flicked my wrist, dropped the large-bore slug-thrower into my palm, and then let them see just a glint of it between my fingers as I followed Mara. They met my eyes and nodded as they circled their employer and made no further effort to interfere with our departure.

Outside on the rooftop as we walked to the hopper pad where our vehicle awaited us, I watched the area and felt uneasy. There was no reason for Fuller to so aggressively approach Mara. I commed the rest of my sec team and put them on alert.

When we were halfway to the hopper, Sanjay shouted, "Sniper!"

I grabbed Mara and wrapped her up, triggering the coat I wore to release the extra sheets of bullet-resistant fabric from my sleeves, creating a protective cone around her. Electricity pulsed through the fabric, stiffening it.

Two high-velocity rounds thudded into the fabric but neither of them penetrated the material. I had swept the large slug-thrower from my hip and had it out as I hustled Mara toward the building. I didn't want to take the chance another assassin waited with a readied rocket launcher or someone had booby-trapped the hopper.

Shots cracked, penetrating the sounds of the megapolis echoing over the rooftop.

"Sniper's down," Sanjay reported.

"Secure the body," I ordered. "I want to know where he came from."

"Roger that."

When we reached the building, several people were in the foyer, drawn by the building's sec movements. NAPD officers on duty for the swearing in ceremony halted me as I entered the building and tried to relieve me of my weapons.

I flashed my e-ID from my PAD and backed them off. "My

employer was the intended victim. My team has put down the sniper."

Four NAPD uniforms were stationed around Mara and me, and I felt more at risk there than I did on the rooftop. Cops could be bought. I tried to keep her wrapped, but she fought free and stood there.

In the crowd, Fuller scowled and looked unhappy. I met his gaze and thought seriously of putting a .50-cal slug between his eyes. I doubted the assassin would be tracked back to Fuller, but I knew where he'd come from, and I knew why the Human First spokesperson had braced Mara.

Maybe he realized what I was thinking, or maybe it showed on my face, because he turned and walked away.

CHAPTER TWENTY-EIGHT

Eight days later, the Screaming Mimis—survivors and new blood—crawled 1,327 klicks northwest of Podkayne colony on a search and rescue mission. A ground supply caravan from the terraforming operations at Persephone 29J was overdue for a check-in.

At that time, we had been on patrol, scouting out the terrain looking for units responsible for strikes against pro-Earth corps. Other merc units were with us, and all of us were operating on "grapevine intel culled from anybody who could hoist a drink and had a creative mind." That was according to the acting major.

I crawled with the soldiers at times, and served on scouting missions as well as a corpsman on minihoppers. No one wanted to fight. I recognized the fear in them, listened to their nightmares when they fitfully slept, and dispensed anti-anxiety patches to help them deal with it.

The constant distress of my companions was having an effect on me as well, which had not been something my programming had been prepared for. I found myself running manual diagnostics checks on my hardware and software even though I knew the automatic ones had turned up nothing. I had self-checked before, but there had always been a reason. This time there was no discernible catalyst that I could find, and I had to prevent myself from cycling endless loops of diagnostics.

"It's not you, Drake." Shelly sat beside me in the crawler as we progressed toward our estimated goal the afternoon of the second day. She was stable and steady, unaffected by the constant lunge and twist of the crawler as it undulated over the rough terrain. I, and the rest of the crawler crew, rocked and rolled with the vehicle's movement. "You're programmed to be sympathetic to the people who work with you as well as the people of interest. It's only natural that a little self-doubt creeps in there."

"I was not made to be self-doubting," I replied. "I am programmed for gathering data, making interpretive conclusions and an action plan, then performing based on that."

"All right, then what do you think needs to be done for these people?"

"They need to be protected."

"Yet they're marching into confrontations that will leave some of them dead and others wounded."

I said nothing.

"You were designed to work at the New Angeles Police Department. The parameters of your work involved protecting people and locking up people who had murdered others you were too late to save. The intention there was to continue to save lives, to lock down murderers and spree killers so other people were not harmed."

"Yes."

"You weren't programmed for watching people risk their lives. I would assume that true medical bioroid officers have different software designs created to view acceptable losses."

"There are no acceptable losses," I replied.

"You can't save them all. You've already seen that."

I had, and the result of our last engagement had been…unacceptable.

"How did you feel toward me when we went into potentially dangerous situations?"

Like when we went to investigate the murder of Cartman Dawes? The question was in my mind, but Shelly didn't acknowledge it. "I knew that risk was inherent in the situation and I accepted it."

"Why?"

There was only one answer for that. "I was programmed to accept such an eventuality of risk and to know that I could provide assistance to you or any other NAPD detective or uniform."

"Yet I ended up killed in action."

"That was unacceptable."

"Yes, it was, and I am no less dead for it."

I started to run a diagnostic again, pulling up the files on the night Shelly was shot and killed, prepared again to go over the situation to see if there was something else I could have done.

"Stop, Drake."

"Perhaps there was something I missed."

"You missed nothing. You did everything you could have done."

"The resolution is unacceptable."

"But not outside the operating parameters of such an engagement."

It was not. Such an eventuality lay within my programming. I did not want to accept it.

"You have to accept it, Drake. It is what it is. And now you're facing another situation like you had days ago, when you lost so many of your team."

"That was not acceptable."

"Yet the eventuality persists. Perhaps it even accelerates and magnifies."

The potential of that made me feel increasingly uncomfortable. "This should not be happening."

"But it is."

"I was programmed to prevent human death."

"You can't prevent a war, Drake."

"War must be prevented."

"It's coming. You know that. If things don't change, and perhaps even if they do, war is going to break out here in the colonies."

That was, indeed, one of the permutations prognosticated by my situational analysis software. Given the variables now in play, war was inevitable. "I do not know how much longer I can do this." I looked at the people around me.

Hayim sat in a loader's ready position. Most of the others were new to the unit, but I had all of their files and could pull up information on them in less than a second. I had access to full medical as well as limited psych profiles, but they were more than just a collection of bytes and data to me.

"A medical bioroid wouldn't see them as more than data," Shelly said. "You're tapping into that part of your programming that is intuitive. Medical bioroids don't intuit more than physical or psychological distress."

I understood that. I had tried to separate what I needed to do as a medical support unit versus a police detective and could not. My system was too integrated with who I was.

"You can do this," Shelly said.

I didn't argue with her.

"You have an edge over those medical bioroids," Shelly went on.

"What?"

"You've been here before as Simon Blake. You know this world. You know this kind of work. Reach into yourself and find more of Simon in order to become more effective here."

"I will try."

* * *

At 1523, one of the airborne drones picked up a comm signal from the missing unit. Major Venturi, his promotion now part of the record for the Screaming Mimis, opened a secure channel, but I'd hacked into all of the links because I needed to know how situations were progressing. I eavesdropped on his conversation.

"This is Major Venturi of the Screaming Mimis. Who am I talking to?"

"Captain Micah Abelard, sir. Acting CO of the Scarlet Chakrams."

"Where is Major Eick?"

"Major Eick became a casualty, sir."

"Understood. What happened?"

"We got hit by Martian terrorists. Ambushed, sir. They came at us hard and fast. We held our own for a little while, but we never stood a chance."

"How long ago?"

"Three days, sir. They crippled us and left us out here to die. We would have been dead too, except that we took seventy-three percent casualties and were able to salvage enough air to keep us going. But if you don't reach us in the next five hours, most of us aren't going to make it."

"Understood. We'll be there in ninety-eight minutes, Captain. You people hang in there."

"Yes, sir. Will do."

* * *

Seventy-three minutes later, I rode on the back of a two-man minihopper that sped only a few centimeters above the nap of the terrain. Dust coiled around us like a storm constantly waiting to close in on us.

Ahead, the remaining fifty-seven men and women that were left of the Scarlet Chakrams lounged in the sun to allow their hardsuits' solar batteries to recharge. Most of them would be in bad shape because the hardsuits only carried enough water and protein sub for two days. They would be hungry and dehydrated.

Even though they knew we were coming and were anticipating our arrival, most of them took up skirmish positions along the ridges and boulders that lay strewn across the hillside.

Clarice Isaacs, the soldier I rode with, halted the minihopper four hundred meters out along a ridgeline and we peered down into the bowl-shaped depression. I accessed the Chakrams' unit frequency, hacked through the sec coding, and started pulling up information on the wounded.

"Captain Abelard, this is Captain Pitts of the Screaming Mimis," our unit commander broadcasted over a hailing frequency. "We're an advance scout group. The main unit is twenty minutes behind us."

"Acknowledged, Captain Pitts. Welcome to come ahead."

Pitts nudged his minihopper over the ridge and descended into the depression. Clarice fell into line behind him and I started prioritizing the wounded. There were two medical bioroids still with the unit.

* * *

"I fear I am not at one hundred percent capability, McDreamy," Welby 4AR9KA told me. "Of course, I will be happy to help in any way I might assist."

The medical bioroid leaned against a boulder and sat in the red powder that shifted restlessly on the bones of Mars that lay below. Shrapnel scars tracked his upper body and he was missing most of his face from the right eye down. His lower body was gone from the waist, ending in a jagged stump that leaked fluids. Most of the capillaries had been tied off to prevent further leakage.

Even if Welby 4AR9KA survived the return trip to Podkayne colony, I knew that he would not be saved. He would be salvaged, parted out, never again an individual. His components would be spread to other units that needed replacement parts. He would never again be Welby 4AR9KA. I was certain he knew that too, yet his programming ran true, putting the welfare of humans ahead of his own. At present, he was a neomort, the living dead.

"You will be of great assistance, Welby 4AR9KA," I told him. "I will see that wounded you are capable of assisting are brought to you."

I thought he tried to smile, a purely human response and not one that was necessary to me, because the underlying musculature along his face shifted. However, there was no mouth to frame whatever his effort had been.

Kildare 5BE3NJ was a more aggressive medical bioroid. Where the Welby had more concern for the emotional side of patients, the Kildare was oriented toward saving lives. If amputations were necessary, the Kildare models performed them as a matter of course. No thought was given to what the patient wanted or how he or she was reacting.

Kildare and I sorted the patients. I looped him under my control, setting him up as a satellite to my master. While I worked on my patients, I provided a second opinion on those he dealt with that had major injuries. When aggressive stabilization was required, I managed those patients myself, providing more of a bedside manner than the Kildare did. As I did, I kept looping memories of Simon Blake in with my real-time experience. Simon Blake had possessed medical training as well.

Modular tents were set up outside the crawlers, providing small bubbles of controlled environment where Welby, Kildare, and I could work, and the survivors of the Scarlet Chakrams could re-outfit themselves. Given the time frames we were working under, those tasks would not be finished until dark.

Major Venturi wasn't happy about spending the night out in the open, especially not since he was using up air and water to do it, but he didn't want to be caught crossing rough terrain at night by hostile forces. Pro-Martian independence forces were deliberately adding to the body count every chance they got.

In my tent, I stayed busy treating the wounded. Of the fifty-seven survivors, thirty-six of them were wounded. Two of them died before I could get them stabilized. One of them was an eighteen-year-old boy who had suffered cerebral damage.

Once I had carried his body out of the tent and laid him to rest in one of the crawlers' cargo spaces, I took in a nineteen-year-old girl named Gabrielle. When she entered the tent and disrobed from her hardsuit, she was weeping.

"Are you in pain?" I asked.

I had given her neuro-blockers to blunt the trauma from the flash burns she'd suffered from a laser blast. The blast had not compromised the integrity of her hardsuit, but it had done secondary tissue damage across her back where some of the heat had seeped through.

"No. The pain is tolerable. Thank you." She sat on folded knees and presented her blistered back for my inspection. Her brunette hair was cut as short as her male counterparts. She looked fragile.

"I knew him."

"Who?"

"Leif Tetsura. Your last patient. The man who just…died." Her voce softened and broke.

"I'm sorry for your loss. There was nothing I could do. His injuries were unrecoverable."

She nodded. "I know. I was surprised he lived as long as he did." She took a deep breath and let it out as I excised dead skin and applied a new layer of synthetic flesh that would protect her wound and keep it clean. The synthetic flesh was akin to what was used to give bioroids their features. "We just weren't given a chance. The Chimeras came out of nowhere and hit us."

I didn't pause in what I was doing, but my investigative subroutine stepped to the forefront. "Your attackers were the Chimeras?"

"Yes."

"You're sure?"

"Their units were clearly marked." She cursed. "I'd heard stories about those people, but I thought they were gone. Dead, maybe. Or back on Earth or the Moon. They haven't been active on Mars in years."

"Why did they attack you?"

"I don't know if they attacked us or if we just caught them by surprise. Our comm team had caught some strange blips on the frequencies. We went to investigate, just keeping the perimeter secure. Strictly by the book. But the way it turned out, we rolled up on a hornet's nest."

* * *

I didn't finish with the last patient, a man with two broken legs, until 0427. Once he was out the door of the tent, I went to see Welby 4AR9KA.

He sat in his tent braced up by a tool vise used by crawler mechanics. No one was with him. Since he was alone and no one was expected to see him for treatment now, the oxygen and CO2 scrubber had been detached to save oxygen as well as battery power. He also had been left without a light and the darkness covered him. His silver eyes glinted as they tracked me, but that was a passive subroutine response because he had 360-degree vision as well.

I accessed his personal frequency. "Permission to enter."

"Of course, McDreamy." Welby waved to me.

I peeled the two openings back and stepped into the small tent.

"Welcome." Welby waved to a camp chair in front of him. "Please be seated."

I sat. "Thank you."

"What brings you to me?"

"Two things. First, I want to thank you for all the work that you did today. The patients are all well cared for."

"I am glad. I wish I were not so handicapped. I could have been of more use." The image of his torn and disfigured face made me uncomfortable to a small degree.

I knew he was not in any pain, but after seeing the injuries I had worked on today and the victims of violence I had observed in the performance of my job at the NAPD, I had a hard time resolving that he was all right.

"You served your unit well."

"Thank you. What is the second thing?"

"Did you witness the attack?"

"I did."

"I was told the attack came from a mercenary unit called the Chimeras."

"I saw several such markings on their vehicles. I could not identify anyone."

"Perhaps I can. May I access your archived memory?"

"Of course."

I put my hand on his chest and linked with his memories. The attacking force had been the Chimeras. I recognized one of them immediately, and I thought I would be able to find her because Simon Blake knew her habits.

I gave Welby a message for Hayim, then told Welby good-bye. Within minutes I was outside the defensive perimeter and walking west. Leigh Bonner and the Chimeras would be out there somewhere. I intended to find them.

Chapter Twenty-Nine

Simon's memories swirled within me as I cycled through the airlock leading to Paxton Node's underground. Like most of the node cities on Mars, Paxton was more way station than a colony, a pocket of civilization that catered to the extra-curricular interests of the terraforming crews in the surrounding area. This was the frontier, raw and uncertain, and law enforcement didn't exist except for roving Martian military units.

I followed the winding staircase down three levels below planet surface. Aboveground, nodes tended to only expose necessary solar collecting wheels and plants grown to produce oxygen, making the most of the surface area. Keeping atmosphere was easier underground, though there were occasional problems with individuals and groups that tried to expand their space without filing the proper requests for those expansions. Smuggling was still a big business in the nodes.

The first two floors housed shops for goods and services and tended to look respectable to visitors that didn't know what the nodes were truly about. Below that, though, the world turned to hedonism and catered to the baser needs of the men and women that reshaped the outer fringe of Martian civilization.

Simon had been here before several times. I knew that although I couldn't latch onto a specific memory of his visits there. I didn't feel comfortable in this place, but Simon did.

"Just remember, partner," Shelly said as she walked at my side, "you're not Simon Blake, and these people you're looking for are dangerous."

"I remember." I passed by Snarky Pete's, a strip club Simon remembered, and then passed by Pandora's Pleasures, a sensie shop specializing in auto-erotica, Battick's House of Smoke, which had its own airlock and CO2 scrubbers, and other clubs. Simon didn't remember all of them. Nodes were constantly undergoing change dictated by their degrees of lawlessness. Paxton served rough trade and was always in transition. All the colors of the rainbow existed in the advertising, but only in neon.

But Mike's Saloon still had its doors open. Simon's yearning for the place stirred within me as I approached the bar.

Dark and unadorned instead of decked in gaudy colors and flashing displays, Mike's looked like a decrepit bar on its last legs. That wasn't the truth, though. Deals were done in Mike's that netted thousands of cred every day as the smugglers made their arrangements, and they all paid a percentage to Mike Dubronsky, the club's owner, for the guaranteed privacy he provided in his institution.

Two huge clones stood guard at the shadowed door. Even the lighting at that end of the tunnel was deliberately subdued. The clones were beefed-up sec models genenginered to look intimidating, hugely muscled, and slightly green. That was only for those who could be frightened by physical prowess. The true danger was the hidden fully automatic slug-throwers recessed in the club's front.

Both clones blocked my entrance to the bar. One of them held up a large hand. "Sorry, friend. No public admittance tonight. Members only. Special meeting is in session."

"I'm a member," I said.

He held up his PAD. “Let’s see your bonafides.”

I pulsed my PAD, sending him the false ID Hayim had constructed for me, and I added a passcode I got from Simon’s memories. The alpha numeric was there waiting for me.

“That’s an old passcode.” The clone frowned at the reading.

“It’s been a long time and I’ve been away,” I replied. “Am I cleared?”

A moment passed and I considered the fact that I didn’t have any options. Reluctantly, the clone nodded and stepped to the side. “Enjoy your visit.”

I passed through the door and into the dark confines of Mike’s. The white noise generator at the entrance blocked the crashing sounds of the music blaring from the speakers; whirling lights burned through the shadows that draped the interior.

I kept moving. Coming to a stop inside a bar like Mike’s was guaranteed to draw immediate attention. I split off to the left, making my way toward a table in the back, avoiding the long bar.

Mike’s didn’t boast much in the way of decoration. In addition to the ochre-tinted transplas bar and the tables and chairs, several holos of sports events, vidcasts carrying stories about the unrest surging through the colonies, and old films played above the bar.

I pulled out a chair and sat, scanning the crowd around me.

Leigh Bonner sat at the bar taking drags off a narc-stick and drinking what Simon knew could only be Irish whiskey. Mike’s had some of the best liquor because a lot of the time he took his fifteen percent of deals in merchandise which he could sell to his patrons at a markup.

Leigh was much as Simon remembered her: tall and lean, with an angular face and a narrow mouth so tight it looked like she’d just bitten into a lemon. The razor-cut hair dyed cobalt blue was new, but I knew her from Simon’s memories and the file on her that Floyd had given me. She wore rough simleathers and had a slug-thrower at her right hip and a laser pistol snugged up under her left arm. Simon knew she carried several bladed weapons with her at all times too, from knives to shuriken.

I considered how best to approach her. She and Simon had worked together well, had even been occasional lovers, which I did not know until that moment and felt uncomfortable about knowing. She had been young back then, and there was a hardness about her eyes now that hadn't been there before.

A server approached me, but I sent him away. Deciding on the direct approach, I got to my feet and walked toward Leigh.

She noticed me at once. She didn't look at me, didn't give any indication that she'd sorted me from the crowd around her, but her gaze lingered on the reflective surface of the screen pulsing advertisements behind the bar. The bar's interior was mirrored there as a grey world of shifting shadows.

I was a little over a meter away when she turned to me with the slug-thrower in her right hand, held close to her side so it couldn't be easily taken from her and the bar crowd couldn't see it.

"Unless you want a new orifice, stop right there," she said softly.

I stopped and slowly held my hands out to my sides. "I just want to talk."

"I'm not in the mood for conversation. Keep moving."

Three men rose from a table behind us. I tracked them in the bar's reflective surface as well. Two of them had chimera tattoos, one on his neck and the other on the back of his left hand. I could not confirm the third man's tattoo because he stood behind the others.

"Is there a problem, Leigh?" one of the men asked.

I spoke first. "I knew Simon Blake. I just wanted to talk about him."

Something flickered in her dark eyes, then it was gone. "That's a name you don't hear much these days."

The three men hovered around me.

"I know that Simon saved your life in Shandakor Heights. You were wounded and he carried you out."

Leigh's gaze flickered over me again, taking a new appraisal. "That's not a story that gets told often, and not many people know it. Mostly because the people who did know it are dead."

I didn't say anything. That revelation was the best I had to offer. If she didn't speak to me, I had at least still found her.

Finally, after a long moment, she shook her head at the three men standing around me. "Give us some space."

The men pulled back, but not before the biggest one of them dropped his hand on my shoulder and said, "We'll be watching."

Leigh nodded to the bar stool beside her. "Have a seat."

I did.

"What's your name?"

"McDreamy K47I19."

"I don't know you."

"No," I agreed. "You don't."

"So how did you find me?"

"Simon mentioned that you often came here when you were in this area. He showed me your image. I don't forget faces."

"He kept a picture of me?" The wistfulness in her voice was so faint I barely caught it.

"He did." It was a white lie to the best of my knowledge. It was possible Simon kept an image of her, and saying so kept our dialogue open.

She sipped her drink. "That begs the question of how you knew I was in the area."

"I heard that the Chimeras hit a supply caravan a couple days ago out in the wilderness."

She flicked ash from her narc-stick and I could tell by the tension in her body and the pulse at her throat that I'd won no confidence from her.

"Simon's dead," she said. "Years ago."

I nodded.

"So why are you here?"

I didn't hesitate. I'd already decided to be up front with her. Trying to lie about my interest was possible because I knew she couldn't read my face, but nothing I could make up would be as convincing—or hopefully as explosive—as the truth. I'd found the Chimeras. Now it remained to be seen if I could find Mara.

"I'm looking for Mara Blake."

She hesitated just for a fraction of a second, but I saw that hesitation. She tried to cover by taking another sip of her drink. "What does that have to do with me?"

"You knew Mara Blake."

"Not well."

"I need to know where she is."

"How would I know?"

"She was taken by the Chimeras."

Leigh laughed and shook her head as if I were deranged. The effort was pretty good, but it was hollow. She knew I was telling the truth, and that recognition sparked anticipation within me. "I don't know anything about that."

I chose to be direct, almost confrontational, knowing that it was risky, but believing anything less would allow her to brush me off. "I think you do."

Her eyes narrowed. "Maybe you're forgetting I'm holding a slug-thrower and have friends in this bar."

"No."

She waited for me to go away. I didn't.

Her brows furrowed. "Who sent you?"

"I came on my own."

"Why are you interested in Mara Blake?"

"I have to find her."

She let out a long breath. "This is where I would ask you—*again*—who sent you."

"And I would tell you, again, that I came on my own."

"How do you know Simon?"

I thought about that question for just a moment. “We got to know each other while he was on Earth.” That was close to the truth, and in some essence, could not be more true.

“While he was at MirrorMorph, Inc.?”

“Yes.”

Leigh’s nostrils flared a little. “You’re a medical bioroid.”

“In this place I am.”

“You were something different before you came here.”

I didn’t care to elaborate.

“Why are you looking for Mara Blake?”

“Because Simon asked me to look after her if she were ever in trouble. I’ve been searching for her since she disappeared.”

She thought for a moment and took another drag on her narc-stick. “How did you know Simon?”

“We worked together.” Again, another claim that was mostly true.

“Where?”

“Off the books.”

“I was at MirrorMorph. I don’t remember you.”

More of Simon’s memories cycled through my mind, and I recalled that Leigh had worked there for a time. In the end, Leigh’s jealousy had caused Simon to ask John Rath to reassign her. I did not think Leigh knew that.

“I was only at MirrorMorph for a short time.” Another truth.

“Who do you belong to?”

“I am independent.”

Leigh spat a curse. “No bioroid is ever truly independent.”

“I am.”

“How?”

“Simon helped.”

“He died eight years ago.” She blew a smoke ring. “With the short lifespan you bioroids have, you must not be long for this world.”

I chose not to respond.

After a moment, Leigh stubbed out her narc-stick and drained her drink. “I don’t know why you came to me.”

“I thought you would help.”

She spat a curse. “If you knew Simon and he told you anything about me, you know I don’t have any love for that woman.”

Don’t. I clung to that word. Present tense. I believed that meant Mara was still alive.

“You cared about Simon.”

“Simon’s dead.” Leigh stood and slotted her credstick to pay her tab.

“Mara’s not.” I didn’t move, aware that her three companions were still watching us intently. If I put a hand on her to stop her, they’d be all over me. Not only that, as Simon remembered, Leigh Bonner was as dangerous as they came.

“She’s not my problem.”

“Did you know that Chimeras killed Simon?”

She stopped, studied me for a moment, then sat back down. “That’s not true.”

“Jonas Salter said it was.”

Her eyes gleamed as she searched my face, but she grimaced when she couldn’t read anything there. “Jonas is dead, too.”

“Yes, and I believe Chimeras killed him as well.”

“Why?”

“I don’t know for certain, but I believe it has something to do with Mara Blake.”

Tension framed her body and made her stiff. “I knew Rath and Simon had a falling out over Mara Blake, but I never suspected anyone from the unit would try to hurt Simon.”

Her words unleashed Simon’s memories within me.

Chapter Thirty

"You don't just go back on a deal, Simon." John Rath leaned casually back against the railing of the observation deck on the Beanstalk. "You know that."

Simon had chosen the meeting place because it was public, and because any violence would immediately draw the attention of the Space Elevator Authority security mercs. A few of them made the rounds on the observation deck as we stood there. Their bright yellow uniforms made them stand out.

"It's not going back on a deal." I felt Simon's anxiety thrumming inside him as he confronted his mentor. He didn't want to take action against Rath, but his fingers were within millimeters of the hidden needle gun he carried. "This...*this* was never part of the deal. You're still getting your fifteen percent of MirrorMorph, Inc. You'll be a rich man."

Rath folded his arms across his chest and I knew there were dozens of ways he could kill a man from that position. When you factored in the small arms weapons he was probably carrying, that number escalated exponentially.

"Riches aren't anything," Rath said quietly. "I thought I taught you that."

"You did."

"Power is what you want, Simon," Rath went on like I hadn't spoken. "What we're talking about here, that can give me a lot of power." He smiled. "Maybe you need to rethink your position on this."

I searched through Simon's memories of this moment, trying to find out what they had been talking about, but images and dialogue slipped through my mind like tiny fish through a net. I only had glimmerings of what the real subject matter was.

"I have rethought it," Simon said. "What I'm telling you now isn't easy. You and I have a lot of history. I don't want to lose the relationship with you."

"Cross me and that relationship is over." Rath's words were flat, like rivets popped into plasteel.

I didn't say anything.

Rath fixed me with his gaze. I prepared for the worst, not knowing if I was going to walk out of that observation deck alive.

"Why are you standing against me, Simon?"

I remained silent.

"Is it the woman?"

"I don't want her harmed." Simon's voice almost cracked. His fingers drifted closer to the hidden weapon he carried.

For a moment Rath was silent, then he chuckled and shook his head. "I'd never hurt Mara. That would be like killing the goose that laid the golden eggs."

"I want your word on that." Simon knew that Rath's word was his bond. No matter the violence he dealt on campaigns, no matter the subterfuge he was capable of, Rath kept his word.

"You have my word, Simon. Mara won't be hurt on my account."

Simon released a tense breath. "Thank you."

"But I'm also not letting this go." Rath's dark eyes flashed. "You betrayed me, buddy. I didn't expect that from you. Out of every man in my unit, I knew you were the one most like me.

I *made* you. Shaped you. Taught you how to think. Everything you are, you owe to me."

"I don't want to lose your friendship."

Rath smiled coldly and shook his head. "Oh, there's a lot more on the table than my friendship." He turned and walked away. "See you around, Simon."

I watched him going, passing easily through the crowd because most of the people moved out of his way as if sensing a predator among them.

* * *

I focused on Leigh. "Do you know the nature of the problem that manifested between Simon and John Rath?"

Leigh tapped her nails on her drink glass. "Simon didn't tell you?"

"No. Only that he wanted me to look out for Mara if anything should happen to her."

"You weren't part of her team?"

"No."

Leigh smiled. "Simon was a lot like Rath. Both of them had their little side games they played outside of the main event. Both of them always planned three steps ahead." She knocked back the last of her drink. "They should have been brothers." Stepping back from me, she turned to go.

The front door to Mike's Saloon burst open and armored Martian army shock troops flooded the room. They ran roughshod over the patrons, knocking them to the floor and shoving them out of the way as they came on like a tsunami. Shouts, curses, and cries of pain filled the bar.

A black armored woman strode in at the forefront of the invading force. Her voice blasted over the confusion. "Martian Colonial Corps! Stand down or you will be put down! Hug the floor! Do it now!"

Four men to my left threw themselves toward the back of

the bar only to be met by stunstick-wielding armored troops pouring through the rear door. They fought, but the struggle was brief because the Colonial Corps soldiers struck viciously.

Most of the patrons gave up immediately, but the ones that moved too slowly or were too inebriated to move quickly got knocked to the floor or shocked into submission. A few of them purged, spreading pools of stomach contents across the floor.

Leigh moved instantly and I went with her, following Simon's instincts before I knew it. She threw herself over the transplas bar and I landed at her heels. Her three companions were a half-step behind me. I wondered what she thought she was doing because the Colonial Corps would have all the exits blocked, and then a split-second later I knew she was headed for an escape route known to only a few mercs that Mike Dubronsky favored with his secrets.

Simon knew of three quick escapes from Mike's Saloon. They'd all been put in place to allow goods to be smuggled in. Leigh went for one of the two in the back room, sprinting through the back room and turning to the wall on the left.

"Get the door!" she ordered.

One of the three men slammed the door closed and locked it, then fired a bullet into the locking mechanism to hold the Colonial Corps at bay. Then he pointed his weapon at me, gazing at me fiercely. "What do we do with this thing, Leigh?"

Leigh pulled a rack of food to the side and glanced at me. She hesitated. "Leave him alone. He knew Simon."

Reluctantly, the man lowered his weapon.

"Thermite," Leigh called, holding her cupped hands out.

One of the men tossed her a ready-made charge. She caught it and slapped it against the wall. Simon had known about the crawl space behind the wall too. There was a cleverly concealed door in the wall, but Leigh obviously didn't want to reveal that because it might have incriminated Dubronsky.

Leigh slapped the charge against the wall and looked at me. "I should probably let McEwen put a bullet through your brain. But you knew Simon." She glanced at the three men. "Pull your oxygen masks on."

All four of them pulled flexible oxygen masks from their thigh pouches. The masks were meant for emergencies only when atmosphere was lost but they would do little against the below-freezing cold that covered Mars. They wore softsuits that would help maintain core heat in their bodies for a few minutes in case of emergencies.

"Once this wall goes, we move fast," Leigh said through her mask. "It won't be as cold underground here as it would be away from the node. Residual heat will keep us warm enough for a few minutes, but if you stop out there, you'll probably die. It's a thousand meters through the caverns till we can regain egress to the node. If any of you don't want to take the chance, stay here."

No one said anything, and the silence was punctuated by a thud at the door as someone tried to break it down.

Leigh tapped a button on the charge and stepped back. Two seconds later, white-hot heat filled the room, turning the plasteel wall to molten slag. Smoke sucked out into the vacuum that lay on the other side of the wall and the cherry-red plasteel started to cool at once.

An alarm sounded within the room and the rhythmic thudding against the locked door stopped as the Colonial Corps realized they were dealing with a breached environment. Opening that door now would allow the atmosphere inside the bar to get sucked away and put everyone inside at risk. They couldn't do that.

Leigh switched on an LED light on the oxygen mask and plunged into the darkness waiting on the other side of the opening.

* * *

We ran through the empty mine tunnel as quickly as we dared. Leigh and her companions had LED lights, but I had infrared vision. Paxton Node had been constructed in a depleted helium-3 mine. Scars left by the huge earthmovers marred the walls and loose rubble covered the uneven ground. The shaft we were in was forty meters wide and twenty meters tall. Behind us, light from the storeroom bled out into the darkness.

Frost formed on Leigh's clothing and skin and I knew that the ambient temperature, even with the residual heat from the node businesses around us, wouldn't allow her or her friends to survive for long.

One of the men cried out in pain and grabbed his leg. A moment later, he crumpled to the ground. Judging from his reaction, he was suffering from a recent injury that hadn't healed or he'd gotten cramped from the cold.

I ran to him, hoisted him over my shoulder, and followed the others. None of them had stopped to help him because they would not have been able to do anything without dying with him.

A thousand and four meters from Mike's Saloon, Leigh stopped in front of a rock wall. For a moment I thought she had succumbed to the cold and was experiencing some kind of dementia, but as I caught up to her, I saw her flip open a section of the rock and punch a keypad with shaking fingers.

I felt the vibration of moving parts, then a section of the wall slid open to reveal a tunnel opening. We plunged inside and Leigh took the lead, running through a maze of tunnels that doubled back on themselves, ascended, then descended, and twisted like a snake. Finally we reached a small airlock in a darkened room. Leigh and the other two men entered and I followed with the unconscious man.

Once inside, Leigh tried to manage the keypad but couldn't keep her light focused on it long enough for her shaking hands to operate correctly. I stepped up beside her.

"What is the code?"

She told me and I entered it. The door sealed behind us and the airlock cycled, bringing atmosphere and heat to us.

I placed the man on the floor and stripped off his mask when the atmosphere became breathable. The ice crystals that had formed in his beard and in his hair began to melt and run down his face and neck. He was breathing on his own, so I massaged his arms and legs to make sure the circulation was flowing properly.

Leigh crouched down beside me. "What's wrong with him?"

"He's gone into shock." I opened his shirt and found a large patch of nu-skin high on the right side of his chest. "He was wounded recently?"

"Yes." Leigh didn't elaborate and I didn't ask, but I assumed that it had been in the attack on the caravan a few days ago.

I reached into my medkit for slappatches to control the man's stress overloads and get his body back to normal functioning.

"Are you sure the Colonial Corps aren't on their way here now?" one of the other men demanded.

"If they were," Leigh answered calmly, "they'd be here by now." Her attention was on the unconscious man. "Is he going to be all right?"

"Yes," I told her. "He needs rest. The meds I've given him will see to that. Doubtless his system crashed because he was drinking too much, was injured, and pushed himself too hard through harsh circumstance."

I glanced around the room. Beyond the airlock, through the transplas door, I could see a larger room that had a few beds in it.

"Where are we?" I asked.

"Mining barracks." Leigh stood and approached the door. "When the mine closed down, smugglers moved in. They took over some of the barracks rooms, reconditioned them, and made them habitable once more. Every now and again, the Colonial Corps sweep the tunnels and find places like these and shut them down. Within a few weeks, the smugglers—or mercs that need a place to lie low for a while—get them set up again. The Colonial

Corps get stretched too thin to keep these places shut down all the time."

The airlock beeped and the locking mechanism disengaged, letting us know that the atmospheres were now matched. It was still far too cold inside the room.

"If this man is to survive, we need more heat," I told Leigh.

"If we turn on the heat," one of the other men said, "the Colonial Corps could sense it. They'll find us."

"Were they looking for you?" I asked. "If not, perhaps they won't be looking."

"We ran," the man replied. "They'll be looking."

I swiveled my attention to Leigh. "Why did you run?"

"Because they were looking for us." She gestured toward the outer room. "Bring him in here. Make him comfortable. Do what you can for him."

I picked up my patient and carried him to one of the beds in the long, narrow room. I stripped blankets from the other beds and wrapped him as best as I could. The room was still cold, but not so cold that it was life-threatening for humans.

"What do we do now?" the soldier asked.

"We wait," Leigh replied in a flat voice. "Either Tallin gets better or he doesn't. If he does, we move out when he's on his feet again. Until then, stay alert and get some rest." She looked at me. "Keep that soldier alive."

"I will do what I can." I settled in beside Tallin and continued to monitor him. I also took advantage of the fact that I could still tie into the Net through my PAD and found out Floyd had sent me a message. I responded, letting him know I could take a meeting at his earliest convenience. Then I sat, silent and still as stone while Leigh and her two men wrapped in blankets and hunkered down to await what would happen next.

Chapter Thirty-One

In the meetbox, responding to the message I had received, Floyd stood in the middle of a virtual crime scene, but it wasn't one I was familiar with. I popped into the holo a few meters from him.

At Floyd's feet, a dead man lay in a crumpled heap. The deceased lay facedown on the carpet and a pool of blood stained the carpet around him. The door to the room lay in pieces on the floor, obviously blasted off its hinges. Closer inspection revealed that the hinges had also been burned through by acid.

Nearby, an automated cleaner sat beeping an emergency code to the NAPD. Low-AI cleaning bots were coded to send out signals to law enforcement when they encountered human bodies. Most of them were, anyway. Some had been reconfigured, but that was hard to do.

Two other men lay against the far wall of the large conference room. Large-caliber slugs stood out starkly in the cracked bullet-resistant transplas, caught like flies in a spider's web. Outside the windows, night hung over the megapolis. Hoppers raced by, their lights bright in the darkness. Two moons hung in the sky and I knew we were on Mars, not Earth, which I found curious. To my knowledge, Floyd had not been to Mars.

"Am I intruding?" I asked.

"No. I wanted you to see this."

I remained standing, secure in the knowledge that the sensors I had set to watch over Leigh Bonner and her merc companions would alert me if they moved. When I had linked to the meet-box, they had been sleeping, waiting for news of the Colonial Corps' search to die down. From what they had gathered, the Martian military was chasing merc units known to associate with rebel forces, and the Chimeras in particular.

"Is this a case you're working on?" I asked.

"In a sense. This is a cold case that is fourteen years old. You are not familiar with it?"

I pulled up the file and read the names of the dead men. They meant nothing to me, but they were all Human First members who worked directly for Alton Fuller.

"No."

"Simon Blake did not know them either."

I searched through Simon's memories, what I had access to. "To my knowledge, no. I have no memory of Simon's meeting with these men. Did he know them?"

"Simon Blake was high on the list of persons of interest regarding these executions."

"Why?"

"He was on Mars at the time these men were killed. The Bradbury colony police detectives tried to build a case against him."

"Why?"

"Trace DNA at the crime scene seemed to link him."

That was interesting. "What trace DNA?"

"Blood."

"Simon was wounded?"

"The Bradbury police believed so. They brought Simon in for questioning."

"Did they find a wound?"

"No. Furthermore, when Simon gave them a DNA sample, it was only a sixty-eight percent match."

"In order to bring Simon in, they had to have had a DNA sample to match against."

"They found one in a hospital database from a few years before. Back when Simon Blake was a mercenary with the Chimeras." Floyd gave me the date and I realized it had to have been from when Simon was wounded and met John Rath.

"A sixty-eight percent match is significant."

"It is, but it wasn't enough to lock Simon down for the executions."

"Where was he at the time of the murders?" I asked.

"At a hotel. Alone."

"So he had no alibi."

"None."

"Was there another reason he was a suspect in these murders?"

"These individuals all had records for doing wetwork for Human First." Floyd pushed more files at me. "They were suspected of murdering Haas-Bioroid and Jinteki R&D people, and also destroying bioroids and clones."

Images of scrapped bioroids and gutted clones popped into view for a moment, then I had them in my PAD.

"They were very good at what they did," Floyd said. "The man who killed them was better."

"One man?"

"Yes." Floyd raised a hand and the three dead men rose to their feet. They stood talking around the conference table, studying a holo that projected above the surface. The door mended itself and floated back into place.

In the holo, Mara Blake—newly married to Simon—arrived at Bradbury Port Authority and made her way along a slidewalk. Simon Blake walked at her side. He was keenly alert but attentive to his wife. They smiled and joked, and I could almost remember that moment.

"The holo was found at the scene," Floyd said. "Bradbury PD assumed that these men had been tasked to kill Mara Blake and possibly Simon Blake as well."

"If that is true, I can see why Simon Blake would target them." I paused. "You say he was alone in his hotel? He wouldn't have left Mara Blake unattended."

"He didn't. She was asleep in an adjoining room."

"So she could provide no alibi."

"Correct."

I considered that. "It would have been better if she had lied for him and said that they were together."

"Simon gave his statement first. He did not try to hide behind his wife."

"Perhaps he didn't wish to involve her until he knew the case against him. He would have protected Mara."

"Possibly."

I studied the three men, thinking about how dangerous they were based on the information Floyd had passed on to me. All of them were augmented, faster and more lethal than anything human. The odds of one man getting all three of them without getting killed were astronomical.

"You're sure there was only one man?"

"The Bradbury PD was." Floyd gestured again and pointed toward the door.

Events progressed in slow motion. The door blew inward and revealed a single figure standing on the other side. The person looked like he or she had been cloaked in ink. A large-bore slug-thrower belched flame before the pieces of the door thudded to the carpet. Lime-green laser lights tracked the paths of the bullets.

One of the bullets chewed through a section of the door, throwing it off-balance, then mushroomed against a man's face, throwing him backward. Another two punched through the second man's chest as he brought out a slug-thrower and opened fire. The paths of those three bullets were marked in bright blue.

Two of them embedded in the bullet-resistant transplas, spider-webbing the panes. The third hit the shadow-person. Blood—marked in lemon yellow highlighter—sprayed from the shadow-person, but I couldn't tell where the bullet hit.

As the second man stumbled back from the impact of the bullets, the shooter took a step to the side, slid one foot through the blood, and fired three more rounds. All of the bullets punched into the last man as he sprinted sideways. His efforts only added to his impetus as the bullets caught him and knocked him from his feet in a rolling death spiral.

Calmly, the shooter entered the room.

"No other blood was found in the conference room," Floyd told me. "So the killer had to have attended the wound."

In no hurry, the shooter walked through the men and shot each one of them through the head to ensure the kills.

"Competent. Professional. And highly skilled," Floyd said. "This is something the Bradbury PD felt certain Simon Blake could have done."

He could have. I didn't say anything for a moment, then I focused on the question that most troubled me. "Why would you investigate a fourteen-year-old crime scene?"

"Because I got a hit on DNA the coroner found on Jonas Salter's body." Floyd touched one of his silver eyes. "Sweat was found inside Salter's right eye that did not belong to him. That trace evidence was not discovered on the preliminary inspection of Salter's body."

"The killer sweated on Salter?"

"Probably as he stood over Salter to confirm the kill. Or perhaps when the trace liquid that tracked back to you was applied."

Around us, the conference room melted away and Jonas Salter's crime scene took its place. A single drop of sweat stood out against Salter's right eye, highlighted in yellow.

"That drop of sweat allowed the coroner to establish a DNA sample."

"Did you connect it to anyone?"

"Only to this crime scene on Mars," Floyd replied.

"You're sure it is the same DNA?" The question felt redundant even as I voiced it. The statement Floyd had given me was a closed loop. There could be no other answer.

"Yes. It also is a sixty-eight percent match to Simon Blake's DNA."

"Curious," I said, and I knew that was an unnecessary assessment.

"I had hoped it might stir more of Simon Blake's memories within you."

"It doesn't."

"Perhaps you will remember something later. You will let me know?"

"Of course."

"In the meantime, I shall endeavor to pursue this latest piece of evidence." Floyd paused. "Things on Mars have gotten very complicated."

"Yes."

"There is talk of the Martian Colonial Authority declaring martial law in the near future."

"It will be a mistake if they do. They should have learned that during the Colony Wars."

"I think so, too, but humans have a tendency to repeat their mistakes. Stay safe, Drake."

I thanked him and faded from the meetbox, returning to the room where Leigh and her companions slept.

* * *

I worked quickly when I got back to the barracks room. My mind buzzed with questions, trying to work out how those two DNA samples—a sixty-eight percent match for Simon Blake—had ended up on Mars and on Jonas Salter's corpse. I could frame no cogent hypothesis. Too many variables still existed.

Instead, I concentrated on Tallin, the man whom I had carried into the barracks after he had fallen. While he was still sedated, I reopened his chest wound just enough to slip in a GPS transponder that I could track through the Net.

I had no illusions about Leigh letting me join her when she left the area. As soon as she deemed it safe to leave, she would be gone, and I would be left behind.

I still believed she knew where Mara Blake was. She was a prominent player among John Rath's plans. In fact, Simon was certain Leigh had been inserted into his security group watching over Mara to spy on him.

I closed the incision with adhesive, made sure it was sterile, and was satisfied that if the adjustment to the wound was noticed I could simply say it had broken open slightly when Tallin had fallen.

Finished, certain my work had gone unnoticed, I sat back and thought about Simon Blake and the three dead Human First assassins.

* * *

"State your name for the record."

I looked at the hard-faced female detective seated on the other side of the interrogation room table. She was in her middle years and wore prominent tattoos that marked her as Marsborn. Her name was Donna Carbo and she was good at her job, focused and unflustered.

I held up my hands, cuffed only a few centimeters apart. A shock collar encircled my neck. "You know who I am. You picked me up at the hotel where I was staying with my wife."

She frowned at me. "This will go faster if you respond in the appropriate manner."

I sighed and told her that I was Simon Blake.

"Where do you live?"

I gave her the address I shared with Mara in New Angeles.

She proceeded down her list, going back through Simon's personal history, first covering his marriage to Mara, then his employment as her security chief, then back to my work as a mercenary on Mars.

"You worked with John Rath?"

"Yes, but that is all I will say about that relationship. That has nothing to do with the murders you're accusing me of."

She tried a few more questions about John Rath. He remained something of an enigma for the Martian Colonial Authority. People could hire him, if they had enough credits—if he wanted the assignment—but not much was known about him.

Simon grew irritated at the repetitive questioning. The emotion was something new in my experience, but I recognized it. Finally, he fell silent and refused to speak.

"What were you doing before you signed up with John Rath and the Chimeras?"

The question threw Simon for a moment. Panic and uncertainty fluttered within him. He spoke succinctly. "I was a mercenary. That's all logged into my file."

"Tell me about those years."

Simon leaned back in his chair. His pulse and respiration picked up tempo. "Why?"

"Because I'd like to know."

"That has no bearing on your investigation."

"Let me be the judge of that."

Simon smiled. "I've been pretty generous about this if you ask me. You brought me in here and I haven't lawyered up yet."

"Getting an attorney would only delay your release."

"I'm beginning to doubt that."

She ignored me. "Tell me about your life before Rath."

"Why?"

She tapped her PAD. "Because I've checked through your history, Mr. Blake, and it's pitifully lacking in detailed information. I've tried to find someone—anyone—who knew you before you signed on with Rath." She paused for effect. "I can't. Maybe you can give me some names that aren't in my files."

Simon's confusion was so alien to me that I almost lost touch with him at that point. I clung to him, though.

"Can you do that, Mr. Blake?" Carbo remained calm, giving no sign of hostility.

Simon leaned back in his chair. "No."

"Why?"

"There was an accident a few years ago. My memory was damaged. Before that time in the hospital, I can't remember much. The doctors told me I was lucky."

"Would you be surprised to learn that I haven't been able to turn up much personal history on you? Like where you've lived? A job history beyond what's put in your files? Friends or references that become flesh and blood at any point along the way?"

Simon's voice turned harsh and I felt his anger and fear surging in a volatile mix within him. I hung onto him, not wanting to let go. "All of those memories are gone, Detective. Did you not hear that?"

"I did, but—"

"No buts." Simon swore. "We've lived through a civil war in the colonies, Detective. Do you know how many lives were lost?"

"I'm well aware of—"

"All those lives, and you're worried about electronic documents that vanished in an electromagnetic surge?" Simon leaned closer to her. "Do you know what I remember most? I remember the night my parents and my sister were killed. I remember that really well." He leaned back in his chair again. "Now either let me go or book me, because I'm not saying another word without my lawyer present."

I lost Simon then and went spinning away from him.

Chapter Thirty-Two

The next morning, Tallin came around and was doing much better. If he noticed any additional pain from the wound in his chest, he didn't say anything about it. He got up with Leigh and the rest of the team and made preparations to leave.

Leigh didn't say much to me and I knew she wasn't sure what to do with me. Shortly after 0800, her comm pulsed and she answered. The device was heavily encrypted, but after I'd worked on Tallin, I'd also hacked into it. I couldn't embed a GPS trace on it because it was equipped with squealies that would notify Leigh of its presence.

But I could listen in.

She took the call and walked to the corner of the room.

"Where are you?" a man's voice asked.

"Paxton Node," Leigh answered.

"Are you still free?"

"Yes."

"Rath heard the Colonial Corps crashed the bars there and rounded up mercenaries they deemed potential terrorists. The Chimeras made the list."

"Lucky us." Leigh frowned and I knew she was thinking

about how much more difficult it was going to be to leave Paxton Node without being noticed.

"You don't know the half of it. The vidcasts are full of the action the Colonial Corps have pulled off. The Martian Colonial Authority thought they were going to be able to shut down the unrest. All they've done is succeeded in accelerating it. Lines have been drawn in all of the major colonies."

"Just like Rath said it would."

"Yeah. Rath's intel people have also told him the Earth corps are shipping special sec units to Mars. They're due to arrive in the next few days."

"The locals are going to read that as an invasion when it happens."

"I know."

Beside me, Shelly cursed. "What are they thinking? The situation on Mars between the pro-Earth groups and those favoring Martian independence has been filled with friction anyway. If Earth lands sec forces here, it's going to start a war."

I silently agreed.

"Rath wants you back here," the man said at the other end of the comm.

"Give us a few hours and we'll be there," Leigh replied.

"Get here before dusk because we've got orders to pull up stakes and get gone by then."

Leigh folded her comm and put it away, returning to me. She crossed her arms and stared at me.

I sat on one of the beds.

"I don't know what to do with you," she admitted.

I remained silent.

"My gut tells me that I should burn you here and be done with it after the way you approached me last night."

I was prepared to move quickly if I had to. A small needler filled with tranquilizers sat hidden in my hand.

Tallin grimaced. "McDreamy saved my life last night. You guys wouldn't have come back for me."

"Would have got us killed if we had," one of the other men said, sounding petulant. "Can't blame us. If it had been one of us, you wouldn't have stopped either."

"And getting emotional about a bioroid doesn't make a lot of sense," the other one said. "We burn this one, Haas-Bioroid will just make another."

Leigh ignored them and studied me. "I've got a lot of questions about you and Simon, but I don't have the time to ask them." She took in a breath and let it out. "Know this: if I see you again, I'll end you."

"I understand," I said.

She turned on her heel, called her men to her, and marched down one of the tunnels.

"She means it, Drake," Shelly told me. "If you go out there, she will destroy you."

"I know," I replied. Leigh had always meant what she said.

I remained seated on the bed for twenty minutes in case she posted someone to stay behind. Then I pinged the GPS transponder I'd placed inside Tallin's wound, locked onto the signal, and started following. They were already three kilometers away and moving.

* * *

Leigh and her team escaped Paxton's Node by joining up with a terraforming group that was undoubtedly part of the smuggling operation in the area. I watched them go, waited a while, then stepped outside the node airlock with a group of bioroids, blending in easily. We rode in the open rear cargo compartment of a crawler.

When we reached the work site, I toiled with the crew for hours, waited until dusk, then stepped away from the group. No one noticed, not even the bioroids I had been working with. They were all Franks and Diesels, purely manual labor to move materials.

By that time Tallin was seventy-six kilometers away and accelerating fast enough that I knew he was traveling in a land vehicle. I took off running, able to see easily in the dark and capable of accelerating almost as fast as their vehicle in the Martian gravity.

Still, I questioned myself, doubting whether I was getting any closer.

Shelly ran at my side, something she would never have been able to do when she'd still been human. "This is the trail, Drake. Don't second-guess yourself. Everything you've been following has been leading up to this place and time. Whatever is going on, the Chimeras, John Rath, and Mara Blake are all connected. You're an investigator. You've investigated. Follow what you know."

I ran quietly, taking great, bounding strides across the mountainous terrain, following the GPS transponder but losing ground. The moons cycled through the dark sky.

At Kline Node, a smaller, seedier version of Paxton, I got lucky just before dawn and found a minihopper that someone had built from salvage parked outside of a pleasure house. I knelt and stripped the GPS beacon, switched the ID with another vehicle, and hot-wired the minihopper.

Throwing a leg over the minihopper, I revved the engine and rose into the air. I drove it to the airlock, got through the lax security easily, and opened it up once all of Mars lay before me. I held onto the controls and focused on the GPS transponder. I wasn't hopeful. Bioroids don't experience that. But I thought a lot of Mara Blake and felt the pressure inside me pushing me to find her.

I realized that Mara might not be there, that I was following a false trail, but there was nowhere else for me to go.

If she wasn't with John Rath as I suspected, then I would begin again searching out her trail. It was all I could do.

* * *

Nine days later, still 342.8 kilometers behind the GPS transponder, I drove toward Bradbury colony. I knew that had to be Leigh's final destination. That was the gathering place for the colonial government committee that had formed to deal with collapsing relations between pro-Earth and pro-Mars. The two sides were still talking only because the rebel forces were flexing their muscles, causing chaos among Earth corps.

According to the vidcasts, access to Bradbury colony was limited. I waited for dusk and rode out to the mag-lev track. The train schedule showed that an inbound train was due at 2341. When it roared by, I chased it on the minihopper and closed on it despite the rough terrain. After I was close enough, I caught the rear railing of the caboose and stepped from the minihopper.

I pulled myself onto the caboose's rear deck as the minihopper sped out of control and slammed into a stand of rocks. Flipping, the minihopper smashed against the ground, coming undone with only a few glimmering parts that reflected Deimos's light.

I waited, but no one came to check on me. I thought the weight tolerance for shifting cargo was enough to cover my added mass. When we were only five minutes out from Bradbury colony's sec gates, I opened the caboose door with a lock subroutine and stepped inside.

Most of the bioroids riding there were Franks. A couple of Brads and a few Davids were thrown into the mix. I found one of the older Franks and mirrored his e-ID. By the time the train stopped a few minutes later, for all intents and purposes I was Frank B07I43, a cargo handler for the train.

I walked to the baggage compartment, picked up a load of cargo on a skiff, and approached the sec gate, following other Franks and cargo bots. I was not nervous as a human might have been, but I knew the likelihood of my ruse depended on a number of things that were out of my control. If the sec guards were overly attentive to bioroids, my duplication of e-ID would be discovered. I also knew they were more concerned with human rebels. Bradbury colony was under martial law and tension was spilling over into the streets.

I moved through the line, awaiting my turn, and focused on the GPS signal I followed. For the last twenty-seven hours, the transponder had been relatively stationary. I knew it was possible that Tallin had been taken to a medical facility under another name, but I also knew he was a wanted man. I'd found a warrant for his arrest on the Colonial Corps site. The highest percentage was that Tallin would be somewhere with the Chimeras.

I hoped that Mara Blake was there as well.

The sec guards barely looked at my e-ID before they waved me through. I placed the cargo I carried at the kiosk where it was to be delivered, shifted my e-ID back to McDreamy, and entered Bradbury colony, still following the transponder signal.

* * *

Three hours and fourteen minutes later, I stood in front of a tall building Simon Blake recognized. I felt his memories shift within me and tried to pin one down and couldn't.

Hoppers serviced the rooftop where the penthouse quarters were, but I knew that the Chimeras wouldn't be there. They would be underground, and that was where the transponder signal came from.

Across the street from the Mahendra Building, the Khondi Tower stood tall and elegant. It was the tallest building in Bradbury. From street level, the spire at the top seemed on the verge of piercing the protective bubble that enclosed the colony. The building was also located in the geographic center of the colony, anchoring the municipal and business centers in concentric streets for twenty blocks.

A security cordon circled the tower, holding back groups that protested against the colonial government committee housed there in the top five stories. The nosies had broadcast their location, and the protestors had wasted no time setting up there.

Angry voices filled the street. Ground vehicles mired between the protestors and the sec forces honked, giving voice to protests of their own. Traffic continued, but it was choked down on all sides, moving by centimeters now.

A woman stepped forward toward the sec line, shouting invective at the guards at their posts. Perhaps she was simply too close, or perhaps she struck at the man, even the vidcast image scrawling across the third and fourth floors of the Khondi Tower in real-time couldn't reveal that. Either way, the sec guard nearest her spun, put his armored hand over her face, and shoved her back using the artificial musculature of his encounter suit.

The woman flew backward into her compatriots. Blood leaked from her split lips. Some of her fellows managed to catch her before she hit the ground. Even as those people returned her to her feet, at least two dozen protestors surged forward across the sec line, most of them pushed by the people behind them.

The sec guards pulled out stunsticks and beat the aggressors back. I took a step toward them.

Shelly's arm dropped onto my shoulder and I felt her holding me back. "No."

"Someone is going to get hurt." I started to shrug her off but she held onto me tightly.

"Let this go, Drake. Those people aren't going to get killed. Mara Blake is in more danger than they are."

I prioritized and realized that though I did not know that for certain, everything indicated that was true. I turned from the battle spreading across the street and entered the Mahendra Building. The transponder signal was 82.6 ahead of me and 64.8 meters down.

I entered the noodle shop on the first floor and pulled down the Mahendra Building's schematics from the fire department.

Chapter Thirty-Three

Most of the noodle shop's clientele were pressed against the windows overlooking the growing riot out on the street. The others watched the vidcast on the shop's holos.

I walked through them unnoticed and stepped through the interior doors into the main hallway that allowed access to the rest of the Mahendra Building.

The hallway was nearly empty. I made my way to the maintenance room, spoofed the sec locks, and entered. I knelt and rearranged my weapons. I holstered the Synap to my right hip and snugged the Gortaub 15mm slug-thrower at my back so I could easily draw it with my left hand. I was completely ambidextrous. I slid the rifle stock and barrel extension into the long pockets of my trouser legs. I had bought dark clothing to replace that which I had worn into Bradbury.

"You seem very familiar with what you're doing," Shelly said as she stood across the room.

"It's not me," I replied. "I'm following Simon Blake's instincts." He was there with me, hovering just out of reach now.

"Be careful, Drake." Shelly's lips compressed into a hard line for a moment. "Don't get so lost in his memories that you forget who you are."

"I won't."

"Even if you come out of this okay, you're not going to be the same again."

I didn't have anything to say to that. I nodded and focused on the GPS transponder signal. I ignored the access to the elevator to the lower floors and instead opened the air duct and went down.

The space was a tight fit and a human would have been hard-pressed to navigate the duct down for sixty-four meters. I experienced no problems using my hands and knees to lock my body into position as I journeyed down.

I thought I could hear Simon Blake whispering in the back of my mind as I continued down. "Be careful, buddy. John Rath is no fool. Every time you think you have him cornered, he's got nine escape plans just waiting in reserve."

"Do you know what this is about?"

Memory of the conversation with Rath on the Beanstalk's observation deck flitted through my mind.

"You betrayed me, buddy. I didn't expect that from you. Out of every man in my unit, I knew you were the one most like me. I made *you. Shaped you. Taught you how to think. Everything you are, you owe to me."*

I wondered at his words, poked at them for hidden meanings and depth. He'd meant more than he had revealed and I knew it. A deeper truth had been spoken.

"I made *you."*

I continued down and I remembered the man with ice-blue eyes who had talked with Mara while I'd lain in my cubicle awaiting final activation. Mara had only referred to him as "John," and I had assumed he was Rath at the time. I recognized him in the memory now. It had been the first time I had seen John Rath as Drake.

Their conversation trickled through my thoughts.

"Where were you when Simon was killed, John?" Mara asked.

Rath took in a breath and let it out. "Away. You know that."

"Simon was murdered."

"I know."

"The thing that bothers me most is that I don't know if his murderer knew that he was killing Simon, or if he thought he was killing you."

Rath shook his head. "I don't know. Simon and I were...close. We worked together for years. We made a lot of enemies. A lot of people wanted us dead." He showed her a twisted smile. "Many of those same people still want me dead."

"That's what you've said. That's what he said. But neither of you ever said how long you worked together or what it was you did."

Rath's jaw knotted up for just a moment, then smoothed out again. "We fought and bled for whoever would pay us in whatever dirty war happened to be going on at the time. That's what we did." He paused. "And unless you've been in situations like that, you don't really want to talk to an outsider about it." His voice softened a little then. "Not even someone you love."

Unshed tears glistened in Mara's eyes. "I've got a party I've got to get back to." Without another word, she walked past him and out of my field of vision.

Rath stood there for a moment after her ringing footsteps vanished. Then he turned to me and studied me some more. "You're not as special as she thinks, golem. You're a copy of a copy. Nothing remarkable." He walked away, his footsteps silent as a shadow on the hard floor.

I thought about his words for a moment. I paused nine meters up from the ductwork that allowed me onto the bottom underground floor. Enough of Simon's memories were in my head to let me know John Rath had a safehouse there.

The GPS transponder pinged inside my head. If I was right, Mara was nearby.

* * *

I checked into the meetbox and pinged Floyd while I continued to monitor the transponder. Four minutes passed before he stepped into the meetbox with me. He gazed around at the NAPD bullpen where detectives continued to work cases and paid no attention to us.

"Interesting choice of location," he told me.

I hadn't made a conscious decision regarding the surroundings. "I have a task I would like you to do."

"Of course. Are you safe? The colonies are rife with violence."

"I am safe at the moment, and I might have found Mara Blake."

"That's good. Do you have any assistance?"

"No."

"That is regrettable."

I didn't bother agreeing with him. "I need you to quietly look into the murder of Simon Blake."

"What am I looking for?"

I told him.

Floyd considered the request for a moment. "That is an interesting supposition. What led you to that conclusion?"

"It was something John Rath told me."

"I was not aware that you had met Rath as Drake."

"Once. For only a moment."

"I will get back to you on this as soon as I am able."

"Thank you."

"Stay safe, Drake. My interest in you deepens."

I left the meetbox and returned to Mars.

* * *

Nine meters farther down, I stepped down onto the ground, and then hunkered down to remove the filter and peer through the slots. My field of view was narrow and heavily restricted.

I waited three seconds, the GPS responder holding steady. Unwilling to wait any longer, I snapped the screws and removed the duct cover. Moving slowly, I eased out into the hallway. Just as I started to put the cover back in place so no one would notice I had entered there, a massive electric shock slammed me back against the wall. My senses swirled, cutting offline then returning in flickers. I tried to move and couldn't.

A section of the wall across from me winked out of existence and revealed John Rath standing there in a hardsuit with an electromagnetic pulse rifle canted over his shoulder in one hand. He didn't look like he'd changed at all since the last time I'd seen him. His hair was still ink black and his eyes were ice-blue.

Leigh stood at his side and looked at me ruefully.

"You owe me twenty credits, Leigh." Rath walked over to me.

"There are six ductworks he could have come down," Leigh complained. "How did you know he would come down this one?"

"You want to answer her, golem?" Rath asked.

I tried to speak, not to answer her question, but to ask about Mara. I couldn't. My systems were locked up in self-repair and running diagnostics.

"This hunk of tin can't tell you, so I will." Rath grinned. "This ductwork? It's a straight shot to the GPS transponder he stuck inside Tallin. This thing isn't that creative. It's single-minded. It didn't even think about subterfuge." He paused and lifted an eyebrow. "Surprisingly dedicated, though. Or maybe it's just stupid."

I still couldn't speak.

"The transponder inside Tallin, though?" Rath nodded. "That was nice. That's something I would have done." He lowered the rifle and shot me again, and this time I went away.

Chapter Thirty-Four

My consciousness came back online in a rush, blurring color and causing audio distortion of the voices and noise around me. I was lying on the floor with my wrists and ankles shackled together. I tried to access the Net and couldn't because someone had attached a damper to the back of my head.

Across from me in the large empty room, four meters away, Mara Blake sat handcuffed to a chair. She looked haggard and worn, but she hadn't lost that fierce independence that Simon Blake had loved. She wore a black one-piece that revealed she had lost weight.

John Rath, Leigh, Tallin, and a half-dozen chimera mercenaries sat at a table and stared at the vidcast of the riot that had swelled enough to fill the streets in front of the Khondi Tower. All of the mercenaries, including Rath, were heavily armed. The vidcast console was the only furniture in the room besides the long table and chairs.

"Mara," I said before I knew it.

She looked at me, not comprehending.

"Are you back with us, golem?" Rath looked back over his shoulder. "I thought maybe I fried your circuits with that last blast."

I knew I should have remained quiet, but I felt closer than ever to Simon Blake at that time. "Not quite," I replied.

Rath grunted in amusement. "You'll disappear soon enough. But only after you play out your swan song. Me and you have got some private time coming as soon as I can manage it."

"What are you talking about?" I struggled to sit up. One of the mercs standing near me kicked me back down.

Unable to balance myself, knowing that the man would only kick me again if I tried once more to sit up, I remained there. The impact had shifted my shackles, though. I managed to seize one of the chain links between my thumb and forefinger. I pinched. Hard. At first I didn't think anything was going to happen, then I felt the metal start to give.

Mara looked at me and I wondered if she could see Simon's features in my face.

"Don't you recognize him, Mara?" Rath asked. He touched his own face. "Something about the eyes? I thought surely you would know him. After all, you created him, and then you programmed him to come after you."

Mara understood then, and another layer of defeat dropped onto her. She had been in Rath's custody—or at least had been held by the Chimeras—for almost a year now. "Drake?" she whispered in disbelief.

"Yes," I replied.

"Where are the others?"

"There is no one else." I pinched harder and felt the chain link part. I searched out another in another strand of chain.

"Your lab experiment didn't quite work out the way you'd planned," Rath said in a mocking tone. His blue eyes watched the riot on the street outside. "I knew about him at the time you made him. I could have ended it then, but I knew I had a use for him when the time came." He looked at me. "You know me. I don't let anything go to waste."

Sec squads employed non-lethal measures to break up the riot on the vidcast. Despite the microwave fields, the tear gas, and the high-pressure water, the rioters remained engaged. In fact, their numbers swelled as their outrage grew, and the level of violence escalated as some of the anti-Earth rebels began firing on the guards. The sec teams tried to bring in more barricades to hold back the tide of outraged citizens.

"Drake 3GI2RC came looking for you," Rath went on, "but he got his partner killed along the way, managed to get framed for the murder of Jonas Salter, and got involved with an illegal arms manufacturing operation."

"Jonas is dead?" Mara's eyes widened.

"Yes. Months ago." Rath manipulated the vidcast feeds, pulling up aerial footage of the floor of the Khondi Tower where colonial government heads had gathered to discuss the outbreak of violence. "Not much of a rescuer, your Drake 3GI2RC, eh? That's one experiment you didn't quite have worked out, Doctor. You've done pretty good on your other neural channeling, though. See? I did find a use for your pet golem."

Rath dialed up the audio as a trio of hoppers lifted from the rooftop hopper pads.

"I've just heard from a source inside that some of the colonial governors are trying to leave the Khondi Tower," the nosie said on the vidcast. "They've released a message that indicates they believe the rioters will disperse if they realize no government agents remain within the building. They're going to meet again on a date to be announced later."

Rath adjusted his comm mike and spoke quickly. "Take them down."

In response, a dozen rockets rose from the surrounding buildings and targeted the three hoppers. Explosions rang out like a string of fireworks. The detonations sounded first on the vidcast, then followed a second later as thunder rolled down the air and elevator shafts.

Burning debris tumbled down from the sky and left black smudges of smoke hanging in the still air.

Mara stared at the vidcast in tired horror and I sensed Simon's frenzy to be at her side within me. Whatever she had been through at Rath's hands had left her jaded and numb.

On the screen, four gold cargo hoppers shot down out of the sky, tearing through the smoky clouds. For a moment, the rioters and the sec teams stood frozen in awe, and then they realized the lethal fallout from the destroyed hoppers was claiming victims. They took shelter where they could.

The gold cargo hoppers stopped their descent about four meters above street level. The doors slid open and figures clad in armored gold suits began dropping down, some of them crashing on top of the rioters, driving those victims into the street under their crushing weight. All of the newcomers carried rifles, and they moved like components in a well-oiled machine.

They opened fire without warning and large-caliber bullets chopped into the crowd, taking off limbs and leaving corpses in their wake. The brutal attack drove the rioters away instantly. More people died trying to help their wounded fellows. Even rioters who tried to surrender were shot down mercilessly.

The inhuman speed and lack of fear told me who was in the armored suits. Nothing flesh and blood could move like that—nothing human, nothing cloned. They showed machine precision and hive mind behavior, all moving toward a single directive.

"Drake," Shelly said beside me, "you know what they are."

Rath stood and watched the screen, and then spoke over his comm. "Light one of them up. Let's let the worlds see what they're dealing with. Time to lift the curtain and have a look at the wizard."

A rocket streaked across the screen and slammed into one of the armored gold figures, driving it back into its fellows. Sections of the armor flew off, including the helmet.

"Do you see what that is?" one of the nosies bellowed over the channel. "Somebody get a vid on that thing!"

The vid zoomed in to magnify the downed armored figure. The immobile metallic surface beneath the helmet had no face.

"That's a bioroid!" one of the nosies shouted in disbelief.

"Bioroids can't kill!" another yelled. "That's against the Three Directives!"

"Tell that to those people they just murdered!"

As the other armored figures continued to march around the fallen one, the downed bioroid forced itself back to its feet. It reached down for its rifle, picked it up, and opened fire again. Methodically, it reloaded its weapon and rejoined its fellows.

Mara stared at Rath. "You did this."

Rath grinned and nodded. "I did."

"How?"

"I installed specialized code into Haas-Bioroid's warroids program."

"The warroids initiative was supposed to be kept separate from the work I was doing."

"You seriously thought Haas-Bioroid was going to develop a secondary neural channeling system for their warroid unit?" Rath snorted. "You're a fool. Maybe you made a fortune from Haas-Bioroid, but they used your software for a lot more than you agreed on. Those warroids are based on one of the best soldiers Mars has ever seen, but it took your software design to implement it." He leaned forward and smiled in open appreciation. "They're the best urban killing machines ever designed. Fast. Ruthless. Precise. Everything a world leader could want in a private army."

The vidcast flickered briefly before centering on a new shot of Bradbury colony governor Albert Bloomfield. He was in his sixties, immaculate and virile, black eyebrows juxtaposed beneath silver hair.

"Are you ready?" he asked in his baritone voice.

"Yes," someone off-screen replied.

Bloomfield looked into the vid, addressing the viewers. "Citizens of Bradbury, remain calm. Those units you're seeing in the streets in front of the Khondi Tower are under colonial government control. They're here to deal with the civil unrest."

Rath touched a control and the projection split. One side continued showing Bloomfield while the other picked up the bloody action in front of the Khondi Tower.

"As we have seen over the last few days, negotiations have broken down within the colonies," Bloomfield said. "The colonies cannot exist if split into factions. We have to remain whole to remain strong. We learned that in the Colony Wars. Therefore, the other colonial governors and I have chosen to take drastic measures to ensure our continued survival on Mars. We will have *one* government."

The sec guards stepped back as the warroids marched toward them. Several of the sec people continued holding their weapons on the bioroids, but they didn't open fire and I could see the fear in them. Some of the officers moved among the soldiers, frantically waving at the guards to stand down.

"This new class of bioroid is not limited by the Three Directives," Bloomfield continued. "These units are capable of taking human life. You have seen that. But responsible colonial citizens have no reason to fear them. These bioroids are here to protect the recognized Martian Colonial Authority. Over the next few days they will be incorporated into the colonies to help stabilize governments and provide safer environments for our citizens."

Like ants, the warroids filed inside the Khondi Tower.

"You've seen today the lawlessness that lies in wait within our megapolis. Those officials in the hoppers that were just shot down were elected by you to represent your needs." Bloomfield clenched a fist and looked determined. "I swear to you that their deaths will be avenged. The murderers that committed this heinous act will be located and punished. No longer will innocents live in a divided Mars. Today we start becoming one world."

"Quite the speech, but he's in for a surprise." Rath punched a button on the console in front of him and the screen blanked. He picked up his assault rifle and glanced around at his troops. "Tallin, pick three and stay here to guard the woman and the golem."

Tallin nodded and called out three names. Two men and one woman stepped forward to join him. "I can understand keeping the woman alive, Colonel, but we don't need the golem."

"No," Rath said, "we don't." He looked at me and flashed a grin. "However, I do. Drake is going to be a sacrificial lamb for the cause. He'll take the rap for a few murders back on Earth and the Moon that could become complications." He paused. "And I'm curious about him. I want to know how much of him reflects the original model he's based on."

"Yes, sir."

Rath stepped forward, heading for the door. "All right. Move out. I've got a world to save from Earth dominion."

Leigh and the other mercs followed him, leaving Mara and me alone with our captors.

Chapter Thirty-Five

"Mara," I called.

She looked at me in confusion.

"Are you all right?" I asked.

"I'm alive and unharmed." Mara looked more closely at me. "Are you really Drake?"

"Yes."

"You came for me?"

"As you instructed, yes."

Tallin walked over to the console and turned the screen back on. He split it into thirds, keeping the views on the street carnage, Bloomfield, and picking up another view that trailed Rath. The mercenary colonel jogged down an underground access tunnel. Although the direction was not indicated, I knew he was heading for the Khondi Tower. John Rath had come looking for a fight. More than that, he wanted a showdown, and he had set everything up to emerge victorious. That was what he did.

"I thought you would find me sooner," Mara said.

"I apologize for not finding you more quickly," I said, "but the trail was difficult."

"It's not your fault." Mara's mouth worked and she had a hard time speaking. "When I created you, when I wrote that sub-program, I never thought it would be used. I just…wanted something to remember him by. To know that somewhere out there, he was still around."

"You're talking about Simon."

"Yes." She nodded.

"Something has been happening to me," I told her. "I have been…remembering."

Interest flickered in her eyes and I remembered how she had always been driven so much toward science. Even though her captors still remained with us, her mind automatically pried at the mystery I presented.

"What have you been remembering?"

"How we met. How I came to work for you. How we fell in love. How I was killed."

"You mean, how Simon was killed." Her eyes rounded fearfully. "You're not Simon. He was killed eight years ago."

As soon as Mara uttered those words, another memory dragged me out of there.

* * *

I sat in the hopper, letting the autopilot do its job. I was on my way back to MirrorMorph, Inc., already thinking about having dinner with Mara.

Then my PAD chirped for my attention. I answered.

"Hello, Simon."

I recognized Rath's voice immediately even though it had been months since we had last spoken on the observation deck of the Beanstalk. "Hello, John." I waited, knowing the situation was his to play out.

"I'm not going to keep you long," Rath said. "I know you're busy. Gotta get back to that wife of yours." His tone was mocking.

I remained silent.

"I just called to say goodbye. I wanted to at least give you that, and to let you know it was coming. Or rather, I should say, *you were going*." Rath paused. "My voice was the first one you ever heard. I figured it should be the last one you ever hear. See you around, Simon."

Too late, I noticed the ruby laser sight on my chest. I reached for the hopper's controls, but at the same instant, a hammer struck me in the chest and knocked me backward. Consciousness already fading, I struggled to hold on, but it was a slippery slope and I couldn't stay there. Then another bullet struck me and everything went black.

* * *

"Your situation must be very confusing," Mara was saying.

"I've learned to cope."

"I have to say, your memory of a past life was not anything I had envisioned." Mara smiled slightly. "I only wanted you equipped to operate independently of the NAPD if you had to."

"It became necessary, but things also became very *complicated*." I gazed around the room.

"How much of Simon is in there?"

"I don't know. The line between Simon and me has gotten blurred. I remain Drake 3GI2RC."

"I left as much of Simon's personality intact as I could, but I buried it within you. That's never been done before. I wasn't sure if a true human mind could withstand coming online inside a bioroid body."

"Simon has not rejected the idea. We have been focused on finding you. I think that has helped. And my personality remains in control."

Tallin and the other mercs had their attention glued onto the screen. Rath had already commandeered an elevator and slaved it to his PAD.

"Did you kill Jonas?" Mara asked.

I was surprised she could think I could do something like that. Then again, in some ways she knew more about me than I did. "I didn't kill Jonas. I found him. He told me that the Chimeras were connected to your disappearance. That's why I came here looking for you. Someone framed me for his murder."

"I'm sorry." Tears glimmered in her eyes.

"For what?"

"For whatever John Rath is going to put you through. And I'm sorry for Simon. He shouldn't be forced to die twice."

I ignored that because speculating on that was a closed loop and I had no intention of allowing that to happen. I was determined to live in spite of the circumstances. "Rath killed Simon."

The sudden pained expression on Mara's thin face told me she hadn't known. "I'd had my suspicions, but Simon never confirmed that. I was there when he died. Did he know?"

"Yes."

Mara opened her mouth, then closed it, then finally asked, "Why didn't he tell me?"

"Perhaps he wanted to spare you." I found another link in the chain and pinched. The plasteel separated and I felt the sudden slack in the chain. I reached for the next and prepared myself. All four guards Rath had left in the room were intently watching the vidcast. Reactions—pro and con—to the presence of the warroids crawled across the bottom of the screen.

"He should have told me."

"If you had known for certain, what would you have done?"

Her grimace told me what she didn't put in words.

"If you had gone up against Rath, he might have killed you."

"Not then. Back then I was too important to him. And to Haas-Bioroid."

"Simon didn't want to take the chance. I don't think he believed Rath would kill you." I looked at the screen where the warroids were now stepping into the chambers where the remaining colonial governors were. “I’m afraid that will change after today.”

Mara didn’t say anything.

The final chain link snapped and I prepared myself, moving as stealthily as possible. I gathered the ends of the chain in my right hand, shifting them slowly so they wouldn’t make any noise as I stood. I knew the mercs in the room didn’t hear me. The aud from the vidcast made more noise than I did.

But Tallin saw my reflection in the screen. He stood at the right angle to notice my movement.

“Look out!” he warned as he drew his weapon and spun to face me.

Moving more quickly than he could ever hope to, I stepped forward and whipped the chains in a glinting arc that wrapped them around his rifle. I yanked and Tallin stumbled toward me, unwilling to relinquish his grip.

The others moved to bring their weapons up.

I held Tallin against me, preventing him from employing the rifle. His sour breath clouded my face and he grinned up at me. “You can’t do anything more, can you? The Three Directives, remember? You’re bound by them.” He let go of the rifle and reached for the pistol belted at his waist.

“Drake!” Shelly screamed in my ear.

“Break him!” Simon yelled. “You can’t let them kill Mara!”

Time slowed and whirred, clicking through my mind. I shed some of my Drake persona and reached for the part of me that remembered being Simon Blake. I was no longer simply a bioroid. I was no longer simply Drake 3GI2RC. I remembered how Shelly had been killed because I hadn’t been able to act, and Simon and I didn’t want that to happen to Mara. Too many people had died to get me here, and there were too many lives at stake if John Rath’s plan worked.

With one hand, I drove the rifle butt into Tallin’s skull, feeling the bone break and seeing blood spray. With my other hand,

I stripped the Gortaub pistol from his hand. The Drake part of me teetered on shutting down, but the Simon part of me relished the kill. I was no longer who I had been. I was no longer stifled as Drake, and I was a more skilled warrior than Simon Blake had ever hoped to be.

I flipped the pistol in my hand, grabbing it by the butt and sliding my finger over the trigger. My other hand caught the rifle as I dropped the chains and brought it around to bear.

One of the mercs got off two rounds that hit me dead center in the chest, but the extra plating over my brain kept them from penetrating, though I was dented. I pointed the pistol at him and put two rounds into his face.

I side-stepped as the dead man fell and brought up the rifle, flipping it to auto-fire. I squeezed the trigger as my targeting programs integrated with the rifle's smart-link and cut a swath through the other two mercs, dropping them where they stood as their bullets cut through the space where I had been.

Frozen for a moment, I looked down at what I had done.

"Drake," Shelly said.

"Simon," Mara called.

I turned toward them, finding Shelly standing behind Mara.

"You've got to get her out of here," Shelly said. "And you've got to stop Rath from doing whatever he has planned."

"Shake it off, buddy," Simon whispered into my ear. "We can do this. We're the wild card even Rath couldn't see coming."

I freed Mara from her restraints and removed the damper from the back of my head. I felt the surge as I returned online and then centered myself. The Simon parts of me kept pulling at my thoughts, struggling to take over. I didn't let that happen. I wasn't willing to let go of myself. Simon had had his day. I still had my life, whatever it would be, ahead of me.

Mara took my face in her hands and looked up at me, her eyes searching. "Simon?" Her voice was strained.

"He's here," I said, "but I am not Simon. I am Drake."

Slowly, she nodded and released my face. "Haas-Bioroid *borrowed* the neural channeling I was doing, but I dipped into their programming as well." She smiled tentatively and coldly. "I knew about their warroid project—Project Ares. I couldn't stop it, couldn't even prove it was there because Director Haas took care to hide it. But her son knew."

"Thomas." I remembered how Thomas Haas had waited on me in my home in New Angeles.

"Yes. Thomas. He and I had an agreement. He has no love for his mother and he has his own desires. He was my second fail-safe. Thomas found you?"

"Yes."

"He unpacked the warroid programming in you, and it's slowly been evolving your personality."

I looked at the dead people lying in the room. "This…is not what I wanted."

"I know." Mara's voice firmed. "But this is necessary, Drake. If you were any less, you wouldn't have been able to find me. You wouldn't be able to stop Rath."

On the vidcast, Bloomfield was still talking, still trying to pacify citizens who were up in arms about the arrival of the warroids. He suddenly fell silent as a burst of gunfire heralded the arrival of John Rath and the Chimeras.

Dead sec guards dropped around them and I felt certain as the warroids spun to confront Rath that the merc colonel and his people were about to die. The warroids leveled their weapons.

Rath grinned and held up a hand, walking fearlessly toward Bloomfield and the other governors. "Execute Chimera Protocol Alpha Tango Frostfire."

The warroids cradled their weapons and stood at attention. Inside, I felt new programming unpack that I had never known was there, and I realized what Thomas Haas had truly done to me. On the Net, a meetbox was already pinging a connect code I didn't recognize. But I had a suspicion who was going to be on the other end.

Rath never broke stride.

"Who are you?" Bloomfield demanded.

"My name is Colonel John Rath," Rath declared. "And I'm here to save Mars." He leveled his pistol and shot Bloomfield through the head.

Bloomfield flew backwards in the lesser gravity and hit the floor at the feet of the other governors. None of them moved.

Rath pointed at the nosies in the group. "Get me on camera now."

All of the nosies pointed their vid equipment at him.

"You people have seen what the colonial governors were prepared to do," Rath said as he reloaded his pistol. "They were going to force you under the thumb of Earth corps and pro-Earth civil service. The time has come to break the ties to Earth. The time has come for Mars to be free. We can stand strong without Earth, and you people need to realize that." He snapped the pistol closed. "Some of you may be afraid right now. That's to be expected. New life and dreams never come without fear. But you don't have to do this alone. I'm going to guide you through it. I will lead you to the destinies you deserve."

Sec reinforcements burst into the large meeting room. At Rath's order, the warroids spun around and shot them down, charging forward to chase down those that did not die in the initial assault. The nosies recorded the carnage immediately.

When the sound of the gunfire died away, Rath called for the nosies again.

"You have a choice," Rath told the viewers. "Follow me as I take you to better lives...or I'll bury you."

Chapter Thirty-Six

I looked at Mara. "You need to get out of here."

"What do you mean?" She looked at me in disbelief.

"When Rath, or one of his seconds, is unable to reach this team, they'll send someone. You need to be gone. Get somewhere safe."

"Simon—*Drake*—no place is safe as long as Rath is out there."

"I know." I bent and began retrieving weapons from the fallen mercenaries. I found a flak jacket with deep pockets for ammo for my weapons and filled them. "I'm going to stop him."

"Rath will kill you."

"I'm going to try to not let that happen."

"Don't do this."

"I have to." I looked at her. "This is who I am, Mara. I was programmed to stop people like Rath. I can't walk away from this. Rath can't be allowed to do what he's doing." I paused and looked at Shelly. "He killed my partner, and when something like that happens, you're supposed to do something. I'm going to bring Rath to justice."

"You won't make it past the warroids."

"I will," I said, and left her there.

On my way to the tunnel Rath had used to infiltrate Khondi Tower, the connection to the meetbox clicked through. I paused against the wall and accepted the connection.

* * *

I stepped into a plush office and found Thomas Haas sitting at an ornate desk with his fingertips braced against each other. He looked much as he had the last time I had seen him. Lean and dressed in an expensive suit, his honey-colored red hair trailing past his shoulders, he looked up at me from behind his signature pink-lensed sunglasses. His Asian features gave him a more youthful look than his nineteen years.

"Hello, Drake 3GI2RC," he greeted in a warm voice.

"What do you want?" I asked.

"Things have gotten out of hand on Mars." Thomas waved an indolent hand over to the vidcast that was lagging several minutes behind real time on Mars.

On the screen, Rath strode into the room and shot Bloomfield through the head again.

"Wow." Thomas leaned forward and tapped the PAD in front of him. "I'm gonna have to save that one. It's a keeper."

"I don't have time to waste."

Thomas relaxed back into his chair. "I'm not wasting your time, Drake 3GI2RC. I'm here to help."

"How?"

"I suppose you know I was aware of the warroid program my mother has unleashed on Mars?"

"Yes."

"And that I was ultimately working with Mara Blake?"

"Get to it."

On the vidcast, Rath was addressing the audience.

"Allow me to savor this a little," Thomas said. "You know my mother and I don't share a lot of...familial feelings. But I do have part ownership in this corporation. I check into more projects than she is aware of. I knew that she was planning to send them to Mars to shore up our corporations there if it ever became necessary. Which it has. I also knew that someone had interfered with that program, putting in a command structure in the neural programming MirrorMorph, Inc. provided."

I thought about that.

"Mara Blake didn't know about that, but she told me about you. She suspected my mother would try something at some point, so she wanted to have a secret project of her own." Thomas Haas shot me with his forefinger and grinned. "That was you."

"Play your games with someone else."

Thomas's face hardened. "I'm not playing games. What are you planning on doing? Confronting Rath in that room? You'll just get yourself killed."

"It will be worth it if I kill him first."

"It's not like you're really going to die either, is it?" Thomas cocked his head. "Of course, Simon Blake has already died once. Maybe it's him that's not afraid of dying again."

I started to break the connection.

"I can tilt the odds in your favor," Thomas said.

I waited.

"I put my own program artifact in the encoding of those warroids. I could have stopped Rath's plan altogether, but I didn't know who was ultimately behind that subterfuge. Trying to excise the program would have been impossible. Besides that, I wanted my mother to get her comeuppance. I wanted her to be embarrassed and have legal repercussions that will consume her attention for a year or more. This will do it. In the meantime, I'll have less attention focused on me and what I'm doing." Thomas paused. "You can shut those warroids down, Drake 3GI2RC. I put a subroutine in there that would allow me to do that, but I hadn't planned on them ending up on Mars." He shrugged.

"Since I'm not there to save the day as I'd hoped, this is my gift to you."

"How?" I asked.

He gave me the password and I dropped out of the meetbox, returning to Mars.

* * *

I didn't know if Thomas Haas was telling me the truth or not, but I knew that secrets didn't hold up much in the corp world. It seemed like everyone had dealt themselves into this one, and the double-crosses and triple-crosses flourished like ragweed.

I headed down the hall again, not knowing if I had an edge or I'd been set up by Thomas Haas.

* * *

Minutes later, I reached the meeting room high in Khondi Tower. I remained tapped into the vidcast, listening to John Rath continue his diatribe.

"I was born on Mars," Rath was saying. "My parents and my sister were killed in a corp attack on what was supposed to be the hidden headquarters of Martian rebels. I vowed then that Earth and pro-Earth Martians would pay. I became a mercenary, and I took Earth corps' credit and pro-Earth Martian profits, plowing it back into my own operations till I could reach this point. Ways for me to accomplish this fell into my hands like it was meant to be. I *am* your *savior*."

Three chimera mercs guarded the entrance to the room. Rath didn't leave things to chance. I was running at full speed by the time they saw me, closing rapidly. They started raising their weapons, but mine were already in my hands and I shot them without mercy, following Simon's instincts, not the Three Directives.

I was past them before they fell to the floor.

Rath whirled on me and I stopped to face him because I was already drawing the attention of the warroids in the room.

"I don't know what you're doing here, golem, but you're dead," Rath growled. "Warroids, kill him."

The warroids swiveled.

I pulsed the disarming code. For a moment the warroids held their ground, then they shouldered their arms, and shut down, slumping to resting positions.

Recovering quickly, Rath pulled up his rifle and opened fire. But I was no longer where I'd been. Bullets tracked me but they didn't catch up to me as I ran behind the closest row of inert warroids. The surviving sec guards realized the odds had shifted as well and grabbed the weapons they'd abandoned earlier when confronted by the warroids. Both sides opened fire immediately, but I had no doubts about the outcome of the battle. The Chimeras were heavily outnumbered in the gubernatorial chamber.

Rath's rifle cycled dry. He cast it from him and reached for his sidearm, but by then I was already closing on him. I fired several rounds into his chest and drove him backward, but he remained standing. Through the rips in his uniform, I saw the ballistic under armor that had protected him.

I aimed for his head, but he was in motion too, moving at superhuman speed. The hardsuit was wired for micro-exo supports, increasing his strength and his speed. He fired his pistol, emptying it into me, blowing holes in my chassis and coming dangerously close to my brain center, but the extra shielding prevented him from killing me.

Weapons empty now, I threw myself at Rath as he tried to reload his pistol. I grabbed the weapon and ripped it out of his grasp. I swung a fist at his head, pulling the punch so it wouldn't kill him, only render him unconscious.

Rath countered my punch with an arm block the way he used to when he fought Simon in their practice bouts. As I regrouped, he pulled a microfilament dagger the length of his forearm and shoved it into my midsection. The monofilament edge sliced easily through my chassis and the extra armor.

I managed to pull away when he was only five centimeters from my brain box. The dagger slid out of me with a metallic shriek. My online servers struggled to work around the injury, nanobots rewiring components and circuits to bring me back to full function.

Rath swept his blade at me again and I jumped back. The monofilament tip scraped a fresh scar across my chest. "So who are you, golem? Simon or Drake 3GI2RC? Do you even know? Or has Mara's tampering got you so screwed up that you don't know?"

I batted his next strike away and launched a kick of my own that sent him scrambling back. "I know who I am, John. And it's not just Mara's programming that has been confusing. You had your hand in it, too."

Rath grinned and the bloodlust glowed in his eyes. He swung at my head, causing me to step back, then performed a spinning back kick that caught me on top of the earlier slash and knocked my chest chassis in a little. Sparks shorted in my chest and part of my systems went down again, slowing me. By the time I'd almost recovered, Rath had spun low, raking both of my legs with his blade, then coming up from my crotch toward my chest again. If I had been human, he would have unmanned me and disemboweled me with the same stroke.

I caught his wrist, but he spun out of my grip before I could lock down on him.

"Then you've figured it all out?"

"Simon Blake was a clone," I said. I exchanged blows with him, blocking and being blocked, locked into the rhythm of the battle now the way he and Simon used to be. "DNA at Jonas Salter's crime scene was a sixty-eight percent match for Simon Blake. There's only one way that could happen."

Rath threw another flurry of blows, but I managed to block them. He stepped back to regroup, breathing rapidly. Displeasure showed on his face as he saw the Chimeras going down under heavy fire. The sec team was drawing blood, too, and the chamber was littered with bodies. The nosies were getting it all on record. Including my battle with Rath.

"Simon was *your* clone," I said. Floyd's investigation into Simon's autopsy had revealed that. "You created Simon. That's how I was able to remember the deaths of your parents and sister and thought they were my family."

"You only remembered that because I told you. I wanted you to have a reason to hate Earth and their toadies here as much as I do. You could have been with me, Simon. You *should* have been. Only you went and fell in love with that woman. That screwed up everything we were doing."

"Everything *you* were doing," I replied. "You made Simon over in your image the same way Mara made me over in Simon's. Neither of us turned out to be you."

"We should have been together. You should have been the perfect partner." Rath whipped and ducked, and he suddenly threw his hand out.

An anti-personnel grenade flipped through the space between us and adhered to my metallic skin. It sat there, no bigger than my thumb, and blinked red lights.

Rath turned and ran for the observation window, stooping long enough to pick up a machine pistol.

The grenade went off and blew me off my feet, knocking me back and down. If I had been flesh and blood, the anti-personnel grenade would have killed me. My chassis withstood the blast and loose shrapnel easily. I hit the floor and skidded across pools of blood and through dead bodies. I righted myself immediately, focused on Rath.

A few meters short of the observation window, Rath fired his weapon and the bullets tore through floor to ceiling transplas window. He followed the chunks out into space. For a moment I thought he'd committed suicide rather than submit to me or die at my hands.

Then a hopper glided under him and I knew he'd already planned on an emergency exit. That was Rath.

I ran after him, ignoring the weapons firing all around me. A few stray rounds slammed into my chassis and knocked me slightly off-balance, but I reached the window and dove headlong for the hopper.

Rath was crawling into the top hatch when I hit the hopper and knocked it off-course.

In the pilot's seat, Leigh Bonner tried to correct the flight but ended up losing control for a moment, allowing the hopper to dip sharply to the left. The vehicle sped within centimeters of nearby buildings.

Rath slid out of the hatch and spilled across the top of the hopper. He screamed a curse and managed to grab a new grip on the hatch opening as I slid to the back end of the vehicle. I kept my left hand against the vehicle's exterior and tried to magnetize a hold, but only succeeded in slowing my fall. I drew back my right hand, stiffened my fingers, and drove my hand through the plasteel with a rending crunch. Secure again, I pulled myself up.

Reaching into the hatch, Rath pulled out a submachine pistol as the wind screamed around us. Leigh ducked between buildings, trying desperately to elude the Martian police hoppers that had targeted us.

"Park the vehicle," one of the policemen ordered over the PA.

Rath aimed the machine pistol at me and opened fire. The steel-jacketed bullets tore through my head. He'd aimed instinctively, forgetting that I wasn't human. My face tore away and my head crumpled inward. The impacts knocked me backward and almost shook me loose from my precarious hold. The plasteel in my grip slipped and tore and the wind whipped at me.

"Park the vehicle," the pursuing officer repeated.

Turning his weapon on the police officer, Rath opened fire again. The rounds tore through the transplas cover on the hopper and bright blooms of crimson spotted the interior.

I couldn't let Rath kill any more people, especially police officers. I was Drake 3GI2RC, designed to uphold the law, to protect the innocent, and to bring the guilty to justice.

I would not fail in that job.

And Rath had been responsible for Shelly's death, for the deaths of a lot of people.

I drew back my other hand and hammered the rear section of the hopper, tearing through the exterior, getting down to the control systems. Then I was battering them, ripping through them, taking away all of Leigh Bonner's control over the vehicle.

The hopper suddenly sped up, lunging out of control. It turned sideways and skidded against a tall building, knocking plascrete loose to fall into the street below.

Rath turned to me once more and fired again, blasting away my fingers on the hand that gripped the hopper. I tried to hang on, tried to find a fresh grip, but I fell.

My internal GPS told me I dropped twenty meters before I landed on a hopper pad on one of the nearby buildings. I lay on my back as nanobots struggled to reconnect my systems and salvage what remained of my chassis.

Above, the hopper screamed toward the glistening dome that protected Bradbury colony. Unable to stop, it wrecked into the thick, reinforced transplas surface and shattered. Even before the pieces fell, an explosion turned it all into a ball of flame. I assumed some of the munitions aboard the hopper had detonated.

I didn't think Rath and Leigh Bonner survived the fire because they were both alight. If that didn't kill them, the long fall to the street did. I got up in time to stagger over to the side of the building and watch them hit.

Epilogue

So you're staying on Mars?" Mara Blake glanced around the small office I'd rented.

It was on the forty-fifth floor of a building in Brackett colony, one of the older colonies. I hadn't ever been there as Simon Blake, so everything was fresh and new to me. Also, no one knew me there. I was simply Drake, a private investigator.

"I'm staying," I told her.

The office contained a desk and a few chairs, no views of anything. It was a quiet and dark place where people could come and discuss their troubles. I knew I wouldn't get any wealthy clients, but I didn't need money and Rachel Beckmann sent me work from time to time. I just needed something to do.

"Why?" Mara sat in one of the client seats in front of my desk.

I sat on the other side. "I can start over new here. I can find a life of my own, be someone I want to be."

"Do you know who that is yet?"

"I'm working on it," I said. "You remember Miranda from Haas-Bioroid?"

"I do."

"I'm working with her."

Mara showed me a tentative smile. "She's good at what she does."

"I know."

"You're looking better than the last time I saw you."

I'd required a lot of custom work done, but I'd found the right people to do it. Hayim's friend Reena had helped me get in touch with them, and it had taken most of the credits I'd earned as a mercenary to pay for the repairs. My right knee still had a hitch that caused occasional distress, but when things got better, I'd get that fixed too. Or I'd learn to fix it myself. I had time.

"Thank you. So are you."

During the month that had passed, Mara had received medical treatment and had put back on a few of the pounds she'd lost. "It's kind of you to say that. Is Haas-Bioroid going to leave you alone?"

"They are. I have files Director Haas doesn't want made public."

"Blackmail?"

"I like to think of it as insurance."

She laughed a little, and I think that surprised her. I had not expected that reaction.

I waited because I knew she had more to ask. During the last month, the relationships between Earth and Mars, between the pro-Earthers and Martians and rebels, had healed some. Things weren't quite back to where they had been, but I felt certain they would get back there. Mars was necessary to everyone, and Earth wasn't going to let it go. And no matter how much the rebels wanted independence, presence of the Earth corps predicated a certain amount of structure that was needed.

I think that no one wanted to truly be alone.

"Is he still with you?" Mara asked.

I knew she was talking about Simon. "Less and less every day." I didn't know if that was because my memory had been damaged, or because new memories were overwriting the old ones, or if it was simply that the neural channeling—now that it had served its purpose and saved Mara—was simply fading away.

Mara smiled, but I knew that her heart wasn't in it. "That's good, I suppose."

There was nothing I could say to that and I didn't try.

"I don't mean to be a bother," Mara said.

"You will never be a bother." I didn't know if that was Simon or me who said that, but we both meant it.

"I just wanted to see you again. Before I left."

"I understand. You're going back to Earth?"

Mara's mouth tightened. "I am. There's a lot Haas-Bioroid has to answer for. Maybe they can convince the nosies that the warroids were all John Rath's doing, but I know the truth. That's not going to happen again."

"Good."

After a while, after a little more small talk that didn't go anywhere, Mara got up and I walked her to the door. She hesitated there for a moment, then kissed my cheek. It was a new face and I hadn't quite gotten used to it, but I felt the heat of her, and the softness, and memories stirred a little, like a reflex that just hadn't quite gone away.

"Take care of yourself, Drake."

"I will. But if you ever need me, you just have to call." I watched her walk to the elevator and enter, then the doors closed and took her away from me.

I returned to my office and sat down at my desk. I had an appointment scheduled for later that afternoon, someone Rachel had referred to me.

"You need to do something with this place, Drake." Shelly suddenly stood in front of my desk.

"What's wrong with it?"

"It looks like a closet. You need to bring some color in here. Hang a picture on the wall. Something that says, 'I'm Drake. I detect.'"

"I don't exactly have a diploma or license to hang there."

"Then make one up. You're building the rest of your life. Get something in here." She smiled at me.

I was comforted to see her. Shelly had all but disappeared as well and I had missed her. Miranda felt that was because I was becoming more and more my own individual self. Shelly held me back to the old life, and I needed to forge the new one.

I hoped that she would never completely disappear.

"Come on," she said.

"Where?"

Shelly waved. "Out there, Drake. This world—this *life*—is yours. Do something with it."

I got up only because she told me to, which was illogical because she was me to a degree and I was telling myself to get out when all I wanted to do was stay put.

"Let's go explore this new world of yours," she insisted.

"I can pull down everything I need to know about Brackett colony from the Net."

"What about the things you need to know that you don't think you need to know?"

That argument almost made sense. I reached into my desk drawer, pulled out the black beanie that was so like the one she had made me, slipped it on, and went out to explore.

Shelly took my arm and walked with me. She wouldn't be there forever, but she was there now.

THE END